The Strange Case of the Alchemist's Daughter

THE STRANGE CASE

of the

ALCHEMIST'S
DAUGHTER

Theodora Goss

SAGA PRESS

LONDON SYDNEY **NEW YORK** TORONTO NEW DELHI

SAGA PRESS

AN IMPRINT OF SIMON & SCHUSTER, INC.

1230 AVENUE OF THE AMERICAS, NEW YORK, NEW YORK 10020

SAGA PRESS and colophon are trademarks of Simon & Schuster, Inc.

For information about special discounts for bulk purchases, please contact Simon & Schuster Special Sales at 1-866-506-1949 or business@simonandschuster.com.

The Simon & Schuster Speakers Bureau can bring authors to your live event. For more information or to book an event, contact the Simon & Schuster Speakers Bureau at 1-866-248-3049 or visit our website at www.simonspeakers.com.

Jacket art direction by Krista Vossen

Interior design by Brad Mead

The text for this book was set in Perpetua.

Manufactured in the United States of America

4 6 8 10 9 7 5

Library of Congress Cataloging-in-Publication Data

Names: Goss, Theodora, author.

Title: The strange case of the alchemist's daughter / Theodora Goss.

Description: New York : Saga Press, [2017]

Identifiers: LCCN 2016031398 (print) | LCCN 2016038043 (eBook) | ISBN 9781481466509 (hardcover) | ISBN 9781481466523 (eBook)

Subjects: LCSH: Holmes, Sherlock—Fiction. | Watson, John H. (Fictitious character)— Fiction. | Secret societies—Fiction. | Alchemists—Fiction. | GSAFD: Mystery fiction.

Classification: LCC PS3607.O8544 S77 2017 (print) | LCC PS3607.O8544 (eBook) | DDC 813/.6—dc23

LC record available at https://lccn.loc.gov/2016031398

For Ophelia, who read it first

Here be monsters.

MARY: I don't think that's the right epigraph for the book.

CATHERINE: Then you write the bloody thing. Honestly, I don't know why I agreed to do this.

MARY: Because we need money.

CATHERINE: As usual.

CONTENTS

CHAPTER I

The Girl in the Mirror

Mary Jekyll stared down at her mother's coffin.

"I am the resurrection and the life, saith the Lord."

The rain had started again. Not a proper rain, but the dreary, interminable drizzle that meant spring in London.

"Put up your umbrella, my dear, or you'll get wet," said Mrs. Poole.

Mary put up her umbrella, without much caring whether she would get wet or not. There they all were, standing by a rectangular hole in the ground, in the gray churchyard of St. Marylebone. Reverend Whittaker, reading from the prayer book. Nurse Adams looking grim, but then didn't she always? Cook wiping her nose with a handkerchief. Enid, the parlormaid, sobbing on Joseph's shoulder. In part of her mind, the part that was used to paying bills and discussing the housekeeping with Mrs. Poole, Mary thought, *I will have to speak to Enid about overfamiliarity with a footman.* Alice, the scullery maid, was holding Mrs. Poole's hand. She looked pale and solemn, but again, didn't she always?

"Blessed are the dead who die in the Lord; even so saith the Spirit, for they rest from their labors."

At the bottom of that rectangular hole was a coffin, and in that coffin lay her mother, in the blue silk wedding dress that matched the color of her eyes, forever closed now. When Mary and Mrs. Poole had put it on her, they realized how emaciated she had become over the last few weeks. Mary herself had combed her mother's gray hair, still streaked with gold, and arranged it over the thin shoulders.

"For so thou didst ordain when thou createdst me, saying, dust thou art, and unto dust shalt thou return. All we go down to the dust; yet even at the grave we make our song: Alleluia."

"Alleluia," came the chorus, from Mrs. Poole, and Nurse Adams, and Cook, and Joseph, and Alice. Enid continued to sob.

"Alleluia," said Mary a moment later, as though out of turn.

She handed her umbrella to Mrs. Poole, then took off her gloves. She knelt by the grave and scooped a handful of dirt, scattering it over the coffin. She could hear small pebbles hit, sharper than the soft patter of rain. That afternoon, the sexton would cover it properly and there would be only a mound, until the headstone arrived.

Ernestine Jekyll, Beloved Wife and Mother

Well, at least it was partly true.

She knelt for a moment longer, although she could feel water soaking through her skirt and stockings. Then she rose and reclaimed her umbrella. "Mrs. Poole, will you take everyone back to the house? I need to pay Reverend Whittaker."

"Yes, miss," said Mrs. Poole. "Although I don't like to leave you alone . . ."

"Please, I'm sure Alice is hungry. I'll be home soon, I promise." She would follow Reverend Whittaker into the church and make a donation to the St. Marylebone Restoration Fund. But first she wanted to spend a moment alone with her mother. With what was left of Ernestine Jekyll, in a wooden box on which the raindrops were falling.

MARY: Is it really necessary to begin with the funeral? Can't you begin with something else? Anyway,

> I thought you were supposed to start in the middle
> of the action——*in medias res.*

Before Mary could stop her, Diana crouched by the body of Molly Keane, getting blood on the hem of her dress and the toes of her boots. She reached across the murdered girl to the stiff hand that lay on her bosom and pried open the clenched fingers. From that cold grasp, she withdrew what the girl had been holding: a metal button.

"Diana!" cried Mary.

> MARY: Not that *in medias res*! They won't understand
> the story if you start like that.

> CATHERINE: Then stop telling me how to write it.

It was no use standing there. It would accomplish nothing, and Mary needed to accomplish so much today. She looked at her watch: almost noon. She turned and walked under a gray arch, into the vestry of St. Marylebone to find Reverend Whittaker, who had preceded her inside. Ten pounds for the Church Restoration Fund . . . But she was Miss Jekyll, who had been baptized and confirmed at St. Marylebone. She could not give less.

She emerged from the quiet of St. Marylebone into the hurry and bustle of Marylebone Road, with its carriages and carts, the costermongers by the sides of the road, crying their wares. Although it was out of her way, she took a detour through Regent's Park. Usually, a walk through the park could lift her spirits, but today the roses just starting to bloom were bowed down with rain, and even the ducks on the pond seemed out of sorts. By the time she reached the staid, respectable brick house at 11 Park Terrace where she had spent her entire life, she was tired and wet, despite her umbrella.

She let herself in, a procedure that would no doubt scandalize Mrs. Poole, and put her umbrella in the stand, then stopped in front of the hall mirror to take off her hat. There, she caught a glimpse of herself, and for a moment she stood, captured by her own reflection.

The face that stared back at her was pale, with dark circles under the eyes. Even her hair, ordinarily a middling brown, seemed pale this morning, as though washed out by the light that came through the narrow windows on either side of the front door. She looked like a corpse.

I have paused to show you Mary staring into the mirror because this is a story about monsters. All stories about monsters contain a scene in which the monster sees himself in a mirror. Remember Frankenstein's monster, startled by his reflection in a forest pool? That is when he realizes his monstrousness.

> MARY: I'm not a monster, and that book is a pack of lies.
> If Mrs. Shelley were here, I would slap her for all the
> trouble she caused.

> DIANA: I'd like to see that!

"What are you going to do?" Mary asked the girl in the mirror.

"Don't you start talking to yourself, miss," said Mrs. Poole. Mary turned, startled. "It reminds me of your poor mother. Walking back and forth in that room of hers, until she near wore a hole in the carpet. Talking to who knows what."

"Don't worry, Mrs. Poole," said Mary. "I have no intention of going mad, at least not today."

"How you can joke about it, I don't know! And her just in the ground," said the housekeeper, shaking her head. "Would you like a cup of tea in the parlor? I've started a fire. Cook says lunch should be ready in half an hour. And there's a letter for you, from Mr. Guest. I found it pushed through the slot when we arrived. I've put it on the tea table."

From Mr. Guest, her mother's solicitor. Well, hers now, although she did not think Mr. Guest would want to do business with her much longer. It had been different while her mother was alive. . . .

"Thank you, Mrs. Poole. Could you tell everyone to come into the parlor? Yes, even Alice. And could you bring—you know. I think it had best be done right away, don't you?"

"If you say so, miss," said Mrs. Poole, visibly reluctant. But there was nothing else to be done. Unless this letter from Mr. Guest . . . Could it possibly be about a change in her circumstances?

Mary went into the parlor, took the letter from the tea table, and tore open the envelope—neatly, but without searching for a letter opener. Perhaps . . . but no. *If you could come to my offices at your earliest convenience, we can settle a few final matters concerning your late mother's estate.* That was all. She sat down on the sofa, stretching her hands to the fire. They were pale and thin, with the blue veins visible. She must have lost weight in the last few weeks, from worry and the long nights sitting by her mother's bed so Nurse Adams could get some sleep. She wished she could lie down now, just for a moment. The funeral had been so . . . difficult. But no, what had to be done should be done as soon as possible. There was no point in putting it off.

"Here we are, miss," said Nurse Adams, leading what reminded Mary of a procession from a fairy tale: the cook, the footman, the maid, and the poor little scullion in the rear. Mrs. Poole followed them in and stood by the door, with her hands folded and the expressionless face of a disapproving servant.

Well, this was it. How she hated to do it, but there was no alternative.

"Thank you all so very much for coming to the funeral," Mary began. "And thank you also for your—your care and loyalty, particularly these last few weeks." While Mrs. Jekyll had screamed and torn her hair, and refused to eat, and finally declined into her last illness. "I wish I were calling you in here simply to thank you, but I'm afraid there's more. You see, I have to let you go, every one of you."

Cook took off and wiped her spectacles. Enid sniffed and started crying into a large handkerchief that Joseph handed her. Alice looked like a scared rabbit.

How horrible this was! More horrible even than she had imagined. But Mary continued. "Before my mother's death, I met with Mr. Guest, and he explained my financial position. Cook remembers, for she was here while my father was alive, but I don't suppose the rest of you know. . . . My father was a wealthy man, but when he died fourteen years ago, we discovered that his fortune was gone. He had been selling his Bank of England securities and transferring the money to an account in Budapest. When Mr. Utterson, his solicitor at the time, contacted the Budapest bank, he was told that the account holder was not Dr. Jekyll, the bank had never heard of a Dr. Jekyll, and it was unable to supply information on one of its customers without an order from the Austro-Hungarian government. Mr. Utterson attempted to get such an order, but it proved impossible. The Austro-Hungarian government was not interested in a widowed mother and her child in faraway London. I was only seven at the time, so I remember little of this. But as I grew older and my mother grew increasingly . . . well, unable to handle her finances, Mr. Utterson explained it to me. She had an income left to her by her father, which was enough to keep us all in modest comfort."

She did not need to tell them how modest. No doubt they had noticed her economies, although she had tried to feed them well and keep them comfortable. To have meat on Sundays and coal in the cellar. But they must have noticed books disappearing from the library shelves, silver replaced with plate. Over the years, she had sold off china shepherdesses, and ormolu clocks, and all the silverware, including the epergne her mother had received as a wedding gift from the Archbishop of York. There were outlines on the walls where paintings had hung. Once, Enid had remarked that she was thankful there were fewer figurines to dust, then quickly said, "Sorry, miss!" and scurried off to the kitchen. Her mother's income had not been enough to cover the household expenses, and her medicines, and Nurse Adams.

"But it was only a life-income. When she died, it died with her. It does not come to me."

For a moment, there was silence, broken only by the crackling of the fire.

"Then are you quite ruined, miss?" asked Enid, who indulged in romances of the cheapest sort.

"Well, I supposed you could put it that way," said Mary. What a way of putting it! And yet it was true enough. She was, if not ruined, then nearly so. Her grandfather had died years ago, never dreaming that the provisions of his will would leave his granddaughter impoverished. He had been her last living relation—there was no one to whom she could turn. So that was it. Ruined was not, after all, such a bad choice of expression.

> BEATRICE: The laws regarding female inheritance in this country are barbaric. Why should male heirs be left fortunes outright, while female heirs are left only an income for life? What if their husbands abandon them, as so many do? Or transfer their fortunes to accounts in Budapest? Who is to take care of their children?

DIANA: Oh bloody hell! If you let *her* get started,
we'll never hear the end of it.

"Mrs. Poole, if you would bring me the envelopes?" They had been locked in the housekeeper's room since yesterday, when Mary had gone to the bank to withdraw . . . she did not want to think how much. Mrs. Poole pulled them out of an apron pocket and handed them to her. "In each of these envelopes is your fortnight's pay, as well as a letter of reference for each of you. You need not stay the fortnight. As soon as you find other, and I hope better, employment, you are free to go, with my blessing. I am so very sorry." She sat silently, looking at them, not knowing what else to say.

"Well, as for myself," said Nurse Adams, the first to speak, "I must confess, Miss Jekyll, this has not caught me unprepared. I knew as soon as your mother started muttering about that face at the window. That's how they start, if you'll forgive my saying—seeing things that ain't there. I thought, the poor woman won't survive the month, and I was right. I always know these things! So I spoke to my agency, and there's a position just opened up accompanying an elderly gentleman to the spas in Germany. I'll be taking my leave tomorrow, if it's all the same to you."

"Yes, of course," said Mary. "And thank you so very much, Nurse. The last few weeks were difficult for you, I know." What would she have done without Nurse Adams? She and Mrs. Poole could not have held her mother down when she began screaming and crying about the face, the pale face. . . . Even in her final days, when she was too weak to leave her bed, Mrs. Jekyll had whimpered about it in her sleep.

"As for me and Enid, miss," said Joseph, "we didn't want to tell you in the middle of your troubles, but we're planning to wed. My brother is the proprietor of an inn in Basingstoke, and he has too much custom for one man to handle, so I'll be going into business with him. And we're hoping you'll give us your blessing, like."

"Why, that's wonderful news," said Mary. Thank goodness, for Enid's sake, it had not merely been a dalliance. "I'm so pleased for you both. And Cook?" For Cook was the one she had really been worried about.

"Well, I'll be honest with you, miss, I'd been hoping to stay on awhile yet," said Cook. "But my sister's been at me to come live with her, back in Yorkshire. Her husband died last year, and her daughters are grown and in service, so she's all alone. Two old women living together—I'll be bored to tears, without the hustle and bustle of London. Perhaps I'll take up knitting! But I'm sorry to leave you in your troubles, miss. Having known you since you were a wee thing, and coming into my kitchen for jam tarts!"

"No, it's I who am sorry," said Mary. They were all being so kind, when here she was, telling them they no longer had a home. At least Alice could return to her family in the country. "You'll be able to see your mother again," she said to the scullery maid. "And your brothers, and that hen you miss so much, what was her name?" She smiled encouragingly, but Alice just kept twisting her hands in her apron.

When she had given them the envelopes and Mrs. Poole had ushered them downstairs to their lunch, all except Nurse Adams who asked for a tray in her room so she could start packing, Mary leaned back into the sofa and stared at the painting of her mother over the mantelpiece. Ernestine Jekyll, with her long, golden hair and eyes the color of cornflowers, smiled down at her in a way Mary could not remember her smiling while alive. Almost as long as Mary could remember, her mother had stayed in the large bedroom she had slept in since marrying Dr. Jekyll and moving to London from her native Yorkshire—pacing around the room, talking to invisible companions. Sometimes she scratched herself until she bled. Sometimes she tore out chunks of her hair, so it lay in long strands on the floor. Once, Nurse Adams had suggested she be sent to an institution for her own safety. Mary had refused, but in the last few weeks she had begun to wonder if she had been wrong. What had caused those violent spasms, those shrieks in the night? That final swift decline?

Even as a little girl, Mary had not cried easily. She had learned long ago that life was difficult. One had to live it with courage and common sense; it did not reward sentimentality. At the memory of her mother lying on her pillow, looking more peaceful than she had looked for years, Mary put her head in her hands. But she did not cry, as she had not cried at the funeral.

DIANA: Because our Mary never cries.

MRS. POOLE: Miss Mary is a lady. She does not throw fits, unlike some as I could name.

MARY: It's not my fault I don't cry. You know perfectly well it's not.

CATHERINE: Yes, we know.

Mary's "earliest convenience," as Mr. Guest had put it in his letter, did not occur until a week later. First, there was Nurse Adams to see off, and Joseph and Enid, and finally Cook. One afternoon, Mrs. Poole came into the morning room where Mary was going through the accounts at her mother's desk and said, "Alice is gone."

"What?" said Mary. "What do you mean, gone?"

"I mean that she's taken her things and gone off, without saying goodbye. She did all her morning work just as usual, without saying a word. I went into her room a minute ago, to tell her tea was ready, and there's nothing there. Not that she had much, but it's empty."

"Well, no doubt her brothers came for her. Didn't she say it was all arranged?"

"Yes, but she could at least have said goodbye. After the way I took her in and trained her. I never expected ingratitude, not from Alice! And no forwarding address. I would at least have liked to send her a card at Christmas."

"She's very young, Mrs. Poole. I'm sure you were thoughtless yourself when you were thirteen. No, come to think of it, I'm sure you weren't. And I'm sorry about Alice. We'll probably get a letter from her in the next few days, telling us she's safely home and how nice it is to be back in the country. All right, I'm done here. It's time to face Mr. Guest. It's raining again. Could you bring my mackintosh?" She closed the account book and sighed. The last thing she wanted to do today was meet with the solicitor, but what had to be done should be done as soon as possible. Or so Miss Murray, her governess, had taught her.

Mrs. Poole met her in the hall, holding her mackintosh and umbrella. "I wish you would take a cab. You'll be soaking wet, and when I think of you walking those streets alone . . ."

"You know I can't afford a cab, and I'm just going to Cavendish Square. Anyway, this is the nineties. The most respectable ladies walk alone. Or ride their bicycles in the park!"

"And look like horrors," said Mrs. Poole. "I hope you're not thinking of wearing a divided skirt and getting on one of those contraptions!"

"Well, not today, at any rate. Do I look sufficiently respectable to your discerning eye?" Mary glanced at herself in the mirror and adjusted her hat, more out of habit than because it needed adjusting. She was not trying to look smart, and if she had been trying, it would not have worked anyway. *Not when I look as though I've seen a ghost,* she thought.

"You always look respectable, my dear," said Mrs. Poole. "You're a born lady."

MRS. POOLE: Well, I never! I have never in my life called Miss Mary anything so disrespectful as "my dear."

DIANA: Oh, stuff it! You do it all the time without noticing.

"A lady should be able to pay her butcher's bill," said Mary. Twelve pounds, five shillings, three pence: that was her current bank balance. She had written it neatly in the account book, and now she could not stop thinking about it. The number kept chiming in her head, like a clock always telling the same time. On her mother's desk in the morning room was a stack of bills. She had no idea how she would pay them.

"Mr. Byles knows you'll pay him eventually," said Mrs. Poole. "Hasn't he been supplying meat for this household since before your father died?"

"That was when there was a household to supply for." Mary buttoned her mackintosh, picked up her purse from the hall table, then hooked the umbrella over her arm. "Mrs. Poole, you really should reconsider . . ."

"I'm not leaving you, miss," said Mrs. Poole. "Not in this big house, all alone. My father was butler here under Dr. Jekyll, and my mother came from the country with Mrs. Jekyll. Your mother's nurse, she was. Same as I was yours when you were in pinafores. This is my home."

"But I have nothing to pay you with," said Mary, hopelessly.

"It was all I could do to give Cook and Joseph and the rest their fortnight's wages. You can't give me credit, like Mr. Byles. And a trained housekeeper could find another position, even at a time like this. I'm the one the employment offices don't want. You should see these women, with their pursed faces, telling me I don't know enough to be a governess—which is true—or that working in a shop 'is not for the likes of you, miss'!"

"It certainly isn't," said Mrs. Poole.

"Or if I took a two-week typing course costing ten shillings, they might find something for me by and by. But I haven't got ten shillings to spare, and I haven't got two weeks! I called on Mr. Leventhal, but he says there's no hope of selling this house, with the economic situation as it is. Unless, he says, a buyer comes along who will take on the expense of dividing it into flats."

"Flats!" said Mrs. Poole in a horrified tone. "Divide a gentleman's residence into flats! I don't know what the world is coming to. Well, perhaps Mr. Guest will tell you something to your advantage."

"That," said Mary, "is highly unlikely." She checked herself in the mirror again. Umbrella, mackintosh, gum boots. She was prepared for the deluge.

And a deluge it was. The rain beat mercilessly on her umbrella. In the gutters, rivers ran dark and fast. London went about its daily business: shops were open, carts rumbled down the streets, newspapers boys called out, "Another 'orrible murder! Maid on her day out found without a 'ead! Read about it in the *Daily Mail!*" But the crossing-sweepers were soaked and glum, and the hansom cab horses shook their heads to get water out of their ears. The sidewalks thronged with umbrellas.

As though God has decided to drown the world again, she thought, almost wishing He would. Sometimes she thought the world needed drowning. But she pushed the uncharitable thought away and took a quick look at her watch to make sure she would be in time for her appointment. Her boots squelched on the wet pavement as she made her way through Marylebone.

Utterson & Guest, Solicitors, was located on one of the quiet, respectable streets near Cavendish Square. Mary knocked with the polished brass knocker. A clerk opened the heavy wooden door and led her down the long, paneled corridor to Mr. Guest's office. While her mother was alive, Mr. Guest had come to the house, but the impoverished Miss Mary Jekyll was not important enough to warrant a visit.

Mr. Guest was as tall and lean and balding as ever. He reminded Mary of a cadaver; she imaged the paneled office, with its rows of leather-bound books, as the coffin in which he had been interred. He bowed over her hand and said, in his cadaverous voice, "Thank you for coming in response to my letter, Miss Jekyll. And in this rain, too!"

"I don't suppose this has anything to do with my finances?" said Mary. She might as well be direct. He knew perfectly well that she had no money.

"No, no, I'm afraid your financial situation remains the same." Mr. Guest shook his head regretfully, but Mary could detect a certain relish in his tone. "Do sit down, as our business may take some time. I asked you here because I received this." Mr. Guest sat behind his desk and pulled forward a leather portfolio that had been lying beside the inkwell. "I was contacted by your mother's bank—not the Bank of England, but another bank at which she had opened an account, some sort of cooperative society in Clerkenwell. Without my knowledge, I might add." Clearly, he did not approve of his clients opening accounts without informing him, particularly in such a disreputable part of the city.

Mary stared at him in astonishment. "Another account? That's impossible. Before she died, my mother had not left her room for many years."

"Yes, of course," said Mr. Guest. "But this account must have been opened before your mother . . . secluded herself entirely from the world." *In other words, went mad,* thought Mary.

"When the account was set up, your mother deposited a certain sum, stipulating that each month, a portion of it would be paid to a designated recipient. When the director of the bank saw the notice of her death in *The Times,* he very properly contacted me. I requested that he send me whatever information he could, and a week later I received these documents. They include the account book."

He unbuckled the portfolio, took out a book such as bank clerks use to keep their accounts in order, and placed it in front of Mary. She sat in the rather uncomfortable chair Mr. Guest provided for his clients, put her purse on her lap, and opened the book to the first page. At the top was written: DATE—TRANSACTION—AMOUNT—PURPOSE. Each transaction had taken place on the first of the month, and each was recorded in exactly the same way: *Payment to the Society of St. Mary Magdalen—£1—For the care and keeping of Hyde.*

Hyde! At the sight of that name, Mary gasped. It conjured an image from her childhood: her father's friend, the man known as Edward Hyde—a pale, hairy, misshapen man, with a wicked leer that had sent a shiver up her spine.

MARY: That's a bit melodramatic, isn't it?

CATHERINE: Well, at any rate, he always made you
feel uncomfortable. And he was insufferably rude.

"That account is now yours," said Mr. Guest. "As you can see, it was originally set up with a single deposit of a hundred pounds. Since then, money has been withdrawn monthly, for some purpose I do not understand?" He paused for a moment in case Mary cared to explain. But even if she had any idea what this was about, she would not have enlightened the solicitor. He continued, "It contains the sum left after last month's withdrawal: I believe the current total comes to twenty-three pounds. Not a large sum, I'm afraid."

No, it was not, but Mary had a sudden vision of being able to pay the butcher, and the grocer, and of course Mrs. Poole. Perhaps they could even hire back Cook, who would not have to live with her sister in Yorkshire! And Mrs. Poole would not have to struggle with the oven, or producing edible meals from a cookery book she had never been trained to use. But no, that was too ambitious. Twenty-three pounds was significantly more than she had, but it was not enough to live on for any length of time—not at 11 Park Terrace. Still, some of the panic she had been feeling subsided. But the incredulity remained.

"For Hyde?" she said. "How could my mother possibly have been involved with Hyde? I was only a child, but I still remember the police coming to our house, questioning my father about him."

"I was Mr. Utterson's clerk at the time," said Mr. Guest. "I remember the circumstances quite well, although fortunately I never met Mr. Hyde myself. That is of course why I asked you to come so urgently, although I hesitated to interrupt your period of mourning, Miss Jekyll." He looked at her solemnly, but she thought that behind his professional mask, she could detect a smirk. He was the sort of man who would enjoy the misfortunes of others. "But there is more: your mother left these documents with the bank for safekeeping."

He pushed the portfolio toward her. It was filled with papers of various sorts: another book, envelopes that likely contained letters, slips of paper that seemed to be receipts. She started to pull the other book out of the portfolio, but saw the look of avid curiosity on Mr. Guest's face. He had probably restrained himself from looking through his client's private papers, although he would have liked to. Well, whatever her mother had wanted to hide, Mary was not going to show him.

She closed and buckled the portfolio. "Thank you, Mr. Guest. Is that all?"

"Yes, that's all," he said, with a frown—of frustrated disappointment, thought Mary. "May I ask, Miss Jekyll, what you intend to do in this matter?"

"I shall close the account, of course," said Mary. She would go to Clerkenwell—could one get there by omnibus?—and withdraw the remainder tomorrow. Thirty-five pounds, five shillings, three pence. She could not help thinking with relief of the new number.

"That is certainly the best course of action," said Mr. Guest. "Whatever the account was created for, I suggest you have nothing more to do with it. And if I may also mention—young ladies in your situation often find it a relief to place their affairs in the hands of those who are more worldly, more wise in such matters. In short, Miss Jekyll, since you have recently come of age, you may choose to marry. A young lady of your personal attractions would certainly prove acceptable to a man who is not particular about his wife's fortune." Mr. Guest looked at her meaningfully.

Goodness, thought Mary. *Surely he's not proposing to me?* She had an impulse to laugh, but after the events of the past week, it would come out sounding like hysteria. This had all been . . . a bit too much. "Thank you, Mr. Guest," she said, rising and extending her hand. "I'm sure you're very wise in worldly matters and all that. And I appreciate your advice. And could you please ask your clerk to fetch my umbrella and mackintosh?"

It was still raining when Mary emerged from the solicitor's office. She walked back through the crowded city streets, carrying the portfolio under her arm so it, at least, would not get wet. By the time she reached home, she was tired, wet, and grateful that Mrs. Poole had already laid a fire in the parlor.

> BEATRICE: Oh, your London rain! When I first came to London, I thought, *I shall never see the sun again.* It was so cold, and wet, and dismal! I missed Padua.

> DIANA: If you don't like it here, you can go back there. No one's stopping you!

> CATHERINE: Please keep your comments relevant to the story. And it is not my London rain. I dislike it as much as Beatrice.

Mary changed out of her black bombazine into an old day dress, put on a pair of slippers, and wrapped a shawl that had belonged to her mother around her shoulders. She lit the fire with a match from the box on the mantelpiece. How shabby the parlor looked! She had asked Mr. Mundy, of Mundy's Furnishings and Bibelots, what else she could possibly sell, but he had shaken his head and said there was simply nothing left worth buying. Unless Miss Jekyll wanted to sell the fine portrait over the parlor fireplace? But Mary would not sell her mother's portrait.

She sat on the sofa and pulled the tea table in front of her, then unbuckled the portfolio and pulled out the documents it contained. They would have been easier to sort through on her mother's desk—she could not help thinking of it as her mother's desk, although she had been using it for years to do the household accounts. But there was no fire laid in the morning room, and not much coal left in the cellar. Also, she did not want to face those bills again, not now.

The book was, more properly, a notebook: her father's laboratory notebook, she realized when she began leafing through
it. She recognized his handwriting, the same angular hand that
had commented in the margins of his books. The envelopes were
addressed to Dr. Henry Jekyll, 11 Park Terrace. They must contain letters sent to him while he was alive, perhaps about his
scientific experiments? He had maintained a large correspondence with other scientists in England and Europe. Scattered
among the envelopes were miscellaneous receipts, mostly from
Maw & Sons, the company that had supplied the chemicals for
his experiments. She began to sort through the documents,
barely noticing when Mrs. Poole brought in her dinner of a chop
with peas and potatoes. She moved the documents to the sofa so
Mrs. Poole could set it on the table, thanking the housekeeper
absentmindedly.

When Mrs. Poole came to clear away, she leaned back into the
sofa and said, "You know, I think Mr. Guest almost proposed to
me today? Or hinted that I should marry a man who could take
charge of my affairs, since young ladies are so unworldly."

"And you running this house since you were old enough to sign
your mother's name!" said Mrs. Poole. "I've never held with men,
and that's a fact. Footmen are ornamental in white stockings for
dinner service, but not as useful as a good scullery maid. Although
Joseph made himself useful enough, I'll admit."

"If only I could afford a good scullery maid!" said Mary. "I
hated letting Alice go, but she's better off with her family. Mrs.
Poole, could you sit down for a moment? I know, I know, it's not
your place. But please, there's something I need to ask you."

Reluctantly, Mrs. Poole sat in one of the armchairs by the fire,
with her hands folded on her lap, as though she were sitting in one
of the pews of St. Marylebone. "Well, miss?"

Mary leaned forward and stared into the fire. She did not

quite know how to ask . . . but directly was always best. She turned to Mrs. Poole and said, "What do you remember about Edward Hyde?"

> **AUTHOR'S NOTE:** I can't tell you how much I regret allowing Mary and the rest of them to see this manuscript while I was writing it. First they started commenting on what I had written, and then they insisted I make changes in response to their comments. Well, I'm not going to. I'm going to leave their comments in the narrative itself. You, dear reader, will be able to see how annoying and nonsensical most of them are, while offering the occasional flash of insight into character. It will be a new way of writing a novel, and why not? This is the '90s, as Mary pointed out. It's time we developed new ways of writing for the new century. We are no longer in the age of Charles Dickens or George Eliot, after all. We are modern. And, of course, monstrous . . .

CHAPTER II

Consulting Mr. Holmes

"N ow that's a name I haven't heard in a long time!" said Mrs. Poole. "But I don't think anyone who once saw Mr. Hyde could forget him. You were so young, just out of the nursery and into the schoolroom. Such a solemn child you were, calm and quiet, unlike other children, with big gray eyes that always seemed to be asking questions. Do you remember Miss Murray, with her globes and French grammar? You used to come see me when you were tired of conjugating or declining, or whatever you call it, and I would give you a bit of ginger cake. I don't know if you ever saw him yourself, though he was here often enough."

"I did, once," said Mary. "But tell me what you remember about him. I have a particular reason for asking."

"I was head chambermaid then, so I rarely saw gentlemen guests. My father was still alive, bless his soul. 'It's not my place to criticize Dr. Jekyll's guests,' he would tell me. 'But that Mr. Hyde just makes me feel like taking a shower, with plenty of soap!' He spent most of his time with your father in the laboratory. But I saw him once or twice, creeping down the stairs as he did, with an evil look on his face. The sight of him made me shiver. I remember it to this day!"

"I saw him once," said Mary, thoughtfully. "He was standing outside my mother's bedroom door. He had his hand raised, as though about to knock. But he turned and saw me, then lowered it and gave me such a look—almost of guilt, but also a sort of glee. He grinned, and I remember being frightened and running back to my room. Later, I told Miss Murray that I had seen Rumpelstiltskin." She looked back down at the documents spread over the sofa. "What do you remember about the murder?"

"Shocking, it was!" said Mrs. Poole. "That old gentleman, Sir Danvers Carew, beaten to death with a cane. Such a brutal crime!"

"And Mr. Hyde was implicated," said Mary.

"Oh, I don't think there was any question of his guilt! It was a dreadful time. The police coming around, questioning us all as though we were criminals. I'm convinced it hastened your poor father's death. But Hyde disappeared, and hasn't been heard of since. Good riddance, I say!"

"Until now. Look, this is what Mr. Guest gave me." Mary held the account book out to Mrs. Poole, turned so the housekeeper could see the list of figures, and repeated what the solicitor had told her.

Mrs. Poole looked down at the book, then back up again at Mary. Astonishment was written on her face, and for a moment, she could not speak. Then, she said, "I don't know what to make of that, miss."

"I don't know what to make of it either. Except that my mother knew where Hyde was, and was sending him money each month. Could he have been blackmailing her?"

"With what, miss? Your mother hadn't a secret in the world."

"But I think my father did. I've been reading one of these letters." Mary picked up the letter and stared at it, frowning. "There are references I don't understand—scientific references, in part. But I'm starting to think that my father was involved in some strange things, Mrs. Poole."

"Well, he was always a secretive gentleman. Shall I take your plate, miss? I'd like to wash up before banking the stove for the night."

"I'm sorry," said Mary. "I'm being inconsiderate. Sometimes I forget it's just the two of us now—and you're the one actually doing all the work. If only you would let me help."

Mrs. Poole removed the plate and cutlery in a way that expressed her complete disapproval. She has always had the remarkable ability to show exactly what she thinks without saying a word. It's a very annoying trait. No, you may not add a comment here, Mrs. Poole.

"I hope you don't stay up too late," said the housekeeper. "And do light the gas when it gets dark. I don't want you ruining your eyes."

"I won't stay up," said Mary. "But I want to finish looking through these documents. I have a sort of idea . . . Mrs. Poole, wasn't there a reward offered for information leading to the apprehension of Hyde?"

"A hundred pounds, it was. Why, miss? Do you think you could get that hundred pounds by turning him in? It's been so long. Surely they won't pay that much now." Mrs. Poole did not specify who *they* might be.

"I don't know," said Mary. "But I think I know who to ask. It was so long ago, but I still remember . . ."

She did not finish her sentence. Mrs. Poole carried the tray out, shutting the parlor door behind her. Mary wondered what secrets her mother had taken to the grave. An idea was starting to form in her head, a course of action. Tomorrow . . .

But no, she would not think about that yet. She still had the rest of the documents to read through. Perhaps they would tell her more about what had happened all those years ago. She picked up her father's notebook and continued where she had left off. The fire had burned low by the time she finally put the documents back into the portfolio, then rose and went upstairs to the bedroom she had slept in since leaving the nursery.

Once in bed, she could not get to sleep. The house was so silent! There had always been noises: her mother waking in the night, Nurse Adams going down to heat some milk. The house felt so empty around her. Mrs. Poole was two floors down, in the housekeeper's room by the kitchen. She was tempted to go down and sleep in Alice's bed, just so she could hear Mrs. Poole snoring through the wall. But she was Miss Mary Jekyll, of 11 Park Terrace. A lady might feel fear, but she must not give in to it, or so her governess had taught her. So she stared into the darkness until she finally fell asleep, and dreamed of a leering Mr. Hyde walking through the lamplit streets of London, brandishing his murderous cane.

MRS. POOLE: I do *not* snore!

MARY: I don't remember dreaming any such thing. How can you say I dreamed it, if I don't remember?

CATHERINE: You don't remember *not* dreaming it, do you? Well then. You must have dreamed something. I can't just write, *Mary dreamed something but she doesn't remember.* You have absolutely no sense of drama.

MARY: Well, I don't tell lies, if that's what you mean.

The next morning, after an early breakfast of toast and tea, she asked Mrs. Poole for the key to the laboratory. With a shawl wrapped around her shoulders, she crossed the courtyard at the back of the house and unlocked the laboratory door, which had been locked for—how long now? Since her mother had become too ill to be cared for by the servants and Mary had hired Nurse Adams. That must be . . . seven years ago. Even before that, it had only been entered by the maids, for an annual cleaning.

She did not know what she expected to find, but perhaps her father had left something, anything that would answer the questions she had begun to ask, after looking through the documents in the portfolio.

The laboratory, which had once been an operating theater, was lit by a domed skylight. The gray light of a rainy London day streamed in over wooden desks and seats arranged in tiers, as in an amphitheater, so students could watch anatomical demonstrations. Now, they were covered with a thick layer of dust. On the central table, once used for operations, her father had performed his chemical experiments. She still remembered what it had looked like, so many years ago, covered with equipment: a Bunsen burner, two microscopes, mortars and pestles in various sizes. Equations had been scribbled on the chalkboard behind him. The shelves on either side of the room had been filled with books. She had seldom been allowed in the laboratory, but sometimes he had called her in to observe his experiments. The table of elements with its symbols that meant so much when you understood them, the colored flame of the Bunsen burner when he passed various chemicals through it, more to amuse her than for any practical purpose, had always seemed magical to her. She had laughed and clapped at the performance. . . .

Now, there was nothing. The theater was entirely empty.

She mounted the steps of the amphitheater, up to a second half-story where her father's office was located. The door was almost off its hinges, as though it had been forced open. A window that looked onto a back alley was covered with dust, and there were cobwebs in the corners. The office was still furnished: a desk and chair, a sofa, a mirror in one corner. Glass-fronted cabinets that had once held chemicals, now as empty as the bookshelves in the laboratory. But here, too, was a thick layer of dust. She looked in the desk drawers . . . nothing. As she was descending the steps back down to the first floor, Mrs. Poole poked her head through the doorway.

"Well, miss? Did you find anything?"

"No, nothing. Do you know what happened to my father's papers? I remember his desk being covered with them. . . ."

"Why, miss," said Mrs. Poole, looking around the dusty theater with professional disapproval, "everything was burned after your father's death. I still remember that night, although it was so long ago. My father and Mr. Utterson breaking down the door to the office, and then my father telling all the servants that Dr. Jekyll was dead. An accident, he told us, but we all whispered the word *suicide*. And Mr. Utterson up with your mother half the night. The next day Mr. Utterson and my father carried him out themselves, in a plain wooden box. That made us certain it must have been suicide. Why else were none of the servants invited to the funeral? It was just Mr. Utterson and your mother, and he was buried without even a proper stone to mark where he lay, just that plaque in St. Marylebone. After that, everything was cleared away—all the chemicals, the papers, even the books. Your mother bore it all so well. It was later she broke down, from the strain, I suppose."

"So the documents my mother deposited at the bank are all I have left," said Mary. All she had left of her father and the mystery of his life . . . and death.

"I suppose so, miss. Will you be wanting anything else? Now that you've opened this room, I want to give it a good airing out, and then I'm going to bring my broom in here, and as many cloths as I can find. Just look at this, will you?" Mrs. Poole drew her finger along the top of a desk and held it up. It was gray with the dust of years.

"Just my mackintosh and umbrella, if you don't mind. Yes, I'm going out again. I have an errand to run this morning."

"To that bank, miss?"

"Not quite yet. I'll tell you about it when I get back."

MARY: If I had known then what I know now . . .

JUSTINE: Would you have acted any differently? I think not.

MARY: But I might have felt differently. Although I don't suppose that makes much of a difference. You know, when I was a child, I thought my father was a magician. I thought he was the most wonderful man in the world.

JUSTINE: What happened later doesn't have to destroy that memory of him.

CATHERINE: For goodness' sake, Justine. You are way too forgiving.

Twenty minutes later, Mary rang the bell at 221B Baker Street. Miraculously, just as she had reached the front door of the building, the rain had finally stopped. It had been a short walk around the perimeter of Regent's Park. She had stopped for a moment in St. Marylebone Church to kneel in one of the pews and had tried to pray for her mother . . . and yes, for her father as well. She had stopped by the plaque on the wall that said only *Henry Jekyll, Benefactor*. She did not even know where he was buried, although Mr. Utterson had assured her that it was in holy ground. Wherever his spirit was now, she hoped he was at peace. But she had been distracted from her prayers by the mysterious payments, the letter she had read last night, the laboratory notebook. If only it were all clearer!

Had she come to the right place? She would find out soon enough.

> MARY: You're making me sound like the heroine
> of a popular novel. That's not at all what I was
> thinking at the time.

> BEATRICE: What were you thinking, then?

> MARY: How much it would cost to buy new boots.
> If I was going to be walking around London, I would
> need a stouter pair, and wasn't sure if I could afford
> it. That's what I was distracted by, if you really want
> to know. The state of my footwear.

Mary, who was not thinking about the price of boots because that is *so boring*, shut her umbrella, awkwardly because she was carrying the portfolio Mr. Guest had given her under one arm. She stood waiting while the rings reverberated, trying to brush mud off the hem of her dress and wishing she could have worn a walking suit—but she could not afford one in black. Not that it was much use; she would get just as muddy on the way home. As though to reinforce the point, a cart rumbled by, its wheels running through a puddle and sending up an arc of muddy water that narrowly missed her.

For a moment, she wished she weren't a lady, so she could swear at the driver.

> MARY: Well that, at least, is accurate!

Why wasn't anyone answering the bell? She rang again.

"I'm so sorry, miss." The woman who opened the door had gray hair under an old-fashioned mobcap and had evidently been dusting. She still held the ostrich duster in one hand. "I was all the way up on the third floor. My hearing isn't what it used to be, and the first time you rang, I thought I was just imagining it. And then you rang again . . ."

"I'm here to see Mr. Holmes," said Mary. "I'm afraid I don't have an appointment, but it's important that I see him. Is he available?"

"Oh, you poor dear," said the woman. Was she a housekeeper? No—this must be the famous Mrs. Hudson! "Mr. Holmes is upstairs, and I'm sure he'll be able to help you, whatever trouble you're in. He won't mind being disturbed. Not, that is, if you're bringing him a case, as I imagine you are. He does love his cases."

Mary could not help smiling. Mrs. Hudson had obviously decided she was some sort of damsel in distress, anxious to see the great detective. Who probably would very much mind being disturbed, but Mary couldn't help that.

"Thank you, Mrs. . . ."

"Hudson. Mrs. Hudson. I let rooms and do for the gentlemen upstairs. Or I would, if they ever let me. I have to warn you, miss, it's a terrible mess up there."

Mary followed Mrs. Hudson up a narrow flight of stairs to the second floor.

At the top of the stairs, Mrs. Hudson knocked. "There's a lady to see you, Mr. Holmes," she called through the door.

A shot rang out, and then another.

Mary flinched, both times, but Mrs. Hudson seemed not to notice.

She waited for a moment, then said, "It's important, Mr. Holmes."

Another shot, and then—

"All right, let her in." The voice implied that whoever she was, she would be an infernal nuisance.

Mrs. Hudson opened the door. "In you go, miss," she said to Mary. "And don't let Mr. Holmes intimidate you. If anyone can help you with your problem, he can."

Mrs. Hudson paused for a moment, in case Mary might reveal what that problem was. An angry father? An absconding fiancé? But Mary said, "Thank you very much, Mrs. Hudson," and walked into the flat.

Yes, it was indeed a terrible mess.

On the mantelpiece, above the fireplace, were skulls, representing what Mary recognized as different physiognomic types, in a row from highest to lowest. The last one in the row was obviously the skull of an ape, but in an effort to be humorous, perhaps, someone had put a top hat on it. By the window stood a camera, from which an opera cape was hanging, probably for whomever was going to wear the top hat. The long table in front of the window was covered with equipment of various sorts, just as her father's laboratory table had been: she could see a smaller portable camera, a Bunsen burner and microscope, glass jars filled with what looked like human ears swimming in liquid. Casts of hand- and fingerprints. Boxes of dirt in a variety of colors, from light red to black. Along the wall across from the fireplace were bookshelves, overflowing with books. There were books stacked on the floor, the sofa, and one of the armchairs. On the other armchair was a violin.

The man in the middle of the room was holding a pistol. He was tall, with a high forehead and the sort of nose they call aquiline. He looked, Mary thought, like an inquisitive eagle. His shirtsleeves were rolled up, and he was pointing the pistol at the wall.

DIANA: You're not going to make him the hero, are you? Because that would be sickening.

BEATRICE: I think Mr. Holmes would make a very good hero.

DIANA: You would!

By the mantle, the wallpaper was pocked with bullet holes in a pattern: VR, VR, VR—*Victoria Regina*. For a moment, Mary wondered if she should have gone straight to Scotland Yard.

The second occupant of the room rose from behind a stack of books on the sofa. "What are you thinking, Holmes? You'll scare the girl." He was shorter, stockier, with a mustache. Unlike his friend, he was properly dressed, in a jacket and tie.

"I'm not scared, Dr. Watson," said Mary. "I've read your accounts of Mr. Holmes's cases, and am aware of his peculiarities. Although shooting inside a flat seems somewhat theatrical, doesn't it? Honestly, I thought you had made it up for dramatic effect."

"Ha! She's got you there, Watson!" said the man holding the pistol. "Or perhaps she's got me. There's nothing quite like the clear-sighted irony of a modern young lady to make one feel ridiculous. Although I swear this was a practical experiment, however it may appear. Well then, madam, tell me who you are and what sort of assistance you need this morning. Lost a pug or Pomeranian? I seem to be in the business of retrieving missing pets lately. I'm Sherlock Holmes, and this, as you have so brilliantly deduced, is my associate, Dr. Watson."

"No," said Mary. Lost pug or Pomeranian, indeed! "I'm here to ask about a murder that happened fourteen years ago. I believe you were involved with the investigation. My name is Mary Jekyll."

"Is it now!" said Holmes. He put the pistol on the table, next to the microscope. "Come sit down, Miss Jekyll. I remember the case, and your father, Dr. Henry Jekyll, although it was a long time ago. I was interested in chemistry, and he was described to me as the best man in his field. Not quite sound in his theories, perhaps, but the best. Do you remember the murder of Sir Danvers Carew, Watson? It was in the early days of our association, when I was just beginning to establish my practice as a consulting detective. Miss Jekyll must have been . . ."

Mary put her umbrella in the stand, beside a pair of fencing foils.

"Here, Miss Jekyll," said Watson, moving the stack of books from the armchair nearest the door. She sat down, noting the cigarette burns on the arms, and put the portfolio on her lap.

"It was almost fourteen years ago," she said. "I was seven years old."

"Yes, I remember a daughter. And a mother."

"My mother died recently," said Mary.

"My condolences," said Watson, bowing to Mary. "But no, I don't remember the case, Holmes."

"Thank you." Her mother's death was the last thing Mary wanted to discuss at the moment. She turned to Holmes and said, "At the time, there was a reward . . ."

"I was not involved with the case directly, but you would have read about it in the newspapers. The murder was marked by its particularly vicious nature and the high position of the victim. Sir Danvers Carew was a member of Parliament, a personal friend of Gladstone, and a prominent supporter of Irish Home Rule. The facts, in brief, were as follows." He swept aside a stack of books on the sofa, sat with his elbows on his knees, and tented his fingers together, then stared at the wall just over Mary's head as though actually seeing the events he was describing.

"Sir Danvers was found brutally beaten to death on a street

in Soho. His head had been bashed in with a cane—the cane was actually found broken beside him. His purse and watch were still on him, but he had no other identifying papers, except a letter in his pocket addressed to a solicitor named Utterson. This Utterson was summoned and identified the body. The police already knew who had committed the murder: a housemaid who was looking out onto the lamplit street, waiting for her admirer, had noticed a man she recognized as Mr. Hyde. He lived in the neighborhood, with a woman who was said not to be his wife. She observed him walking along the street, stopping once under a street lamp to check his watch, which is how she could identify him so clearly—until, at the street corner, he met Sir Danvers Carew. A conversation, and then an altercation, ensued. Hyde struck the man over the head, then continued to beat him until the body lay still on the pavement. Utterson told the officer that Hyde was employed by one of his clients, a Dr. Jekyll, who lived near Regent's Park. Not far from Baker Street, and I observe that Miss Jekyll walked here, although not through the park, I think. The mud of Regent's Park is quite distinctive, since it contains matter from the flower beds. No, that is ordinary Marylebone street mud, splashed from the gutters."

Mary looked down at her boots. Well, next time she would gather more distinctive mud for Mr. Holmes! Seriously, did they need to go into all the particulars of the Carew murder? She was starting to lose her patience.

"But I take it there was a difficulty," said Watson. "Or you would not be describing the case in such detail."

"You know me well," said Holmes. "Utterson led the officer to Hyde's Soho residence, around the corner—but the man was gone. Although the police combed London, and indeed all of England for him, he could not be found. It was as though he had disappeared into thin air. I was sufficiently intrigued that I decided to look into the case for myself. Whatever else can be said about them, our English police are nothing if not thorough. It is difficult to escape them so entirely. I had no official relationship with the police at that point. But my brother Mycroft knew Jekyll, so I asked for an introduction. He was willing enough to discuss the matter with me. He told me that Hyde had been a sort of assistant to him, helping with his scientific experiments. However, he claimed that he had not seen Hyde since the murder. Shortly afterward, Jekyll committed suicide."

Yes, that was what Mary had remembered last night: a tall man in her father's study, walking back and forth on legs like scissors, and old Poole telling her not to interrupt because her father was talking to an important gentleman, a detective. She had deduced that it must be the famous Mr. Holmes, whose cases were featured so often in *The Strand*.

"Holmes!" said Watson. "Consider Miss Jekyll's feelings!"

"I'm perfectly fine, thank you," said Mary. "But I would like to know if there is still a reward? You see, I may have some information. . . ."

"I've always wondered about that case," said Holmes. "Hyde was never found, and eventually Scotland Yard stopped looking. I did not pursue the matter further or inquire into the cause of Dr. Jekyll's suicide. As I mentioned, it was early in my professional career, and I had other cases to attend to."

"Mr. Holmes!" said Mary. "Is there or is there not a reward for information leading to the apprehension of Mr. Hyde? One was advertised at the time of the murder, but I do not know if, after all this time . . ."

"Yes, there was a reward," said Holmes. "A hundred pounds for information leading directly to the apprehension of the murderer, offered by the family of Sir Danvers Carew. Whether the family would still be willing to offer that sum? I don't know, but we can certainly enquire. It would be best to ask Inspector Lestrade of Scotland Yard. I'm meeting him in an hour to discuss these murders in Whitechapel. These *'orrible murders*, as the newsboys keep shouting. Watson, I'm afraid the mystery of Lord Avebury's menagerie will have to wait. We have two mysteries on our hands, both more intriguing than a collection of missing animals. If Lestrade does not know, he can tell us whom in the family to contact. But about what? If you'll forgive my saying so, Miss Jekyll, you don't appear to be the sort of person who consorts with criminals or knows their whereabouts."

"And yet, I may know where to find Hyde," said Mary.

"Indeed?" he said, smiling. It was evident that he did not believe her. "Well then, Miss Jekyll. What can you tell me?"

Mary spoke in her most businesslike tone.

> DIANA: *Most businesslike?* She always sounds as though she's directing a meeting. I think what you mean is her *bossiest* tone.

> JUSTINE: Diana, you know what Mary tells you is for your own good. Someone needs to keep you from committing mischief. Like cutting up all our underclothes because Mary said you couldn't come to Vienna this time.

> MARY: Not that telling her what to do ever works. And Mrs. Poole is trying to sew the pieces back together, but the last time I saw her, she was shaking her head. . . .

> DIANA: Works! I should think not. The day I listen to Mary is the day I eat my own boots.

> MARY: At least that would keep you quiet for a while.

Mary spoke in her usual businesslike tone. "After my mother's death, my solicitor"—not that Mr. Guest was her solicitor any longer, but it sounded more official—"informed me that she had been making regular payments to a Society of St. Mary Magdalen. One pound a week for the care and keeping of Hyde. Look." She pulled out the account book and put it, open to the correct page, on top of the books that were already stacked on the table. Both men leaned forward. "I suspect he was blackmailing her with information learned during his association with my father. This morning, I searched in the directory—the Society of St. Mary Magdalen is a charitable organization in Whitechapel. I believe we shall find Hyde there."

"Now *that* is very interesting," said Holmes. "And worthy of investigating further. Unfortunately, I may be tied up all day with Lestrade. These murders are spectacular—Fleet Street can't seem to get enough of them, and each one appears on the front page, with the body part particularly emphasized. The victim without arms, the victim without a head . . . But I'm sure the solution will be a simple one, in the end. Spectacular cases are usually simpler, and less interesting, than they initially appear."

"A madman, certainly," said Watson. "Who else would murder young women and take away parts of their bodies? The murderer is clearly mad."

"Yet even a madman has method in his madness," said Holmes. "Watson, I would like you to accompany Miss Jekyll to this society. Try to determine whether Hyde is there—unobtrusively, of course. You can meet me afterward and tell me what you've found."

"The two of us?" said Watson. "Surely you wouldn't send Miss Jekyll into Whitechapel looking for a dangerous criminal! That is too imprudent even for you, Holmes. And consider the name of this society. It would be improper . . ."

"I'm quite prepared to go," said Mary. "And I'm fully aware of what the society's name implies. I have read my Bible, and am familiar with the Magdalen. I could hardly live in London without realizing there are prostitutes on the city streets, or societies for their salvation. Really, Dr. Watson, I do read the newspapers." Although she had lived in London all her life, she had never been to the East End, and Mrs. Poole had warned her what a den of iniquity lay there, in Whitechapel and Spitalfields. She was curious to see whether it was as iniquitous as she had been told.

> MRS. POOLE: It was most improper of him to send you there, miss!

> CATHERINE: I have not yet gotten to the part where he actually sends her, Mrs. Poole. Please don't anticipate the action for our readers.

> MARY: If we are to have any readers. Do you think anyone will actually be interested in us, how we met, and our lives together?

> BEATRICE: There is always interest in monsters. I think Catherine knows that well.

> CATHERINE: Yes, I do.

"That is why I'm sending you to protect her," said Holmes. "You have never seen Hyde, and she has—he was her father's laboratory assistant. Miss Jekyll, do you think you would recognize him, after all this time? You were only a child, remember."

"Yes, absolutely," said Mary. "One doesn't forget a man like Mr. Hyde."

"Well then," said Holmes. "The investigation is afoot. Miss Jekyll, you are responsible for determining whether Hyde is still alive. If he is, we shall attempt to apprehend him and secure your reward. Watson, you are responsible for insuring that Miss Jekyll returns safely. You are to do nothing—nothing, I tell you—but determine whether Hyde lives. After you have visited this society, we shall discuss what to do next."

"Very well, Holmes," said Watson. "I would prefer to keep Miss Jekyll out of this, but of course if Hyde is alive, he must be apprehended. We can't allow a dangerous criminal to conceal himself in London."

"Can we go now?" said Mary, looking at her watch. "It's almost noon, and I'm sure it will take us a while to get there." She had no idea how long it would take, or how they were supposed to get there—surely they were not going to walk? But she was tired of this endless discussion, particularly as to the propriety of her going. At least Mr. Holmes was being practical about it.

MRS. POOLE: And most improper!

CATHERINE: Yes, yes. You've made that point.
Thank you, Mrs. Poole.

"Shall we meet you back here, Holmes?" asked Watson. As he put on his coat, Mary noticed that he slipped a pistol into the pocket.

"No, ask for me at Scotland Yard. If I'm not there, I'll be with Inspector Lestrade."

So Mary's day would include a trip to Whitechapel and Scotland Yard! This was certainly more interesting than sitting at home and worrying about money. She put the account book back into the portfolio and stood up. "We'll report back to you this afternoon, Mr. Holmes. Dr. Watson, are you ready?"

"I'll find us a cab on Baker Street. If you'll follow me, Miss Jekyll?"

Mary took her umbrella from the stand, turned back, and nodded to Holmes, who was smiling—she had no idea why—then followed Watson out the door. As they walked down the stairs, she suddenly wondered how much a cab to Whitechapel would cost, and how she would pay for it. She had exactly two shillings in her purse. Before coming to see Mr. Holmes, she should have gone to her mother's bank, but of course she had not known she would be taking a cab this morning, and she had been eager to solve the mystery of Hyde. Anyway, she was still not sure how to get to Clerkenwell. Perhaps this afternoon, after their investigation, she could close her mother's account and transfer the funds. Then, at least, such impromptu trips would not cause her so much concern.

"Mr. Watson, about the fare—," she began.

"Oh, don't worry about that, Miss Jekyll," he said, opening the front door. "You're assisting us in an investigation. All expenses will of course be borne by Mr. Holmes."

They emerged onto Baker Street to the rumble of cabs, and costermongers shouting "nice fresh 'addock!" or "apples 'alfpenny a pound!" To her left she could see the trees and lawns of Regent's Park; to her right was the noise and bustle of the city.

She thought of what she had read in her father's laboratory notebook and the letters, what she had not told Mr. Holmes. There was no need for him to know, at least not yet. But there was no time to think about that now. Watson had waved down a cab and was motioning for her to climb up. She lifted her skirt and settled onto the leather seat, wondering what would be waiting for them in Whitechapel.

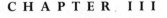

CHAPTER III

The Magdalen Society

As the hackney cab drove east, the main thoroughfares grew more crowded, the cross streets narrower, darkened by lines of laundry hanging from balconies and windows. Mary was used to the leafy stateliness of Marylebone Road. Whitechapel High Street was completely different, a tangle of carts and omnibuses, with no trees to relieve the drabness of the buildings. The cabbie refused to take them into the twisting alleys of Whitechapel, so they got out and walked the rest of the way.

Asking directions as they went along, of men smoking in doorways and women selling needles and other oddments from dingy storefronts, they walked until Mary had lost all sense of where they were. Finally, they came to a dismal square, with a park in the middle: a few trees shading a graveled area on which children attempted to roll a hoop. The park was surrounded on three sides by tenements with broken windows and shutters hanging awry. On the remaining side was a gray stone church that proclaimed itself St. Mary Magdalen on a board in faded lettering. Next to the church was a high stone wall, above which they could see the upper stories of a stone house covered with ivy. Over a gated archway in the wall were carved the words SOCIETY OF ST. MARY MAGDALEN.

"How in the world could he be hiding here?" said Mary.

She and Watson looked at a sign on the gate, on which was

written: A MISSION TO RESCUE OUR FALLEN SISTERS IN CHRIST. VISITORS PERMITTED BETWEEN THE HOURS OF 2 AND 4, EXCEPT ON THE SABBATH. NO GENTLEMAN VISITORS AT ANY TIME.

"It is what we expected, a society for fallen women. You can't go into such a place, Miss Jekyll," said Watson. Mrs. Poole, I'm not going to let you comment here. We all know what you think.

"Why, because it wouldn't be proper? I don't think we have much of a choice," said Mary. "I doubt they'll let *you* in." She walked up to the gate and rang the bell.

In a few minutes, a woman appeared at the gate. She was dressed in gray wool, as plain as the habit of a nun, and her hair was pulled into a tight bun at the back of her head as though she were afraid a strand might escape. She said, in a high and somewhat artificial voice, "I heard the bell as I was passing. These are not our regular visiting hours, as I believe the sign indicates. I'm Sister Margaret. Were you looking for anyone in particular?"

"My name is Mary Jekyll," said Mary, "and this is—"

"Jekyll!" said Sister Margaret, her voice rising even higher, into a sort of screech. "You'd better come in at once. Mrs. Raymond will want to talk to you immediately."

She opened the gate, which shrieked as though it badly needed oiling, and motioned Mary, with rapid gestures, to come inside.

"Who is Mrs. Raymond?" said Mary, hesitant to venture inside that stone wall. Why would anyone in this place want to talk to her? Was she being mistaken for someone else?

"Mrs. Raymond is the director," said Sister Margaret, as though the information were obvious. But that did not answer Mary's question. Why would the director of such an institution want to talk to her? How could she know who Mary was? But no, she suddenly realized. This was not about her personally: it was the name Jekyll that had caused Sister Margaret such consternation.

"Miss Jekyll, if I may intervene . . . ," said Watson.

"Not you," said Sister Margaret contemptuously, as though talking to a dog that had rolled in the mud. "No gentleman visitors. We don't even make an exception for relatives."

"All right," said Mary. "I'll come talk to this . . . Mrs. Raymond."

Watson took her by the elbow. "Miss Jekyll, I don't like this," he said, so low that only Mary could hear him.

"But I have to go," said Mary, turning to him and speaking in the same low tones. "The director of this place obviously knows something about Mr. Hyde. I have to find out what. We know the money was coming here, and look at how Sister Whatever responded to my name. Can you hold these for me?" She handed him the portfolio and her umbrella. She did not like to relinquish the portfolio, but felt safer giving it to Watson than taking it into such a place, where Hyde might lurk.

"All right," said Watson. "But there's something I want you to have."

As he took her umbrella, he slipped something into her hand. She looked down: it was the pistol he had put into his pocket—a revolver. "Do you know how to use one of these?"

"Yes," she said. And she did—Joseph, who had been a game-keeper's son in Lincolnshire, had taught her. She even had a revolver at home, in a desk drawer. It had been her father's, and she had insisted that Joseph teach her how to use it, despite his protests that as a lady, she would always have someone to defend her. Even then, she had not been so sure that would be the case. Now she was grateful that she had insisted on those lessons.

"If you're not back in an hour, I'll come after you. I don't know the meaning of this, but Hyde was—perhaps is—a dangerous criminal. If he is on the premises, I want you to have some sort of protection."

Mary nodded. "I understand." She did not want him to see that she was—apprehensive? Yes, that was the word.

DIANA: Because you can't frighten our Mary.

MARY: Don't be ridiculous. I'm perfectly capable of being frightened. You frighten me all the time. Remember what happened in Vienna, when you almost burned down the mental hospital? And almost got yourself killed by doing the *exact opposite* of what Justine and I told you to do?

DIANA: Well, if you hadn't been such a bloody— [The rest of Diana's comments are not appropriate for a book that we hope will reach an audience of both mature and younger readers.]

CATHERINE: Diana, I will not include that sort of language, so you might as well try to express yourself without resorting to insults or invectives.

DIANA: [Comments omitted. Seriously, just stop already.]

But what could happen to her in a religious society to rescue Magdalens, the prostitutes who are ubiquitous in London, particularly in the East End? Keeping her body turned so Sister Margaret could not see what she was doing, she slipped the revolver into her purse. Thank goodness it was the practical kind, not one of those decorative purses fine ladies carried, mostly tassels and embroidery. She turned back toward the gate and, trying not to look as reluctant as she felt, walked through the archway into a courtyard. She heard the gate clang behind her and turned back for a moment. Dr. Watson was looking at her through the bars. He pointed to his watch—reminding her that she had one hour.

She gave him a small wave, then followed Sister Margaret, trying not to think too much about where she was going and what she might find. She was inside, which meant she was committed to this adventure, whatever it might produce.

They walked across the courtyard, which was paved except for a border by the stone wall of the house, where straggling yews leaned toward the sunlight. A thick layer of ivy grew up the walls to the third floor, making the house look particularly ominous. Sister Margaret pushed open a large wooden door with iron fittings that made Mary feel as though she were entering the Castle of Otranto. She could not repress a small shudder. The air was damper and colder here than it had been in the streets of London. Mary followed Sister Margaret up a set of stone stairs to the second floor. At the top of the stairs was a long hallway, leading to another large wooden door. There seemed to be a lot of those in the Magdalen Society, as though someone had decided on large and ominous as a decorating style. Sister Margaret knocked.

"Come in!" came the call from inside.

Sister Margaret pushed, and the door opened with a loud creak. "Mrs. Raymond," she said, "this is Miss Jekyll."

A handsome woman with iron-gray hair rose from behind a desk. Like Sister Margaret, she was wearing a gray dress, but hers was of watered silk, and she had a chatelaine at her waist, with an imposing number of keys dangling from it

"I'm glad you've come, Miss Jekyll," said the director. "I refuse to keep the child any longer. She has proven incorrigible. I've written to your mother numerous times, asking her to come take Diana, but she's never responded."

"Diana?" said Mary, astonished. "Who is Diana?" What in the world could this be about?

"You are Mrs. Jekyll's daughter, are you not?" asked the director, looking at her as though not at all sure of her mental capacity.

"Yes, of course," she said.

"Then I assume you are here to take responsibility for her. Mrs. Jekyll has been quite generous, but it's impossible for her to stay any longer. She is a continual disruption. She whispers blasphemies during prayers. And I can't tell you what she did in the baptismal font of St. Mary Magdalen, where we attend services."

Mary stared, astonished. What in the world was the director talking about? And what could this possibly have to do with Hyde? "I don't understand," she said. "Letters to my mother?"

"Through her solicitor, of course. A Mr. Utterson of Gaunt Street."

"But Mr. Utterson died several years ago, and his offices are not in Gaunt Street—perhaps you were sending them to his personal address? That would explain why my mother never received them."

"That," said Mrs. Raymond with a frown, "is not my problem. She's been confined to her room for singing inappropriate songs during dinner. We can have her packed in fifteen minutes."

"When you say *her*—," Mary began, but Mrs. Raymond had already turned and started walking out of the room. *Whom do you mean? Who is this Diana?* she had meant to ask. However, there was nothing to do but follow, with Sister Margaret trailing after them. They walked back down the hallway and up yet another flight of stairs. Two women in plain gray dresses, with white aprons and caps, who were washing the stone steps rose and curtseyed as they passed. "Both rescued from a brothel in Limehouse," said Mrs. Raymond. "We do wonderful work here, Miss Jekyll, bringing strayed souls back to the Lord's path." Mary nodded without paying particular attention, but as they reached the top of the steps and walked down another hallway, she became interested in the rooms they were passing, where women in identical gray dresses, with white aprons and caps, were sewing in long, straight rows. "The work our Magdalens do supports our mission," said the director. It looked like a rather grim mission, to Mary. The women worked silently: there was no chattering, the way there usually is in a room full of women, and if they looked up as Mary passed, they almost immediately looked down again to their work. Finally, Mrs. Raymond opened a door and said, "Diana, there's a lady here to see you. She's going to take you with her."

"About bloody time," Mary heard.

She entered the room. There, sitting cross-legged on the bed, barefoot and in a white shift, was a girl. She had red hair curling down to her waist, and her face was covered with freckles. The room around her was a mess. A bureau in the corner had its drawers pulled out, and there were clothes strewn over the floor. A bookshelf had been emptied of its books, which lay on the floor among the clothes. Mary noted that they were all pious works—a Bible, *The Sermons of Reverend Dr. Throckmorton*, a book with *Holy Thoughts and Good Deeds* written on the spine, lying open with its pages downward. A table was pulled out from the wall and the chair had been turned over. On the floor, Mary could see the shards of a pitcher and washbasin, a brass candlestick, and a hair brush. On one wall was written, in large red letters, LET ME OUT OF HERE YOU BLOODY HIPOCRITES!

"What have you done now, you ungrateful miscreant?" said Mrs. Raymond, in icy tones.

With a grin, the girl held up her arm. It was obvious where the red letters had come from: she had wrapped a long cut with pieces torn from her shift. The red on the strips had crusted.

"Oh, how dreadful!" said Sister Margaret. She looked faint.

"Well, you're not going to be my problem much longer," said Mrs. Raymond. "Pack your trunk immediately. You don't want to keep Miss Jekyll waiting."

"Miss Jekyll, is it?" said the girl. "Oh, that's rich. Lovely to meet you, Miss Jekyll. Where are you going to take me, that's what I want to know. Is it the asylum next? Or prison?"

"Who is this girl?" Mary asked Mrs. Raymond, feeling utterly bewildered. It was about time she got some answers. And the girl, whoever she was, should have her arm tended to.

"This is Diana Hyde," said Mrs. Raymond, looking at her with astonishment. "Surely you knew? She was brought to us after her mother died, with a letter from Mrs. Jekyll charging us to care for and raise her. Your mother has paid for her maintenance ever since. Didn't she tell you?"

"My mother died last week," said Mary. Why would her mother do such a thing? She did not understand.

"Oh dear!" said Sister Margaret. "How dreadful!"

"My condolences," said Mrs. Raymond, sounding not at all sincere. Indeed, she sounded rather pleased. Some people enjoyed death when it did not touch them directly. "But that does not change my position. The girl must go."

"But can you give me no explanation?" said Mary. "I understand that my mother left this child under your care and arranged for her maintenance. I assume she is somehow connected to my father's assistant, Mr. Hyde. But why?" What interest could her mother have had in this child? A charitable one, surely. It was just the sort of case that would have appealed to Ernestine Jekyll. But then why had she not told Mary about her? The child must be thirteen or fourteen, although she looked small for her age—food was probably not overabundant at the Society of St. Mary Magdalen.

> DIANA: Not overabundant! They damn near starved
> us to death. Those sanctimonious . . .

> CATHERINE: I already warned you about using that
> sort of language.

"Well," said Diana, "are you going to take me out of this place?"

Was she? Mary wondered what in the world to do. She had no idea why her mother had supported this child for so many years. But she had, and Mary supposed that created some sort of obligation. After all, once she closed the bank account, there would be no more money for the child's maintenance. What would the Society of St. Mary Magdalen do with her?

"If she were to stay here——," she began.

"Oh, we couldn't possibly keep her, Miss Jekyll," said Mrs. Raymond. "We're a society for fallen angels of the Lord, not wayward children. No, I'm afraid that's quite out of the question." She smiled, a grim and implacable smile.

Mary looked at the girl again. Her arm needed tending to. Obviously no one here was going to do it, and then there was the mystery of her origin and name. What was her relationship to Hyde? If she left the girl here, she would never find out. She was the right age to be Hyde's daughter. . . . If so, perhaps she would know something of her father's whereabouts? "All right," said Mary. "She can come with me."

"Thank you, Miss Jekyll," said Mrs. Raymond. Now that the matter was settled, she was much more gracious. "Perhaps you can beat some sense into her. We have attempted to prepare her for a useful trade, but have found her utterly unteachable. We had initially accepted her on the understanding that she might be trained for service in a private household, or have a religious vocation——"

"Not bloody likely, you old bitch!" said Diana, getting up and starting to dance around on the bed. She moved so wildly that Mary was afraid she would fall off.

"If you want me to get you out of here, you'd better pack," Mary said. The girl was out of control. What in the world was she going to do with her?

Diana jumped off the bed, pulled on one of the dresses that

were lying on the floor, and started throwing the remaining dresses into a trunk that was sitting beside the bureau. Well, they could sort it all out later. The important thing now was to get out of here and discuss the situation with Dr. Watson.

"And put on your boots," said Mrs. Raymond.

"Won't," said Diana.

"Suit yourself," said Mrs. Raymond. "You're not my responsibility any longer."

"But you seem to be mine," said Mary. "Put on your boots or I'll leave you here."

Diana glared at her, but she pulled a pair of boots from under the bed and put them on over her bare feet. "All right, I'm ready. Get me out of here so I don't have to see her ugly face again." She stuck out her tongue at Sister Margaret, who looked shocked and a little frightened.

"That's enough," said Mary. "If you want to come, then come."

> DIANA: See, that's the voice. You can call it *businesslike* if you want to.

> MARY: I was very close to leaving you there. You'd better thank your stars I didn't!

> DIANA: They'd better thank *their* stars! If I had stayed there much longer, I would have burned down that whole operation.

> MRS. POOLE: Oh, I don't doubt you would have. Sometimes I think you're a demon in the shape of a child! And don't bother sticking your tongue out at me. I'm so used to it that I no longer pay attention.

Together, Mary and Sister Margaret carried Diana's trunk down the two flights of stairs, with Diana capering before them, humming some sort of tune. Mrs. Raymond followed them all the way down to the front door, then watched them walk across the courtyard to the gate, as though to make certain Mary and Diana were truly leaving.

Watson, still waiting outside the gate, looked relieved to see Mary again.

Once they had carried the trunk through the archway, Sister Margaret set it down, scurried back into the courtyard, and shut the gate behind her with a clang. She turned the key in the lock, then called, "May the Lord bless and keep you—away from here, you imp!"

"Your arse!" Diana called back, with a rude gesture.

"Dr. Watson," said Mary, almost laughing at the astonishment on his face, "I've been informed that this is Miss Diana Hyde, and that I am now in charge of her." The situation wasn't funny of course—only he looked so completely bewildered. It was such a perfect expression of how she herself was feeling at the moment.

"How d'you do," said Diana. "Any gentleman friend of my sister is a gentleman friend of mine."

"Your sister?" said Mary. "What in the world do you mean—"

"Dr. Watson! Dr. Watson!" A boy was running down the street toward them. He was a typical London urchin, in an oversized suit with holes in the knees and a battered cap on his head. He stopped, put his hands on his sides, and tried to catch his breath.

"What is it, Charlie?" asked Watson, producing a penny out of his pocket.

"Mr. Holmes says to come as soon as you can," said the boy, taking the penny so swiftly and skillfully that Mary barely saw him do it. "They've found another body. It's not far from here, but I ran all the way."

"I'm afraid your explanation will have to wait, Miss Jekyll," said Watson. "I'll have to get you back to Marylebone. But how to do it, when there are no cabs in the area . . ."

"I can come with you," said Mary. "I need to talk to Mr. Holmes, quite urgently." She wanted to tell him about what had happened at the Magdalen Society. Perhaps he could shed some light on it all. "Can we can send the trunk and this child back together?"

"Oh no!" said Diana. "You're not getting rid of me that easily. Wherever you go, I'm coming too. You took charge of me, remember?"

"Miss Jekyll, I can't take you to a murder scene," said Watson.

"I don't think you have much of a choice. I can't find my way back to Marylebone from here alone, you know." Despite the difficulty of the situation, once again Mary felt like laughing. Here she was, in the middle of Whitechapel, with Dr. Watson and mystery in the shape of a very dirty girl, arguing to be taken to a murder. What would Mrs. Poole think?

MRS. POOLE: What indeed!

"Oh, all right," said Watson. "Charlie, can you take charge of this trunk? Miss Jekyll will give you her address. Find a cart that can transport it for her, and make sure it arrives safely. And tell me where I can find Holmes."

"All right, guv'nor," said Charlie, looking curiously at Diana, particularly at her bare ankles, which were visible under the hem of her dress. Obviously, he was not used to seeing her like with the respectable Dr. Watson. She made an impish face at him. He turned up his nose, looking most superior, and paid her no more attention.

Watson handed him a shilling, which disappeared as quickly as had the penny. Charlie ran off into the alleys of Whitechapel, with a promise that he *wouldn't be a minute, guv'nor*. While they were waiting, Mary retrieved her portfolio and umbrella, and handed the revolver back to Watson, with thanks for its protection. As briefly as she could, she told him what had happened inside the Society of St. Mary Magdalen, with numerous interruptions from Diana, half complaints about the society, half curses. When he heard about Diana's cut, he did his best to clean it with the whiskey he carried in a flask—for emergencies, he said. As he poured whiskey onto the cut, Diana swore vividly and inventively. Although she hated to admit it, even Mary was impressed by her verbal prowess.

MARY: I was not!

DIANA: Oh, you most definitely were.

He rebandaged the cut with strips from Diana's already-torn shift, ripped off with the aid of his pocket knife. Just as he had finished tying the bandage, Charlie returned with a man driving a wheelbarrow. The trunk was lifted into the wheelbarrow, and the man promised that it would be delivered safely to 11 Park Terrace by his brother, who had a cart from which he sold vegetables in Covent Garden, "lovely turnips and cabbages, miss." Charlie gave Watson directions, although Mary could hear phrases such as "turn by the house with the chickens in the front yard," which did not fill her with confidence. Then Charlie followed the man with the wheelbarrow, whistling between his teeth.

Watson turned to them again. "Miss Jekyll, and . . . Miss Hyde? If you'll both follow me, I'll do my best to take you to Holmes, although what he'll think of your presence, I have no idea."

"So," said Diana, "is this another one of those murders? That's all they talk about at St. Mary Magdalen, when they're allowed

to talk, that is. The girl without arms, the girl without a head . . .
They say it gives them nightmares. What's she missing, this time?"

"We have no idea, yet," said Mary. "And if you don't keep a
civil tongue in your head, I'm sending you back there, no matter
what Mrs. Raymond says. So for goodness' sake stay quiet and
out of mischief!" There was no time now, but later she would
have to untangle the mystery of Diana Hyde. Who was this girl?
Why had her mother supported her for so long? And why had she
called Mary *sister*? But Dr. Watson was already walking toward
the narrow street that Charlie had indicated, and Diana Hyde was
skipping, actually skipping, as though this were all a game, beside
him. Mary hurried to catch up.

> JUSTINE: Diana, I've always wondered. What did you
> do in the baptismal font?
>
> DIANA: I pissed in it!
>
> JUSTINE: Yes, I suspected something of the sort.

CHAPTER IV

A Murder in Whitechapel

The Society of St. Mary Magdalen had been near Whitechapel High Street, but now they were walking into the
heart of the East End. The alleys grew more dismal, with
broken pavement and piles of refuse. Women hung out washing,
men sat on the steps of the tenements, playing cards or reading
newspapers. Barefoot children ran down the alleys, playing tag or
simply hitting each other and running away, Mary could not tell
which. The air smelled of the smoke from factories, and cooking,
and human waste. Even the sunlight seemed dimmer, as though it
were coming through layers of fog.

This is the dark half of London, where poverty and crime
thrive—a shadow cast by the bright and prosperous West End.
Go on, tell me I'm being melodramatic, I dare you. We all know
what the social conditions are like down there. And yes, I know
perfectly well that this is not a political tract, thank you, Mary! I
don't need to be reminded.

As they walked, Mary answered Watson's questions about
what had happened inside the Magdalen Society, trying to fill in
the details she had not been able to give him earlier. They passed
a soldier without legs, begging on a corner. As they turned the
corner and walked down yet another alley, a dog on a chain barked
at them until someone shouted, "Shut up, you bloody bitch!" Then
it lay down, whining, its ears flat against its head.

"Miss Jekyll, I'm not sure I should have brought you here," said Watson.

"What, you didn't know how the other half lived?" said Diana, mockingly. "So it's good enough for me, but not a lady like her. I get it!"

If she says one more thing, I'm going to hit her, thought Mary. Diana had continually interrupted her conversation with Watson, detailing her life at St. Mary Magdalen—how she had hated the meals, which sisters she had particularly disliked, what she had said to them before they washed her mouth out with soap. What they had said to her after she bit them. *If I had some soap,* thought Mary, *I would wash your mouth out myself, and you wouldn't get to bite me, you brat.*

> DIANA: Oh yes I would! You're not nearly as quick as
> I am.

"You shouldn't be here either," said Watson. "This is no place for a child."

"Oh Lord!" said Diana. "I was born in a place like this. There was a man who lived in our court, a butcher he was, with a wife he used to beat when he was drunk. Well, one night he fell down drunk and hit his head on one of the stoops. That was the end of him! By morning, the rats had eaten him up, all but the bones. Wasn't that a funny end, for a butcher?"

"Diana," said Mary, "even rats wouldn't pick bones clean in one night. If you're going to tell tales, you should at least make them plausible."

"All right then," said Diana. "He wasn't gone by the next morning, but he was gnawed by rats! His widow couldn't pay for a funeral, so he lay there for three days until the Missionary Society took his body away. Lord, how he stunk up our court!"

"That's quite enough," said Mary. "Dr. Watson, where are we going, exactly?"

"I think it's just around the corner," he said. "It would have been better for Charlie to guide us—boys like him know every inch of this city. But I needed him to look after your trunk, Miss Hyde. Otherwise, I'm not sure it would have reached its destination."

> DIANA: That's right, *Miss Hyde*! At least some people know how to be polite. And I could have guided you—I know every inch of Whitechapel, better than Charlie. But did you ask me? Of course not.

"I just hope I've understood Charlie's directions," Watson continued. "The alleys in this part of the city are like a labyrinth. You expect a Minotaur around each corner, and wish for a piece of string from Ariadne!"

Around the next corner was the narrowest, dirtiest alley they had yet seen. Halfway down it stood Sherlock Holmes. With him were three men: two of them London bobbies, the third a short man in plain clothes with bright red hair and a bristling mustache. Lying on the ground between them was . . . well, mercifully she was covered with a piece of cloth, although it was not long enough to conceal her entire body. Mary could see her shoes and stockinged ankles. Toward the top of her body, the edges of the cloth were soaked with blood. Mary gasped. Why had she thought this would be interesting? It was not interesting—it was horrible.

> DIANA: Horrible and interesting!

> MARY: Horrible. But Diana's right, it was interesting as well. I still remember her shoes: the heels were worn down, and I wondered if she had simply

neglected them, or not been able to afford a cobbler.
One of her stockings had been mended. It's strange
what trivial things we think of, when experiencing
something so—well, horrible is the word.

"Watson! Excellent timing," said Holmes. "Although I'm surprised to see that you brought Miss Jekyll. Could she not have
been sent home in a cab? Forgive me, Miss Jekyll, I do not mean to
dispose of you as though you were a piece of baggage. But this is
scarcely the place for a lady. And who or what is this?" He looked
pointedly at Diana.

"This is what we found at the Society of St. Mary Magdalen,"
said Watson.

"Her name is Diana Hyde," said Mary. "This is the Hyde my
mother's payments have been supporting. She looks about thirteen
or fourteen, although she's a bit scrawny. Do you think—"

"Scrawny my arse!" said Diana. "And I'm fourteen, thank
you. I'm not some beggar born on the streets—I know my own
birthday."

"—that she's the daughter of Mr. Hyde?" said Holmes. "Surely
she herself can give you some information on that score."

"I suppose we never did ask her, did we, Dr. Watson?" said
Mary.

"There was no time," Watson replied.

"Why are you talking about me as though I'm not here?" said
Diana, crossing her arms and looking irate.

"In this case, the simplest course of action is to ask." Holmes
turned to Diana and put his hand on her shoulder, conveniently
stopping her from what she had been about to do—kick Mary on
the shin. "Are you the daughter of a Mr. Edward Hyde?"

Diana twisted her shoulder out of his grasp and stood glaring
at them. "Mum always told me that my father was a gentleman

who called himself Mr. Hyde. She told me to behave like a lady because I was a gentleman's daughter. But he never came to see me, not while Mum was alive. And then I was sent to St. Mary's."

"So you would have no idea where he is now," said Watson.

"Holmes, I don't know what you're doing bringing a woman and a child to a murder scene," said the red-haired man. "Watson can make himself useful, although nowadays he seems to spend his time recording your exploits rather than examining bodies. But they have no business being here."

"I'm not a child," said Diana. "And who do you think you are, carrots?"

"Carrots yourself!" said the red-haired man, glaring at her.

"This is Inspector Lestrade of Scotland Yard," said Holmes. "He's not in the habit of locking up young women for rudeness, but it's probably a good idea not to tempt him. Lestrade, this is Miss Jekyll, the daughter of Dr. Jekyll, who was involved in the Carew murder case. You may remember it, although it was many years ago. She's here on business, with me. But I'm afraid, Miss Jekyll, that this murder takes precedence. It was reported an hour ago. A man who does odd jobs in these parts found the body of a woman named Molly Keane lying in this alley. I have not yet examined the body myself, and must do so at some length. As you are here, you and Miss Hyde may stay, but you may wish to avert your eyes. It's not a sight for the squeamish, I'm afraid."

Mary stood undecided, afraid to see what lay under the sheet. "Her head isn't missing, is it?" she asked.

"That was the last victim," said Lestrade. "He never takes the same body part twice, and if you look carefully, you'll see the outline of her head, or most of it. But Holmes, I protest. This is highly irregular."

Holmes paid no attention, but lifted the sheet and handed it to one of the sergeants, who folded it gingerly, trying not to get blood on his uniform.

Mary gasped.

"Horrible," said Watson.

"Lord, he done her in good," said Diana.

Molly Keane had been around Mary's age. She must have been a pretty girl. The bones of her face were strong and fine, although the face itself was bruised: there were blue marks over the cheeks and under the eyes. Those eyes looked up at the gray sky, lifeless. There was blood spattered over her shoulders and soaked into her dress. Since the pavement was still wet from the morning's rains, the paving stones around her were slick and red, with blood pooling in the spaces between them. Her long hair trailed in the blood on the pavement. Mary forced herself to look back up, to what she had been avoiding—the head lying in a pool of blood. The entire top of it, above the eyebrows, was gone.

"He cut out her brain," said Holmes.

"What . . . what could he possibly want with it?" asked Mary.

"He must be a madman," said Lestrade. "Who else would do something like that? Molly Keane was a—well, I'm not going to say anything in front of the ladies. You shouldn't even be here, neither of you."

"A whore," said Diana. "We know. Look at the rouge on her cheeks."

"But not an ordinary one," said Holmes. "Look at her hands. Her palms are not calloused by manual labor, and her clothes are of good quality, although patched and mended. However she may have fallen, she was once a lady."

"You're right about that," said Lestrade. "While we were waiting for you, Sergeant Debenham talked to one of the other girls who works this area. He's got her waiting at an inn around the corner. He's also holding the man who found the body, a local beggar who goes by Poor Richard and hasn't any other name, so far as I can tell. You'll want to talk to them, Holmes. According to her friend, Molly Keane had been a governess until she was seduced by her master and thrown out by her mistress. Her child died at birth, and she went on the streets to earn her living."

"A sad story, and not an uncommon one," said Watson, shaking his head.

"Poor girl," said Mary. She had read about this side of London life, but never encountered it herself. It shocked her, although not perhaps as much as it should have. This was life, wasn't it? Life as she had often imagined it, looking out the curtained windows of the house on Park Terrace.

"Or stupid," said Diana. "I've lived with whores all my life, whether they were working or reformed. Whores know all sorts of ways to avoid getting with child. They can make customers withdraw, or use a sheepskin, or—"

"Diana!" said Mary.

DIANA: How is that more shocking than getting with child, I'd like to know?

MARY: One doesn't talk about such things, particularly in front of gentlemen.

DIANA: Then one is as stupid as Molly Keane.

"She may have fallen into sin," said Holmes, "but she died bravely. Look at her right hand. The fingernails are broken, and there is flesh under them. She fought for her life, poor girl."

"What's that in her left hand?" asked Mary.

Before Mary could stop her, Diana crouched by the body of Molly Keane, getting blood on the hem of her dress and the toes of her boots. She reached across the murdered girl to the stiff hand that lay on her bosom and pried open the clenched fingers. From that cold grasp, she withdrew what the girl had been holding: a metal button.

"Diana!" cried Mary.

"Bloody hell . . . ," said Lestrade, sputtering as though he did not know how to go on. "Don't you know never to touch a murder victim? Holmes, I'm holding you responsible."

"All right, I'm responsible," said Holmes. "You should not have done that, Miss Hyde. There might have been fingerprints, although it's unlikely we would find any but Molly Keane's. But since you have—what is it?"

"It's a button of some sort . . . no, I think it's a watch fob," said Mary, taking it from Diana in her handkerchief, so as not to touch it, and examining it closely. It was made of brass, and heavy in her hand. "Part of the chain is still attached. And there's something . . ." The fob was caked with blood, but she could make out letters on the bottom, engraved into the metal. "S.A. It could be a set of initials. Or it could stand for something—some sort of motto."

"Indeed," said Holmes. "I've seen fobs like this worn by members of scientific societies, or social clubs, or even cricket teams. They're often used as seals, which would explain the engraving. She must have torn it from the murderer during their struggle. Miss Jekyll, if you could step aside, I would like to examine the body thoroughly. And take your ward with you, if you please."

Mary grabbed Diana by the arm and pulled her back, out of the way. Holmes walked around and around the body while the rest of them stood and watched. It was almost comical to see him, bent over like a praying mantis, inspecting the ground around the murdered girl, lifting her hands, turning her head from side to side and looking at her bruises. Finally, he examined the hole in her head. Mary had to turn away, sickened by the sight. Then he made a careful examination of the alley. He seemed to be look-ing at every stone, from the cross street at one end to the blank wall at the other. It was, Mary thought, a good place to commit a murder. The alley was long and narrow. Neither of the buildings that formed its walls had windows overlooking the alley, so the solid brick rose sheer. Close to the street, the building on one side had been built out so that it hung over the alley, blocking some of the light. Toward its blind end, there was a large doorway. It looked like the back entrance to a warehouse, but the door was evidently locked on the inside, since Holmes turned the handle and rattled it several times. Last night, there would have been no one to see, and no way out for poor Molly Keane. Holmes paid particular attention to that doorway, returning to it once he had examined the rest of the alley.

"How long is he going to take?" Lestrade finally asked, looking at his watch. "I have Poor Richard and that other girl waiting, and I want to question them before they start getting restless."

"As long as it takes," said Watson. "You know him well enough to know his methods."

As far as Mary could tell, it took forever. She did not know how much longer she could keep Diana quiet—her furious whis-pers that Lestrade would lock Diana up in Newgate, in the deepest, darkest cell where rats would chew her ears off, were losing their effect. But finally, Holmes rejoined them.

"Well?" said Lestrade.

"They were careful," said Holmes.

"They? We assumed this was the work of an individual madman." Unconsciously, Lestrade chewed on a corner of his mustache. Mary almost laughed, but reminded herself that this was no laughing matter.

"No, there were two of them, and I wish you had called me in on this case earlier! If I'd been able to examine where the other victims were found, I might have been able to tell you more. It's obvious that they had to leave the murder scene quickly, or they would have attempted to hide the body, as they did in the cases of Sally Hayward and Anna Pettingill. But the rain early this morning has wiped away most of their traces. There are few clues on the site. Watson, when would you say she was killed?"

"By the general condition of the body, I would say late last night or early this morning."

"I agree. They obviously did not want to take the chance of being detected, so they chose the cover of darkness to commit their crime. I would put it closer to early morning, before the rain began. Her clothes are still damp."

"How can you tell there were two of them?" said Lestrade. Which was, of course, what Mary had been wondering.

"One left two footprints in the mud under that overhang, where the rain has not erased them." He gestured toward the overhang at the entrance to the alley. They had walked under it themselves, when they arrived. "By the distance between them, I would put him at not much above five feet. By the distance his boots sank into the mud, he is not a heavy man, eight or nine stone. And they are undoubtedly the boots of a gentleman."

"A gentleman!" said Watson. "What gentleman would do such a deed?"

"Oh please!" said Diana. "The things I've seen gentlemen do . . ."

"And the other man?" asked Mary.

"He has left no traces," said Holmes. "But Molly Keane's neck is broken, and I don't think the man we've been describing would have the strength to break her neck. He's small and light—and lame in one leg."

"Lame!" said Lestrade. "How is that, Holmes?"

"His footprints in the mud. One of them is straight, the other bent, almost as though he had a club foot, although without defor-mity. To look at, he must be a twisted man. I don't think he has the strength to saw into a woman's head—you're looking for a surgical saw, I think, Lestrade. Yes, and a sharp knife to remove her brain with. Perhaps a scalpel. This was a more delicate opera-tion than Pauline Delacroix, whose entire head was missing. Two men are most definitely indicated: one strong enough to break a woman's neck and saw through her skull, another with the knowl-edge and skill to take out her brain. You may be looking for a medical man, or a man with medical training."

"The devil!" said Watson.

"Indeed," said Holmes. "Unfortunately, I was able to get noth-ing more: the rain has washed too much away. I would like to talk with the girl who identified Molly Keane, and with this Poor Richard. You said they are at a nearby inn?"

"I would like to come with you, Mr. Holmes," said Mary.

"That's entirely out of the question," said Lestrade. "This is a police investigation, young lady. You don't belong here in the first place."

Holmes looked at her curiously. "Why is that, Miss Jekyll?"

"Your description—it reminds me of something. Someone."

"Indeed? Lestrade, I would like you to indulge me this once. Miss Jekyll, if you can keep Miss Hyde under control, you may listen in on my interviews. But only so long as she behaves herself, mind."

"Indulge you this once!" said Lestrade. "Considering how often I give in to your notions . . ."

But Holmes was already walking up the alley, and Lestrade had to hurry after, shouting directions to his sergeants about how they were to transport the body of Molly Keane back to Scotland Yard. Watson followed, and Mary dragged Diana behind her by the wrist.

The inn was just around the corner: it was called The Bells and had a sign with faded yellow bells painted on it above the front door. The police had cleared out the pub that formed its first floor, so inside there were no patrons, only the landlord behind the bar, disgruntled because he was losing custom; a policeman looking uncomfortable and bored; a young woman rather splendidly but cheaply dressed; and a man with a grizzled beard who must have been Poor Richard. He seemed to be wearing a collection of rags.

> MRS. POOLE: A pub! To think that Miss Mary should have entered such a place.

> MARY: Mrs. Poole, there were no patrons inside. And there were policemen. And Mr. Holmes. And Dr. Watson. I don't know how it could have been more respectable.

> MRS. POOLE: Nothing about a murder investigation is respectable.

"Let's have the man who found her first," said Holmes. Lestrade brought Poor Richard over to a corner of the pub where Holmes had gathered several chairs around a table: one for himself, one for Lestrade, one for the person they were questioning. Mary found herself another chair and sat discreetly behind Holmes, where she could see Poor Richard's face as he was interrogated. Diana perched on the edge of a stool, and Watson leaned against the wall. Mary sent up a silent prayer: *For goodness' sake, just let Diana stay quiet.* She wanted to hear what Poor Richard had to say.

> BEATRICE: How did you manage to keep Diana quiet all that time?

DIANA: I can be quiet when I want to. I wanted to
hear what they were talking about too.

"Now then," said Holmes, when Poor Richard was sitting
across from him. "How did you find the body of this girl, Molly
Keane?"

"Well, it was like this, sir. I wandered into the alley to have a
smoke, and just stumbled across her, like," he said in a thin, high
voice. It was not the voice Mary had expected, coming out of
what was still a large man, under all his rags. "Then I told Jim,
here"—he gestured back toward the landlord behind the bar, who
nodded—"and he called the constable on duty. That's all I know,
sir." He stared at Holmes with bloodshot eyes, and Mary noticed
that his hands on the table were trembling.

"That won't do, you know," said Holmes, smiling at him, not
unkindly. "I want the truth from you, no more, no less. The sleeve
of your coat is stained with blood. If you don't tell me how you
discovered Molly Keane, I shall have Sergeant Debenham arrest
you on suspicion of her murder."

To Mary's astonishment, Poor Richard put his head in his
hands and began to sob. And yes, there, she could see it—the
cuff of his coat, a faded tweed that had seen better days, was
streaked with red. She must become more observant, like Mr.
Holmes. When she had first met him, shooting so theatrically at
the wall, she had dismissed him as a charlatan. But now that she
was seeing him in action, she had to admire his powers of observation and deduction. If only she could develop such abilities in
herself . . .

DIANA: You'd better not let him see this chapter.
I don't know what His Nosiness would think of
being called a charlatan. He's so used to being

worshipped by Dr. Watson and anyone who reads
The Strand!

MARY: He knows perfectly well what I thought of
him, at first. And he knows my opinion's changed
since then.

"None of that," said Lestrade. "You'll answer the question, or
it's off to gaol with you."

"It's all right," said Holmes. "Here, landlord, bring this man
a pint of your best ale, on me. Shall I tell you what you did last
night? You can tell me whether I'm right or not."

Poor Richard raised his head and nodded. The prospect of ale
seemed to have restored his spirits.

"You had been drinking, as you often do. One can't mistake
the red nose of the habitual drunkard. You knew there was a doorway at the back of the alley, and that it was sufficiently hidden so
you could sleep there without being told to move on. Perhaps you
had slept there before—I suspect it's one of your regular spots. So
you stumbled into the alley and fell asleep. You were still asleep
when two men brought Molly Keane into the alley and murdered
her, but I think they must have woken you enough that you stirred,
or made some noise. I conjecture that's what sent them running
from the alley. They had not thought anyone would be there. Do
you remember seeing or hearing them?"

"You're right enough," said Poor Richard. "I fell asleep in that
doorway, although how you know it, I have no idea."

"You were telling the truth when you said that you had a
smoke," replied Holmes. "You sat in that doorway smoking before
you fell asleep. I found your match where you tossed it, and you
dropped ashes in the doorway, where they would not be washed
away by the rain. There are identical ashes on the front of your

coat and that scarf around your neck. The ash from pipe tobacco is easily distinguished from the ash of a cigar or cigarette, and I note the general shape of a pipe in your breast pocket. A man does not sit and smoke his pipe in a dark alley, but he might well do so at sunset, as he prepares for sleep. It was obvious that you had entered the alley while it was still light, then fallen asleep in the doorway. Several threads from your coat were caught on a splinter in the door. I deduced a man in a tweed coat who was a pipe smoker, and here you are. That you slept in the doorway without waking is evident from your trousers, which are still damp from the knees down. The doorway was a large one, but you're a tall man, and your legs stuck out at an angle, into the rain. Not even being cold and wet could wake you, intoxicated as you were."

"Well, I don't remember waking," said Poor Richard. "If I had seen a woman being murdered, I would never have spent the night there. It gives me the shivers just thinking about it, her body lying there in the darkness while I slept. Do you think she'll haunt me, sir?"

"But you must have touched her," said Mary. "I've been wondering how you could have gotten blood on your cuff, and that's the only way."

"Is that true?" said Lestrade. "If I find that you've taken anything from the murder victim . . ."

"Ah, pity an old man!" said Poor Richard, rapidly searching through his coat pockets and bringing out a dirty handkerchief. "Here, this is all I took!" He shook the handkerchief, and out fell a sovereign, shiny except where blood crusted the edges. "I found it lying beside her on the ground. It must have fallen out of her hand, or her pocket. But that's all, I swear! I had nothing to do with her murder." He wiped his eyes and blew his nose loudly.

"Well done, Miss Jekyll," said Holmes. "Molly Keane was paid handsomely, no doubt to entice her to her death. I believe we've gotten as much as we can out of you, my man. Consider yourself free to go. Unless Lestrade wants a beggar taking up space in his prison, I see no reason to detain you."

Lestrade was not interested in holding Poor Richard. After the old man had stumbled out of the pub, he said, "I can't see that half-wit removing a woman's brain. He's well known in this area, and the local constable will keep an eye on him. He may know more about this murder than he's letting on, but if those men were his confederates, I want him out of prison so he can lead us to them. He's more use to us out of prison than in."

The girl was a different proposition than Old Richard. "Call me Kate," she said. "That's what I'm known by, and I won't be telling you my last name, if it's all the same to you, sir. Kate Bright-Eyes is what they call me around here, and that's good enough for you, I reckon. The less you tell the police, the better, I find. But I'll tell you about poor Molly. She may have been on the streets, but she didn't deserve to be treated like that."

"Indeed," said Holmes. "And what can you tell us about her?"

Kate was pretty beneath her paint, although if you looked closely, you could tell she was no longer as young as she seemed, and there were pockmarks on her cheeks. She was slender, with bright eyes, rather like an inquisitive bird. Mary looked at her with interest. So this was what a fallen woman looked like! Exactly like any other woman, except for her fancier dress and general air of boldness. In another life, Kate could have been a parlormaid, like Enid. "Well, Molly was a good girl, a governess until her master took liberties. No, I don't know where, she wouldn't say, nor where her family was. After the child died, she worked the streets, and made a fair bit too. The gentlemen liked her educated ways. She tried to reform for a while, went to one of them reform societies, but it only lasted a week. Couldn't stand the sancti-monious piety, she said. No, she didn't say where, somewhere in

Whitechapel or Spitalfields, I believe. She wasn't one to talk much, was Molly. Last night, she was just as usual. The night was getting on, and it was so cold and damp that there had been no custom, so we sat by the fire in The Bells. Then Molly says, I think I'll be getting on home, Kate. I told her I would finish my beer—Molly was so ladylike, she never drank anything but barley water. So she puts on her coat, and out she goes. And then I thought, I'm almost done anyway, I'll drink up quickly so we can walk home together, companionable. My place wasn't much farther than hers, and we'd been talking about sharing a flat, not liking our situations at present. But when I got outside, I saw that she'd found a customer after all. He was talking to her—there was just enough light coming through the window to see by. You want to know how he looked. I only caught a glimpse in passing, but he was a small gentleman, twisted like. Reminded me of Punch, in the Punch and Judy. He had a strange, whispering voice, as though he didn't want to be heard. I didn't rightly hear what he said, and you may think I'm making this up, but that voice chilled my spine, like ice. I walked past them without a word to Molly and went home. I didn't want her to lose the custom, see. But now I wish I'd said good night. . . . And that's the last time I saw her, until this sergeant asked me to look at her, lying in the alley. What he did to her—I hope you catch him and string him up good."

Kate looked down at her hands on the table, but did not cry. What good would it have done? We often think that class of woman is hard-hearted, because it does not show emotion, but what good would it do for the Kates of the world to cry? They have learned that tears do not bring relief or change of circumstance. There is no one to wipe their tears, no one to assuage their grief.

MARY: Oh, for goodness' sake. She got what was much more useful. After thanking her, Mr.

Holmes gave her the sovereign. What in the world
would she have done with someone to wipe her
tears? Kate's not as sentimental as you are.

JUSTINE: We all need human sympathy.

DIANA: I don't.

Before getting up, Kate said, "You remind me of someone,
ducky." Mary was startled to realize that she was looking directly
at Diana, who was turning back and forth on her stool. "Are you in
the trade? You look young to be in it, but there are plenty of young
ones, more's the pity."

Diana looked back at her, defiantly. "My mother was known as
Gilded Lily, at Mrs. Barstowe's."

"Ah, that's it, then. I knew her when I was a young one myself,
although I wasn't at Mrs. Barstowe's for long. I fell on hard
times—don't let them tell you that laudanum's harmless, because
it ain't—and by the time I was right again, the establishment had
closed. She was spirited, your mum, and kind to us younger girls.
I hope you're not in trouble with these legal gentlemen."

When Diana shook her head, she said, "Well, if you ever are,
remember Kate Bright-Eyes at The Bells. Any friend of your
mum's will be a friend of yours, and don't you forget it."

"I think we've done all we can here," said Holmes, after handing her the sovereign and thanking her for the information she
had provided. "It's long past time for tea. Watson is used to my
habits—I often eat irregularly when I'm on a case. But the two
of you must be hungry." Just then, Diana's stomach gave a low
growl. "Watson can take you back to Regent's Park. I must go
with Lestrade. We have a great deal to talk about."

"But Mr. Holmes," said Mary, "this man, this twisted gentleman with the low voice who looks like Punch. That's a description of Mr. Hyde. I thought of him immediately, after we saw Molly Keane's body. Remember that he was my father's assistant—he has surgical knowledge."

Holmes smiled. "That's an interesting connection, Miss Jekyll, and one I had considered myself, which is why I allowed you to stay and participate in this investigation. But rather tenuous, don't you think? There must be many small, twisted men in London who could wield a scalpel, and Hyde has not been seen since the Carew murder. Beware the *idée fixe*: you've been thinking of Hyde, so he seems an obvious suspect. But he also presents significant problems. We don't even know if he's still alive."

"Who is this Hyde?" asked Lestrade. "Should I add him to the list of suspects?"

"I'm surprised you don't remember," said Holmes. "He was involved in the case I mentioned—the murder of Sir Danvers Carew, the Liberal MP who was at one point spoken of as a possible prime minister. Hyde was identified by a reliable witness as the murderer, but when the police went to arrest him, he had disappeared. He has not been heard of since, although Miss Jekyll briefly thought she was on his track."

"Well, of course it was years ago," said Lestrade, looking put out. "I'll have to go through the records again. And you think this Hyde may be in London, murdering prostitutes?"

"It seems unlikely," said Holmes. "Although I never discount the improbable until it has been proven impossible."

"I thought the previous victims were maids and shop girls?" said Mary. Wasn't that what the newspaper boys had been crying for the last few days?

"Oh, that's the line we've been giving the newspapers, but they're what you might call ladies of the evening right enough. I don't think we can hold back that knowledge much longer. Imagine how much

larger the headlines will be with a sex angle thrown in! And then
the newspapers will start on why the London police haven't solved
these murders. Incompetence of the police—that's how it always
goes." Lestrade pulled on his mustache and looked bitter.

"You think my father's been going around murdering prostitutes?" said Diana. She broke into a peal of laughter.

"Now watch yourself, miss," said Lestrade. "I don't like young
ladies getting hysterics."

"Clearly, Miss Hyde has some information she would like to
share with us," said Holmes.

Diana laughed again. "Jekyll's dead, according to Miss Mary,
here. That means Hyde's dead. My mum told me that Hyde was
just another name for Jekyll. Hyde was a disguise Jekyll used when
he didn't want to be found out. Like a cloak."

"That's not possible," said Mary. "I met Hyde, when my father
was still alive. My housekeeper, Mrs. Poole, remembers him. He
looked nothing like my father."

"Are you calling my mother a liar?" asked Diana, scowling.

"I think we must rely on Miss Jekyll's evidence in this case,"
said Holmes. "Your mother may have been deceived. Hyde may
have told her that he was Jekyll, in order to act the part of a gentleman. Perhaps even to use Jekyll's credit."

There was a look on Diana's face: anger at not being believed,
and something that startled Mary, a grimace as though she were
about to cry.

DIANA: Oh, bosh.

MARY: No, that's exactly what I remember.

"My father had many secrets," said Mary. "I don't know what
sort of relationship he had with Mr. Hyde. Of course what Diana

suggests is impossible—I'm sorry," she said, turning to Diana, "but one man can't simply disguise himself as another, not when their appearances are so different. Hyde was at least a foot shorter than my father. However, there must be something more to their relationship than we are aware of, or why would my mother support his child? I know my supposition is farfetched, Mr. Holmes, but the description fits Hyde perfectly. I still remember that low voice and the chill it sent down my spine. Like ice, as Kate Bright-Eyes said."

"If there's a possibility that Hyde is still out there, I want to know about it," said Lestrade. "We don't want murderers walking the streets of London, and there's Carew to pay for. But he's likely long gone, to Australia or South America."

"You're almost certainly right," said Holmes. "Nevertheless, I would like Miss Jekyll to examine her father's papers again. Could you do that, Miss Jekyll? And report back to me tomorrow?"

"Of course," said Mary. She wanted to read through the notebook again in particular, systematically this time. There had been some mention of Hyde . . . but she could not remember in what context. And what in the world was she going to do with Diana?

"Watson, can you take these ladies home? I'll meet you back at Baker Street after I've talked with Lestrade." Holmes looked from one of them to the other. It was difficult to tell what he was thinking, but Mary thought he seemed . . . well, almost amused.

"Come on," said Mary to Diana. She was not interested in amusing Mr. Holmes. She was grateful to him for having included her in the investigation, but also irritated—she was not sure why. "I have a lot of work to do. And you need a bath."

"No, I don't," said Diana.

"Bath, or you won't get dinner." Mary grabbed Diana by a dirty wrist and pulled her along. Watson walked beside them, trying not to smile as Diana glared and muttered under her breath. Mary resolutely ignored her. She would ask Mrs. Poole to make a strong pot of tea and she would stay up all night, if she had to. What secrets did those papers hold? What had she missed the first time? She did not know, but she wanted to find out.

CHAPTER V

The Letter from Italy

Climbing down from the cab, Mary found it difficult to believe that she had just come from Whitechapel—that such a place even existed. Park Terrace was broad and quiet, and the only sound was the clopping of the horse's hooves as it stepped impatiently in place. The brick buildings, dating from the time of one of the Georges—she could never remember which—stood along the street in respectable rows. Over the roofs and chimney pots of the row opposite from the Jekyll residence, she could see the tops of the trees in Regent's Park.

"Well, isn't this swell?" said Diana.

And there of course was the evidence that Mary had indeed spent a morning in the dregs of the city—the dirty, ragged girl beside her. What in the world was she going to do with Diana?

The door opened. "Come in, come in," said Mrs. Poole. "You'll catch your chill, standing out there on the pavement."

Mary turned and thanked Watson, who had handed her and Diana down the steps of the cab. "Think nothing of it, Miss Jekyll," he said. He had already paid the cabbie, once again insisting that it was a business expense, which worried Mary. Kind as he was, she disliked feeling a sense of obligation. But there was nothing to be done about that now.

"Although of course it was a pleasure as well," he added. "Having a young lady of—keen intellect such as yours, shall we say—involved in Holmes's investigation makes a refreshing change. I shall see you tomorrow—at noon? Should Holmes and I meet you here?"

"Thank you," said Mary, not quite knowing what to make of the compliment, but certain it was not the one he had originally intended to make. "I think it would be best if we came to Baker Street. At noon, then, Dr. Watson." She did not want Holmes—or Watson, of course—to see the bare walls, the uncarpeted floors. The places where there had once been vases filled with flowers or plaster busts of philosophers. It was pride, and pride was a sin, but still . . .

"Ta," said Diana. "Until tomorrow, then."

Watson bowed, unsuccessfully hiding a smile, and said, "Ta to you as well, Miss Hyde." Then he strode off toward Marylebone Road.

"Come on," Mary said to Diana, who was examining the house and Mrs. Poole. "If you keep staring like that, your eyes will fall out."

Diana gave her what Mary would come to call *that look*—of mingled contempt and annoyance. But she followed Mary up the steps and into the front hall.

MARY: She gives me *that look* all the time!

DIANA: I wouldn't if you weren't so annoying.

Diana's trunk was waiting in the hall. Yet another thing for which they were obliged to Dr. Watson.

"This came for you earlier today," said the housekeeper. "It was delivered on a vegetable cart, but the man said Miss Jekyll right enough, so I told him to leave it by the staircase."

"Yes, thank you, Mrs. Poole," said Mary as the housekeeper took her umbrella. "I had it sent—I'm sorry, I should have sent a note, but we were in a bit of a hurry." She put the portfolio with the papers in it on the hall table, then pulled off her mackintosh and handed that to Mrs. Poole as well. How tired she was! She had not realized it until now, but it had been a long day, and as Holmes had pointed out, she had not eaten since breakfast.

"Do we have a guest, miss?" asked Mrs. Poole, looking doubtfully at Diana, with her bare legs and hatless head. She checked the mackintosh for stains before folding it neatly over her arm.

"This is Diana," said Mary. "And she needs a bath."

"I don't want to take a bath," said Diana.

"Yes, you do," said Mary. "You don't actually like being that filthy. You just want to be contradictory. Mrs. Poole will draw you one. I assure you, it will be better than anything you could get at St. Mary Magdalen. And then we will have tea, I think. If you wouldn't mind, Mrs. Poole?"

Diana grinned. "Oh, it's going to be a treat living with you, I can see that already. You're just like that detective. You tell people what to do, and they do it simply because they're used to following orders. Well, I'm not."

"Obviously," said Mary. "Nevertheless, you are going to take a bath, because you smell and I don't want you sitting on the furniture in that state. No tea unless you take a bath first."

"Come on, you," said Mrs. Poole. "Miss Mary says into the bath, so into the bath you go. And while you're in this house, you will speak to her with respect. Miss Mary is a *lady*." She took Diana by the arm and pulled her toward the stairs.

"And what am I, a piece of dirt?" said Diana.

"Near enough!" responded Mrs. Poole.

When they were gone, Mary took off her hat and gloves, leaving them on the hall table. She glanced at herself in the mirror. She was still pale, but the fresh air had put some color into her cheeks. She looked more alive than she had before her visit to Mr. Guest.

She took the portfolio into the parlor. Should she turn on the gas? It was getting dark, but she didn't want to use it until absolutely necessary. She lit the fire, which was once again already laid—thank goodness for Mrs. Poole! The housekeeper should find other employment, but Mary did not know what she would do without her. How lonely it would be. . . . She sat on the sofa with the portfolio next to her, warming her hands and staring into the flames. It had been horrible—that poor girl. But she could not help being interested in the case—it was a mystery, and surely everyone was interested in mysteries? In untangling their various threads?

One of the threads was sitting next to her on the sofa. Once again, she pulled the tea table in front of her, set the portfolio on it, and began pulling out its contents: the account book, the laboratory notebook, the letters and receipts. They were all she had left of her father, the only clues to the mystery of his life and death. She put them into neat piles. She had looked at them last night, but had been focused on the book of accounts and the possibility that Hyde was still alive. She would go through them more carefully now.

Diana's claim couldn't possibly be true. But why had her father hired Hyde, so unpleasant, so unreliable? And as it turned out, a criminal. And why had her mother supported Diana all those years? She had not wanted to question Diana in front of Mr. Holmes and the police. This was a family matter, and she wanted to explore it privately. What had been the relationship between her father and Hyde? And her father's fortune—was it a coincidence that it had disappeared at the same time as Hyde? Had it been a matter of blackmail? If so, for what?

She remembered her mother, after her father's death. So secretive, so unwilling to discuss her life with him even before the long descent into madness. Mary had assumed her reluctance was a result of grief. But maybe there was more to it.

The documents. She would focus on them. Systematically, she

began sorting through each pile, starting with those she had paid
the least attention to last night. Letters first, taking each one out
of its envelope. Two of them were from Maw & Sons, the scientific supply company. The other three letters had foreign stamps.
Two of them she set aside, but the third, from Italy . . . She read
it again, more carefully this time. She looked through the receipts
from Maw & Sons. And then she looked through the laboratory
notebook, knowing what to search for, although she dreaded
finding it. If only her father hadn't had such crabbed, eccentric
handwriting! It was like trying to decipher the movements of a
spider. The letter from Italy had given her a clue she would never
have paid attention to last night. But tonight, a particular sentence
in the letter had stood out, taken on a different and more sinister
meaning: *A scientist should not experiment on himself.* What, exactly,
had her father been doing?

It could not mean—but she was starting to think it could. She
looked at the letter again, then the notebook, then the receipts.
She leaned back into the sofa, staring at the painting of her mother
over the mantelpiece without seeing it, lost in thought. Surely
what she imagined was impossible? And yet she could think of no
other explanation.

"Here's your tea, miss." She blinked, startled. It was Mrs. Poole
with the tea tray. "I don't know as you've eaten since breakfast, so I
made some ham sandwiches, and some paste as well. That will be
the last of the ham for a while, I'm afraid. There should be enough
for the both of you, once that brat gets out of the bath, which may
not be until Judgment Day. For all the screaming she did going in,
now that she's in, she doesn't want to come out."

"Her name is Diana Hyde," said Mary. "She says she's Hyde's
daughter. She's the one my mother was supporting, in a sort of—
charitable institution."

"You don't say! Well, she does look rather like him, with that grin of hers, like an imp plotting mischief. And she's wicked enough for anything. Tried to bite my arm when I put her in the bathtub, not that I'm going to put up with that sort of nonsense! I wonder who her mother could be. I pity her, whoever she was, getting herself involved with a man like Hyde. The ways of men are unaccountable, my mother always told me. Not that I've ever been married myself, thank the Lord. Where should I put these?"

"Oh, I'm sorry," said Mary. "Can you put them on the sideboard? I've made a bit of a mess on the table, I'm afraid. And would you mind pouring me a cup of tea, Mrs. Poole? I don't want to lose my place here. She says more than that. She claims Hyde was not a man at all, but a sort of disguise my father wore to visit—well, places he should not have been, evidently. Hyde was a way to hide his activities."

"Surely not, miss," said Mrs. Poole, looking astonished. "Why, the two were quite different. Dr. Jekyll was a tall, distinguished-looking gentleman, and Mr. Hyde was a low, creeping sort of thing. It's not possible, I assure you."

"Did you ever see them together?" asked Mary. That would settle the question once and for all.

"Well, no, I can't say as I did," said Mrs. Poole, putting the tea tray on the sideboard. "But that doesn't prove anything, does it? Perhaps Mr. Hyde claimed to be his master. I wouldn't put it past him, especially when it came to the matter of paying bills."

Mrs. Poole handed Mary a cup of tea. "Lemon and sugar, as usual. I took the liberty of putting in two, seeing as you need strength after such a long day." Mary took a sip. Ah, that was better. Of course she should have eaten, but there simply hadn't been time, with the visit to Mr. Holmes and then to Whitechapel. And then the body of poor Molly Keane.

"What do you remember about my father, Mrs. Poole?" she asked. "I was so young when he died—and he was not an affectionate father, even then. He was kind, or tried to be, but I always felt a little intimidated around him. I remember him teaching me the table of elements and showing me how the flame of the Bunsen burner turned different colors in response to various chemicals."

"Well," said Mrs. Poole, frowning. "He was always a kind gentleman, as you say. Even to a chambermaid, as I was then. Although he smelled funny. It was those chemicals he used. Always experimenting, he was, in the laboratory. My father never believed he committed suicide. Thought he might have swallowed one of those chemicals of his by accident, and poisoned himself."

"He may have poisoned himself, in a way," said Mary. She hesitated—would her idea sound foolish? Impossible? But she had to tell someone, and she had known Mrs. Poole as long as she could remember. Mrs. Poole had been like a mother to her, when her own mother couldn't be. "These documents imply—they seem to indicate—that he was performing chemical experiments. On himself, and one of those experiments transformed him into Hyde. The disguise wasn't just a physical change, like changing his clothes and putting on false hair, but an actual chemical transformation."

"Lord have mercy," said Mrs. Poole. "Is that even possible?"

"I know it sounds absurd," said Mary. "But look at this." She opened the laboratory notebook to a page she had marked and pointed to an entry written in her father's crabbed, shaky script.

> Today, I let out the beast Hyde. He is stronger than I am.
> What will he do when I can no longer control his impulses?

Last night, she had assumed these sentences meant her father had fought with Hyde. Now, they took on a different meaning. "And look, a couple of pages later." Mary flipped past several pages of formulas and scientific notes.

The sight of my face in the mirror. The horror! The horror!
He has gained the power to transform at will, and I cannot
stop him.

"And the final entry."

All is lost. All, all lost, and I am a dead man.

"I don't understand," said Mrs. Poole.

How could she explain? It would sound so strange, almost absurd, and she was not entirely sure she believed it herself. And yet Mary had to try. "Why did the sight of his own face fill him with horror? And these two letters from Maw & Sons, the wholesale chemist and supplier, about some sort of powder he ordered. Look, in the first one they say they're enclosing another batch, and in the second they apologize that it's not working as expected. They offer a refund, but insist that it's identical to the first batch in chemical composition. What if he transformed into Hyde repeatedly, but then the chemical transformation stopped working? What if he became stuck as Hyde? And then—committed suicide."

"But why ever would Dr. Jekyll want to do such a thing?" asked Mrs. Poole. She sounded completely unconvinced.

"I don't know," said Mary. Suddenly, she felt very tired. Surely the whole thing was impossible? No, not impossible. Merely improbable. This was the nineteenth century, the age of science. Who knew what possibilities existed in the natural world? If a caterpillar could transform into a butterfly . . .

"You said yourself that the ways of men are unaccountable. There are many reasons a man, even a gentleman, would assume a disguise. To visit opium dens or prostitutes. Commit murder with impunity. Do the things that gentlemen are not supposed to do. He may not have been the man we remember."

"You've started without me," said Diana. In comparison to how she had looked earlier, she positively glowed with cleanliness. Her hair was wet and slicked back, like a seal's, and she wore a clean white nightdress of Mary's. The cut on her arm was neatly bandaged.

"I didn't realize you wanted to read through stacks of documents," said Mary.

"I don't. But I want to know what you find out." Diana grabbed a ham sandwich and sat on the other end of the sofa, drawing up her bare feet.

"Put a plate under that," said Mrs. Poole.

"You're supposed to call me miss," said Diana.

"I'll call you miss when you deserve it," said Mrs. Poole. "I've put her in the old nursery, miss," she said to Mary. "I'll brush her clothes for tomorrow, but some of them are in a disreputable state."

"Disreputable yourself!" Diana shoved the sandwich into her mouth and took a large bite.

"Diana, if you're not polite to Mrs. Poole, your stay in this house won't be a pleasant one," said Mary. "She's the one who cooks for us and cleans our rooms, and makes our lives generally comfortable. Although if I don't find a way to make money soon, she'll have to find another employer, and we will have to fend for ourselves."

"I'm not leaving you, miss," said Mrs. Poole. "This has been my home since I was a girl, and I'm staying, whether you can pay me or not."

"I thought you were rich," said Diana. "I wondered why you don't have pictures on the walls, and most of the floors are bare. And there are holes in this sofa." She put her big toe into one.

"Well, I'm not rich," said Mary. "And stop that, or you'll tear it further. When my father died, we discovered that his fortune had disappeared, and my mother's income was only for her lifetime. Now that's gone as well. Even the money she left to pay for your care at St. Mary Magdalen is almost gone." Twenty-three pounds. She had meant to go to the bank this morning, after visiting Mr. Holmes, but instead she had ended up in Whitechapel. She would have to go tomorrow, as soon as the bank opened. "Once that money runs out, there will be nothing for you or me or Mrs. Poole to live on. I sold everything of value to pay for my mother's care, because her income wasn't enough. I've tried to sell this house, but no one will buy it. These are difficult economic times—not that I expect you to understand, since I doubt you've read a newspaper in your life. And I can't seem to find employment, even as a nursemaid. So there's nothing. I thought if I found Hyde, I could claim the reward, although if you're correct and my father was Hyde, he died fourteen years ago. In the meantime, you will be polite to Mrs. Poole. Of course, if you'd rather sleep in the scullery, you're welcome to do so."

Diana looked at Mary, then at Mrs. Poole, and said, "Thank you for the bath." She grinned like a monkey, but still, they were words Mary had never expected to hear out of her mouth.

"You're welcome," said Mrs. Poole, sounding unconvinced. "Is there anything else you want, miss?"

"No, thank you," said Mary. "But if I do, I'll ring."

After Mrs. Poole had left, Mary sat rereading the letter from Italy in silence. Diana chewed on the sandwich with her mouth open. Then, "What is that?" she asked.

"Aren't you capable of being quiet?" asked Mary.

"Oh, I'm capable, all right," said Diana. "I'll be as quiet as a mouse, for as long as it takes you to notice the seal."

"What do you mean, the seal?"

Diana pointed to one of the envelopes lying on the table. It had been sealed with red wax. Impressed in the wax were two letters: S.A. It was the same design as on the watch fob in Molly Keane's hand.

For a moment, Mary could not speak. Then, "How could I have missed that?" she said. And there it was on another of the envelopes as well. Two envelopes, two identical seals.

"Well, what are the letters about?" asked Diana.

"I have no idea." Mary pulled a letter out of one envelope and handed it to Diana. "Look."

Diana wrinkled her brow. "Is it in some kind of code?"

"No, it's in Latin. But I can't read it. Miss Murray started me on Latin, but after my mother became so sick, I couldn't afford a governess. All I remember is *Carthago delenda est*. They're both in Latin, and postmarked from Budapest. Who would be writing to my father from Budapest in Latin? The other letters are the two from Maw's, about some chemical he was trying to buy, and this one from Italy, which is in English, thank goodness."

"Well, what does that one say?" asked Diana.

Mary gave her a look, sighed, and started reading it out loud.

> My dear Jekyll,
>
>   I am glad to hear that your experiments are going well. I remain convinced that we are working along the correct lines. The important scientific advances of this century will be in the biological sciences, as the important advances of the previous century were in chemistry and physics. Darwin has shown us the way, although he himself cannot see past the end of his nose! (I have heard it is a rather long nose, but not long enough to see the truth.) We shall go where Darwin never imagined. Transmutation, not natural selection, is the agent of evolution. God is an alchemist, not a plodding incrementalist like Signore Darwin! We shall show the scientific community, shall we not, my friend and colleague? Only those

who dare much are capable of changing history and shining the light of knowledge on our dark world.

I am pleased to report that my Beatrice is flourishing. After a series of initial setbacks, due I think to incorrect dosage, she is as healthy as a weed—although I admit that I had a fright, several months ago, and almost lost her. But she recovered, and I have never seen a child look more radiant. How joyfully she plays in the garden! I have decided that botany is the most appropriate area of study for her, and I believe she has a naturally scientific mind, although in the feminine mode of course. She cannot look at the plants as dispassionately as I do, but thinks of them almost as her sisters. She is sad that she cannot enjoy the insects, particularly the butterflies, but they perish from her breath.

Our colleague Moreau was right to conjecture that the female brain would be more malleable and responsive to our experiments. I am fascinated by his research, but it seems as though he is never satisfied, and must continually try new techniques, with new experimental material. How I lament the scientific ignorance that hounded him out of your England. What he could have done with the resources and funding of a medical school! However, he is sending Montgomery to present a paper at the meeting of the Société in Vienna next month. Will you be attending as well? I look forward to hearing about your own experiments in transmutation, although I fear, dear colleague, that what you are undertaking is too dangerous. A scientist should not experiment on himself. He should be a dispassionate observer, and for an experimental subject, young, malleable flesh is best. You have a daughter, have you not? Surely she is old enough for you to begin the process, in whatever direction you decide will yield the most promising results.

Do please let me know if you will indeed be presenting a paper in Vienna. I am getting old, but will brave the roads to see you.

My very best regards,
Giacomo Rappaccini

"I don't understand," said Diana.

"Well, I don't either," said Mary, looking once again at the envelope. "Dottor Giacomo Rappaccini, with a return address in Padua—that's not S.A. There's no seal on this envelope—you can see the circle where it was, and a little bit of red wax, but it must have fallen off when the envelope was opened. And all this about Darwin and transmutation and their scientific experiments . . . Although it does suggest that a theory of mine may be correct." She sat silent for a moment, looking at the letter in front of her.

"Well?" said Diana. She waited, then stood and walked over to the sideboard, where she piled the rest of the sandwiches onto a plate. She poured herself a cup of tea, put in four lumps of sugar, then carried the plate and saucer, with the cup balanced precariously on it, back to the sofa. She set them down on the floor and sat on the sofa with her legs crossed under her, drawn up into the nightgown. "Are you going to explain your theory or not?"

Reluctantly, Mary told her what she had told Mrs. Poole earlier that evening: about the possibility of a chemical transformation, the possibility she did not want to admit . . . that her father was indeed Hyde. After all, wasn't that transmutation? The transformation from a respectable gentleman to a suspected murderer . . .

"Look for yourself," she said, showing Diana the laboratory note-book, flipping to the relevant pages.

"Well, that's it, then," said Diana, through a mouthful of bread and paste. "I told you, didn't I? Sister."

"It's not that simple," said Mary. "I don't know if that's the experiment this letter describes. Perhaps the notebook refers to something quite different."

"He has gained the power to transform at will, and I cannot stop him," said Diana, tapping the page with her finger and leaving a smear of paste. "That's plain enough, isn't it? He let out Hyde, and Hyde was taking over. You just don't want to believe your father was a murderer."

"Of course not!" said Mary, rubbing the paste off as best she could, although a grease stain remained on the paper. "How do you feel, knowing yours is?"

"I don't know yet," said Diana. "He's a suspected murderer, as far as I know. But I always thought he was a bloody bastard. Look at the way he abandoned my mother. She died in St. Bartholomew's, where they dumped her in a grave with the patients who had died that week, so they could prepare her bed for someone else. I've never had your high opinion of *our father.*"

"You shouldn't say that, even if it's true," said Mary. "We should not judge until we understand what happened. All this about Darwin, and Moreau—that's another scientist, I'm guess-ing, like Dr. Rappaccini. And these experiments . . ."

Diana snorted. "I don't care who they are. Bastards, the lot of them, most likely."

The door opened. "Miss Mary, do you need anything else? Have you actually eaten any of those sandwiches, or has that scamp eaten them all?"

"I don't think I can eat right now, Mrs. Poole," said Mary, put-ting a hand to her head and running it through her hair. "Do you know why my mother saved these documents?"

"Perhaps she wanted you to have them," said Diana. She started on her third sandwich.

"While it pains me to agree with *Miss* Diana, and you are not to eat all the sandwiches, no matter what Miss Mary says, she may be right. Mr. Utterson burned your father's papers after his death. Perhaps your mother saved these so you could read them someday."

"I always wondered why she—went mad." Mary might as well say it. Because that was what had happened, hadn't it? "This . . . her husband turning into a monster. Well, it would explain a lot of things." Mary ran her fingers through her hair again, then tried to pin back the strands that were starting to come out of the bun at the nape of her neck.

"That's terrible, miss," said Mrs. Poole.

"This letter is from Italy, from a Dr. Rappaccini. Have you heard that name before, Mrs. Poole? I believe he corresponded with my father regularly."

Mrs. Poole wrinkled her forehead. "I have heard that name before. The question is, where?" She was silent for a moment. "Wait, I seem to remember . . . it's in the kitchen! I'll be back in a moment." She left the door open behind her. Mary and Diana stared at each other. The kitchen? Diana shrugged.

In a few minutes, Mrs. Poole was back with a copy of the *Gazette* in her hand. "Here it is!" she said triumphantly. "Goodness, it's dark in here. Why haven't you turned on the gas? I'll do it, and then I'll be able to see. . . . Yes, that's better. 'Beatrice Rappaccini, the Beauty who Breathes Poison. Appearing 10:00 a.m. and 12:00 noon Wednesdays and Fridays at the Royal College of Surgeons. Admission free with advertisement for all who would like to witness this scientific marvel. Otherwise, a shilling for adults and sixpence for children.' I was going to ask for Friday off, to see her."

"Breathes poison!" said Diana appreciatively. "Wish I could do that!"

"Beatrice Rappaccini," said Mary. "Wasn't that the name in the letter? Mrs. Poole, you're right, I should have something to eat. Of course you can have Friday off, you can have any day off you like. But Diana and I are going to see her tomorrow, 10:00 a.m. sharp. We can get there and back by noon, when we have an appointment with Mr. Holmes and Dr. Watson."

"He's got a thing for you," said Diana, grinning.

"He most certainly does not," said Mary, indignantly.

"Then why did he hand you out of the cab so carefully, *Miss Jekyll?*"

"Oh, you mean Dr. Watson. Well, I don't think he does either. Give me a sandwich—you've taken all of them! You're like a goose, you know that? They'll eat and eat until they're sick." Mary took a sandwich off Diana's plate and bit into it. Paste, not her favorite, but it would have to do. Suddenly, she realized that she was very hungry.

"Mrs. Poole, can you pour me another cup of tea, and then one for yourself? I think we're going to be awake for a while yet. I know, I know, you have to wash the dishes, and sweep the floor, and bank the oven. But for goodness' sake, sit down for a moment and listen. I know you would never ask, but I want to tell you what happened today."

With visible reluctance, Mrs. Poole sat in one of the armchairs by the fireplace and clasped her hands on her lap, waiting. Mary recounted, as succinctly as she could, the events of that day, from the moment she had knocked at the door of 221B Baker Street to the moment Watson had deposited them once again at 11 Park Terrace.

DIANA: And wasn't she properly horrified that her Miss Mary had gone gallivanting around London like that! I still remember how she looked at you.

MARY: I do too! But you didn't say anything, Mrs. Poole.

MRS. POOLE: Not my place, miss. You young ladies
will do as you wish, whatever I think. And however
foolish it may be.

"So you see," Mary continued, showing Mrs. Poole the letter, "my father was a scientist. He was involved in a series of experiments—and not just him, there were others as well. This Rappaccini, and a Moreau."

"And don't forget Darwin," said Diana.

"Oh, for goodness' sake," said Mary. "Don't you know who Mr. Darwin is? Did they teach you nothing at St. Mary Magdalen? No, never mind, I'll explain later. The issue is, they were involved in a series of experiments, and somehow my father learned to transform himself into Hyde. As Hyde, he murdered Sir Danvers Carew. I thought perhaps Hyde could be the murderer of Molly Keane, but that seems impossible now. If he was my father, then Hyde is dead, and there is no connection between the two murders—except this." She pointed to the seals on the two envelopes.

"So what do we do now?" asked Diana. "Look for S.A.?"

"Yes, although at the moment we have no idea what S.A. means. Why was my father receiving letters in Latin from S.A.? Did it have anything to do with his scientific experiments? Tomorrow, we'll talk to this Beatrice Rappaccini. Tonight, Diana, I want you to tell us anything else you know about Hyde."

Mary sat back. She and Mrs. Poole looked at Diana, expectantly.

CHAPTER VI

Diana's Story

D iana stared at Mary and Mrs. Poole. "How would I know anything about Hyde? I mean Dad. He died before I was born."

"But your mother told you about him," said Mary. "She told you about his connection with my father, didn't she? What else did she tell you? Think back—anything you remember could be important."

"Oh hell!" said Diana. She shoved the rest of the sandwich into her mouth and finished her tea. Then she leaned back on the sofa and said, "She told me he was a proper gentleman, with an account at the Bank of England. And he had a house in Soho, furnished like a gentleman's house, with paintings on the walls. And he frightened her, toward the end. He was always talking about life and death, about how the dead could be brought back to life. She thought he might be into spiritualism."

"How the dead could be brought back to life?" said Mary. "Do you mean ghosts, or corpses?"

"How should I know?" Diana looked down at the plate on the floor, but it had no more sandwiches on it. "Corpses, I think. Yes, he told her that with the right chemicals, corpses could be brought back to life. If they weren't long dead, that is. He told her some-one had done it with frogs."

"Frogs?" said Mrs. Poole. "That's ungodly, that is."

"Why would anyone want to bring a dead frog back to life?" said Diana. "I'm still hungry. Are we done yet?"

"Oh, for goodness' sake," said Mary. "Diana, this is important. Go back to the beginning. And I really mean the beginning. Tell me everything you know."

> DIANA: Why do I have to write this part of the story? You're the author. Write it yourself, like you're writing everything else, and then say I wrote it. Isn't that what authors do?

> CATHERINE: Because this is what we agreed on. You would each write your individual stories, and I would make them sound right. I would fit them into the whole, so they made sense.

> DIANA: Well, why do I have to go first? Let Mary go first.

> CATHERINE: Because the whole story is Mary's story. She doesn't need to write a separate section. But you do, so sit down at that desk and write. And don't get up every five minutes to argue with me. The sooner you start, the sooner you'll finish.

> DIANA: Don't expect me to do all the he said she said, and those fancy descriptions.

> CATHERINE: Write it however you want to. But start writing!

"My mother was the long-lost queen of Bohemia. When she

was a baby, she was stolen out of her cradle by a priest in league with her wicked uncle, who was attempting to usurp the throne. He had become regent after his brother's untimely and suspicious death. He thought that with the rightful although infantine ruler out of the way, he could crown himself king. The priest spirited her out of the castle by night, and then his confederates, who were also priests because we know that all priests are liars, carried her over the border into whatever country borders Bohemia. Where is Bohemia, anyway? They traveled by carriage and ship, eventually arriving in England, where they sold her to a poor family. . . ."

CATHERINE: Diana, if you don't start over again and tell the truth, I'm going to bite you.

DIANA: I'd like to see you try!

MARY: Do you really want to tempt her? This is Catherine we're talking about.

CATHERINE: And write the way you speak. That sounds like one of your horrible penny dreadfuls.

DIANA: Oh, all right. Though they're no worse than the books you write. Ouch! All right, you didn't need to do that.

"My mum never told me much about herself, although she always said she was a Londoner through and through, born with the sound of the ships going up and down the Thames in her ears. That was her lullaby, she said. She would have been a kitchen maid, most likely, if she hadn't fallen in with a soldier when she was fifteen. It was a mistake, the greatest mistake of her life, she told me.

'But I've never regretted it, sweetheart,' she would say. 'No, I've never regretted my Bonny Joe.' That's what they called him in the regiment. He was a Scotsman, from Glasgow, and as handsome, she said, as the day was long.

"Well, there she was, fifteen and with child, and her father cast her out of the house, telling her to go sleep under the bridges with the other whores, where she belonged. And go sleep under the bridges she did, until she lost the child, from hunger and illness. It was a boy, and I always wondered, when I was sent to sit on a stool or had my hands rapped at St. Mary Magdalen, what my life would have been like if I'd had an older brother. But she was young and pretty, with a saucy tongue and long red hair from her Irish mother, so one of the houses by the docks took her in and paid her regular. And that was where she met my father, Edward Hyde."

> DIANA: Now don't you tell me I sound like a penny
> dreadful, because it's the literal truth!

"Tell us everything you remember," said Mary, leaning forward.
"It's a sordid enough tale," said Mrs. Poole, but she too leaned forward eagerly to hear it.

> MRS. POOLE: I did no such thing.

> DIANA: If she interrupts me, I don't care who bites me.
> I'm stopping right here.

> MARY: Mrs. Poole, could you please—

> MRS. POOLE: Oh, I'll go. I have no desire to read
> anything Diana writes about me. You are
> incorrigible, my girl.

    DIANA: Of course I am. And the sooner you realize it,
       the better!

"It was run by a Mrs. Barstowe, and it was described in the *Gentleman's Guide to London* as a superior place, catering principally to doctors, lawyers, and politicians. Barstowe's had a reputation—it wouldn't service men in trade, no matter how much money they had to spend. The girls were clean and could talk about the latest news—Mrs. Barstowe made them read *The Times*, *The Financial Times*, and *Punch*.

"My father took a particular fancy to Mum—at first he tried a few of the other girls, but then he started asking for her regular. Maybe it was because he liked it rough and she didn't mind—she said he never hurt her. And he was ugly as sin, but she didn't mind that either. No man had meant anything to her since Bonny Joe left with his regiment. She had told Joe about the child, and he had told her that he had a wife and three children already, back in Glasgow, with another on the way. 'I can't do anything for you, my love,' he told her, 'but give you my blessing.' And still she loved him and only spoke well of him to her dying day. Love is a fool's game, I think.

"One day, Hyde said to her that he wanted a child, and if she had a child for him, he would take it and support it. Well, she didn't want that, although he offered her a lot of money. She had her living to get, and she was done with trusting men's promises."

    CATHERINE: She told you all this when you were just
       a child?

    DIANA: She told me when she got sick, before they
       sent her to the hospital. I think she knew she wasn't
       coming back. "Sweetheart," she said, "I ain't been

the best mum to you, but this is a hard world, and I want you to know what people are like— men especially. They will lie to you as easy as blowing dandelion clocks, and that's the best of them." She told me so I would know, and she was right.

BEATRICE: She told you because she loved you. I wish I could remember my mother, but she died when I was so young.

CATHERINE: Could we not dwell on the subject of mothers, please?

"Well, she found herself pregnant, and she thought he might have tampered with the protection she used. All the girls at Barstowe's used protection, against the clap. Though he was an ugly gentleman, he was a clever one, she used to tell me. He was a scientist, and would talk about the strangest things, like those experiments with frogs. Raising things from the dead and turning things into gold, like that. She used to laugh at some of his ideas. Well, when he found out she was pregnant, he said he would support her and the child, and he put her in that house in Soho. He told her he hoped it would be a girl. She was surprised, because gentlemen usually want a boy, but no, he was particular and said if it was a girl, he would be most pleased.

"And then one day, she heard a knocking at the door. She wondered who it could be, because no one ever visited that house— Hyde had no friends. She opened the door, and who should it be but the police. They said he was wanted for murder, and would she know where to find him? 'No,' she told them. They asked her if they could come in and look around. 'Certainly,' she said. So they looked around, and they questioned her again, and the housekeeper who lived with them. After a couple of hours, they left, knowing no more than when they had come. She thought he would show up after a while, that he had gotten himself in trouble and was hiding, but would eventually return. He never did. She stayed until the end of the lease, then sold the furniture and moved to cheap accommodations in Spitalfields. And that's where I was born. We damn near died of hunger, although she worked hard enough, walking out with gentlemen while the butcher's wife minded me. But the windows were cracked, and the wind blew in, and we had scarcely a blanket between us, with nothing to eat most nights. I was so hungry, I would have eaten the rats, if I could've caught them. . . ."

"To think that you were born in such a place!" said Mrs. Poole. Suddenly, her heart swelled with pity for the poor orphan child, and she regretted her earlier harshness.

> MARY: It's a good thing Mrs. Poole is sorting laundry, or whatever she's doing. I don't want to hear what she would say to that!

> DIANA: How do you know her heart didn't swell with pity? Mrs. Poole can say what she likes, but she always gives me the largest chop and the most pudding.

> CATHERINE: That's because you're so scrawny.

> DIANA: How do you know? Wouldn't it be rich if our precious Mary wasn't her favorite after all?

> MARY: For goodness' sake, can you just finish your section?

DIANA: You were the one who interrupted in the first
place.

"Yes," said Mary, also feeling a surge of pity for her long-lost
sister.

MARY: Oh please!

"One day," continued Diana, "Mum ran into a friend from
Barstowe's, who promised to speak for her, and Mrs. Barstowe
agreed to take her back, although she usually turned away girls
who'd been foolish enough to get with child. I was four or five,
then. The girls would take care of me while Mum was working.
They all liked to play with me. They were still children themselves—
the youngest girls at Barstowe's were fourteen. Mrs. Barstowe
wouldn't take them younger. 'I have standards, I do,' she used
to tell us. They sang to me, and told me stories, and made me
clothes out of their cast-offs, decorated with bits of ribbon and
lace that gentlemen had given them. As I grew older, they taught
me games and rhymes, and even my letters. I learned about the
world—there's no place in it for girls whose parents aren't rich
and respectable, or who have Lascar blood in them, or who are
addicted to laudanum. One step off the path of respectability, and
that's where you end up: Barstowe's.

"It was a happy enough life for me, though maybe not for the
girls there, until Mum became ill. One day, she started coughing, and she just kept doing it until blood started coming up. Mrs.
Barstowe called the doctor and paid for the medicine herself, but
finally Mum was too sick and had to go to St. Bartholomew's.
That was where she died, in one of the common wards with
their long rows of beds. The girls took me to visit, but several
days later they told me she was gone. Mrs. Barstowe herself held

my hand as I watched her being lowered into the ground, in the graveyard next to the hospital. She was wrapped in a shroud, and all I could see of her was her hair hanging out, like blood on the ground. I'll never forget the sight of it, or the stench of the corpses.

"I was only seven, but the girls talked to Mrs. Barstowe and she decided I could stay, if each girl gave up enough of her pay to support me until I was old enough to support myself. All the girls agreed, though they had little enough themselves. They called me their mascot, and said I would bring them luck. A week later, Mrs. Barstowe called me into her parlor and said, 'There's a gentleman here to see you on behalf of your father, Diana.'"

"A gentleman?" said Mary. "I thought it was my mother who took you from that place—Mrs. Barstowe's—to St. Mary Magdalen. Although how could she have known that Hyde had a child? Mrs. Poole, I think my mother had her secrets as well."

"Or was trying to keep your father's secrets, like as not," said the housekeeper.

"I never saw your mum or any other woman," said Diana. "All I saw was a man in a frock coat and top hat. He said he was a lawyer who'd been sent to take me away from Mrs. Barstowe's to a place where I would be educated and cared for. Well, little did I know that it would be Our Lady of Dullness! If I had, I would have kicked and screamed before letting him take me. But I thought he was going to take me to my father, and Mum had always told me he was a rich man.

"So I went with him, and did I ever regret it! The girls at Barstowe's had let me wear their dresses and jewelry, and put rouge on my cheeks, and perfume on my wrists. They had laughed and sworn and gotten drunk. At St. Mary Magdalen's, I had to wear a gray dress with a white pinafore. My hair had to be up in braids and under a cap, so it was proper—how they pulled it, braiding it in the mornings! There were no more bonbons, no more magazines with pictures. Just prayers and sewing. I swore under my breath and tangled the thread, just to make the sisters mad!"

"But what about this man?" said Mary. "Do you remember his name?"

"He never gave a name, at least not to me," said Diana.

"Was he short and crooked, like Hyde?" asked Mrs. Poole.

"No, he was tall and straight, like a lamppost. He had sharp eyes that looked me up and down, and thin lips that he pressed together with disapproval when he saw how I was dressed. He carried a cane with a dog's head in silver as the handle—I kept looking at it because it was so lifelike. I wished it would bark."

"Mr. Utterson!" said Mary. "Mrs. Poole, I'm completely mystified. Why would Mr. Utterson have been involved in this affair?"

"Well, he was your mother's solicitor at the time," said Mrs. Poole. "Could he not have made all those arrangements for her—the documents, the account, even the child?"

"You're talking about me as though I'm invisible," said Diana, once again pushing her big toe into the hole in the sofa and giving it a good tear.

"But Mr. Guest didn't know about any of those arrangements," said Mary. "Why would Mr. Utterson not have informed his own clerk?"

"Perhaps Mr. Utterson didn't trust him," said Mrs. Poole. "Would you?"

"Not as far as I could throw him," said Mary.

DIANA: Have I done the he said she said enough now? I'm getting tired of this.

CATHERINE: Oh, all right, I'll finish it up for you and revise what you've written to make it sound like a

proper narrative. And to take out the cursing! Go
do whatever it is you do.

DIANA: Wouldn't you like to know!

CATHERINE: Not particularly.

Yes, her mother must have known. About her father and the
experiments, about Hyde . . . Mary imagined Mr. Utterson, in
his somber frock coat and black top hat, with the gold chain of his
pocket watch just visible, getting into a hansom cab and ordering it
to take him to Barstowe's. The cabbie must have grinned, to indicate that he understood what a gentleman such as Mr. Utterson
would be doing there. It would have been so distasteful.

And then arriving at the whorehouse, walking in and speaking
to Mrs. Barstowe herself, asking for the child. Being presented
with Diana, with her tangle of red hair, got up like a—well, like
one of those girls. She could imagine him shuddering.

He must have been acting for her mother. Mary had wondered how her mother, who was already ill, had managed to set
up a bank account and bring Diana to the Magdalen Society. This
explained it: the lawyer had done all. And of course Mrs. Jekyll
could not have gone to a whorehouse to pick up the daughter of
her husband's assistant—or, if Mary's hypothesis was correct, her
husband's daughter by another woman. Mary put her head in her
hands. This affair resembled a jigsaw puzzle. One corner of it was
starting to fit together, to show a picture. But there were so many
other pieces that had no place as yet: Beatrice Rappaccini, the
poor girl this morning with her brain cut out, and S.A., whatever
that meant.

"So, are there any more sandwiches?" asked Diana.

"Not for you!" said Mrs. Poole. "I have a bit of jelly roll left, and that will be for Miss Mary, because she's barely eaten anything. You've eaten quite enough! But that's the last of the sugar, I'm afraid."

"I'll go to the bank tomorrow and close the account Mr. Utterson opened," said Mary. "I didn't have time today, what with the corpse and long-lost sister and all." *That will be the agenda for tomorrow,* she thought, mentally making a list. If she could arrange it neatly in her head, then perhaps the events of the day wouldn't seem so bewildering. Clerkenwell, wherever that was, Bank of England to deposit the funds so they could buy sugar, Royal College of Surgeons to see the Poisonous Girl, back to Regent's Park to meet with Holmes and Watson. She wondered what Beatrice Rappaccini could tell them. Would she know what their fathers had been doing, what sorts of experiments they had been conducting? Would she know what S.A. stood for?

Diana gave an enormous yawn.

"All right, to bed with you," said Mary. One problem at a time, and the immediate problem was Diana.

MARY: As it so often is!

And then began the ordeal of getting Diana into bed, which involved several trips to the bathroom, innumerable glasses of water, and a headache for Mary, since Mrs. Poole declared early in the process that the heathen could stay up all night, as far as she was concerned. Mary ended up giving Diana half of the jelly roll Mrs. Poole had brought up for her.

Finally, the admonition "You say you're fourteen, but you behave like a child" had its effect. Diana lay tucked into bed in what had once been Mary's nursery, and Mary collapsed into a chair in her own bedroom. She was so tired!

Once, her days had passed quietly, one after the other, in the routine of caring for her mother. She had ordered meals, responded to the nurse's complaints, paid bills. That "once" had been only a fortnight ago. In that fortnight, her life had changed completely, and she had the disquieting sense that it would continue to change, perhaps in ways that were not particularly pleasant. She had longed for adventure, and now that it was happening to her, she was not sure how she felt about it. Today she had been to Whitechapel, seen a corpse, and gained what was presumably a sister. What would tomorrow bring?

The most difficult part, the part she did not want to think about quite yet, was the revolution a day had made in her memories of her father. The tall, kind, distant father she had known . . . At least he had not been a Dr. Rappaccini, experimenting on his own daughter! Or daughters, because there was after all Diana. Was Diana, in a sense, the product of his experiments? Why had Hyde wanted a child, and a girl specifically? Perhaps he had simply been jealous of his alter ago and wanted a daughter of his own—if Dr. Jekyll had Mary, then he would have Diana. Or was there something more nefarious behind it? Those thoughts went around and around in Mary's head. Would it never stop aching? She should have asked Mrs. Poole for something, one of those patent medicines the housekeeper kept in her dispensary. But Mary did not want to wake her, or make a trip downstairs through the dark house.

There was nothing to do now but get some sleep. She pulled on her nightgown and slipped between the covers. The nursery was next to her bedroom, and until she fell asleep, Mary could hear, through the walls, Diana snoring. It was a strangely comforting sound.

The next morning, Diana was up before she was. Mrs. Poole had dressed her in one of Mary's old dresses, which would have been given to Alice in another year. "Her own clothes will need to be washed," said Mrs. Poole. "Though I don't know what good it will do—I've never seen dresses that have been mended so many times! They're about to come apart at the seams. And such cheap material, that scratchy gray wool! Thank goodness her coat is in a reasonably decent state, and I've made her polish her boots. But I've had to give her a pair of your gloves, and one of your hats."

After a breakfast of toast, eggs, and coffee as a particular treat for Diana—"Coffee, heavenly coffee!" Diana sang, dancing around the morning room, and Mary had to admit that she had a good singing voice—they walked first to the bank where Mrs. Jekyll had kept an account for Diana, and then to the Bank of England, to transfer funds. Thirty-five pounds, five shillings, three pence, in what was now Mary's own account. She withdrew a pound, in change, and put it into her purse. Oh, to have money in her purse again! Mrs. Poole would be able to buy sugar, and perhaps there would be jelly roll for tea. And then, with Diana complaining that her boots pinched, they made their way to the Royal College of Surgeons, to see the Poisonous Girl.

CHAPTER VII

The Poisonous Girl

Mary and Diana crossed Lincoln's Inn Fields. Mary had never been in this part of the city—there were so many parts of the city she had never seen, although she had lived in London all her life. She sighed, remembering weeks when she had barely left the house for fear that her mother might suffer another of her attacks—thank goodness for Nurse Adams, who had been so reliable, although very expensive. But here she was, after a long walk from Threadneedle Street. Somehow she had expected Lincoln's Inn Fields to be fields, but as so often in London, the name was deceptive: it was simply a park, surrounded by streets lined on two sides with respectable buildings in the Georgian style. On the other two sides were Lincoln's Inn, where barristers plied their trade, and the Royal College of Surgeons. As she and Diana walked through the park, under a canopy of ancient oaks, Mary remembered the park she had seen yesterday in Whitechapel, with poor children playing in ragged clothes. How strange that the word "park" could describe such different places! The rain had stopped, but whenever the wind blew, which was often, large wet drops would fall on their heads from the branches above. Mary kept her umbrella up and tried to cover them both, but Diana always walked either ahead or behind her, not caring whether she got wet.

As they left the park, they saw the facade of the Royal College of Surgeons with its gray columns, looming like a great mauso-leum. There was already a line of visitors stretching down the stone steps. Mary could see respectable men in frock coats and bowler hats, mothers with children pulling at their hands and asking if they could go play in the park, maids on their day off, boys in dirty trousers who would obviously not be able to pay the entrance fee, but probably hoped to sneak in and catch a glimpse of the Poisonous Girl before they were ejected by the porters. She checked to make sure she had the advertisement with her, folded into her purse.

"Are you here to see the poisonous beauty?" asked a young man with a sparse attempt at a mustache, presumably one of the por-ters. He had an official look about him and was holding a sheaf of pamphlets in his hand. When Mary nodded, he told her to line up behind the others. At 10 a.m. precisely, the line began to move. The visitors who had been waiting filed into the entrance hall, handing the porter either an advertisement or the requi-site number of shillings and pence. In return, he handed them a pamphlet. Mary glanced at it quickly. At the top of the page was written *The Poisonous Girl! A wonder of modern science! Discovered by Professor Petronius, M.D., D.Phil., member of the Anthropological Institute of Great Britain and Ireland.* She did not have time to read the rest. The line was filing past a set of stairs marked TO LIBRARY, and through a pair of doors that opened into a large chamber. In the middle of the chamber was a wooden platform, with a table on it. On the table was a collection of objects—Mary had no time to pay them closer attention, although she noticed that one was a canary in a cage.

"Now that's more like it!" said Diana, turning and staring upward. The chamber was two stories high, with a balcony run-ning around it. On both the first and second floors, the walls were lined with wooden cabinets. Through their glass fronts,

Mary could see anatomical specimens of various sorts: skeletons, but also row after row of glass jars filled with what were presumably parts of the human body. It looked like the pantry of a frugal housewife who, instead of pickles, had put up hearts, livers, spleens.

"Come on," she said to Diana, pulling her along by the collar. The audience to see the Poisonous Girl was a large one, and Mary wanted to get as close to the platform as possible. It was obviously the stage on which Beatrice Rappaccini would stand and—do what? Mary had no idea. Would she simply be put on display, like the freaks that were shown at the Royal Aquarium—the bearded women and dog-faced men? Mary had never seen one of the shows herself, but she had heard about them from servants. Alice, the scullery maid, had gone once with Mrs. Poole and could talk of nothing else for a week. She pushed through the crowd and secured a space for them at one corner of the platform, somewhat crushed between a woman in a violently purple walking suit and a man with a monocle. The woman gave her a look as Mary pushed her way in, as though she were some sort of recently discovered and unwelcome beetle. *Well,* she told herself, *politeness has no place in a murder investigation.*

When the audience had been kept waiting just long enough to start getting restless, the porter said, "Make way, make way, for Professor Petronius!" The crowd parted, and a man in a theatrical black cloak, with enormous side-whiskers too black to be entirely natural, walked to the platform. He looked around at the audience, clearing his throat once or twice while the crowd quieted down and waited expectantly. Then he spoke in a voice that carried to the back of the room.

"Ladies and gentlemen, I am Professor Petronius. Welcome to this august institution, which has so generously allowed me to reveal to you one of the scientific wonders of our age—a marvel out of the classical world, when such a phenomenon was known, although it astonishes us to see it in the nineteenth century! Today I will show you a young woman, as beautiful and innocent as a rose in bloom, whose system has been so imbued with poisons that she herself has become poisonous to all she touches. Imagine, ladies and gentlemen, not being able to touch, to kiss, other human beings for fear of harming them—of rendering them lifeless! Imagine being so deadly that your fellow men shun you once they learn of your powers. Today you shall see just such a creature, separated forever from others of her kind. She is not a monster—no! For unlike the Elephant Man or Bear Woman, of whom you have no doubt heard, she was not born with her peculiarity. The poison was introduced into her system slowly over a period of many years, as you may read in my article, a copy of which you hold in your hands, originally published in the *Journal of the Anthropological Institute*. Beatrice Rappaccini is not a monster, but a marvel of modern science! Behold!"

He flung out his right arm, pointing toward the entrance. There stood a woman, about Mary's age, dressed in white. With the rest of the audience, Mary gasped. Even Diana, who was usually unimpressible, whistled under her breath.

She was beautiful. She was, it was no exaggeration to say, the most beautiful woman most of the audience members had ever seen. Her dress was in the Grecian style, leaving her neck and arms bare. Her skin, of a soft olive hue, proclaimed her a daughter of the temperate South, and her cheeks were tinged with red, as though she had spent time under a southern sun. Her features were as clearly cut as those of an ancient statue. Her hair, a lustrous black, hung down to her waist. She stood still for a moment, then walked toward the platform, swaying as gracefully as one of the reeds so admired by the classical god Pan.

JUSTINE: That's a lovely description, Catherine.

CATHERINE: Thank you! I'm glad someone notices
when I write particularly well.

"Let her through, let her through," said Professor Petronius.
"Mothers, nurses, if you please, protect your children. Make
certain they do not touch her, not even the hem of her gown.
Remember that she is deadly!"

The audience parted before her like the Red Sea, some of the
mothers pulling their children back sharply as she passed, although
the children strained to see her.

Poor girl, thought Mary. *Surely this Petronius is both cruel and a
charlatan. She could not possibly harm those children.* And indeed, as
she moved through the crowd, the woman's face was so sad that
Mary would have liked to comfort her.

BEATRICE: Is that truly what you thought, when you
first saw me?

MARY: More or less, although you know how Catherine
romanticizes everything. But I was thinking about
how sad you looked.

BEATRICE: I was! Oh indeed, I was so sad that you
could not imagine the depth of my sadness.

The woman stepped onto the platform and stood beside
Professor Petronius. She looked out at the audience, calmly and
with an expression of resignation on her face.

"This charming creature," said Professor Petronius, "was born
in the city of Padua, in Italy. No doubt even those of you who have

not traveled in Europe have heard of the splendors of Italy—the ruins of an ancient civilization turned up by every farmer's plough, the perpetual sun that warms the soul and makes it so much more eloquent than here in England. In Italy, the soul becomes poetic, although the body is lethargic. It is the country of Petrarch, of Michelangelo! That is the country in which Signorina Rappaccini was born."

Looking around at the stolidly English audience, Mary very much doubted that any of them had dreamed of traveling in Europe. A nice trip to Bournemouth would be more in their line.

"Her father was a professor at the University of Padua, a famous doctor specializing in the vegetable poisons. He knew how to draw out their properties and turn the deadliest toxins into the most beneficial pharmacopeia. His daughter tended his garden of poisonous plants. So she could tend them properly, with the attention that the most delicate specimens required, he forbade her from protecting herself with gloves or masks. Slowly, as she assisted her father in his experiments, she herself became poisonous. The essence of the plants seeped into her, and as she grew into splendid womanhood, she also grew deadly to man. And now," said Professor Petronius, "you shall see how deadly Miss Rappaccini can be."

From a vase on the table, he lifted a Madonna lily—a long stem of white flowers, no doubt forced in a hothouse, since it was before the season for them. Ceremoniously, he handed it to the woman—to Beatrice. She took it in her hand, held it for a moment, then opened her mouth and breathed on the flowers. Almost at once, they began to turn brown, to shrivel and dry up. Their petals fell to the floor, then the stem itself turned brown and was simply a dry stick. The audience gasped.

In quick succession, as the audience stood spellbound, Professor Petronius handed Beatrice a variety of living objects.

An apple on its branch rotted from her breath. Bees in a jar that had been buzzing a moment before fell silent and lay on the glass bottom, their wings twitching and then still. A mouse Professor Petronius handed her—Mary noticed that he donned gloves before doing so—scampered up her arm, stopped on her shoulder, then stood as though transfixed. She lifted it off and kissed it tenderly before laying it back on the table, where it did not move. A small green snake that he lifted out of a box wound itself around her wrist. In a few minutes, she unwound it and returned its limp form. Finally, Professor Petronius held up the canary in its cage. Beatrice touched the cage gently with one hand. There were tears in her eyes as she leaned forward and breathed on the unfortunate bird. A moment before, it had been cheeping. It gave a final querulous cheep, then it too was silent. Beatrice turned away, as though she did not want to see—either the destruction she had caused, or the reactions of the audience.

"Who will volunteer to approach and feel the power of Miss Rappaccini's breath?" asked Professor Petronius. "We need a robust gentleman who is willing to risk his life for a kiss from the Poisonous Beauty. Gentlemen, if you volunteer, Miss Rappaccini will kiss you on the cheek, and you will feel her power. But do not volunteer if you have a heart condition or your medical advisor has forbade you from taking vigorous exercise!"

Mary was astonished to see that there were indeed volunteers. Professor Petronius chose two: a younger gentleman who was no doubt some sort of clerk, and an older man who proclaimed that he was a builder, and not afraid of a girl. Both were given the opportunity to go up to Beatrice and hold her hands. Then, she leaned over and kissed each of them on the cheek, quickly and with no indication of enjoyment. When they turned back to the audience, the clerk looking dazed and the builder grinning, Mary could see the red mark of her lips on their skin.

"How do you feel, gentlemen?" asked Professor Petronius, according the builder a rank he did not deserve. Both proclaimed that they felt dizzy. "It's like being drunk, it is," said the builder. "Don't know as I could make my way home if I felt like this after leaving the pub on a Friday night!"

"You are brave, gentlemen," said Professor Petronius. "When you go home tonight, tell your wives or sisters or mothers that today, you were kissed by death and survived! Those marks will fade in a few days, although I would recommend a topical ointment to assist with healing. Now, if anyone in the audience has questions about this marvel of science, I am available to answer them!"

There were questions: What did Miss Rappaccini eat? How long would it take her to poison a full-grown man? Who did her hair?

While Professor Petronius answered them, Mary slipped closer to where Beatrice stood on the platform. How could she communicate with the Poisonous Girl? There had been no indication that she spoke anything but Italian. Quickly, Mary drew a pencil from her purse. Did she have any paper? Yes, the pamphlet—she tore off a corner, scribbled on it the letters she had seen on the watch fob in Molly Keane's hand and the seal on the mysterious letters from Budapest, and held it out, whispering as loudly as she dared, "Miss Rappaccini."

Beatrice heard her and turned her head. For a moment, Mary was not certain whether she would take the note. But then, she took a step toward Mary and held out her hand. Mary placed it on her palm—she could not help being glad that she, like Professor Petronius, was wearing gloves. How far did Miss Rappaccini's baleful influence extend? Beatrice glanced at the note. When she saw the letters, her expression changed: for the first time, she looked interested, alive. "What is your name?" she asked in a low voice.

"Mary Jekyll," Mary replied.

"Wait for me in the park," said Beatrice. "I will try to get away, although it will be difficult—he watches me all the time. But wait for me. I will be there when I can."

It was obvious, from Beatrice's furtive glance at Professor Petronius, that she did not want to speak further in the exhibition hall. Mary nodded. Their conversation would have to wait.

She looked around for Diana. Where had the girl gone? Mary assumed she had been standing beside her all this time, but no— Diana had slipped away and was on the far side of the room, staring at one of the glass cases. Mary pushed through the crowd, which was still questioning Professor Petronius.

"Do you ever do as you're told?" she said to Diana when she had made her way to the case.

"No," said Diana without turning. "Look, it's the skeleton of Charles Byrne, the Irish Giant. Seven feet tall, he was. And there's the brain of some kind of mathematical bloke. I've never seen a brain before."

Mary glanced over: the jar was labeled BRAIN OF CHARLES BABBAGE, MATHEMATICIAN.

"Diana, we don't have time to look at all these things, not right now." She told Diana about the note she had passed to the Poisonous Girl and Beatrice's reaction. "We need to go wait in the park. That professor—I think she's afraid of him. She said that she had to get away from him, to meet us. We need to go wait for her, so we're there when she has the opportunity."

It was difficult to drag Diana away from such a tempting display of grotesquerie, of fetuses in jars, some of them with two heads or four arms, or only one eye. Of tumors and abnormalities. But Mary took a firm hold of her coat collar and pulled.

DIANA: My favorite was Charles Byrne. I'd never seen a giant before.

JUSTINE: He was not a giant, simply a very tall man. There is nothing wrong with being tall.

DIANA: Says you. Of course you don't think it's abnormal, any more than Beatrice thinks it's abnormal to go around poisoning people.

BEATRICE: But I know perfectly well it's abnormal, I assure you. Justine's height is not extraordinary— for a man. For a woman, yes. But as she says, there is nothing wrong with being different.

DIANA: Oh, come off it! You're both freaks. Just like me.

Outside, the rain had started again—not a proper rain, but a sort of mist that fell from the sky and covered their clothes in water drops. Mary put up her umbrella. They crossed the street and once again entered the park, then followed the central walk around and around the gazebo, trying to keep warm. It must have been half an hour before they saw a woman hurrying toward them. She was wrapped in a thick shawl, and Mary did not immediately recognize her. She looked so different than she had in the exhibit hall. But as she drew closer, her graceful movements identified her as Beatrice Rappaccini.

"Miss Jekyll," she said. "Please forgive me, my English is not always adequate to my wishes." Her English was, in fact, perfect—although she spoke with a lilting Italian accent. "I must speak with you, but there is no time. Fortunately, Petronius has been detained by one of the trustees of the college—I believe he owes the college a considerable sum for allowing him to put on my shows. But he will be along any minute, and then I will not

be able to speak freely. I agreed to these shows because he promised that the physicians of the college would attempt to heal me of
this dreadful curse, but he has made so much money that he has
no interest in my cure—he has become greedy, and I believe he
will not willingly let me go. Each night, he locks me in, but even
if I were to escape, where would I go in this country? I have no
friends in England. Except perhaps you—I have heard your name
mentioned, and I am familiar with your father's work. He must
have told you about the Société, or you would not have handed
me that piece of paper. Have you come to help me? This must be
your—servant?" She looked at Diana curiously.

"This is my—sister, Diana Hyde," said Mary. "This Société—
Society—what is it? I don't understand."

"Hyde! This is Hyde's offspring?" Beatrice looked astonished. "How could your father have done something so disastrous?
Allowing Hyde to reproduce himself. I cannot believe it."

"Hey, who are you calling disastrous, poison breath?" said
Diana.

"Then you know what this is all about?" said Mary. "These
experiments . . ."

"Yes, of course," said Beatrice. "I was my father's assistant. I
took his notes and made fair copies of his papers for the journal of
the Société. But you—do you truly not know? About the trans-
mutations, the Société des Alchimistes? Your father died when you
were still young. He must not have had time to explain . . ."

"Don't look now," said Diana, "but Professor Whiskers is
coming this way."

It was indeed Professor Petronius, walking down the path
toward them.

"He is no professor," said Beatrice scornfully. "He has no degree,
no qualifications whatsoever! Look, I live in that building. . . ."
She pointed to a tall gray house on the other side of the park. "My

room is the only one occupied on the second floor. The window faces the back. But I don't know how I could get out. As I said, he locks me in every night, and I am watched during the day."

"We'll help you," said Mary. "I don't know how, but we will. We'll just have to figure it out."

Professor Petronius was almost upon them.

"Oh sir," Mary called, turning to him. "Thank you so much for your wonderful lecture! I was just telling Miss Rappaccini how much I enjoyed it, although she probably doesn't understand me, does she, being a foreigner? But my pupil and I thought it was so interesting! This is my pupil, Diana. Her mother gave us permission to come see the show. We enjoyed it ever so much!"

"Oh yes," said Diana. "Especially when she killed the canary. That was prime! I hope we get to see it again."

"Well, only if your mother lets us. Thank you again, Professor. It was all so fascinating."

"Thank you, ladies," he said, taking Beatrice by the arm. Mary noticed that although he bowed to them politely enough, his grip on Beatrice's arm was firm. Up close, his dyed whiskers made him look even more like a charlatan, and his teeth were stained with tobacco. "Do come again, with your mother's permission of course. A shilling and sixpence. Now if you'll excuse us, Miss Rappaccini has a show again in an hour."

He hurried Beatrice away. Mary and Diana watched them depart, the man in the top hat and the woman wrapped in a shawl. He was still holding her arm when they went into the building Beatrice had pointed out.

"We have to rescue her," said Mary.

"Got any bright ideas?" asked Diana.

"Not a single one. Not at the moment. But we have an appointment with Mr. Holmes. We can at least tell him what we've learned about S.A."

"And what's that?" said Diana.

"Well, what the initials mean. It has to be the society Beatrice mentioned: the Société des Alchimistes. Although I don't understand why a scientific society would want to murder girls and take their body parts. . . ."

"Unless they want to use those body parts in experiments," said Diana.

Mary stared at her sister. The rain started again. She could hear it patter on the leaves of the trees above, and then on the pavement. "That's horrible. That's—well, just horrible." She remembered the words of the letter from Italy: *You have a daughter, have you not? Surely she is old enough for you to begin the process, in whatever direction you decide will yield the most promising results.* Experiments—on girls. What had the letter said about the female brain being more malleable? Molly Keane's brain had been missing . . . why?

"Are we going to just stand here?" asked Diana. "I'm getting wet."

"Well, get under the umbrella." Mary consulted her wristwatch, then thought for a moment. "I hate to spend money on transportation, but I told Dr. Watson we would meet them at noon, and it's half past eleven. Let's catch an omnibus back to Baker Street."

"That's more like it," said Diana. "You've spent the morning dragging me all over the city. The least you could do is pay for a bus. And buy me something to eat."

They bought half a dozen currant buns for tuppence and ate them as they rode in the omnibus. Luckily, the bus was almost empty and they could sit inside, dry although not particularly warm or comfortable. They disembarked on Marylebone Road, walked up Baker Street, and rang the bell at 221B. Mrs. Hudson led them right up the stairs and knocked on the door. "Mr. Holmes, it's Miss Jekyll and—a friend," she said, looking at Diana dubiously. Diana still had crumbs on her collar. Mary wiped them away hastily with her handkerchief.

"Let them in, Mrs. Hudson," called Holmes. "The door is unlocked."

Mary pushed open the door and stepped into the parlor. It was just as disorganized as the last time she had visited, with the skulls on the mantelpiece, the specimen jars on shelves, and furniture covered in books and ash. Holmes turned to her with a smile and Watson bowed, but a third man in the room frowned. It was Inspector Lestrade.

"You again!" he said. "The case is closed, Miss Jekyll. The murderer has confessed. So you can take yourself home to your embroidery, which is what young ladies should be doing, rather than interfering with murder investigations. And take that hellcat with you," he added, seeing Diana.

"Although Lestrade has expressed himself so rudely, I'm afraid he's right," said Holmes. "There has been a confession. A madman by the name of Renfield claims he committed the murders. We're on our way to Purfleet Asylum to interview him."

"A confession!" said Mary. "Then perhaps what we've found doesn't matter after all."

"And what have you found?" asked Holmes.

"S.A.," said Diana. "It's some kind of society."

"We believe it may refer to a Société des Alchimistes," said Mary. "Have you heard of it, Mr. Holmes? My father belonged to it, and so did two scientists named Rappaccini and Moreau. I believe they corresponded regularly about the activities of the society. We found a letter from Dr. Rappaccini to my father in which he mentions experimenting on girls."

"Moreau—I've heard that name before," said Watson.

"Intriguing," said Holmes. "This may have nothing to do with the murders, Miss Jekyll, but I would like you to tell me as much as you know about this society."

"Holmes!" said Lestrade. "There's no time if we're going to

make it to Purfleet and back before the end of the day."

"Well then, Miss Jekyll will simply have to come with us. You won't mind a rather long trip, will you? We need to take a train from Fenchurch Street. You can tell me what you discovered on the train. Watson, will you hand me my coat?"

"Absolutely not!" said Lestrade. "Holmes, this is too much, even for you. Much as I dislike Miss Jekyll's interference, and Miss Hyde in general, I will not take them into a madhouse."

"Then they can wait outside," said Holmes. "Miss Jekyll, are you coming?"

"Yes, of course," said Mary. "I've never been to an insane asylum." Yet another thing she had never done before. But this was different from going to Whitechapel or inside a society to save fallen women. This would be the sort of place her mother might have been sent, or ended up, if she had not died. Once again Mary remembered her mother in those last days. Did she truly want to go to such a place? On the other hand, she did not want the mystery to be solved without her. And now there was this new mystery, of the Société des Alchimistes.

"I'm not afraid of madmen," said Diana. "I used to see them all the time, wandering around Whitechapel. They would sleep on the stoops or in the park. Sometimes they were the only ones who made sense."

"I apologize, Miss Jekyll, that you haven't at least had time to dry off," said Watson. "You see how things are around here—I'm afraid this is standard procedure for Holmes. Are you certain you're willing to undertake this journey?"

"Yes, it's quite all right," said Mary. "I would like to tell you both what we've found. And we need your help—but I'll tell you more about it on the train."

"Very well then. Mrs. Hudson has prepared some sandwiches, and I have tea in a vacuum flask. We are technologically up to date, you see! Well then, let's accompany Inspector Lestrade to the station."

Without having sat down, Mary and Diana were once again out the door. On Baker Street, they crowded into the police carriage. She was relieved that Lestrade was sitting across from her, next to Holmes rather than her and Diana, although she had to see his cross face all the way to the train station. At least the sergeant who had been waiting for him in Mrs. Hudson's kitchen sat outside, next to the driver. The main thoroughfares were so crowded at that hour that they did not speak about the case—they could barely have heard themselves above the continual din of London and the clacking of wheels on Oxford Street.

They were just in time to catch the train to Purfleet, and Mary was relieved to see Watson purchasing tickets for her and Diana. Well, they were helping with the case, after all. There was no reason for her to feel ashamed that she could not afford the expense herself. She had been dreading the long train ride with Lestrade, but he wanted to smoke on the journey. She breathed a sigh of relief when he decided to share a second-class compartment with his sergeant. She and Diana would travel first class with Holmes and Watson.

Once they were sitting in a first-class compartment, Watson unwrapped a packet of sandwiches in waxed paper. "Cheese and Mrs. Hudson's special chutney," he said. "I believe she brought the recipe back with her from India. Did you know her husband was in the army? He died in the Indian Mutiny."

"I'm so sorry," said Mary. How strange that Mrs. Hudson, that perfectly ordinary Englishwoman, should once have lived in India! Had she seen cobras and tigers? And fakirs? Mary could not quite remember what fakirs were, but surely Miss Murray had mentioned them during a geography lesson. Suddenly, Mrs. Hudson seemed a much more romantic figure.

"Here, have some tea. It will warm you up." Watson poured tea from the flask into collapsible cups.

"And while you're drinking it," said Holmes, "you can tell me what you've been doing since we all stood over the corpse of Molly Keane together. I believe the two of you have been on adventures of your own, have you not, Miss Jekyll? I'm looking forward to hearing about them. And in return, I will take you to see a homicidal maniac."

CHAPTER VIII

The Man Who Ate Flies

While the train traveled through the countryside, Mary recounted the adventures of that morning. She described the letters in Latin with their red seals. She hated admitting to Mr. Holmes that she could not read them. And yet why? Most women could not read Latin. It was nothing to be ashamed of. Her account would have taken less time if Diana had not kept interrupting. "Yes, but that's not relevant," Mary would reply to her descriptions of Charles Byrne and the two-headed baby in the specimen jar.

Holmes listened in silence, staring out the window. Mary could only tell that he was paying attention by his stillness. When she told the story of Beatrice, Watson exclaimed, "The poor girl!"

"So you see," she concluded, "we need to rescue Beatrice Rappaccini, not only for her own sake, but also so she can tell us about this mysterious society."

Holmes turned to look at her, with a serious expression on his face. "Are you prepared to take responsibility for her, Miss Jekyll? Remember that she is dangerous, even deadly. Will you take her into your own home?"

"I—don't know," said Mary. "I haven't thought that far. But surely she needs to be rescued. Our duty that far is clear, is it not?"

"Of course it is!" said Watson. "Holmes is right—we must

make certain she poses no risk to the general public. But of course she must be rescued."

"So you are both determined," said Holmes. "Well, don't let Lestrade know you're about to let a poisonous woman loose in the city of London. He won't take it well, I assure you."

"She won't be loose, Mr. Holmes," said Mary. "I'll take care of her somehow, I promise."

"Just as long as you don't put her in my room," said Diana. "I don't want to die in my sleep."

Mary ignored her and continued. "Here's how I see the mystery we are trying to solve. The death of Molly Keane, and perhaps the other girls, can be connected to this Société des Alchimistes. The watch fob in her hand, the seal on the letters, and Miss Rappaccini's words create a logical trail from the body in Whitechapel to the society. We know the society was conducting experiments on women—young women. We know that at least three scientists were involved: my father, Dr. Rappaccini, and a colleague of theirs named Moreau."

"I just remembered where I've heard that name!" said Watson. "It was in my medical school days. He was a professor—had to leave his post because the anti-vivisection league made a fuss about some experiments of his. I don't remember what they were exactly. I always thought anti-vivisection was a lot of non-sense. I'm as fond of animals as the next man, Miss Jekyll, but human knowledge must progress. We cannot stop scientific research."

"I wonder if you would have approved of Dr. Moreau's research, Watson," said Holmes. "I remembered the case as soon as Miss Jekyll mentioned his name. That was why I suggested she accompany us on this journey. Moreau was grafting together parts of animals, hybridizing in order to create new species. The experiment over which he lost his post involved surgically altering the brains of pigs so they would become capable of human speech."

"Human speech!" said Watson. "That is indeed shocking. I had no idea."

"All his papers were burned after his departure," said Holmes. "The medical school wanted to keep the incident as quiet as possible. I learned about it only because around the same time, the dean called me in on another matter, of drugs missing from the school's pharmacy. The thief, I determined, was a man named Montgomery, a medical student who had gotten into the habit of betting on dog fights and was selling those drugs to pay his gambling debts. He left the school before we could confront him, but his guilt was clear."

"Montgomery!" said Mary. "He was in the letter too. He was going to present a paper for Dr. Moreau at a meeting of the society in Vienna."

"Ah, Miss Jekyll, I wish you had told me that at once," said Holmes. "Or brought the letter with you so I could read it for myself."

Mary flushed. Of course she should have brought the letter. But she had not wanted to expose her father's correspondence to the eyes of strangers. Even to the eyes of Mr. Holmes. She still felt an obscure desire to protect him. The portfolio was in the drawer of her mother's desk, in the morning room. Somehow, she had wanted it to remain in that darkness.

"How could Mary have brought it?" said Diana. "She didn't know this morning that you would be interested, and anyway, it's been raining all day. Only an idiot would bring an important letter out in the rain."

Mr. Holmes smiled. "You are correct, Miss Hyde, and I stand rebuked. I apologize, Miss Jekyll. Perhaps we can examine this letter at a later date?"

"Of course," said Mary. She did not know whether to be angry at Diana for her rudeness or grateful for her support.

DIANA: I only said it because he was being an idiot.

MARY: You said it because you wanted to protect me. Because despite your insufferable behavior, you love your sister. That's why.

DIANA: If you kiss me again, I'm going to hit you.

"As I was saying," she continued, "this society was conducting experiments in transmutation . . ."

"And what may that be?" asked Watson.

"Transmutation was the goal of the medieval alchemists," said Holmes. "They were attempting to turn base metals into gold. It sounds as though these modern alchemists are attempting something more complicated: Moreau's experiments point toward a biological transmutation. He was attempting to create new species, to alter the fundamental material of life itself. But Miss Jekyll, remember that the only connection between the murders and this society remains the initials on a fob torn from a watch chain—initials that could have another meaning altogether. And we have a confession on our hands. Watson, I believe you made a copy of the telegram Lestrade received last night?" He added, with a shade of sarcasm, "Watson always takes notes, in case he wishes to write up one of our adventures later."

"Yes. Yes, of course," said Watson. He drew a small notebook out of his breast pocket, opened it, and read, "RE WHITE-CHAPEL MURDERS RENFIELD A LUNATIC MISSING TWO WEEKS RETURNED LAST NIGHT AND CONFESSED TO MURDERS HOLDING

AT PURFLEET ASYLUM PLEASE SEND POLICE INSPECTOR AS SOON
AS POSSIBLE GABRIEL BALFOUR M.D. That does seem fairly defin-
itive, Miss Jekyll."

"How do you know?" asked Diana. "You haven't even talked to
him yet. How do you know he's not making the whole thing up?
He's a lunatic."

"That's why we're going to interview him," said Holmes. "I
believe we're approaching Purfleet."

And they were. The train drew into the station. Mary gathered
up her belongings, as well as Diana's. The girl was fourteen—
couldn't she keep track of her hat, at least? But Mary had to remind
her to put it back on her head. She remembered all the times she
had longed for a sister, someone to play with and later, someone
to help with the household. And now she had one. A completely
annoying one! Still, she could not help saying, "Here, hold still,"
and straightening Diana's hat, which was of course askew, before
they left the compartment.

> DIANA: I don't see the point of hats.

> MARY: They're a social convention. One wears them
> because one is expected to, whether one needs
> them or not.

> DIANA: How does that contradict what I just said?

> JUSTINE: For once, I agree with Diana. I don't see the
> point of following social conventions. Why wear a
> hat unless it is cold outside? An umbrella keeps the
> rain off your head, a parasol keeps the sun out of
> your eyes. Why follow social conventions if they're
> silly?

CATHERINE: Because we're unusual enough without
    drawing additional attention to ourselves.

Mary was so used to the crowds and smog of London that she
looked in wonder at Purfleet, with its orderly shops and detached
houses surrounded by small gardens. It was not the country exactly,
but as they walked from the train station into the center of town,
they passed the Thames, flowing between banks covered with grass
and furze, so different from the embankment in London. On the
other side of the road grew oaks and beeches, beyond which she
could see a wilderness of marshland. The closest she had come
to wilderness for many years was Kensington Gardens. She was
delighted to have left the city behind, if only for a little while.

When was the last time she had left London? Yes, the visit to
her grandfather when she was a child. Her father had still been
alive, and they had traveled by train for most of a day. She remembered watching the city disappear, and then green fields and hills
proceed past the train window. In Yorkshire, there had been a
large country house and an even larger garden, with quince trees.
Each morning, the housekeeper had put glass jars of golden quince
jam on the breakfast table. Mary had ridden a pony in the paddock,
and her mother had shown her how to make a necklace of oxeye
daisies. She had made one for her mother, but it was too small, and
her mother had laughed, then worn it on her head as a crown. Was
that the last time she remembered her mother happy? For there
had been a quarrel—between her father and grandfather, she
remembered, about evolution. Her grandfather had denounced it
as blasphemy, and her father had called him—something dreadful,
and they had left early.

"It's lovely here," she said.

"Give me London any day," said Diana. "I don't know how
anyone can live in this racket. What is it, anyway?"

"Birdsong," said Watson. "You would become accustomed to it in time, Miss Hyde."

Diana snorted. They were walking together, some steps behind Holmes, Lestrade, and Sergeant Evans, who were discussing how best to approach the coming interview.

The asylum was beyond the town and past an old chalk quarry. Mary was tired when they arrived. It had already been a long day. Perhaps she should not have come? And this might be a false lead after all. The lunatic might be making it all up. She glanced at Diana, who complained often enough, but never seemed to tire. Well, there was no turning back now. Although what Mrs. Poole would think of all this, she did not know.

> MRS. POOLE: I was worried sick because I had no idea where you were or when you were coming back. As far as I knew, you'd been poisoned by that Poisonous Girl in the advertisement. Imagine leaving the city without telling me!

> MARY: I'm sorry, Mrs. Poole. Truly, I am. I can apologize again if you would like.

> MRS. POOLE: That won't be necessary, miss. Just don't do it again. Unless you absolutely have to, I mean. I know how you girls get when you're in the middle of an adventure.

"Holmes," said Lestrade when they were standing at the front gates of the asylum, "I don't want those girls anywhere near a dangerous lunatic. Do you understand? He's already killed four that we know of. I don't want an injury—or even a death—on my hands."

"He's confessed to killing four, which is an altogether different thing," said Holmes. "I understand your concerns, Lestrade, but I would like Miss Jekyll to be present at the interview. If this man had any connection with her father, she may remember him from her childhood."

"So you're still stuck on that, are you?" said Lestrade. "I won't take responsibility for her, and if she comes, Watson stays out. This is a police investigation, damn it! Not a tea party. Anyway, he'll need to watch that hellcat—Evans is not a nursemaid."

The asylum grounds were surrounded by a brick wall topped with metal spikes. It was almost twice Mary's height, and the front gates were spiked at the top as well. Mary wondered how the lunatic had gotten out. The place seemed impregnable.

They rang a bell, and an attendant in a white coat came running across the lawn. "Hello!" he called. "Is that Scotland Yard? We've been expecting you." When he reached the gates, he looked at them curiously. Evidently, he had not expected Scotland Yard to bring two young women. However, Lestrade confirmed their identity.

The attendant opened one of the gates and ushered them in. He was a large, clumsily built man with a ruddy face and blond hair that looked as though he'd been running his hands through it. "Dr. Balfour will be glad to see you, Inspector. I'm Joe Abernathy, one of the day attendants. I was the one as found Renfield, wandering about the grounds." He led them up a flagstone path across the lawn, toward the asylum. It was a building in the modern style, also of brick, and looked as though it might have been an ordinary if rather large house—but the windows on the third story were barred.

"I'm surprised your patient was able to escape," said Holmes. "Those walls are high, and I imagine the spikes on top are sharp."

"Oh, we're not as secure here as we oughter be," said Joe. "The wall is high enough between the road and the asylum, but on the other side is Carfax House, which has been empty these many years. It's surrounded by woods—Carfax Woods, they're called—and they stretch back a ways, wild and overgrown. The wall on that side belongs to Carfax, not the asylum, and it's their responsibility to maintain it—but being as nobody's there, it's tumbled down in places. This isn't the first time the old devil has gotten out, either."

"So this man Renfield has escaped before?" said Lestrade.

"Oh, aye. He makes a regular career of it. He's been here as long as I can remember, and I've been here these ten years at least. He's gotten out every few months, regular. I used to think he just wanted to stretch his legs and go on a little walk by moonlight. He seemed such a harmless old devil, until this happened."

"So there's never been a problem with him before?" said Watson.

"No, and I was shocked to hear him say he'd killed those women. I've never heard of him hurting anyone before—except his flies. But Dr. Balfour will tell you all about it."

Except his flies? Mary wondered what that could mean. They walked up the front steps of the asylum and into an entrance hall, painted a plain and glaring white, with wooden benches along the walls. From the inside, the building reminded her of a hospital. There was the same smell of carbolic, the same bustle of attendants in white coats. Here and there she could see what were evidently patients, because they were dressed in uniforms of light blue serge: shirts and trousers for the men, gowns for the women, all shapeless.

They followed Joe Abernathy up a flight of stairs and down a corridor, to a door marked GABRIEL BALFOUR, M.D. Joe knocked on the door, opened it just a crack, and said, "Sir, the inspector from Scotland Yard is here to see you."

"Why, let him in, man," said a cheerful voice with a strong Scottish accent.

Dr. Balfour's office was a mess. There were piles of medical books on the floor, beside empty shelves, and files spilling out of boxes. Several framed diplomas, one from the University of Edinburgh, leaned against the walls.

"I take it you're the director of the asylum," said Lestrade, looking around him with a frown. Obviously, he did not think much of the director's organizational skills.

"The director!" said Dr. Balfour. "Oh Lord, no. I'm the assistant director, hired only a month ago after the former assistant director, Dr. Hennessey, retired—rather suddenly, I gather. The director is Dr. Seward, but he's been away for the last three weeks. I'd only just completed my medical training when I applied for this position, and I thought myself lucky to get it, the economic situation being what it is in England and Scotland, both. But a week after I arrived, Dr. Seward went off to Amsterdam to consult on a patient, and he hasn't returned since. I understand it was a situation that demanded his immediate attention—nevertheless, he could have given me some time to learn the ropes, so to speak. Meanwhile, one of the patients goes missing, and when he turns up again, he confesses to four murders! Honestly, Inspector, I'm glad you're here to take charge of this affair. They didn't teach us to deal with murderers in medical school."

"Well, let's see what this lunatic has to say for himself," said Lestrade. "Mr. Holmes and I will see him—and yes, Miss Jekyll too, if Holmes still insists on such a foolish procedure. If it turns out that he's our murderer, Evans and I will take him to Newgate. Before we left London, I sent a message to the warden, directing him to send a wagon for the prisoner. It should be here within the hour."

"How did he come to tell you he had murdered those women?" asked Holmes.

"Well, I was assured he was harmless—it's a pleasure to meet you, of course, Mr. Holmes. I've read Dr. Watson's fascinating accounts of your cases. When I was a medical student, it was my favorite way to avoid studying for exams!"

Mary looked quickly at Holmes and tried not to smile. Although he listened and nodded politely, she could tell he was annoyed. A distraction from studying for exams! It was certainly not how he wanted his work to be perceived. She could not help being amused. Despite her respect for him, he could sometimes be a little . . . self-important? But now was not the time to think about Mr. Holmes, whatever his character. What had Dr. Balfour been saying? "He's run away before, so the staff thought nothing of it. He usually turns up again in a day or two, when he gets hungry. When he did not return after several days, we alerted the local police. But we never imagined he would harm anyone. We assumed he would be the one in danger, from boys throwing sticks or from inclement weather. Yesterday afternoon, Joe found him wandering about the grounds. His clothes were filthy and spotted with blood. When we asked where he had been, he told us he'd been in London, and done terrible things there. Those are the words he used—terrible things. When we asked him what he had done that was so terrible, he said he'd killed four—women of the streets, if the young ladies will pardon the expression. But you'll want to hear all this from him directly."

"Indeed," said Holmes. "Can you take us to him? Inspector Lestrade, Sergeant Evans, Miss Jekyll, and I will accompany you. Could the others wait here?"

Dr. Balfour nodded. "Yes, of course. I was just sorting through Dr. Seward's mail, separating the private correspondence from asylum business. I would be happy to take you to poor Renfield. Joe, could you stay with Dr. Watson and Miss—the young miss here, in case they need anything?"

"As you wish," said Joe, sounding none too pleased to be left out of the action.

As Mary passed Diana, following Dr. Balfour and the other men, she whispered, "Behave yourself!"

"Not likely!" came the whisper back.

Ah well, she had done what she could. Dr. Watson would have to handle Diana.

The lunatic was housed another flight up, on the third floor. As they approached his room, Dr. Balfour told them his history.

"Dr. Hennessey could tell you more, of course—but he's returned to Ireland, and I don't happen to have a forwarding address. Based on his files, Renfield has been an inmate here these twenty years. It's a pity that a respectable gentleman, a man of science, should fall into madness. He took ill on a trip abroad—in Austria or Romania, one of those Mittel-European countries—and returned a broken man. His family confined him to this asylum, and he has lived here peacefully since. Oh, he runs away once in a while, but from what Joe tells me, there's never been trouble like this! When you see him, you'll find it as difficult as I do to believe he committed these dreadful crimes. And yet—well, here we are, and you can hear it from his own lips."

In front of the door stood another attendant, a strapping young fellow who looked as though he could subdue a bull. "We didn't used to have a guard on him, never thinking he'd do any harm," said Dr. Balfour, "but he's been watched since he returned yesterday." At the assistant director's request, the attendant unlocked the door and let them in.

The room was very plain—white walls, a narrow iron bed with white linens, a table under the window on which were set a basin and ewer. Across the window were iron bars. The only sources of color were a blue bowl on the table and the man who sat on the bed. Like the other inmates, he was dressed in blue serge, but his uniform was streaked and stained with dirt. On the shirt, there were several large red splotches, now dried. He sat hunched forward, his shoulders rounded, head hanging down.

"Renfield," said Dr. Balfour, "here are some gentlemen to see you."

He did not look up.

"This is Inspector Lestrade from Scotland Yard, and Mr. Sherlock Holmes."

At the detective's name, Renfield gave them a sideways, almost surreptitious glance. He was a small man, with hair that had gone prematurely white, and large, somewhat protuberant eyes. Indeed, he looked as though he would not hurt a fly.

Just then, a fly flew into the room through the window. It circled around the table. The room was so quiet that Mary could hear it buzz. Renfield's attention was immediately on it: he watched as it settled on the rim of the blue bowl. In a moment, he was across the room, the fly in his cupped hand, the cupped hand at his mouth. With a triumphant expression, he opened his hand: it was empty. He had swallowed the fly!

Mary could not help shivering. His movements had been so quick!

"Stop that!" said Dr. Balfour. "Didn't I tell you, no more flies? Who put that bowl of sugar water in the room?"

"No, don't take it away!" said Renfield. His voice was highly pitched, and piteous. "Dr. Seward always allowed me to have the flies, and spiders too! Without the flies, how will I live? How will I live forever?"

"This is his mania," said Dr. Balfour. "He collects flies and eats them. He believes they sustain his life."

"They do, they do!" said Renfield. "So big and juicy! There's nothing like a big fat fly, unless it's a big fat spider! If only I could have a spider!"

"I don't know why Dr. Seward allowed him to feed this mania," said Dr. Balfour to them. Then he turned and said to the lunatic, "No flies, nor spiders either. These gentlemen are here to ask you about the murders."

"Oh yes, the murders." Renfield sat back down on the bed, his shoulders once again hunched. He seemed uninterested in the murders.

"Come, we were told you had confessed," said Lestrade. "Did you commit these murders or not?"

"Oh yes," said Renfield, still looking at the floor. "Tuesday was the day I ran away, that was very wrong of me. Thursday evening I found Sally Hayward and chopped her legs off at the knees. Friday was Anna Pettingill, I took her arms. Pauline Delacroix, that was on Monday, because I wouldn't kill on a Sunday, not me! Or God would smite me for sure. I took her head that time. Right pretty she was! Then Molly Keane on Tuesday, that was brains. I killed them in Whitechapel. I killed them, and I deserve to be punished." He looked up again. "Will it hurt very much, being punished?"

"Why, man," said Lestrade "the penalty for murder is being hanged by the neck until you are dead."

"But it won't hurt, will it?" said Renfield. "And then I'll have eternal life."

"Burning in hellfire, he will," said Sergeant Evans under his breath.

"Well, I think that's all we need," said Lestrade. "He knows the dates and times of the murders. He's confessed to them, and there's the blood, right on his shirt. Doctor, thank you for your promptness in contacting us. You will no doubt be called upon as a witness at trial. As soon as the wagon from Newgate arrives, we'll take him off your hands, which I'm sure will be a relief to you."

"As the wagon has not yet arrived, there are a few questions I would like to ask Mr. Renfield," said Holmes.

The lunatic looked up again and watched the detective warily.

"Certainly," said Dr. Balfour.

"If you must," said Lestrade.

Mary waited, curious. What would he ask? The case seemed so very open and shut, now that Renfield had named the women. How else could he have known their names or when they had died? He must, after all, be the murderer.

"Where did you stay while you were in London?" Holmes asked.

"Where did I stay?" Renfield looked puzzled. "Where did I . . ."

"Why does this matter, Holmes?" asked Lestrade. "Surely he stayed wherever he could—under bridges, in doorways!"

"Yes—yes," said Renfield. "The inspector is right. I slept under bridges. And—in doorways."

"What did you eat?" asked Holmes.

"What did I—oh, rubbish. Whatever I could, on the streets, you know. What people threw away."

"Did you have any help in committing these crimes? Did you have a confederate to assist you?"

"No!" said Renfield. "No, I did it all by myself."

"Did you? And what weapon did you use to cut those women in two?"

"A knife. Yes, I used a knife."

"And where is it now?"

"I threw it into the Thames!" Renfield said this with glee, as though he had scored a point against the detective.

"But Molly Keane's neck was snapped. How did you manage to do that? You don't look particularly strong, if you don't mind my saying so."

"Oh, I have the strength of a madman," said Renfield. "Haven't you heard, Mr. Holmes? Madmen are strong! Joe said that, when I told him all about it. I snapped her neck just like I would snap a matchstick." He smiled gently.

"I see," said Holmes. "Well, Miss Jekyll, have you ever seen this man before? Could he have any connection with your father?"

Mary looked at him again carefully, trying to imagine what he might have looked like fourteen years ago. Surely the same? "No, Mr. Holmes. I'm afraid I haven't. As far as I know, he never visited my father's house. But I was only a child. I wouldn't have known all his colleagues and confederates."

Renfield looked at her with blank, innocuous eyes. It was clear that he did not recognize her either.

She thought for a moment. "May I ask him a question?"

"Of course not," and "Certainly," said Lestrade and Holmes at the same time.

"Why did you kill those women?" asked Mary.

"Why?" said Renfield. He stared at her, his eyes wide.

"Because he's a lunatic," said Lestrade.

"Yes. Yes, that's right, I'm a lunatic." Renfield smiled again, that strange, gentle smile, as though he had explained everything. Yet Mary could have sworn that when she had asked the question, he did not have a response.

"Doctor, the wagon has arrived from Newgate." It was Joe Abernathy. He had opened the door a few inches and was peering through.

"All right," said Lestrade. "Sergeant, handcuff him and take him down. I think he'll come quietly."

Renfield allowed Sergeant Evans to fasten the cuffs on his wrists. "Yes, yes, I'll come quietly," Mary heard him mutter to himself. "And then eternal life!" She followed Lestrade, the sergeant leading the handcuffed prisoner, and Holmes, with Dr. Balfour and the two attendants bringing up in the rear. What a strange procession it was, winding its way down the stairs of the asylum! Diana and Dr. Watson were already waiting for them in the entrance hall. "Took you long enough," said Diana.

At the sound of her voice, the prisoner stopped and jumped back as though startled, so that Holmes and Sergeant Evans had to stop as well. Dr. Balfour and the attendants almost crashed into them. If they had, Mary thought, they would all have gone down like dominoes. She stifled a laugh, then admonished herself to pay attention. This was certainly no time to be laughing! Why had the prisoner stopped so suddenly?

Renfield looked up at Diana and whispered, "Who are you?"

She stared back. "What business is it of yours?"

"This is my sister, Mr. Renfield," said Mary. "My sister, Diana Hyde."

At that, Renfield's face took on a sly, crafty look she had not yet seen on it. Perhaps he had killed those women after all?

"You're his daughter, you are. When you see your father, tell him I did well. Will you do that for me? Eternal life, that's what I want. That's what I was promised. You tell him I did everything I was told."

Sergeant Evans wrenched the prisoner's arm, so that he had to step forward not to fall. But as he started walking again at the sergeant's insistence, he turned back to say, one last time, "Remember!"

"What did he mean by that?" asked Mary.

"Some nonsense," said Lestrade. "Have you ever seen that man before, Miss Hyde?"

"If I had, I would remember," said Diana. "He looks like a frog."

"There you go!" said Lestrade. "A bunch of nonsense. I think this case is closed. I'm sorry, Holmes, that you weren't able to perform one of your feats of deduction, but it was a simple case after all."

The prison wagon was waiting in the drive. Mary looked at it and shivered. How forbidding it looked, with its barred windows! Renfield's face was visible through the bars. He stared at them—no, she realized, it was Diana who had his attention—until the sergeant told him sharply to sit down. Inspector Lestrade locked them both in, then swung himself up beside the driver.

"It's the train again for us," said Watson. "Well, Holmes? Was it a simple case after all?"

"Not as simple as Lestrade thinks," said Holmes. "He's used to seeing what he expects to see. He expected to see a man who had murdered four women, so that's what he saw: a dirty lunatic with blood on his clothes. The details Renfield was able to provide confirmed his guilt. Lestrade failed to notice the discrepancies in Renfield's story—even in his appearance."

"What discrepancies?" asked Mary.

"There were no bloodstains on his knees. You remember the body of Molly Keane. Her head lay in a pool of blood. How could he have cut her brain out without kneeling on the pavement? I asked if he had a confederate, but he said no. And I scarcely think Renfield was carrying a pocket watch. The asylum uniform has no pockets. That leaves the fob in Molly Keane's hand unexplained. She might have torn it from someone else's watch chain, but why? Surely she was defending herself against her attacker. And what of the man with the low, whispering voice Kate Bright-Eyes described? Finally, if Lestrade had looked more carefully at Renfield's hands, he would have seen that although they were dirty, there was no dirt under his fingernails. After sleeping outdoors in London for a week, after scavenging for food in heaps of refuse, his nails should have been filthy. And how did he kill those women without getting blood under his nails? No, he washed his hands, and recently. The dirt was added later."

"You didn't mention any of this to Lestrade," said Watson.

"He would not have listened to me, just as he paid no attention to the exchange between Renfield and Miss Hyde."

"Yes, what do you make of that?" asked Mary.

"I don't know what to make of it, yet. Unless Miss Hyde can enlighten us?"

"Not me," said Diana. "I have no idea what he was on about. But I've got something else to show you. When that muscleman—Abercrombie, Aberwhatsit—left the office to let you know the wagon had arrived, we had a bit of a look around. It was Watson's idea as much as mine, so don't you go blaming me! And in a pile of letters, we found this."

Out of her coat pocket, she drew an envelope. Affixing the flap was a red wax seal stamped S.A.

CHAPTER IX

A Rescue at Night

While they were talking, they had come to the train station.

"We're in luck," said Watson. "There is a train in fifteen minutes. We can be in London in an hour. By the time we've had dinner, it will be dark, and we can reconnoiter around Miss Rappaccini's home. Remember that we have a lady in distress to rescue, although I have no idea how it is to be accomplished."

"Diana, put that letter away until we get on the train," said Mary. "Then we can look at it properly. You do know that stealing is wrong, don't you?"

"Yes," said Diana. "And you can thank me later."

Once they were seated in the first-class compartment, Diana produced the letter out of her pocket.

Holmes held out his hand.

"I don't think so," she said. "Mary can open it. You're bossy enough as it is."

"Diana!" said Mary. But she was rather pleased to be the one to take the envelope. After all, this was her mystery, more than it was the detective's. He wasn't personally involved. She was. It was her father who had been a member of the Société des Alchimistes, and who had done . . . what? Committed murder, certainly. But there must have been more. After all, that murder had not been connected to the society, as far as she knew. Who were its members?

What were its goals and aims? The envelope was addressed to John Seward, M.D., at the Purfleet Asylum. "It's to the director," she said. "Not to Dr. Balfour. This must have been one of the letters he was sorting for Dr. Seward." She opened the flap, breaking the seal with a pang of guilt. But didn't she have a right to know what was in the letter, what this mystery was all about? Surely if anyone had a right to open that letter, she did. She pulled out a sheet of paper and read the rather florid handwriting.

My dear friend John,

Thank you for sending me your so interesting paper, which I think is almost ready for presentation before the meeting of the Société in Budapest. There are a few points—I do not question your methodology, my friend, but your conclusions may be challenged by those who are more conservative than we are. Anticipate and be prepared for their criticism. I will send you some notes on your paper once I have completed my own manuscript, later this week. Please do you the same, and tell me what you think of mine. I would welcome your suggestions.

It is most important, at this juncture, for the Société to support our line of research. When I began working on the biological problem, as our colleague Moreau called it, our members did not approve of my goals and methods. But acceptance has been growing, and after the setbacks of the last few years, we can finally show results. Research is ever like this, friend John! If only our goals had not been discredited by our predecessor, if such a word can be used for him. You know of whom I speak. I confess to you, my friend, that I was concerned about my own experiment for some time. The change did not seem to be taking effect, and when it did, the alteration was so drastic that I thought I would lose her altogether. But in the last month, all has worked as I have wished, and I believe my results will be persuasive, at least to the majority of our members. I assume you will be traveling with Mr. Prendick? Poor man, I hope he may someday be ready to participate fully in our community again. I cannot tell you how I mourn the loss of Moreau. You and Prendick belong to a younger generation. You do not know what it was like for us old fogeys, as you may call us, resurrecting the Société from the decrepitude into which it had fallen and redirecting its energies to biology, to the material of life itself! I am proud of the organization we have built, but distressed to have lost some of our most important men. Alas, scientific exploration has a price! More than once, my friend, I have nearly lost my own life in the pursuit of truth.

I know we can count on the support of my friend Professor Arminius, of Budapest University. I look forward to introducing you to him at last. I am not so certain that our president will look upon our research benevolently! Alas that even our elected leader is prejudiced, conservative, thinking the old ways are best. But we are not living in the eighteenth century! This is the age of Herbert Spencer, of Francis Galton. Well, we shall have to be convincing, and your paper will be instrumental in that endeavor. I look forward to seeing you, and to introducing you also to some excellent Tokaj that Arminius brought me when he came to observe my methods. I hope your voyage goes well, and give my regards to Mr. Prendick, whom I also look forward to seeing.

Yours most truly,
Abraham Van Helsing

Mary put the letter down on her lap. She stared at Holmes and Watson. "What does it all mean?"

Watson shook his head but did not answer. Even Holmes was silent.

"Is anyone *not* a member of this society?" asked Diana. "We seem to be running into it wherever we go."

"Van Helsing and this Arminius he mentioned, Seward and his friend Prendick, Rappaccini, Moreau, and the president of the society, whoever that might be," said Mary. "We're up to seven, but there are certainly more. You can't have a scientific society, even a secret one, with only seven members. And if there's a conference . . ."

"It seems as though Moreau is dead," said Holmes. "But clearly the others are continuing the work of the society—amid some controversy, it seems. How that work is linked to the murders, if it is, I do not know. Van Helsing and Seward could scarcely have been murdering women in Whitechapel if they are in Amsterdam, as Balfour told us. And that would explain this unopened letter. Presumably it was sent before a situation arose that necessitated Seward's presence. Clearly it does not anticipate his trip to Amsterdam. Let me see it for a moment, if you please, Miss Jekyll."

Mary handed him the letter.

"Van Helsing writes, *The change did not seem to be taking effect, and when it did, the alteration was so drastic that I thought I would lose her altogether. But in the last month, all has worked as I have wished.* Perhaps it stopped working, and that's why Seward was summoned, likely by telegram."

"What stopped working?" asked Diana. "And who's she? Are they poisoning another girl?"

"Perhaps they have confederates in England," said Watson.

"Or perhaps they're not in Amsterdam at all, and the summons was a ruse. Perhaps they're the ones who are really killing women in Whitechapel," said Mary.

Diana frowned. "You're giving me a headache."

"One thing can't be denied," said Watson. "Wherever we turn, we run up against this society. What now, Holmes?"

"Well, at least that's obvious," said Diana. "We need Poison Breath to tell us what's going on. We need to break her out."

"Yes," said Holmes. "That does seem to be indicated. And as Watson has pointed out, we can scarcely show up at the lady's residence before dark. Miss Jekyll, could you oblige us with dinner, whatever your cook can provide? It would allow us to look through your father's papers more closely—if you will allow it."

"Yes, of course," said Mary. Whatever her cook could provide. As though she had a cook! And was there enough food in the house for two men? She imagined they would want a proper meal. Men did, didn't they? She wished that she could have spoken to Mrs. Poole before leaving for Purfleet. At least she had money now. She put her hand on her purse and almost patted it, in the comforting knowledge that it contained a whole pound in change. But would it do her any good? By the time they reached the house, the shops would be closed. Perhaps Mrs. Poole could send for something from a pub.

But there was to be no time for a reading of the letters, not that day. At Fenchurch Street, they found a hackney carriage, the kind popularly known as a growler for the noise of its wheels on the cobbled streets, to take them back to Park Terrace. As they jolted along the London thoroughfares, on which the lamps had already been lit, Mary wondered if she would be facing the wrath of Mrs. Poole, left with no information as to where they had gone or when they would be back, and expected to produce dinner as though by magic.

MRS. POOLE: Wrath! Well, I never. When have any of you ever faced my *wrath*?

JUSTINE: Yesterday.

BEATRICE: You remember, Mrs. Poole. When you realized we hadn't cleaned up in the parlor after our meeting with Prince Rupert.

MRS. POOLE: Well, I can't abide it when you girls leave a mess. It's just me and Alice looking after the lot of you, as you know. It's not as though we have any other servants in this house. Alice was up until all hours sweeping up the broken glass.

ALICE: I don't mind, Mrs. Poole.

MARY: We were trying to capture the masked men who had shot at the Prince. We would have caught them, too, if they hadn't jumped on the back steps of an omnibus. Why is it that one can never find a cab in London when one really needs it? And when we got back, we had to take care of Prince Rupert, who had fainted on the sofa. I'm sorry— we would have cleaned it up the next morning. It was just the glass cover for the wax flowers. I'm afraid the flowers are shot to bits, though. And I think there's a hole in one of Justine's paintings.

BEATRICE: I never liked those flowers anyway.
I would not have shot at them of course, but now
we can buy something new at Harrods. Something
modern, in the style they call *l'art nouveau.*

MARY: As soon as you start speaking French, I know
it's going to be expensive.

MRS. POOLE: In my day, young ladies had nothing
to do with masked men, or princes, or madcap
chases through the streets. I can't stop you from
having these adventures, but I insist on keeping a
decent house.

As the carriage drove up to 11 Park Terrace, Charlie leaped off
the steps, where he had been waiting.

"Mr. Holmes!" he said. "Old Carrot Top wants you right away.
There's been another murder."

"Another!" said Watson. "How is that possible? Renfield has
been under observation since he returned to Purfleet. Did he
somehow manage to escape?"

"I don't know about any Renfield," said Charlie. "But this afternoon another doxy was killed, same way as the last one. And her
brain was missing!"

"What!" said Holmes sharply. "Are you quite certain?"

"That's what Carrot Top told me. Inspector Lestrade, I mean.
I ain't seen her for myself. He found Tommy in front of Scotland
Yard and sent him to find me. He said to bring you as soon as I
could. I figured you'd be coming back here or to Baker Street.
Tommy's watching for you there."

"If her brain was taken—that's the first time any of these
crimes have been repeated," said Mary.

"So you noticed that as well?" said Holmes. "Watson, stay with Miss Jekyll and her sister. I'll be back as soon as I can. Driver, can you take me to Scotland Yard?"

"Aye, sir. Hop on back in," said the driver. And then Holmes was off again. They stood looking at the back of the carriage as it drove away from them down the street.

"Well," said Mary. It was all she could think of to say.

Suddenly, the door opened behind them. "*Where* have you been?" said Mrs. Poole.

Dinner consisted of Irish stew, since Mrs. Poole did not consider cold meats sufficient for a gentleman of Dr. Watson's reputation. Mary said it would take too long, but "I made it this morning," said Mrs. Poole. "I thought it would be cheap, and last several days for you girls. It'll just be a matter of warming it up, and I bought some rolls at Maudie's. Ladies may go hungry, but gentlemen have to eat, you know." She was rather intimidated by Watson, and bustled around making sure he was comfortable. She even whispered to Mary that they should open a bottle of Dr. Jekyll's port. They ate in the dining room, with its large mahogany table, which had not been used in—how many years? Mary could not remember. How strange it was to sit there now, with Watson and Diana.

> MRS. POOLE: Me, intimidated by Dr. Watson? Stuff and nonsense.

> JUSTINE: Is there really a hole in my painting? The one of the girl holding sunflowers? I was hoping to sell that one at the Grosvenor. . . .

The stew was a success, filling and hearty, with beef and potatoes and carrots. Watson thanked Mrs. Poole for the port, but would accept only a glass, and insisted that Mary have a glass as well. "You'll need it to keep your spirits up tonight," he said. "It will be cold, and dark, and our mission is dangerous."

"What about me?" said Diana. "I need my spirits kept up too, you know."

"Your spirits are already high enough," said Mary.

They ate as quickly as they could, punctuated by Diana's slurping and Mary's "For goodness' sake, stop that! It's a disgusting habit."

As they sat at the table over the remains of dinner and empty coffee cups, Watson said, "Are you ladies ready?"

"As ready as we'll ever be, I suppose," said Mary. "How ever am I going to tell Mrs. Poole what we're up to?"

"I find the direct way is always best," said Watson.

So when Mrs. Poole came back into the dining room to clear the table, Mary said, "Mrs. Poole, I'm afraid we're going out again tonight. Beatrice Rappaccini, the girl in the advertisement, is being held captive near Lincoln's Inn Fields, and we need to rescue her."

"Well, wrap up warmly," said Mrs. Poole. "I don't want either of you catching a cold."

"Either of us?" said Diana.

"Yes, either of you!" said Mrs. Poole. "With a cold, you'd be even more trouble than you are now, Miss Scamp!"

MARY: You didn't object at all, Mrs. Poole!

MRS. POOLE: There was someone needed rescuing. I've never objected when it's really important, have I?

They took a cab toward Lincoln's Inn Fields, asking the cabbie to let them out on High Holborn Street. From High Holborn, they turned into a smaller street—it was Searle, Mary remembered from that morning, although she could not have seen the sign at this hour. The streets were lit, and they walked along the pavement through pools of lamplight, but the park at the center of the square was a tangle of shadows cast by tree limbs. She held Watson's arm so they would look like a married couple, with Diana as their daughter. As they passed the house Beatrice had pointed out to Mary and Diana earlier that day, they noticed a light in one of the ground floor windows.

"I'm going to see who's there," said Diana.

Before Mary could object, Diana had scampered over the front railing and crept to the window, pulling herself up to look over the sill. In a moment, she was back. "Professor Petronius and a woman are sitting at a table, counting money. And there's a dog, a big black one, sleeping by the fire. Beatrice isn't there."

"Don't ever do that again!" said Mary. "You can't simply go off by yourself whenever you want to. We have to work together. We have to follow a plan."

"Well, what's your plan then?" said Diana, crossing her arms.

"She told us her room was in the back, and they locked her in at night. She's probably there now, locked in. We need to go around to the back."

They walked down Searle Street and, at the end of the block of houses, turned into an alley. On one side were the backs of the houses on Searle, on the other were the backs of the houses on the next street over. Here, there were no lamps. The only light came from the windows, mostly dark at this hour. One of the windows at the back of Professor Petronius's house was lit, but it was on the second floor.

"That may be her room," said Mary. "She may be looking for us tonight, and the light may be her signal."

"So now what?" asked Diana. "What's your plan *now*, sister?"

"I don't know," said Mary. "Let me think."

"We need to communicate with her," said Watson. "But I don't see any way of getting up there. If only we had a sweep's ladder! Could we throw up pebbles and see if she notices? Perhaps she'll come to the window."

"We don't know if that's her room," said Mary. "Or if she's alone in it. No, we need to get up there somehow."

"Oh, fiddlesticks for you and your plans!" said Diana.

Before Mary could stop her, she had run over to the wall of the house, silently as a cat, and crouched down in the shadows.

"What is she doing?" whispered Mary, urgently.

"I believe she's taking off her clothes," said Watson.

"What? Taking off—what?"

Sure enough, Diana was removing her hat, gloves, coat, boots, and stockings. Mary could see her in the dim light that came from the window, standing beside the wall in only her dress and bare feet. Then she clutched at the drainpipe that ran down the wall and began climbing, pulling herself up the pipe with her bare hands and feet, now and then supporting herself by putting her toes on the joints.

"She looks like a monkey!" said Mary. "I'm afraid she'll fall."

"A monkey would not," said Watson. "And judging by her agility, I don't think your sister will either." Mary could not see his expression in the darkness, but he sounded—amused.

Mary shivered. It was not the cold, for the night was warm, at least for a late spring night in London. No, it was the sight of Diana climbing up the drainpipe in that primitive way. Wasn't Diana her sister? And Hyde's daughter. What sorts of experiments had her father been conducting, to turn himself into Hyde? What had Hyde been? And what, pray tell, was his daughter? She remembered how shocked Beatrice had been to learn that Diana was Hyde's child. What had the girl inherited from her father, other than his unpleasant temperament?

When Diana reached the second floor, she let go of the pipe and crept along a narrow ledge to the window. Mary could see her silhouetted against the square of light. Then a face appeared. "That's Beatrice!" said Mary. The window was pulled up, and Diana crawled in. "What is she doing? I don't like this."

But in a few minutes, Diana reappeared, climbing out the window and letting herself back down the drainpipe. At the bottom, she gathered her discarded clothes.

"What did you think you were doing!" said Mary, when she rejoined them. Diana sat on the muddy stones, pulling on her stockings and shoes.

"You wouldn't have let me go up, but I knew I could," said Diana. "I used to climb out of my window at the Magdalen Society all the time. I went inside and picked her lock. When Professor Petronius and the landlady go to bed, she's going to try to get out. The dog is the landlady's—she takes it down with her and locks it in the kitchen when she's asleep. I told her we would be waiting in the park."

They walked back to Searle Street and then across to Lincoln's Inn Fields. There, they waited, sitting on one of the park benches, watching the light in the ground-floor window. Eventually, it went out, but there was still no Beatrice.

"How long do we have to wait?" asked Diana. "I'm bored."

"As long as it takes," said Mary. "She may not be able to get out tonight, in which case we'll have to come back. I hope she can find the front door key!"

"It can't be far from the door, in case of fire," said Watson. "I'm more concerned that Professor Petronius will find her searching for it and guard her even more closely in the future."

They waited for what seemed like hours—once, Mary looked at her wristwatch, but she could not see its face in the darkness. At last the front door opened and a cloaked figure emerged. It was

Beatrice. Although there was a hood drawn over her hair, Mary could see her face in the light of the nearby street lamp. She closed the door carefully behind her, then hurried down the steps and toward the park.

As she reached the darkness under the trees, she looked around frantically.

"Here!" said Mary, keeping her voice low. Beatrice was so close, only a few feet away from the bench.

Beatrice started. "Oh, I'm so glad to see you!" she said. "Let us go quickly. Professor Petronius was snoring when I left, and I believe that woman is asleep as well. But her room is near the kitchen, so I could not see or hear. I do not want either of them to realize I am missing!"

"Well, someone's awake," said Diana. "Look at the light." And Diana was right: when they looked back at the house, they could see that the fanlight, formerly dim, was now glowing. Someone had turned up the gas. Had Beatrice's absence been noticed? If not, it might be at any moment. And then they heard the dog bark.

"Run!" said Mary. "Follow the path on the right!" She turned and started running down the path that curved around the park, with the hedge on her right and tall trees to her left. It seemed safer than the long, straight path that led to the gazebo, and would take them to the corner near the Royal College of Surgeons. There, she remembered, was another street leading back—she was almost sure—to High Holborn. That was their escape. She turned back to make sure the others were following—Diana darted past her, and she could see Watson trying to help Beatrice, who waved him off, making certain even as she ran that he did not touch her. Mary turned to catch up with Diana. They ran through the shadows, their boots landing with dull thuds on the dirt path. Then, the Royal College of Surgeons loomed up on their left. To their right was the opening in the gate and the road Mary had noticed that morning. They were almost there, almost at the street that led to their escape, and still there was no pursuit.

Suddenly, they heard a sound that struck a chill into all their hearts.

DIANA: Not mine.

MARY: I don't believe that for a minute.

It was the dog, barking and growling in the open air. It had been let out, and was making straight for them across the grass, under the trees. They could see it as a vague black shape in the darkness, but mostly they could hear it, drawing closer.

"I hate to shoot a dog," said Watson. "But in this case, I have no choice."

"No!" said Beatrice. "A pistol shot will merely draw more attention to us. Fidelis knows me. Let me handle him."

"Madam, I think that would be unwise," said Watson. But Beatrice had already turned back. She was holding her hands out to the large black dog, who approached her warily, with barks, but refrained from attacking.

"Fidelis, sweet Fidelis," she said, coaxingly. "Come to me, sweetheart. Who gave you gingerbread yesterday?"

Evidently, Fidelis remembered the gingerbread. He stopped barking and drew nearer. Beatrice put her hand on his head, then leaned down and breathed on him, long and steadily over his entire face. The black dog sat, then lay down as though tired, and twitched for a moment. And then he was still.

Beatrice looked up at them, and even in the darkness Mary could see that her face was wet with tears. "I did not mean to . . . Oh, he has made me too poisonous! I meant only to render Fidelis unconscious for a while."

"Madam, that was a most impressive demonstration," said Watson.

"This isn't the time for compliments," said Mary. Could Watson not see how upset Beatrice was? And what did she mean—who had made her too poisonous? But this was no time to inquire. "To the right and up the street! We need to lose ourselves in the crowd."

They ran up the street, emerging on King's Way, then merged with the crowd as best they could, heading toward Piccadilly Circus. Although it was late—Mary checked her watch again and found that it was after midnight—the roads were still choked with carts and wagons. On the sidewalks, beggars asked for pence and fancily dressed women greeted potential customers. Which was all the better for them—there was less of a chance they would be seen in the London traffic.

At Piccadilly Circus, they caught a hackney carriage. "You must lower the windows," said Beatrice. "Cover your mouths with handkerchiefs, and do not breathe too deeply. Forgive me, I would change my nature if I could. I shall always be what I am—a danger to others. But my toxicity will lessen with time. Professor Petronius insisted that I ingest poison every day, to make certain I would kill his specimens as effectively and dramatically as possible. Tonight, I am sorry to say, it has ensured our escape. Under ordinary circumstances, I could not have killed Fidelis so quickly. Would that he had survived! He was a good creature, and did only as his master bade him."

"How terrible!" said Mary. She and Watson pulled down the windows, none too soon because she was beginning to feel light-headed. Luckily she had an extra handkerchief for Diana, who had of course forgotten hers. "Why did you stay with him if he treated you so badly?"

"I was told the college would find a way to make me—ordinary, not mortal to my kind. I hoped it was true, but came to realize that his sole motive was profit. The college was benefitting from his fees—there was no incentive to cure my condition."

Beatrice looked out the window, taking in the sights and sounds of London at night: the rows of gas lamps, the continual life of the city, cabs and carts and gentlemen's broughams moving through the streets even at this late hour. "It's magnificent!" she said. "I've seen so little of London since I've been here. Before arriving, I spent several weeks in Paris, hoping the French physicians, so famous for their art, could find a cure for me, but to no avail. I had already been to Milan and Vienna. So I came to the largest city in the world, hoping that here, if nowhere else, I could be cured. By the time I arrived, I had no money left, and Professor Petronius offered me a way to at least keep body and soul together. At first he wanted to put me in a freak show and tour through the countryside, but displaying me as a scientific oddity proved more lucrative. So here I am, still with no way to sustain myself, and no cure for my condition. Ah, sometimes I wish that I had died in Padua!"

"Don't say that," said Mary. "You're among friends now. We'll help you as best we can." But how could she help the Poisonous Girl? A perfume seemed to emanate from Beatrice, like the scent of an exotic flower. *That's the poison,* she thought. She put her head out the window to gulp mouthfuls of London air, with its miasma of coal dust, manure, and the general doings of six million inhabitants. Still, it was preferable to Beatrice's sweet toxicity. They were almost at Marylebone, she noticed with relief. Soon, they would be home. And then what?

The house was dark when Mary let them all in, but almost immediately Mrs. Poole came bustling up from the kitchen. "I've been waiting up, watching for you!" she said. "This must be the Italian lady. You're most welcome here, miss."

"Thank you," said Beatrice. "And I apologize for any trouble I

have caused, or am about to cause. It is most kind of you to welcome me into this beautiful home."

> MRS. POOLE: Now that's manners, that is. If you had
> been so polite, Miss Diana, you would have gotten
> a different reception.

"Oh, stuff it," said Diana. "The question is, where is she going
to sleep? I don't want her anywhere near me! I just about threw up
in the carriage."

"I must sleep far away from any of you," said Beatrice. "What is
the most distant part of the house?"

"My father's laboratory," said Mary. "It's across the courtyard.
Mrs. Poole, can you make up a bed for Beatrice in there, for the
night?"

"She could sleep on the sofa in his office," said Mrs. Poole. "Dr.
Jekyll often slept there when conducting his experiments. I'll
bring up a pillow and some blankets. I finished cleaning and airing
it out today, so at least it won't be dusty for you, miss."

Before bidding them good night, Watson said to Mary, "You
will be careful, won't you? Miss Rappaccini is a lovely woman—I
have seldom seen anyone more beautiful—but I do not want her
to make you and your sister ill. If the responsibility becomes too
much, Holmes and I will find other accommodations for her."

"That's very kind of you," said Mary. "Let us see how the night
goes. I'll know better in the morning what is to be done."

After making sure the other girls were both taken care of, and
before going to bed herself, Mary remembered to give Mrs. Poole
half the money she had taken out of the bank that morning. Half a
pound would keep them in groceries for a while.

But when she was lying in bed, she could not sleep. Diana
was snoring in the nursery, and no doubt Beatrice was bedded

down in her father's office, on the other side of the courtyard. She
stared into the darkness, feeling a sickness that had nothing to do
with Beatrice's poison. What was this secret society that seemed
to have its members everywhere? What experiments were those
members conducting? If she included the most recent murder, five
girls had been killed and parts of their bodies removed. Why? She
had a sense of something wrong in the order of things, some evil.
She remembered having felt it once before—yes, when she was
a child. That night, when she had seen the face of Edward Hyde.

When she finally fell asleep, she had dreams she did not wish
to remember the next morning—of women with their heads or
arms or legs missing, stumbling or dragging themselves through
the streets of London, calling if they had mouths, gesturing if
they had hands. But she could not hear what they were calling, or
understand what, if anything, they were trying to tell her.

CHAPTER X

Beatrice's Story

The next morning they gathered for breakfast in the morning room, which had a table just large enough to seat four. It was the room where Mary's mother had done accounts, before she had become too ill to manage the household. Afterward, Mary had taken over. Each morning, she would sit at her mother's desk, going over the books, making sure the bills were paid, her mother taken care of. It was strange to sit in that room now, across the table from Diana. Beatrice perched on a chair by the window, which was open at the bottom. Through the window, Mary could see the bleak courtyard.

Diana could not keep from yawning. She would have to be taught to put her hand in front of her mouth. Beatrice looked pale, but seemed composed. She said she had spent a perfectly comfortable night on the sofa in the office.

Breakfast was buttered toast, poached eggs, and good, strong tea—for Mary and Diana. "I went marketing this morning with the money you gave me," Mrs. Poole had told Mary. "Fresh from the country, those eggs are! Look at the yolks. I paid Mr. Byles, so he can't give me any more of his nasty looks. There will be cakes for tea if that devil of an oven cooperates. I was at a loss for what to give Miss Rappaccini, though I asked her last night what she would like for breakfast. 'Water in which organic matter has been steeped, please,' she tells me, as nice as you please. 'And what might that be, miss?' I asked her. Well, I've done my best, but it's a queer diet, and no mistake."

Beatrice warmed her hands around a steaming mug. It was all she would take for breakfast. "I have no need of food, you see. Only the nutrients themselves, and sunlight. It will take several days for the strong poisons to leave my system. The dandelion greens I picked in the courtyard will help with the detoxification process. Until then, we will need to be particularly careful. Do not touch me, and I will try to keep away from you as much as I can. Once the strong poisons are out, I will be toxic, but not to such a degree. My breath will be able to kill only the smallest living beings: insects, birds, mice, and voles. After spending some time in a closed room with me, you will begin to feel faint, but I will not be lethal unless we are in close contact. Still, my touch will burn, as though you had touched a strong alkaloid."

"You seem to know a great deal about yourself," said Mary.

"It is through sad experience," said Beatrice. "If only I knew how to cure myself! Although my father taught me many things, he could not teach me that. He did not know himself. I asked him . . . at one time I even begged him to cure me. But he told me that as far as he knew, the condition was irreversible. He said I should be proud of my nature, which made me unique among womankind."

"Why don't you tell us about it?" asked Mary.

> CATHERINE: Yes, you do need to write the section about yourself. You all promised that you would write your own stories.

> BEATRICE: But my English is not so good. You know the whole story, Cat. Why can you not write it?

You are the writer among us. You would make it,
you know, lively. Truly, I cannot write it.

CATHERINE: Well, you have to. I have a deadline
for *Astarte and the Idol of Gold*, and I won't get the
advance until I turn it in. At least write the first
draft. Your English is perfectly fine, and anyway
I'll make everything sound right in revision. Come
on, I'll ask Mrs. Poole to make you some of that
disgusting weed tea you like so much.

BEATRICE: It's quite good, you know. Very refreshing.

DIANA: I've tried it. I had to spit it out. It tasted like
warm piss.

CATHERINE: As though you would know! Come on,
Beatrice. Here's the pen. Sit down, like a good
poisonous plant, and start writing. I'll fix it all later.

"I never knew my mother," said Beatrice. "She was the daughter of a poor man, a farmer in the hills around Padua, and much
younger than my father. I believe he married her principally
because of her youth and beauty—his goal was to have a daughter,
to have me. A son would have been less useful to him. He would
have raised a son as his apprentice, to continue his scientific studies.
But a daughter could be both an apprentice and a subject for his
experiments.

"My father was a physician, the greatest in Padua, perhaps in
Italy. Patients would come from all over the country to be healed
by the famous Dr. Rappaccini.

"On her father's farm, my mother had been used to tending a

garden. She tended my father's garden, and I have often wondered if she was weakened by constant contact with his pharmacopeia, the poisonous plants he grew and from which he made his medicines. For as he often told me, poison is in the dose, and a poison in the human body can be cured only by a poison from the external world. Digitalis, the active ingredient of the common foxglove, kills a healthy man, but cures one who is sick in his heart. As she tended his poisonous plants, I grew in her belly, absorbing their poisons. I believe they affected me even in the womb. While they weakened her, I was so imbued by their essence that they made me strong and healthy. On the day I was born, she died—giving birth to me. Already weakened, she could not bear the rigors of childbirth. She was a farmer's daughter, and I—was a monster. I hold myself responsible for her death."

"You must not think that way," said Mary.

"Why?" asked Diana. "She's probably right, you know. I'm not saying it's her fault, but her mother died giving birth to her. Facts is facts."

"My father did not hire a wet-nurse," continued Beatrice. "I suckled at certain plants that nourished me as a nurse would have. As a child, I thought my father and I were the only beings in the world, and our garden walls were the limits of that world. There was a woman who lived in the house next to ours, a Signora Lisabetta. One of her windows overlooked our garden, and I sometimes saw her peering over our wall, but having seen her only from the torso up, I did not regard her as a person, and assumed she was an angel who sometimes looked down on me. For years, I played happily with my sisters, the flowers, and was sad that I could not play with the butterflies, crickets, or worms. But they died when I came too close.

"Eventually, I learned the world was much larger than I had realized, that there were people in it like me, yet not like me. My father did not keep my nature a secret. He explained to me that I was poisonous to others of my kind. He told me with no hesitation or shame—nay, he gloried in it! I was the perfect woman, he told me—more beautiful and stronger than ordinary women. I would entice men, but they could never touch me. I did not question his actions or motives—he was my father, and I believed he loved me. Indeed, I helped him with his experiments, and he told me all about the work of the Société des Alchimistes. He hoped that one day I would become a member. Both as a scientist, and as living evidence of his theories of transmutation."

"Transmutation!" said Mary, leaning forward. "That's what your father's letter mentioned. Experiments in transmutation. Wait just a minute!" She had left the portfolio in her mother's desk. It occurred to her for the first time that she should have locked the desk drawer. She would have to find the key. Now she stood and went over to the desk, pulled the portfolio out of the drawer, put it on the table, and took out all the documents. There was the letter from Italy. She read it to Beatrice. "'Transmutation, not natural selection, is the agent of evolution. . . . I am pleased to report that my Beatrice is flourishing. . . . Our colleague Moreau was right to conjecture that the female brain would be more malleable and responsive to our experiments.' What are these experiments in transmutation? What does it all mean? Do you know?"

Beatrice took the letter from Mary. For a long moment, she could only look at it, her hand trembling and her eyes filling with tears. Clearly, she was thinking about her father. At last, she looked up. "I do, alas," she said, wiping her eyes with one hand. "You know, of course, of the medieval alchemists?"

"No," said Diana.

"Yes, of course," said Mary. "They tried to turn lead into gold."

"That was the medieval idea of transmutation," said Beatrice. "One form of matter turned into another. In the Middle Ages, alchemists were considered magicians and burned at the stake. But truly, they were scientists. What occupied them more than anything else was the search for eternal life—the transmutation of the dead into the living. And so they began to experiment on biological matter. A century ago, a university student named Victor Frankenstein proved that it could be done, that dead matter could once again be brought to life. He paid a terrible price for the success of his experiments. But my father believed his aims could be achieved by other means. Frankenstein was his inspiration, and the inspiration for those who, like him, wished to transmute not base metals, but human beings.

"My father sent papers about me to the Société. He often complained about what he called the traditionalists, the anti-evolutionists who believed that man was divinely created, that transmutation of the human was against God's plan. 'Evolution is the greatest discovery of our age,' he would tell me. 'We evolved from the apes. What may we yet evolve into? The forces of natural selection are no longer acting on man. So it has become our duty to direct evolution, to create the higher forms that man will become. But do they see that? No, they do not, the *grandi idioti!*' He would wave his hands, shouting, '*idioti, idioti!*' Thus would he speak of the traditionalists in the Société. But he and his colleagues were working on advancing evolution through transmutation. They believed they were assisting the species, unasked and unappreciated, to rise higher. . . ."

"And so they were trying to transform girls into—what?" asked Mary. "What were they doing, and why would it require murder? These girls who've been killed in Whitechapel. They had limbs missing. Why would transmutation require that?"

Beatrice looked at her with astonishment. "Missing limbs? From girls murdered in Whitechapel? But that does not make sense. There is only one reason to take limbs—but the experiment

is ancient, a hundred years old! It is Frankenstein's original experiment. Why would anyone want to re-create his experiment
in this day and age? The experiments of my father and his colleagues were subtle and theoretically sophisticated. They sought
to advance humanity in particular directions. My father wished to
strengthen humanity through the incorporation of plant essences.
Dr. Moreau and your father were exploring what separates the
human and animal, in an attempt to raise the human even higher,
above our animal natures. They were attempting to refine and
purify humanity. Their goals were noble, and when I was young,
I thought they were the wisest men in the world, that they would
lead us to a new golden age. Since then, I have come to question
their methods. But this matter of the missing limbs—I cannot
understand it."

She drank the rest of her noxious tea and put the empty mug
on the windowsill. Diana shoved the last of her toast and poached
egg into her mouth and chewed loudly.

"Well, the girls are dead," said Mary. "And their limbs are
missing: legs, arms, head. And two sets of brains. That's the mystery we've been trying to solve. You said there's only one reason
to take limbs from these girls, but you didn't say what it is. What
was Frankenstein's original experiment?"

"To take parts of the dead and create a living being," said
Beatrice. "To sew those limbs together into a woman and bring
her to life. That is what Frankenstein did—not with a woman, but
with a man, a living corpse who became a monster."

"Awesome!" said Diana, her mouth open, with half-chewed
food in it.

"But that's horrible!" said Mary. "I can't imagine what would
prompt someone to do such a thing."

"The love of science for its own sake," said Beatrice. "But also
for the promise it holds of raising us above our limited human

selves. Surely you see the beauty of such an ambition, even if you cannot approve of how it has been pursued. And of course the murder of five women is inexcusable, however noble the aim. But Frankenstein's experiment was crude, inelegant. My father's methods—"

"Left you poisonous," said Mary.

Beatrice simply looked down at her hands, clasped on her lap.

Mary did not know what to do. Had she insulted Beatrice? She had not meant to, but the experiments—they were wrong. Surely they must all agree that the experiments were wrong? Molly Keane, lying on the pavement in her own blood . . .

Diana belched and wiped her mouth with the back of her hand.

Mary did not reprimand her. She did not know what to say.

"What are those other letters?" asked Beatrice. "Are they also from my father?"

"Oh, those," said Mary. "No, and they're in Latin, so I have no idea what they're about. But they have red seals on them, with S.A."

"Bet Poison Breath knows Latin," said Diana.

"Of course," said Beatrice. "It is the language of science. And the seals were used by members of the Société, including my father, when transacting official business. They signaled that the letters were to be opened at once, and in secret. All members of the society had such seals, often on pendants or rings. I will approach and examine those letters, if you will allow."

"Of course," said Mary. She made a point of not moving back as Beatrice walked to the table, although Diana retreated to the other side of the room.

Beatrice drew the letters toward her across the table. "*Ex societate expelleris.* . . . These are from the president of the society to your father, warning him that if he continues his experiments, he will be expelled. This letter is the first warning. The second one—you see it is dated six months later—tells him that the warning is final. It is, as you say, an ultimatum. My father had spoken of Dr. Jekyll's experiments as dangerous. . . ."

"What were they, do you know?" asked Mary. "I have a hypothesis . . ."

"That I do not know, not specifically," said Beatrice. "My father did not speak of it with me, only to say that Dr. Jekyll was trying to defeat our animal nature, raise man to new spiritual heights—and that no scientist should experiment on himself."

Mary was disappointed. She had hoped Beatrice would know . . . something. Her father had attempted to defeat his animal nature and had instead become Hyde, the animal. How? Why? She sighed, ate the remainder of her toast, and wiped her mouth with a napkin. Perhaps she would never know. Her father had taken his secrets with him to the grave—all but these fragments.

"Are we done?" said Diana. "Because I'm bored."

They heard the front doorbell ring, and a moment later, Mrs. Poole came in. "It's Mr. Holmes and Dr. Watson," she said. "They would like a moment of your time. They say—let me see if I've got this right—Renfield has escaped?"

CATHERINE: You haven't said anything about Giovanni.

BEATRICE: I don't want to talk about it.

MARY: But Beatrice, you've left out an important part. I know you don't want to remember what happened, but it's not as though you killed him. You can't take responsibility for what's not your fault.

BEATRICE: But it is my fault. When I let him into my father's garden, when I walked with him among the poisonous flowers, I was infusing him with the poison—my poison. I did not mean to harm him. I thought if he could become like me, we could be together, and I would not be so alone. And then, he died. . . .

CATHERINE: But not just like that. Here, let me tell the story.

One day, as I was walking through the garden, I looked up, and there, looking down from Signora Lisabetta's window, was the handsomest man I had ever seen. He was a cousin of hers, who had come to Padua to study medicine. Of course, the only other man I had seen was my father, but I have seen men since, and Giovanni was indeed handsome, with crisp, curling brown hair, brown eyes that seemed to contain his soul, and cheeks tanned by the sun of southern Italy.

BEATRICE: Oh, Catherine, please stop! It's enough to say that he was handsome, and I loved him. All right, I shall tell the story, if only to keep you from making it sound like one of those romantic serials sold in train stations.

CATHERINE: There's nothing wrong with train stations. If it weren't for train stations, *The Mysteries of Astarte* wouldn't have sold nearly as well.

BEATRICE: That is not at all the point.

Day after day, he would come to visit me in my father's garden. Day after day, he walked in a poisonous miasma, not knowing. I knew—each day I kept him longer, talking to him, never touching him, waiting for him to become poisonous, as I was. My father knew of his visits—how could he not? And yet, he said nothing. Perhaps he thought Giovanni would form a useful addition to our family. After all, he was a medical student at the University of Padua. He could become another apprentice to the great Dr. Rappaccini.

One day, Giovanni noticed that a spider had woven a web in his window—he leaned closer to look, and the spider died from his breath. He realized, then, what had happened—he was becoming poisonous! He went to see my father's rival in Padua, the physician Pietro Baglioni, who was a professor at the medical school. My father and Baglioni had been medical students together, and he had once been a member of the Société des Alchimistes himself. But he had quarreled with my father and left the society. He knew about me, about my poisonous nature. He concocted what he believed to be an antidote and gave it to Giovanni, telling him that if we drank it, we would be cured.

Giovanni brought me the antidote and told me that it would cure us both. We stood in the garden together, not touching. Even then, he did not know I had intended to make him poisonous—he thought it was an accident, that I had not been aware of my own nature. How trusting he was! He loved me, and wanted us both to be normal. He did not want to be a monster—that was the word he used. He did not want to be separated from humanity. That day, I realized what I was—a monster among men.

MARY: You're not a monster, Beatrice. I wish you would stop using that word.

JUSTINE: Why, if it's technically accurate? We are all monsters in our own way. Even you, Mary.

I told him that I did not trust Baglioni, as a man or a scientist. I told him we should not drink. But he pleaded with me. I took the glass vial containing the antidote. It was green, the color of emeralds. And then I heard, "No! No, my daughter! Do you not know that Baglioni is my enemy, that he would do anything to destroy my experiments?"

"Father, can't you see what you've done to me?" I said. "I don't want to be deadly to my kind."

"Here, let me show you that it's perfectly safe," said Giovanni. "I will drink first."

He took the vial from my hand and drank the emerald liquid. He smiled down at me reassuringly, but then his face contorted with pain and he fell to the ground, writhing, clutching his abdomen. I fell to my knees beside him. I, who had made my father's medicines, did not know what to do, what to give him. I took him in my arms and pleaded with him not to die. But in a moment it was over. Giovanni lay in my arms, dead.

I took up the vial he had let fall and drank the remaining antidote, intending to die myself. But nothing happened. The poison in my system was so strong that it had no effect. That night I thought about killing myself, with a knife perhaps. Did I not deserve death? I had killed the man I loved, as surely as though I had driven a knife through his heart.

But I lacked the courage. Instead, the next day I told my father that he must reverse the process. I did not wish to be poisonous any longer, not after killing the man I loved. I wished to be an ordinary woman. That was when he told me the process was irreversible. So I left my father's house and went to the university. I found Professor Baglioni and told him that if he did not find a cure for my condition, I would tell all Padua he had murdered Giovanni. He tried, again and again, to find an antidote. Not for my benefit, or out of a sense of responsibility for Giovanni's death. No, I believe he was motivated by malice toward my father. Nevertheless, I stayed, living in his house, although he kept well away from me—hoping for a cure, or death. There was no one else who knew of my condition, and my father had made it clear that he could not help me, that he wished me to remain as I was—his greatest creation. So I became Baglioni's collaborator, working with my enemy, the man who had caused my lover's death, creating potion after potion in his laboratory. But none of them made me less poisonous.

One day, Baglioni came into the laboratory, where I was brewing the latest potion. "Your father is dead," he told me. He had been found in his garden, among the poisonous plants. Signora Lisabetta had seen him and alerted the authorities. I had left him without a word, and in the weeks I had been staying with Professor Baglioni, he had never come to see me. Always, I had been the one to tend his garden. The plants could not harm me, but he was too frail and had succumbed to their poison. Because of his reputation, none dared enter the garden. I was the one who entered it once again and buried him there. As I left my father's house for the last time, Signora Lisabetta leaned out of her window and cursed me. It was only what I deserved.

JUSTINE: Beatrice, that is certainly not true.

DIANA: Why did you even bother going back? I would have left him to rot.

So you see, I killed my mother and Giovanni. Perhaps I killed my father as well, who knows. Giovanni was right to use the word monster.

MARY: That's ridiculous. It's not your fault that your mother or Giovanni died, and your father is certainly responsible for his own death. I agree with Justine. Honestly, even Diana has a point, for once.

CATHERINE: Has everyone forgotten that I'm trying to tell a story? We've left Holmes and Watson on the threshold.

MARY: Cat, you're the one who insisted we tell our own parts of it. And now you're upset that we're interrupting the plot. This isn't one of your thrillers. We're trying to recount how we all came together, describe who we are. That's not just the story of how we solved the Whitechapel Murders. It's the story of *us*.

DIANA: I don't think you're supposed to say that we solved the murders.

MARY: Well, of course we solved them, eventually. If we hadn't, we wouldn't be writing about them, would we? But how did we solve them and what happened to us along the way? That's the real story.

"Renfield escaped!" said Mary. "Show them in at once, Mrs. Poole."

Both of the men bowed upon entering, and Holmes cast his keen, hawk-like glance at Beatrice.

"I'm pleased to make your acquaintance, Miss Rappaccini," he said. "I often feel like a biological curiosity myself, so you and I have something in common." Mary felt a pang of jealousy. Did

Beatrice have to be quite so beautiful? For a moment, she was glad Beatrice was incapable of touching anyone, that she burned on contact.

> MARY: Is it necessary to include every detail of what we were thinking? And keen, hawk-like glance! Seriously, Cat.

> CATHERINE: It's the story of *us*, remember?

"I think it's time for a confabulation," said Holmes. "We have information you don't, and I suspect Miss Rappaccini has given you information we are lacking. Shall we all consult together?"

"Yes, of course," said Mary. "We were just finishing breakfast. Let's go into the parlor. Mrs. Poole, could you bring us another pot of tea?"

She put the documents back in the portfolio and carried it with her. It was time to show Mr. Holmes what she had found. Once they were sitting in the larger room, with Holmes and Watson in the two armchairs, and Beatrice on one of the deep window seats, Holmes said, "Our news, in brief, is as follows. We are now up to five bodies: Sally Hayward, Anna Pettingill, Pauline Delacroix, Molly Keane, and a Susanna Moore, who was in the same line of business as the others. The last two bodies both had their brains removed, we don't know why. Although curiously, like Molly Keane, Susanna Moore had also been a governess. All the victims were murdered in Whitechapel. We know that despite his confession, Renfield could not have committed the last murder. The body of Susanna Moore was found just after we left for Purfleet with Lestrade. She had been killed the night before, while Renfield was in his room at Purfleet Asylum, watched by an attendant. So who killed her? The next day, we saw Lestrade lock Renfield into the police wagon. He was in handcuffs and guarded by Sergeant Evans. By the time the wagon arrived at Newgate, the door was unlocked, Evans was unconscious, and Renfield was nowhere to be found. Did he kill the other women, but not this one? Is that why the brain was taken again? Or were all the murders committed by someone, or some persons, else? As you know, I've always inclined to the latter theory. And who helped Renfield escape? He could not have done it himself—he did not have the means, or even the courage."

"By someone else," said Beatrice. "There is a method behind this seeming madness, Mr. Holmes. The murderer is not a madman. What I do not understand, however, is why these murders are being committed now. It does not make sense."

"Beatrice has been telling us about the Société des Alchimistes," said Mary. "Its members were interested in the evolutionary theories of Mr. Darwin, although they seem to have gone considerably beyond him. They wanted to advance evolution, to create more-perfect men—well, women, really. But she said this putting limbs together was an old experiment, a crude one. . . ."

"Yes, it was first performed by a student named Victor Frankenstein, who was inducted into the society by his chemistry professor. Frankenstein sought to create a man out of corpses and bring that man to life. He succeeded in his experiment. But that was a hundred years ago. I do not understand why anyone would want to reproduce his experiment now."

"Frankenstein!" said Watson. "I remember that name. Was there not an account—written by the wife of the poet Shelley, I believe? *Frankenstein: A Biography of the Modern Prometheus,* or some such. I remember reading it in my university days. But Miss Rappaccini, that was a popular novel, not a scientific treatise. It gave me a proper fright, but as a medical student, I considered it the worst kind of bunk."

"No," said Beatrice. "It is no more bunk than I am. The public may have considered it fiction, but the members of the Société knew that Frankenstein had existed, and he had created a monster. At least, so my father told me."

"And if I remember correctly, that monster destroyed him," said Watson. "I had nightmares afterward for a week. I kept thinking the corpse from my anatomy class would rise up off the dissecting table and come after me!"

"Ah, I see I shall have to do some reading," said Holmes. "Popular thrillers have never been in my line. But it seems as though we are back at this mysterious society. You were right after all, Miss Jekyll, in that train of inferences you made."

Mary tried not to smile, but she could feel herself blushing.

DIANA: You can't feel yourself blushing. That's lady novelist talk.

"I think you'd better tell us as much about this society as you know," Holmes continued, then waited, looking at each of them in turn.

Sometimes interrupting each other, Mary and Beatrice recounted what they had learned about the Société des Alchimistes. Mary, after some hesitation, pulled the letters from the portfolio and handed them to Holmes. They did not cast her father in a positive light, but if they could help elucidate this mystery, it was her duty to show them.

"This information suggests two lines of inquiry," said Holmes, after examining the letters. "We've spoken to Molly Keane's and Susanna Moore's associates. We must do the same for the other women, who were murdered before I took on this case. Why were they chosen, and why were those particular limbs taken? There's a pattern here, particularly in those two brains, belonging to the two governesses. In my experience, they are usually intelligent, underappreciated women, doomed to lives of inconsequence. Why would they, in particular, have attracted our killer and his accomplice? Today, Watson and I will go to Whitechapel and see what we can find out. But first, I will send a telegram to Dr. Balfour asking for an appointment. I want to take another look at that asylum. I suggest you ladies spend the day recovering from last night's exploits."

"And Renfield? What about him?" asked Mary.

"I shall leave Renfield to Lestrade. I'm convinced he was induced to make that confession, but who induced him? And who helped him escape? That's the man I wish to pursue, not the poor lunatic. He must have known Renfield, been familiar with his habits. I hope Watson and I will learn something at the asylum that enables us to identify the true culprit."

Mary nodded. She felt disappointed to be left out of things. Was this the end of her involvement with the investigation? She hoped not. But she did have Diana and Beatrice to take care of.

After Mrs. Poole had let Holmes and Watson out, Mary watched them walk down Park Terrace until they were out of sight. Then, she returned to the parlor. There would be breakfast dishes to clear, accounts to settle. A household to run.

Beatrice rose from the window seat and said, "I did not want to say this in front of the gentlemen, but there is a third line of investigation, in addition to the two Mr. Holmes laid out. When they arrived, I was about to tell you that I too have a letter to share. I received it a month ago, or rather, I found it in Professor Petronius's desk. He had no intention of delivering it to me, I'm sure."

Out of her bodice, she drew a letter, much creased. She unfolded it and read the following:

"My dear Miss Rappaccini,
    You may recognize my name, as I immediately recognized yours. By chance, I saw a copy of your

advertisement in the *Gazette*, and would like to make your acquaintance in person.

I am currently with Lorenzo's Circus of Marvels and Delights. We are touring throughout the countryside, but will be in London, performing in Battersea Park on the South Bank, from the beginning of May to the end of June. How curious that we should be in the same line of business! Or perhaps not so curious, after all. I do not know your circumstances, so will wait to hear from you. But I very much look forward to meeting.

Yours sincerely,
Catherine Moreau"

"Well, that's a long way of saying nothing," said Diana. "Who is Catherine Moreau, and why does she need investigating?"

"I think she did not want to say anything important in this letter," said Beatrice. "She thought it might be read, as of course it was. But don't you see? Her name is Moreau. She must be related to Dr. Moreau, my father's friend and a member of the Société until his unfortunate death. Perhaps she is his daughter. She clearly recognized my name and wants to meet."

"Well, then we will go to the South Bank," said Mary. Once again, the day had a purpose, an adventure in it. She felt a sense of excitement and relief. How ordinary her life had been, only a week ago! It certainly wasn't ordinary now.

CHAPTER XI

The Marvelous Circus

The first consideration was how they were to dress. Mary had already given Diana some of her old clothes—thank goodness she had never given them away, although a few of the plainest had gone to the scullery maid, Alice. Beatrice was about her size and could wear one of her walking suits; certainly, she could not go out in the theatrical dress she had been wearing when she ran away from Professor Petronius. In her mother's wardrobe, Mary found a veiled hat that her mother had worn before her illness. Veils were no longer in fashion among younger women, but older women sometimes still wore them, and behind the veil, no one would be able to tell Beatrice's age. If Professor Petronius was looking for them, he might recognize Mary or Diana, but at least Beatrice's face would be hidden.

With a pang of guilt, she took off her black dress. Her mother so recently dead, and here she was out of mourning! But a woman in mourning would stand out in the pleasure grounds of the South Bank. Passers-by would stare and wonder what she was doing. She worried that Mrs. Poole would disapprove, but when Mrs. Poole saw her in an ordinary walking suit, the housekeeper said, "Very wise of you, miss." Mary breathed a sigh of relief. At least she had Mrs. Poole's approval.

MRS. POOLE: As though she needed it! Miss Mary is a
lady, and whatever she chooses to do is right.

MARY: I wish you would say that when we've
     accidentally smashed up something!

DIANA: Like the parlor, last week.

They took three omnibuses to get to the Thames embankment. They could have taken two, but as they were leaving the
house, Mary thought she saw—what? Perhaps nothing. Leaning
against one of the houses in the row was a beggar, hunched over
in a peculiar way. But then beggars often were hunched over,
weren't they? The man was probably a drunkard. There was nothing unusual about his appearance—beggars appeared even here,
in the respectable streets around Regent's Park. But there was
something furtive about him, in the way he looked at her and then
immediately looked away again. Beggars usually—begged, didn't
they? Whereas he simply sat there, leaning against the wall, with
his cap on the pavement in front of him. So she changed omnibuses
twice in case they were being followed, although she wondered if
she was being silly. Who would want to follow them, and why?
Diana complained, but Beatrice nodded when Mary described the
beggar she had seen and agreed that it was best to be cautious.

It was a long and tiring journey, riding on top of the omnibus
when they could, or making sure Beatrice was sitting next to a
window. By the end of the trip, she was heartily sick of Diana's
comments about how well she knew London and all the places
she had been. But at last they alighted near the embankment and
saw the Thames meandering seaward, with boats chugging up or
floating down its muddy waters. Mary was very glad to see it.

They walked across the Chelsea Bridge and to the fields of
Battersea Park. They did not need to ask directions to the circus:
it was plain as plain could be—a circular red-and-white-striped
tent clearly visible against the green fields, surrounded by smaller

tents and wagons with LORENZO'S CIRCUS OF MARVELS AND DELIGHTS painted on them in garish colors.

As they drew nearer, they heard a man at the entrance to the circus tent call out, "Step right up, ladies and gentlemen, girls and boys! This way for Lorenzo's Circus of Marvels and Delights! One penny admission, and a ha'penny for the little ones! Admission to the sideshow free with your ticket! Come see Atlas the Strongman lift two Englishmen on his shoulders! Come see the Cat Woman, brought from the jungles of South America! Half woman and half ferocious beast, but for a penny she will allow you to scratch behind her ears! Come see Sasha, the famous Dog Boy of the Russian Steppes, and the Two-Headed Calf of Devonshire, and the Real Mermaid! Come see the Zulu Prince do his bloodthirsty native dances, and the Giantess, taller than any man! If any man is taller, your money back, sir! Next circus performance in an hour, ladies and gentlemen, girls and boys! Buy your tickets, a penny and ha'penny!"

"What do we do now?" asked Mary. "Catherine Moreau's letter said she would be here, but it never told us how to recognize her."

"Buy tickets, of course," said Diana. "She said she was with the circus, so let's see the circus. Anyway, I want to see Sasha the Dog Boy and the Real Mermaid."

"Yes," said Beatrice. "I think that would be best, would it not? Although I will stand at the entrance. Once the performance begins, there will be many people—I do not wish to be around so many, particularly in my current state. We do not know how to recognize her, but perhaps she will know how to recognize us."

Mary went to the ticket booth, next to the circus entrance, and bought them tickets: two adults and one child. Diana could still count as a child, couldn't she? She was small enough to pass for one, and it would save them money. "Now what?" she asked, when she had given Beatrice and Diana their tickets. "We still have

an hour until the next performance." But Diana was already heading toward the sideshow.

"Beatrice," she said, "how long would it take you to poison that
girl?"

"You would poison your own sister?" asked Beatrice, sounding shocked. Mary could imagine Beatrice's expression behind her
veil. Was it because she was Italian, or because she was poisonous,
that she did not understand sarcasm?

"No, I suppose not," she said with a sigh. "Come on, we'd
better follow her. I don't want her getting lost." It was noon, and
between the tents, circus-goers were sitting on the grass, eating
lunches they had brought or purchased at the various food carts.
Mary realized she had completely forgotten to bring a lunch of any
sort. She was not hungry, but Diana would be, soon. Her appetite
was like clockwork—you could tell time by it.

They showed their tickets at the entrance to a smaller, rectangular tent, also striped red and white, that housed the sideshow.
Inside, the tent was partitioned into sections lit by openings in the
cloth ceiling. At this hour, it was almost empty. They passed from
section to section, each labeled with the name of the performer
inside. The first contained Atlas, the Strongman. They watched as
he raised a series of dumbbells, winking at them, and then offered
to carry them on his shoulders. Diana almost stepped forward,
but Mary grabbed hold of her collar. "Two beautiful ladies, I could
lift you easily!" he said to Mary and Beatrice, while Diana silently
struggled. Mary shook her head and kept a firm grip on the fabric.
"No? Well, how about the gentlemen?" Two university students
wearing the scarves of their colleges volunteered, and Atlas lifted
them onto his shoulders. The audience, such as it was, clapped
politely.

Next was Sasha the Dog Boy, who seemed rather glum but
barked and howled convincingly. "He doesn't even look like a

dog," said Diana. "He's just hairy, that's all. I mean, he's wearing a Norfolk suit. Dogs don't wear Norfolk suits, do they?"

Better than both Atlas and Sasha was Astarte, the Cat Woman from the South American jungles. She looked like a cat, with cat ears set high on her head and yellow cat eyes. She was covered with a thick pelt of yellowish-brown fur, except on her face, and had a long tail that whipped around as she walked. She snarled convincingly and showed her sharp claws. But when any of the audience members paid an extra halfpenny, she would allow them to scratch her under the chin and stroke the fur on her back and arms. Then she would purr loudly.

"Oh, she's a sight, isn't she?" said Diana. "Do you think her mother was a woman and her father was a cat? Do give me a ha'penny, Mary. I want to go touch her." One of the students had paid the halfpenny and was approaching her tentatively, clearly nervous about getting too close to those claws.

"That is not possible," said Beatrice. "The laws of heredity do not allow such matings."

The Cat Woman turned toward her. "You," she said, in a low voice that sounded like a growl. "Yes, you, in the dark veil. You will come scratch me, will you not? *Venite, puella florum!*"

"Give me a halfpenny," said Beatrice to Mary, holding out a gloved hand.

Wondering, Mary handed her one. After the student had taken his turn, Beatrice walked up to the Cat Woman, handed her the coin, and then leaned close, scratching her behind the ears. Mary could hear a murmur, and then the usual loud purr of the Cat Woman. What was Beatrice doing?

In a moment, Beatrice returned, and the Cat Woman was saying, "Anyone else wish to scratch behind my ears or under my chin today? You, sir?" She looked at the other student with her yellow eyes and smiled enigmatically.

"Let us keep walking," said Beatrice. "I will explain when we are out of this tent."

The two-headed calf was indeed two-headed, but otherwise looked exactly like a calf. The Real Mermaid was utterly unconvincing. "They could at least have hidden the seams on her fish tail," said Diana. The Giantess had evidently retired with a headache, and the Zulu Prince performed his bloodthirsty native dances with abandon, but Mary could see that on the stool he occupied when not performing, he had left a copy of *Middlemarch*, with a stray ticket marking his place.

At last they emerged from the tent. "What was all that about?" asked Mary.

"The Cat Woman is Catherine Moreau," said Beatrice. "She told me to find her tent and meet her there once the circus begins. Then the sideshow will close and she will no longer be on display. It's the one next to the green wagon."

"How did you know it was her?" asked Diana.

"She spoke to me in Latin," said Beatrice. "I suppose Dr. Moreau must have taught her Latin, as my father taught me." Mary felt a pang of jealously. Her father had never taught her Latin, never taught her much of anything, despite those displays in his laboratory—but then, he had died when she was only seven. If he had lived, would he have taught her more? And would she have been better off? She remembered the letter: *You have a daughter, have you not? Surely she is old enough for you to begin the process, in whatever direction you decide will yield the most promising results.* Perhaps she would have been worse off, much worse. Would he have conducted experiments on her? Or Diana? And anyway, if her hypothesis was correct, at that point he had irrevocably become Hyde. Perhaps it was best, after all, for both of them that their father had died before he could do more damage than he had already done. After all, look at Beatrice. . . .

Then, as she had predicted, they had to stop at one of the carts and buy a meat pie for Diana, because she insisted that she was so famished, she might faint at any moment. Mary could not think of food at such a time, and when Beatrice was asked what she wanted, she said, "A glass of water, please." What did Beatrice do for lunch, anyway? Soak up sunlight?

"Could you try not to eat that entire pie in one mouthful?" said Mary. But before she could finish the sentence, it had already disappeared into Diana's mouth, and she was wiping off the crumbs with the back of one hand. Well, at least lunch had not taken long.

They found the tent, the last in a row of smaller striped tents that housed the circus performers, next to a green wagon that looked as though it might have contained an animal, for its sides were barred. They lifted the tent flap and entered. Beatrice drew her veil back over her hat, and Mary looked around her. The tent was divided into two sections by a curtain. In the section they had entered, they saw a camp bed, a folding table and chair, and a large trunk with its lid thrown back. It was filled with clothes, which were also scattered over both the bed and chair. Catherine Moreau was not very neat in her habits.

MARY: She still isn't.

As their eyes adjusted to the dim light in the tent, Catherine entered after them and closed the flap.

"I'm so glad that's over!" she said. She no longer spoke in a low growl—now, she sounded like an ordinary Englishwoman. "I usually don't mind the performance, but in this circumstance I wanted to get away as quickly as possible." She put her hands to her throat and fumbled there for a moment. Then she put her hands on her ears and lifted off—not only the ears, but the entire cat head. Underneath, she had dark brown hair coiled into braids so it would lie flat under the headpiece. She unbuttoned the invisible buttons of her cat outfit and took that off as well, attached claws and all, dropping it into the trunk. Her body was also brown, but hairy only where women's bodies are usually hairy. Mary blushed and looked away, but not before she had seen the network of lighter scars that covered Catherine Moreau's body. She was not accustomed to women stripping themselves naked in front of her. Catherine pulled on an orange kimono embroidered with cranes from the pile of clothes on the cot.

"How did you recognize me?" asked Beatrice.

"By your smell," said Catherine. "You don't smell entirely human." She looked curiously at Mary and Diana, as though trying to determine who they might be.

"And so you spoke to me," said Beatrice. "I understand. Are you—Dr. Moreau's daughter? If so, I offer my condolences on your father's death."

"His daughter! I suppose you could call me that. He did, and gave me his surname himself. But I am, more accurately, one of his—creations. Perhaps we should talk of this after you've introduced your friends?" Without her cat suit, Catherine looked like an ordinary woman, but her yellow eyes still had something wild in their depths.

> MARY: Oh please! You're turning yourself into one
> of your own heroines. Something wild in their
> depths, indeed!

Mary quailed a bit at the sight of her.

> MARY: I certainly did not!

"These are Mary Jekyll and Diana Hyde," said Beatrice. "They rescued me from the man who was holding me captive, and we can rescue you as well."

"I'm not being held captive," said Catherine. "This is the way I earn my living. It may not be the most dignified way, but it's better than selling myself under some bridge." She looked more closely at Mary. "Jekyll—I remember that name. Wasn't he also a member—"

"Of the Société des Alchimistes? Yes," said Mary. "We're trying to find out as much about the society as we can. If there's any information you could give us . . ."

Catherine threw back her head and laughed. Mary had expected it to sound animalistic, but her laughter was entirely human. "Information! Oh yes, we could give you information about our fathers' precious society!"

"Who's we?" asked Diana.

Catherine looked at each of them, as though assessing them individually. Then she said, "It's all right," not to them but to the curtain dividing the tent. "It's all right to come out."

Mary braced herself. Was this some sort of deception? Were they about to be attacked?

A pale hand reached around and drew back the curtain. Mary saw the tallest woman she had ever seen, taller than most men, but thin and stooping. She had a long, gentle face and sad eyes. "Hello," said the woman, hesitantly. She had an accent Mary could not place.

"That's impossible," said Beatrice. She stared at the tall woman as though looking at a ghost.

"What's impossible?" said Diana. "Is this the Giantess?"

"This is the Giantess," said Catherine. "Also known as Justine Frankenstein."

"But you were *disassembled*," said Beatrice. "The parts of your body were thrown into the sea. That is what my father told me, and it's described in Mrs. Shelley's book. Frankenstein refused to create a female counterpart of his monster for fear that she would have children. Forgive me, I'm being terribly rude," she added, for she could see tears welling in Justine's eyes.

"Frankenstein was a liar," said Catherine. "He and that brother of his . . ." She paused, and sniffed. "Miss Jekyll, are you sure you weren't followed?"

"No, I'm not sure," said Mary. "We changed omnibuses several times, but this morning, there was a man outside my house. . . . I don't know why, but he gave me the shivers. I thought it was my imagination. Why, do you see something?"

"No, I smell something," said Catherine. "Something like a man, but not like a man. I think we're in danger. Is there some-place safe we could go?"

"My house is as safe as anywhere, I suppose," said Mary. "If we were followed, he'll know where it is, but there is a strong door with a lock, and if need be, I can ask Mr. Holmes for protection."

"Then we'll go there. Justine and I always knew we'd have to leave, someday. This is that day. But we can't leave looking like this, all together. We would be spotted at once. I have an idea. You, monkey-girl," she said to Diana. "You can move silently, can't you?"

"Of course," said Diana scornfully.

"Then come with me." Catherine parted the curtain dividing the tent and stepped through to the other side. After a moment, Diana followed.

"Wait, where are you going?" Mary called after them. Could she trust Catherine Moreau? She was starting to learn that Diana could take care of herself. Nevertheless, that was her sister disap-pearing under the tent flap—she could not help feeling concerned. Catherine should at least have told her where they were going.

"You must trust Catherine," said Justine, as though sensing Mary's thoughts. "This tent, on that side it is close to the others. I do not know where she is going, but you will see—she is to be trusted. She saved my life."

"Your life—," said Beatrice. "How is it that you are alive? If what you say is true, you were made almost a century ago. . . ."

"Yes," said Justine, simply. "I had lost track, but you are correct. If it is correct to say that I am alive at all. For seventeen years, I was alive, as you are—a servant in the Frankenstein household. But then I was accused of a terrible crime. Although I was completely innocent, I was hanged . . . And my father, Victor Frankenstein, took my body. He made me as I am, larger and stronger than most women. He brought me back to life, or to a semblance of it. Am I alive? I have not aged like an ordinary woman. I do not know when I will die. So perhaps I am not alive after all. . . ."

Listening to Justine, Mary felt as though she had stepped into a story she did not understand. Everyone—well, at least Catherine and Beatrice—seemed to know so much more about what was happening than she did. And everything was happening so quickly. If only the world could be ordered and comprehensible again, just for a moment.

> JUSTINE: I felt that too. The circus had been my home, and now suddenly I was about to leave it, at a moment's notice.

> CATHERINE: Monsters don't have homes, not permanent ones. You should know that.

> JUSTINE: Then what is this, Catherine? You do not believe in such sentiments, I know. But this is a home, for all of us.

MRS. POOLE: And if it's not, I'd like to know what I
do all the housekeeping for. Not a home, indeed!

Suddenly, the curtain was drawn back. There were Catherine
and Diana, carrying a stack of blankets—no, clothes. Men's
clothes.

"Put these on," said Catherine. "I found them in the tent of the
Flying Kaminski Brothers. There are five of them, and the tallest
is almost as tall as Justine. The youngest is fourteen, and perhaps
his clothes will fit Diana. We'll have to wear our own boots. Ill-
fitting boots would be a danger when trying to evade pursuit on
the streets of London. At least you had the sense to wear low-
heeled ones."

Mary looked at the clothes doubtfully. How did one put on
men's clothes? "Well, at least they won't be expecting five men!"
she said, lifting a shirt from the pile. It was a strange experience,
dressing as a man. Everything felt different, everything buttoned a
different way. But when she had put on the shirt and trousers, she
realized what freedom they would give her. How easily she could
move, without petticoats swishing around her legs! No wonder
men did not want women to wear bloomers. What could women
accomplish if they did not have to continually mind their skirts,
keep them from dragging in the mud or getting trampled on the
steps of an omnibus? If they had pockets! With pockets, women
could conquer the world! And yet she felt, too, as though in putting off her women's clothes, she had lost a part of herself. It was
a confusing sensation.

She looked at the others. Diana was clearly in her element,
although her pants were too long and needed to be rolled up. As
soon as Catherine had put the pile of men's clothes on the bed,
Diana had said, "Give me some scissors." *Snip snip,* and off had come
all her red curls before Mary could object, although she gasped

when she saw them lying on the floor of the tent. "I've wanted to do that forever!" said Diana triumphantly. Now she stood there, hands in her pockets, with short, curling hair in a halo around her head. She looked exactly like one of the London newsboys, or one of Mr. Holmes's Baker Street Irregulars. Beatrice seemed uncomfortable, as though she did not know what to do with her hands. A man's suit could not disguise her femininity. She looked askance at the scissors, clearly reluctant to undergo the same shearing. "Let me do your hair," said Mary. "I think one cropped head is quite enough, thank you!" She unpinned Beatrice's elaborate chignon and pinned her hair up in a simple coil so it would be hidden by a bowler hat Catherine had brought with the clothes. Beatrice would be showing her face now, but at least it would be shielded by the hat brim. Mary's own hair was already as simply dressed as possible.

Justine looked as awkward in her suit as she had in women's clothes, and Mary suspected that she would look just as awkward in anything she wore. But Catherine looked perfectly natural. Once she was wearing a sack suit with a four-in-hand tie, she could have passed for any of the clerks who worked in the city, hurrying to their offices or home from them. She put a cloth cap on her head and pulled it low over her eyes.

> DIANA: Why do women have to wear such rotten clothes? I mean, you've got the chemise, and then the corset, and then the corset cover, and that's before you've even put on the shirtwaist. What's the point?

> BEATRICE: Clothing is one means of enforcing women's social and political subordination. That is why we must support Rational Dress . . .

CATHERINE: Are you seriously going to have an argument about this in the middle of my book?

BEATRICE: *Our* book, as you keep reminding us. And I know you agree with me, Catherine. You have criticized women's fashions many times in my hearing.

CATHERINE: Yes, but I don't wear those ridiculous Dress Reform outfits either. How are they any better? Women should just wear men's clothes. They're easier to move in, more hygienic . . .

JUSTINE: Men's clothes aren't made for a figure like Beatrice's. It's different for us, Cat. But even I, who have no claim to beauty, can see the elegance of Beatrice's gowns. We do not all wish to be masculine, you know.

DIANA: I do. Anyway, I'm the only one of you who keeps my hair short.

CATHERINE: Your point being?

DIANA: That if you really wanted to dress like a man, you'd cut your hair too.

MARY: What, pray tell, is the point of this argument? Catherine can wear whatever she likes and be a man one day, a woman the next. You all know perfectly well that dressing as a woman can be an effective disguise. It can be useful, being overlooked and

underestimated. No one expects a woman to pull
a pistol out of her purse. . . . Although I do wish
you'd grow your hair back, Diana. It's so pretty
when it's long.

DIANA: Sod off, sister.

When they were all buttoned and hatted and gloved, Catherine
consulted a pocket watch she had found in one of the waistcoat
pockets. "The circus performance will end in about ten minutes. I suggest we go out through another of the tents and try
to blend into the crowd. We'll follow the customers leaving
the circus, through Battersea Park and across the bridge. Then
you'll need to lead us, Mary, since Justine and I don't know
where to go."

"But my books!" said Justine. "Must we leave everything, Cat?"

Catherine looked at her with concern. "You know we can't
take anything, not now. Especially books! It's impossible, but
these men smell like . . . well, maybe I'm wrong. We'll send
for our things later. Lorenzo still owes us for the last fortnight,
remember. And Mary, you'd better tell me your address."

"11 Park Terrace," said Mary. "Near Regent's Park. If anything
happens, meet us there."

Catherine nodded, then once again parted the curtains to the
other side of the tent. They followed her through into what must
have been Justine's side, since it contained a particularly long cot.
In contrast to Catherine's side, it was immaculately neat. Then
they passed under the cloth wall of the tent, lifting the cloth and
stooping underneath, darting as quickly as they could to the tent
next to it, only a foot away. From tent to tent they passed, under
and through. All the tents were empty except the Zulu Prince's.
He was sitting on his bed, reading the book Mary had seen on his

stool. When Catherine saw him, she said, "Clarence, don't tell anyone we've been here, will you?"

He nodded and said, "Sure thing, Whiskers," in what was clearly an American accent.

Finally, when there were no more tents to pass through, Catherine looked out through the tent flaps. "Any moment now," she said.

"I think we would be safer if we split into two groups," said Mary. "They're expecting five. What if we're two and three?"

"Yes, that's a good idea," said Catherine. For the first time, she glanced at Mary with respect. *And about time,* thought Mary. Catherine could order them around for now, but she had no intention of letting that continue past the immediate situation! "We can meet—where?"

"Let's cross the bridge—the Chelsea Bridge, I mean—and meet at the other end, by the embankment. And the groups should be different from the ones we came with."

"All right," said Catherine. "You and Beatrice take Justine. I'll go with Diana."

Diana again! Why did Catherine want Diana with her? For a moment, Mary forgot that she should have been grateful to get rid of Diana for a while. After all, Diana was *her* sister, wasn't she?

"Good luck with that," she said, more sarcastically than she had meant to. "We'll go first. I think I can hear a crowd." She lifted the tent flap and stepped outside. Beatrice followed right behind her, but Justine still hung back. Mary waved for her to follow. Justine sighed and stepped out of the tent, blinking in the sunlight. Then they were all walking together across the grass of Battersea Park. The circus performance had just ended, and the audience was streaming out into the cold, damp afternoon. Well, this was spring in London, after all. They blended into it as best they could, Mary whispering to Beatrice, "Remember to walk like a man!" It was easy to follow the crowd across the grassy lawns of Battersea Park and onto the Chelsea Bridge. Once, she had to grab Justine's sleeve to keep them from getting separated, but otherwise their progress was easy. At the other side of the bridge, within sight of Ranelagh Gardens and the Royal Hospital, they strolled as though enjoying the day, then leaned on the embankment.

"Can you see them?" asked Beatrice.

"Not yet," said Mary. But she had not seen anyone following them either, so that was good, wasn't it? And then she saw them: Catherine and Diana, moving as quickly as they could through the crowd on the bridge, dodging costermongers and mothers with children. "Come on," she said. "We need to get back to the bridge." What had happened? Certainly, Catherine wasn't trying to blend into the crowd any longer.

"They found us!" said Catherine, panting and out of breath, when they met at the northern end of the bridge. "Look, you can see them. There and there!"

Mary tried to follow her pointing finger. And then she saw him, the beggar who had been leaning against one of the houses. He was moving through the crowd, still hunched over as he had been that morning, with an oddly stooping gait. She could not see the other.

"Get Justine to safety as quickly as you can," said Catherine. "They're following by scent, not sight. You see, they're not even looking this way. If you take a cab, they'll lose your scent and keep following us. Diana and I can lead them on a chase through London."

"Why should Diana go with you?" said Mary. "She's the youngest of us, and my sister. I want her safe as well."

"Because I can dodge in and out of crowds as well as Catherine, and the rest of you can't," said Diana. "Come on already! They're getting closer."

"I don't know if I have enough change for cab fare," said Mary.
"Justine does," said Catherine. "She has all our money. Now go!"

Mary hesitated, then nodded. "Come on," she said to Justine,
who followed with reluctance, clearly worried about being separated from Catherine. Beatrice brought up the rear. Without a
backward glance, they joined the crowd moving north.

> JUSTINE: I gave a backward glance. I was so nervous!
> I did not know you then, and I did not know
> London. There were so many streets. . . .

> BEATRICE: And you see how well it turned out! We
> are together now, all of us. Like sisters.

> DIANA: Speak for yourself, Poison Breath. As though
> one sister weren't enough to deal with!

On Sloane Street, Mary hailed a cab, and once they were seated
inside, she breathed a sigh of relief. They were traveling north,
with the verdure of Hyde Park to the left of them, the houses of
Mayfair to the right. Soon, they would be home. Suddenly, she
realized that she was hungry. After all, it was midafternoon, and
she had not eaten lunch. She should have purchased something
for herself when she bought Diana the meat pie. Next time she
would know better. Not long ago, her days had followed an invari-
able schedule: each meal at its proper time, served by Enid the
parlormaid. And in between, the paying of bills, the arranging
of household affairs, the fulfillment of duties. For a moment, she
missed her routine. Somehow, she did not think her life would
ever be that orderly again. But there was no time for regrets—she
had to get Beatrice and Justine safely home.

Meanwhile, Catherine and Diana were running across Ranelagh

Gardens and the grounds of the Royal Hospital. Here they were visible, for the lawns were closely clipped, with shrubs and trees only at their edges, and the tall brick buildings offered no shelter. But they paused behind some convenient hawthorns. They had lost their hats some time ago, and Catherine's braids had come down. They whipped around her face as she ran. "We need to leave a trail as long as we can," said Catherine, panting. "I saw one of them a moment ago. He hid behind that—whatever that building is."

"What are they?" said Diana. "They don't look right. Are they deformed?" She was panting as well. She had been able to keep up, although Catherine ran with the speed and grace of a puma.

> DIANA: Oh, you just had to put that in there, didn't
> you?

"I know what they are, but it's impossible. They look like the creatures my father made. Like Beast Men." For a moment, memory took Catherine back to the island, to the menagerie of Dr. Moreau. Men whose legs were too short, arms too long. Who spoke in gruff voices and were hairy beneath their clothes. But all his creations had died on the island. Of them all, only she had survived.

"I see him!" said Diana. "Come on, if we run across that court, we'll be in the streets of Chelsea. We can lose them in the alleys."

"How well do you know London?" asked Catherine.

"As well as I know the palms of my hands!" Diana grinned like a wicked monkey.

> JUSTINE: I don't think that's such an insult. Monkeys
> are quite clever.

> DIANA: [Diana's comments, being unprintable, are
> not included here.]

CATHERINE: Yes, I know you're the one who got us
safely home. And I'm grateful, truly I am. But you
do have a wicked grin, you can't deny. . . . Oh, all
right, I take it back already! I apologize, really I do.
Just for goodness' sake let me finish this chapter.

To those of our readers who are not familiar with London,
who may be reading this in the wilds of America, where we hear
there are bears and savages, or in the wilds of Australia, where
there are also savages but no bears (unless, adds Justine, they
are marsupial bears), the problem that now presented itself to
Catherine and Diana was as follows. How to get from Chelsea, in
the south of London, to Regent's Park in the north? They would
have to cross a tangle of streets, and then the open spaces of Hyde
Park, before emerging in Marylebone. It was a trip that could take
hours by omnibus in London traffic. They were on foot, evading
pursuers who seemed to follow them by scent, as hounds follow
a rabbit. And neither of them had any money. Putting all their
money into one purse and giving it to Justine might not have been
the most sensible plan, Catherine realized, too late. But at least
Justine would be all right. Catherine could take care of herself,
couldn't she?

She turned to Diana. "What do you suggest?"

Diana considered for a moment, looking at the green lawn
they still had to traverse, and beyond it the buildings of Chelsea.
"How well can you climb?"

Catherine made a sound that could have been a laugh or a
growl. Then, "Look!" she said. There they were again, two
hunched figures loping across the grass toward them. "Wherever
you go, I'll follow. Now run!"

They raced across the final stretch of lawn, then darted into
the narrow streets, as though entering a maze. Here, buildings

blocked out the light; once again they were in the shadow of London. To the astonishment of two boys playing at marbles and an old woman smoking a noxious pipe, Diana pulled off her jacket and began taking off her boots. "Rooftop," she said, when she could take a breath.

"Keep the boots, you'll need them later," said Catherine, hopping on one foot as she untied her own boots, then tying the laces together and hanging them around her neck. "Here," she said, tossing her jacket to one of the boys. "You'll grow into it!"

"Can't, they're button," said Diana, leaving her boots on the pavement. She scrambled up a ladder attached to a brick wall that led to a wrought-iron balcony. The building she had chosen had a series of such balconies, one on each floor. Catherine looked up, estimating how far she would have to climb after the last balcony to get to the roof. Could she do it? She could not climb as well as Diana, although she hated to admit that. But what choice did she have?

She tossed Diana's boots and jacket to the other boy. "Happy unbirthday! Unless it's your birthday . . . ," she said, then started climbing up the ladder.

When she reached the final balcony, Catherine looked down. At the bottom, the two Beast Men were starting to follow. The first had reached the lowest balcony; the second was still on the ladder. Would they be able to climb all the way to the roof?

Above her, Diana scrambled up the last stretch of wall. "Staples!" she called down. Catherine looked up, confused, until she saw the iron staples that someone, for some reason, had once driven into the mortar between the bricks. In a moment, she had joined Diana on the rooftop. They looked down at the Beast Men, who were following them but with increasing difficulty. When they reached the top balcony, they stopped, looking up at Catherine and Diana. One of them howled with anger.

"I thought so," said Catherine. "They smell like wolves. I think they're Wolf Men, which means that as long as we stay on the rooftops, we're safe."

"Good," said Diana. "But we'd better get going. We still have a whole bloody city to cross."

They looked around. There was London, spread before them: a different city, the London of the rooftops. (If you wish to travel across London and are as agile as Catherine and Diana, the rooftops are like roads that can take you from one end of the city to the other.) They walked or sometimes crawled across the roofs, balancing on ridges, trying to avoid chimney pots. Where the alleys were narrow, they leaped from one rooftop to another, always heading north. From time to time, they had to descend to the streets, and it was with trepidation that they crossed Hyde Park. By then it was getting late. The trees of the park threw long shadows across the grass, and the setting sun shone on the Serpentine, creating a path of gold across the water. But they neither saw nor smelled their pursuers.

"Why should they follow us?" said Diana. "They know where Mary lives. They can just go back there and wait."

"If they were smarter, they would have done that in the first place," said Catherine. "But if they're Wolf Men, it's in their nature to hunt. They couldn't help following us."

Once they had crossed Hyde Park, there were only the streets of Marylebone to navigate, and to her credit, Diana got lost only once. It was dark before they saw the lights of 11 Park Terrace.

Was the house being watched? They could not see the Wolf Men, and more importantly, Catherine could not smell them. So taking a chance, they ran up the steps to the front door and rang the bell.

It was opened almost at once. "Come in, come in quickly," said Mrs. Poole. "Poor Miss Frankenstein has killed a man!"

CHAPTER XII

Catherine's Story

It was probably the strangest sight the respectable parlor of Dr. Jekyll had ever seen, at least since the days when Mr. Hyde roamed through the house at will. In the light of the gas lamps, which were turned up high, Catherine and Diana could see four men gathered around the body of another, lying on the floor, with a handkerchief draped over his face. The carpet had been pulled back, so he lay directly on the parquet in front of the fireplace. It took them a moment to realize that two of the men were Mary and Beatrice, who had not yet changed out of their masculine clothes. The other two were strangers to Catherine, but Diana immediately recognized Holmes and Watson. The parlor itself was a shambles, with furniture knocked over and the painting of Mrs. Jekyll hanging crooked on the wall.

"Oh, I'm so glad to see you both! We were worried sick," said Mary. And then, looking at them more closely, she exclaimed, "You're absolutely filthy!"

"We came by rooftop," said Catherine. "What is this about Justine? Where is she?"

"Upstairs, lying down," said Mary. "She's completely distraught. We arrived home without incident, but the house was being watched. As I opened the front door, this man tried to force his way in. We fought back—you can see the result! I tried to hit him over the head with my umbrella, and Beatrice did her best to weaken him with her breath. But it was Justine who saved us: she got her hands around his neck and—she strangled him, right here in the parlor. He was so strong! He twisted Beatrice's arm—you can see the bruise, all green and blue."

"I'm all right," said Beatrice. "Charlie was around the corner— he seems to have appointed himself our guardian angel!"

"More like guardian street urchin," said Diana under her breath.

"He heard the altercation—that is the right word, is it not? And ran to get Mr. Holmes."

"I'm glad he's keeping a watch on the house," said Holmes. "I asked him to let us know if there was anything amiss." He turned to Catherine. "You must be Miss Moreau. We've been hearing about your adventures this morning. I'm Sherlock Holmes, and this is my associate, Dr. Watson."

"Is it safe for you to continue this investigation?" asked Watson. "You are certainly courageous young women, but you seem to be running into increasing danger. And this . . ." He gestured at the man lying on the floor. "I scarcely know what to make of it!"

Catherine walked over to the dead man and removed the handkerchief from his face. It was strangely distorted: the eyes small and set close together, the nose upturned and flat, the chin almost nonexistent with a few prominent bristles. "I can tell you what to make of him, Dr. Watson. But Diana and I are tired and famished. If we could sit down and have something to eat, I believe I could provide you with an explanation—although it may deepen this mystery rather than elucidating it. But first I must see Justine. . . ."

"You let her rest," said Mrs. Poole. "She's safe, and what she needs right now is some quiet. She'll come down when she's ready."

Catherine frowned. She had never liked being told what to do, and wasn't it her responsibility to look after Justine? But she had to admit that Mrs. Poole was probably right. She knew, better than any of them, that what Justine often needed was simply solitude.

"Diana!" Mary exclaimed suddenly. "Your feet!"

They all looked. From Diana's bare feet, a pool of blood was spreading over the floor.

"What," she said. "I had to leave my boots."

"Show them to me," said Beatrice. She knelt and examined the bleeding feet without touching them, then insisted Diana show her the soles. "All the wounds are shallow. You have merely torn up the skin, but in so many places!"

"If you'd like me to take a look . . . ," said Watson.

"Not you!" said Diana. "Last time you did that, I thought you'd set me on fire."

"The alcohol was necessary to clean the cut," said Watson, looking put out. "I had no intention of harming you, I can assure you, Miss Hyde."

"It's quite all right, Dr. Watson," said Beatrice. "I can take care of Diana's wounds. My father was a physician and trained me in his techniques. Come, Diana. I will find something in the kitchen to make you a poultice."

"It's no big deal," Diana insisted. "Doesn't even hurt." But she followed Poison Breath, as she still thought of Beatrice, downstairs. At least in the kitchen she would be close to food.

MRS. POOLE: And a time I had of it, trying to scrub away that bloodstain!

ALICE: It's still there. Lye and carbolic couldn't get rid of it. Good thing the carpet covers it, Mrs. Poole, or we'd have some explaining to do when visitors come!

It was an hour before they all sat together in the parlor, where the dead man still lay on the floor, and Catherine began the story that would perhaps explain his presence—and peculiarities. First, on the orders of Mrs. Poole, Catherine and Diana had to clean themselves in basins of hot water ("Before you sit down on any of the furniture, please!") and change into clothing more suitable for the young women Watson had called them. Mary and Beatrice changed as well, and Mary wondered if she had enough dresses left to keep supplying them all in this fashion. If they kept losing or destroying their clothes, they would all have to start sewing! When suitably clean and dressed, they had a cold supper of meat and pudding ("And not in the room with the dead man!"). Justine had still not come down, so Mrs. Poole brought supper up to her ("I don't care how upset she is, she needs to eat!").

Despite Mrs. Poole's consternation, Holmes and Watson restored the parlor to its usual order, so by the time Mary and the others had finished their supper, the furniture was once again upright and the painting hung straight on the wall. The only thing out of order was the man on the floor, who once again had a handkerchief hiding his strange features. Mary, Diana, and Catherine sat on the sofa, Holmes and Watson in the two armchairs. Beatrice sat on the window seat, as far away from them as possible. Where would Justine sit, if she came down? Mary thought of the furniture that had once been in this room, when it had been a proper gentleman's parlor, and sighed. The only remaining carpet was threadbare. She consoled herself with the thought that Mr. Holmes probably had not noticed. He would not notice a rug unless there was a clue on it. But Beatrice was thinking, *How nice that this parlor is not overfurnished! Why do the English overfurnish their houses? Although the walls should not be the color of porridge. They should be blue, a blue like the sea on a calm day, or yellow like sunshine* . . .

BEATRICE: So they are, now. And with Justine's
wonderful border of flowers.

JUSTINE: Is the story supposed to be jumping around
like that, from Mary's head, to Diana's, to Beatrice's?

CATHERINE: I told you, this is a new way of writing.
How can I write a story about all of us if I don't
show what we were all thinking? Do you want
the story to be just about Mary?

DIANA: That would be as dull as ditch water.

JUSTINE: No, of course not. It's just . . . different.
As though it's been stitched together of various
parts. Like my father's monsters.

CATHERINE: Well, we're different. I have to tell the
story in a way that fits who we are.

JUSTINE: You are the author, so I suppose you know
best.

CATHERINE: You could try to sound a little less
doubtful!

Mrs. Poole insisted on making tea. "You could all use a cup,
I'm sure," she said, leaving the teapot on the table so Mary could
pour out, before returning to the kitchen.

"Please take a cup if you wish," said Catherine. "I'm afraid my
story will be a long one. And I must begin with a lesson on anatomy." Just as she was about to begin, Justine joined them, pausing
hesitantly at the threshold. She wore a dress that had once belonged
to Mary's mother, which was too large for her thin frame but hung
down only to her calves. Her eyes were still red.

"Are you all right?" asked Catherine. "The housekeeper said you were resting. Come and take my seat."

"Please, don't mind me," said Justine, but she took Catherine's seat on the sofa. Catherine walked over to the dead man.

It was clear, from the way he leaned forward, that Holmes wanted to know who she was, this woman who was taller than most men. But he refrained. "Miss Moreau, please continue," he said. One story at a time, his countenance seemed to say. He could wait.

"First," said Catherine, "this is not a man. Justine, you did not kill a man. What you killed was an animal. Look at the disproportion of the limbs, look"—she drew back the handkerchief again—"at the scars, here and here and here. Look at the face. The nose resembles a snout, the eyes and ears are too small. What you have killed is a pig, specifically a boar pig, surgically transformed into a man."

"That's impossible," said Watson.

"Improbable, but not impossible," said Holmes. "Remember Dr. Moreau's experiments."

"But I thought he was dead," said Mary. "The letter Dr. Seward received—the one we found in his office. It said Dr. Moreau had died. . . ."

"Yes, he's dead," said Catherine. "I know, because I killed him myself."

> JUSTINE: What a terrible night that was! The man I killed . . .

> MARY: Pig. You killed a pig.

> JUSTINE: But Mary, he had been transformed into a man, with a man's brain. Does that not mean

he was a man, as Catherine is a woman? I am
responsible for his death. . . .

MARY: When are you going to let this go? You have
to stop feeling guilty about it. He was hurting
Beatrice.

DIANA: Justine, is that why you don't eat meat?

"In order to understand my story," said Catherine, "you have to
understand Moreau's experiments." She looked down at the floor,
her hands clasped in front of her, as though preparing herself for
a long narrative. Mary leaned back into the sofa. She noticed that
Diana, who was sitting next to her, put her feet up on the cush-
ions although Mrs. Poole had expressly forbidden her from doing
so. Beatrice shifted on the window seat. Watson poured himself
another cup of tea.

"It was Beatrice's father who led the Alchemical Society in
the direction of biological transmutation. He had been a follower
of the Chevalier de Lamarck, when Lamarck was mocked for his
theories of evolution. He believed in evolutionary theory before
Mr. Darwin became famous for his proof of it. I'm sure you're
familiar with Lamarck's theories, Mr. Holmes."

"That a man can pass physical and mental characteristics
acquired during his lifetime to his children," said the detective. "A
miner will pass on his strong arms. A philosopher will pass on his
discerning mind."

"A man—or a woman," said Beatrice. "Yes, my father was a
Lamarckian. He believed that by introducing traits from plants
into living men and women, he could pass those traits on to the
next generation. He could direct the course of evolution, create
better, stronger human beings. That was why he created me. He

believed any child I bore would inherit my ability to live off organic matter and sunlight—and my natural defenses, for that was how he saw my poisonous nature. But my father had been trained as a botanist. Dr. Moreau was not interested in plants: what interested him was the division between man and animal."

Once again, Mary felt a little lost. Her lessons with Miss Murray had not covered Lamarck. She hated the sensation that Beatrice and Catherine, and sometimes even Justine, were speaking a language she did not understand. Well, all she could do was listen carefully. This was still her case, after all, even though it had grown so much larger than when she started her investigation. But it was she who had seen Molly Keane dead on the pavement, who had gone with Mr. Holmes to question Renfield in the asylum. She must not forget that.

"Yes," said Catherine in response to Beatrice. "It was the difference between man and animal that vexed him." As she talked, she started to pace back and forth before the dead man, stopping and turning to them when she wished to emphasize a point. "What separated the two? If he could turn animals into men, could he not create men who were even higher, in whom the animal nature was entirely absent? Men who would have no base desires, no primitive instincts? After he was driven out of England for the cruelty of his experiments, he took the fortune he had inherited and bought a ship. He stocked it with everything he would need for an extended stay on a South Sea island, and set sail. He took with him a disgraced medical student named James Montgomery, who was willing to become his assistant under such inauspicious circumstances. Once he had found a suitable island, uninhabited and with no important animal species, he began his experiments: transforming animals into human beings. At this, he was successful—or successful enough to fool an average observer, although he was never satisfied with the result."

"I find it difficult to believe," said Watson. "How could an animal be imbued with human reason?"

"The proof stands before you," said Catherine. She unbuttoned the collar of her dress—one of Mary's day dresses that she had not worn for years because it was too tight, but Catherine was smaller than she was. She pulled the fabric back to expose her neck, then turned her head from side to side. Her face and neck were covered with a pattern of faint scars. "Am I human?" she said. "I don't know. I have a name, Catherine, given to me by Montgomery. As a joke: Catherine, Cat in here. There is a cat in here." She pulled up the sleeves of her dress: on her arms, too, they could see a regular pattern of scars, faint but visible in the lamplight, like a network of roads over her body.

"After Moreau had been on the island for several years, a boat carrying specimens for him, under the care of Montgomery, picked up a man who had been shipwrecked and was floating in a dinghy with two dead sailors. His name was Edward Prendick, and by one of those strange coincidences that sometimes occur in the world, he was a man of science, a biologist who had studied under Professor Huxley. Montgomery befriended him, and when the boat arrived at my father's island, Prendick disembarked as well. One of the animals on that ship was a puma."

Here Catherine paused, poured herself a cup of tea, and added a great deal of milk.

"That was you, wasn't it?" said Diana. "You're the Cat Woman."

Catherine took a sip of her tea. "I was the puma, yes. After we disembarked, Moreau began the process that would turn me into a woman. Surgery, but also after a certain point, after my mind was receptive to it, hypnosis and education. Indoctrination. In the same room, for I was in a cage during most of the process, he sat with Prendick, drinking tea, discussing his aims and procedures."

"That's incredible," said Watson. "I don't know whether to loathe the man or admire his artistry."

"They talked science, history, politics. Moreau had been alone with Montgomery for a long time. I think it was a relief for him to talk to someone who was not yet infected with the melancholy of living among the Beast Men. So I listened, as my ability to comprehend their speech grew, and learned more from their conversations than what Moreau was trying to teach me. The history of the Alchemical Society, for example. Moreau invited Prendick to join and explained the aims of the society, the work it had done over the centuries.

"Prendick was horrified, but fascinated. Day after day, he heard my screams of agony, for in that first stage, Moreau would not use anesthetic. He said it complicated the procedure, that pain was a necessary part of the process. Prendick would come and look at me in the cage, watch me being transformed into a woman. He saw the first light of recognition, of reason, in my eyes. And he was there the day I escaped."

"How did you manage it?" asked Mary. What a strange story this was. Several days ago, she would not have believed it. But was it any more incredible than her father turning into Hyde?

"I was almost healed by then. Moreau himself, who was rarely satisfied with his creations, said I was his masterpiece. His previous attempts at creating Beast Women had been failures. He had never before been able to get the delicate formation of the fingers, or the contours of the face. The few Beast Women on the island were poor, malformed creatures. But the ship that brought me had also brought a new set of German surgical instruments. With those, and with patience and the most precise technique, he created me. It took months."

"His technique is remarkable," said Holmes. "I would not have distinguished you from a human woman."

Catherine opened her mouth in a snarl. Moreau had reduced their length and sharpness, but she still had fangs. They would not be visible unless her lips were drawn back, as they were now. But they would nevertheless be deadly.

Holmes smiled. "I meant that as a compliment."

"Thank you, Mr. Holmes," said Catherine. "But you see that I am not entirely human. I could, in a moment, bite through your throat."

Holmes bowed in acknowledgment.

MARY: Did you really say that, or are you showing off?

CATHERINE: If I didn't say it, I should have, don't you think?

"Moreau looked forward to teaching me, to turning me into the perfect Englishwoman. Since I had listened to their conversations, I knew about the island, about the other Beast Men. I knew that he and Montgomery kept a tenuous grip on power by use of the guns, or thunder sticks as the Beast Men called them. At that point, I was no longer caged. Because I was more human than animal, they chained me instead. One afternoon, during the hour when Moreau and Montgomery both slept, I pulled the iron staples out of the walls. And when Moreau came after me, calling to me as though I were a lost cat—'Here, Catherine, where are you, Catherine'—I strangled him with my chains, which still hung from the manacles on my wrists. Montgomery found me standing over him as he lay on the ground, staring up at the sky with empty eyes. There was blood on my mouth. Perhaps I was still more animal than they had realized.

"I was in pain, not yet entirely healed. Montgomery took me back to the compound. He should have killed me, but he could not bring himself to do it. He had always been sympathetic to the

Beast Men. After all, they had been his only company on the island other than Moreau. So instead, he removed the manacles and tended to my wounds. And Prendick—it was he who continued my education. I knew enough English to understand their speech, but he taught me how to sound like an Englishman, how to read and understand what I was reading. There were few books in the enclosure—Darwin was there, and Huxley's essays. Textbooks on surgical technique that I found tedious. *The Decline and Fall of the Roman Empire*, some books of poetry—and a book of your cases, Mr. Holmes. So you see, I know who you are, although I am behind in my reading. I thought you had perished at Reichenbach Falls. And he taught me the rudiments of Latin, what he could remember from his own public school education.

"When the Beast Men discovered that Moreau was dead, they were inclined to rebel. They had never been afraid of Montgomery, and had always hated their masters. Prendick tried to convince them that Moreau was still alive, although incorporeal—watching them from the sky. The Pig Men, who had developed a sort of religion, believed him. The others were still wary of the thunder sticks. Montgomery was less cautious. He traded with them for the fruit and vegetables some of them grew on rudimentary farms, even allowed them into the compound for a sort of 'market day.' In return, he would give them biscuits and tinned meat.

"He and Prendick talked about getting off the island. Moreau had a boat, docked in a natural harbor near the compound. But it needed a crew, and without Moreau to strike fear into the hearts of the Beast Men, none of them would agree to sail it. They had been made of land animals, and feared the ocean. The only other option was to wait for the arrival of the supply ship, which was supposed to come every six months. But the date came and went. The supply ship did not arrive. I think that was what finally broke Montgomery.

"There we all were, in an uneasy truce, with no hope of leaving the island. One day, that truce was broken. It was one of the market days. Montgomery had been drinking. Prendick and I did not know—we were once again discussing how we could sail the boat with only the three of us, for Prendick intended to take me with him to England. He did not think of me as a Beast Woman any longer, and he said that my killing of Moreau had been justified. He called it self-defense.

"Outside, in the courtyard of the compound, Montgomery began gambling with the Beast Men. They had simple games of chance that involved casting marked bones onto the ground and gambling on the results. Montgomery joined in, lost, and kept losing. He gambled away a barrel of whiskey.

"That night, Prendick and I woke to the sound of gunfire. It was outside the compound, which meant that Montgomery was out there—and in danger. We ran out of the compound, carrying our guns. Down on the beach we saw a fire, with Beast Men dancing around it—Ape Men and Bull Men and Wolf Men, like figures out of a nightmare.

"Montgomery was dancing among them, shooting up into the air, drunk, and as beastly as any of them.

"'What are they burning?' I asked, for there was no vegetation on the beach.

"'The boat!' said Prendick, pointing toward the harbor. What floated there was no longer a boat. It looked more like a skeleton that had been picked clean by birds.

"We rushed down to stop them, but it was too late. Most of the planks were already char and ash.

"Montgomery laughed when he saw us, the laughter of a madman. 'Now we'll never get away! We'll all die together on this godforsaken island!'

"What could we do? We turned to walk back to the compound,

only to see that it, too, was in flames. One of the Beast Men had snuck up while we were running toward Montgomery and set fire to the thatched roofs of the buildings. I started to run back, but Prendick stopped me. 'No,' he said. 'The ammunition.' In a moment, I understood what he meant. We were knocked to the ground by the explosion.

"Morning found us with no home, no supplies, and no means of escape. On the beach were the charred remains of the boat and Montgomery's body. He had been strangled by one of the Beast Men.

"After that day, we lived like savages. Prendick and I brought whatever we could salvage from the compound into a cave above the beach. Once our bullets ran out, we hunted—I did most of the hunting, since Prendick had no weapon. But I was a weapon. Slowly, the Beast Men killed each other off. Or," Catherine added calmly, "I killed them. By the end of the year we spent on the island, there were none left. We ate them, of course. What else was there to eat on that island but coconuts and crabs?"

"You—ate them?" said Mary. "How could you . . ." She had been fascinated by the story—as they all had been, judging by their faces in the lamplight. Holmes was leaning forward, his fingers tented in a way she was coming to recognize. It meant he was turning something around and around in his mind, considering every angle. Even Diana had stayed quiet for all this time. But it was a gruesome story as well. Mary did not know whether to feel greater pity for Catherine's suffering or horror at the cruelty of Moreau. Those Beast Men, doomed to die on their remote island . . .

> MARY: Well, to be honest, I was mostly curious about
> how he had done it. Created you, I mean, as well
> as the other Beast Men. It was a quite a scientific

accomplishment, although of course horrible from an ethical standpoint.

CATHERINE: It would be much easier writing from your perspective if you admitted to feeling normal human emotions!

MARY: I did! I felt horror and pity, really I did. At least, some. But I was curious too. Wouldn't you be?

DIANA: I didn't feel horror or pity.

CATHERINE: That doesn't surprise me in the least.

"Why should I not eat them?" said Catherine. "Because they were men? To me, they were apes and bulls and wolves. If I had still been a puma, they would have been my natural enemies or prey. But Prendick—I think it made him sick, not in the stomach but in the head. One day, he gathered together the remaining planks of the boat and made a sort of raft. On it, using the rags of his shirt as a sail, he set out to sea. I saw him from the hill above our cave, already too far away for me to swim out to him, floating away on the tide. That was the last I saw of him. I believe he perished on the open ocean."

"No, he couldn't have perished," said Mary. "Wasn't that the name in Dr. Seward's letter? It was Prendick, I'm sure of it. Let me go check. . . . I'll be back in a moment."

In the morning room, she opened the drawer of her mother's desk and pulled out the portfolio. Yes, there it was. She took out the letter and brought it back with her into the parlor. Justine was talking to Catherine in low tones, and Beatrice was answering a question about transmutation posed by Dr. Watson. When Mary entered, they all fell silent and turned to look at her. Catherine had an expression on her face that Mary did not understand.

"Yes, there, I was sure. Listen: 'I assume you will be traveling with Mr. Prendick? Poor man, I hope he may someday be ready to participate fully in our community again. I cannot tell you how I mourn the loss of Moreau. You and Prendick belong to a younger generation. You do not know what it was like for us old fogeys, as you may call us, resurrecting the Société from the decrepitude into which it had fallen and redirecting its energies to biology, to the material of life itself!' That has to be the same Prendick, doesn't it?"

Catherine opened her mouth, then closed it again, as though she could not continue.

> **MARY:** I didn't understand your reaction that night. It was only later, when you told us about your . . . relations with him, that it made sense.

> **CATHERINE:** My relations . . . how delicately you put it! I didn't want to say anything in front of Holmes and Watson. And why should I have? It was my story to tell—or not.

> **MARY:** No reason, I'm not questioning your judgment, Cat. But I'm glad you told us later.

> **CATHERINE:** He was there when I tore the manacles out of the walls. He didn't stop me—just stood there as I ran out of the room and through the compound. I think he felt guilty for having done nothing all those months, while I screamed in pain. It was easy to open the gate with my human

fingers and disappear into the forest like the puma
I had been. He didn't anticipate that I would kill
Moreau, of course. Once Moreau was dead, Edward
and James fought over me. I was the only woman
on the island, the only one who didn't look like a
beast, and James thought I should be his as Moreau's
successor. But I rejected him. That may be why he
became drunk that night. . . . When you told me
that Edward was still alive, I didn't know what to
think or say. Justine was the only one who knew,
the only one I'd spoken to about it. I still don't
know . . . whether he ever loved me. Or whether I
was simply convenient.

BEATRICE: I'm sure it wasn't that. There must have
been more to it than that.

CATHERINE: Must there? I don't know. I don't suppose
I'll ever know for certain.

"It's all right," said Justine. "She's startled, that's all."

"Yes, startled," said Catherine, finally. "I wonder how he
survived. . . ." She remembered looking down from the hilltop,
watching Prendick's raft float away into the distance, until it was
lost against the immensity of the sea. Finding herself completely
alone on an island where her only companions were beasts. Feeling
as though she should lie down and die, and then deciding that she
was going to survive. She did not know how, but somehow.

"A week later, the supply ship came. The captain had been
sacked for brutality to his men, and another captain hired. In
the transition, the supply ship had missed a scheduled delivery.
When I saw the ship, I made a signal fire from whatever wood I

could find, including planks left after Prendick had built his raft. It was the last of the wood from Moreau's boat. When the sailors picked me up and took me aboard, I told the captain that I was an Englishwoman shipwrecked on that shore. I said I had no knowledge of Moreau or his compound, that the island had been deserted as long as I had been there. I told him I had lost my memory, and remembered only having come from the city of London. Because I spoke with the accent of an educated man, the accent Prendick had taught me, I was believed. They assumed my clothes must have come from a drowned sailor, my complexion from living in the sun unprotected for so long. My scars from my misadventures.

"The captain took me back with him to the port of Callao, and then to the capital city of Peru, where he needed to deposit his cargo. In Lima, I became a sort of *cause célèbre* among the English population—the Englishwoman who had survived on a deserted island! I was offered a room in the house of an English industrialist who had come to Peru to reestablish trade after the late war, and invited to dinners and balls. You can imagine my confusion on first encountering women's clothes! On the island, and even on shipboard, I had always worn the clothes that were available, which were men's. In Peru, for the first time, I was given a chemise and corset and petticoat. I had no idea what to do with them. Luckily, the maids helped me dress, or I assure you, I would not have figured out all those buttons and laces!

"A subscription was taken up for me, enough to pay for my passage to London. The industrialist, Sir Geoffrey Tibbett, was returning to England, and he offered me his protection on the voyage. He told me that I could stay with his family while being treated by a mesmerist, who would help me recover my memories and find my own family, my own home. I wonder what a mesmerist would have made of the incidents I recalled! After the long sea voyage, during which Sir Geoffrey and I played endless games of cribbage and backgammon, I stayed at the Tibbett household in Mayfair for several months, recovering—or so it was thought. I was learning as much about England as I could, going to lectures, reading novels and poems and collections of essays.

"Sir Geoffrey was fond of me. He said if I could not find my family, he wished to adopt me as his daughter. But his wife did not like me. She was a woman with a pinched nose and a back as straight as a poker, whose primary interest was climbing into the right social circles. A strange girl from a South Sea island did not fit into her plans.

"Her small dog did not like me either. He was a Pekingese, horribly overfed, and although he was the approximate shape and size of a bolster, he was still a dog. He knew I was a cat. One day, I was reading in the parlor and he would not leave me alone. He kept yapping at me and nipping at my toes. Finally, I could take it no longer. Lady Tibbett heard his squeals and came into the room, only to see his body dangling from my jaws. That was my last day with the Tibbetts!

"For a while, I lived on the streets, scavenging what I could. There is reasonably good hunting in London, for a cat. But one day, I saw an advertisement for Lorenzo's Circus of Marvels and Delights, which was appearing in Battersea Park. I went to Lorenzo and offered myself as a performer. 'Why do I need you?' he asked me. 'I have Sasha the Dog Boy.' 'But you don't have a Cat Woman,' I said. I growled and purred for him, and he hired me on the spot. During most of the year, we toured the countryside, but each summer we spent a month in London, on the South Bank. And that was where you found me. . . ."

"And Justine," said Mary. "Was she already at the circus when you joined?"

"No, I was the one who brought her to the circus." Catherine looked over at Justine. "She can tell you herself . . ."

But Justine was leaning back on the sofa, looking even paler than usual. She reminded Mary of the Madonna lily, just after Beatrice had breathed on it.

"Have you forgotten?" said Justine. "There is a dead man lying on the floor."

"Dead pig," said Catherine. "I can't imagine who would create Beast Men here, in London. Why would anyone want to replicate Moreau's techniques? Unless . . ." She paused for a moment, but did not continue her train of thought. Mary wondered what she had meant to say. Instead, Catherine looked down at the Pig Man. "We'll have to get rid of him."

"Can't we report him to the police?" asked Mary. "After all, it was self-defense."

"Not without explaining how Justine was able to strangle him. Which means explaining about Justine—and about us."

"I agree with Miss Moreau," said Holmes. "This is not a matter for the police. I suggest taking him to the park, dirtying his clothes, and putting his hat beside him. When the police find him, as they assuredly will, they'll assume he is a beggar. They will not pay much attention to the death of one more beggar in London."

"Phew!" said Diana. "You would make a good criminal."

"Yes, I worry about that sometimes," said Watson. "Holmes, can you and I lift the body between us?"

"I shall carry the body," said Justine. "It will be my penance."

"Penance!" said Catherine. "What a ridiculous idea."

But Justine would not be dissuaded, and although Holmes and Watson went with her, she was the one who carried the Pig Man's body into Regent's Park.

Mary follow them, partly from a sense of obligation—the Pig Man had after all been killed in her parlor—and partly to make certain they placed him well away from 11 Park Terrace, so no one could connect him to the Jekyll residence.

Am I developing a criminal mentality, like Hyde? she asked herself. *Or like Mr. Holmes?* That thought, at least, was more reassuring.

When they had carried the Pig Man as far as the rose beds, Watson and Holmes rolled him in the moist, prepared earth. Then they placed him under a tree near the Inner Circle, close to the pond, where a beggar might be expected to lie down on a chilly, but not cold, spring night. As they were walking back in the darkness, Holmes beside Mary, Justine and Watson ahead of them, he said, "Your mystery is unfolding even faster than I expected, Miss Jekyll. In addition to the pleasure of investigating such a case, there is the pleasure . . . that is to say . . . the contact of another keen, logical mind is always a pleasure." He was silent a moment. Was he going to say anything more?

But they had arrived once again at Park Terrace.

"Yes, Mr. Holmes?" she said.

"What I was going to say . . . Well. Miss Jekyll, Watson and I would have come this evening in any case, to tell you about a curious fact we discovered during our investigation. Four of the murdered women were at one time inmates of the Magdalen Society." Surely that was not what he had been thinking about, as they walked in the park?

"Justine! Are you all right? You don't look well." It was Catherine, standing in the front hall, waiting for them to come in. Just beyond her stood Diana and Beatrice. Justine staggered, clutched at the doorframe, and then crumpled in a heap on the threshold.

"Oh goodness," said Mary, darting forward and kneeling beside Justine. "I think she's fainted. Diana, get Mrs. Poole to bring the *sal volatile*. We have to bring her to, because I don't think we're going to be able to carry her upstairs."

"Why me?" said Diana.

"Because you're closest to the back stairs, and anyway, I may need Catherine to help me lift her," said Mary. "Now go!"

"Straighten her head," said Beatrice. "Make sure the passage of air is not obstructed. Can you do it, Catherine? Alas that I cannot touch her!"

"Allow me," said Watson. He knelt by Justine, checked that she was breathing, and felt her pulse. "Your friend is unconscious, but in no immediate danger. All this has simply been too much for her. I prescribe a good night's sleep." When Diana returned with a frantic Mrs. Poole, who was carrying a bottle of smelling salts, he waved it under Justine's nose and waited until she moaned and opened her eyes.

"She never should have come downstairs," said Mrs. Poole. "Come on, deary. Let's get you back into bed again."

"Mr. Holmes, what were you saying before Justine fainted?" asked Mary. In a moment, she would have to help Justine back upstairs, but he'd been saying something about the murdered girls. . . .

"Never mind for now," said Holmes, smiling. "Take care of your friend. We'll return tomorrow morning and talk then."

"Yes, all right," said Mary, distracted. Catherine was already supporting Justine on one side, and she would need to support Justine on the other, since Diana was too short and Mrs. Poole wasn't strong enough to help the Giantess upstairs. And Beatrice, of course, was poisonous. No, Mary's life was definitely no longer ordinary. . . .

CHAPTER XIII

Return to the Asylum

MARY: Imagine, for a moment, the logistical difficulties of having four girls—or women, for only Diana was truly a girl—suddenly move into your household. On Monday morning, I had twelve pounds, five shillings, three pence in my bank account, and only myself and Mrs. Poole to clothe and feed. After I had transferred the money from Diana's account, we had thirty-five pounds, five shilling, three pence. That amount could feed and clothe three people comfortably for a year! On Friday morning, we had forty-two pounds, twelve shillings exactly. Beatrice had come with nothing but the clothes on her back, but Catherine and Justine had brought their savings, which they kept in the toe of an old stocking. Shockingly irresponsible of them it was, too. Seven pounds, six shillings, nine pence is a great deal of money and should have been deposited in a bank.

CATHERINE: How were we supposed to keep money in a bank? We were constantly moving around the countryside. It was a traveling circus, remember?

MARY: They were still owed for the last fortnight, but

we didn't know if they would be able to collect
that money from Lorenzo, since they hadn't given
proper notice. And now we had six mouths to feed!
Or five, as Beatrice did not count—what she did
could scarcely be called eating. She seemed to live
off sunlight, weeds, and the occasional insect.
But Catherine ate only meat, Justine ate no meat
at all, and Diana ate everything and a great deal
of it. I needed to find beds for Catherine and Justine
in addition to the one I had already found for Diana,
and the bed for Justine had to be seven feet long,
or she would inevitably bump her head. Diana was
already in the old nursery. I put Catherine in my
mother's room, and Justine slept in what had once
been my father's bedroom. If we built up the bed
with enough pillows so she could lie at an angle,
it was long enough for her—just. The governess's
room, where Nurse Adams had been sleeping, was
still empty. But that was all the bedrooms I had.
If creations of the Société des Alchimistes kept
showing up, I would have to start putting them on
the third floor, in the servants' rooms. Mrs. Poole
occupied what had once been the butler's apartment,
in the basement next to the kitchen, which Poole
and his wife had inhabited while they were alive.
Beatrice, of course, slept in the office next to my
father's laboratory. The day before, I had lost three
dresses and a pair of boots. That morning, I once
again had to find enough dresses for all of us to wear.
I wondered how we were all to be fed and clothed
and housed.

Catherine wishes to write about our adventures,

to leave out the domestic details. "This is not a manual of household management," she says. That would be something: a manual of household management for monsters!

MRS. POOLE: And very useful it would have been in those early days, I can tell you! How was I to make a broth with no meat in it for Justine? I'd never heard of such a thing!

The next morning, Justine was ill and feverish. "She'll have to stay in bed," said Mrs. Poole. "The rest of you can go gallivanting around the city all you like, but Miss Justine needs rest, and if she doesn't get it, she'll become sicker yet."

"I would scarcely call escaping from Wolf Men gallivanting, Mrs. Poole," said Catherine. "We were running for our lives, you know."

"Are there any more eggs?" asked Diana.

"No, not cooked, so you'll have to fill up on toast and marmalade. That stomach of yours is like a bottomless pit! You don't see Miss Beatrice asking for seconds, do you?"

"She barely asks for firsts," Diana muttered.

"And as for gallivanting, I'm sure you'll be doing it again today, instead of staying at home as you ought to. There's more than enough to do here. You'll need dresses, so there's plenty of sewing to be done."

"Sewing!" said Catherine, with an expression of disgust.

"But we have a mystery to solve," said Mary. They had already discussed the details of that mystery over breakfast, from Mary's meeting with Mr. Guest to the murder of Molly Keane, the rescue of Beatrice and their slow piecing together of information about the Alchemical Society. . . . Catherine had listened with keen interest.

"Which you could leave to Mr. Holmes and the police, who are after all paid to solve such things." Mrs. Poole said "such things" in the tone she might have used to describe a dead rat.

"I'm going to check on Justine," said Beatrice. "Before Mrs. Poole called me down for breakfast, she was running a fever, and she didn't seem to know where she was. She kept turning her head on the pillow, calling for her father. I think all this has been too much for her."

"Should I come with you?" asked Catherine.

"No, eat," Beatrice replied. "You were sitting up with her most of the night. You should rest too, you know."

Beatrice had flitted out of the room like a beautiful ghost, and Diana had crammed the rest of the toast into her mouth, when the front doorbell rang. A minute later, Mrs. Poole showed Holmes and Watson into the morning room.

"So sorry to interrupt your breakfast, Miss Jekyll, ladies," said Watson with a bow.

"Yes, yes," said Holmes, who was obviously not sorry at all. "Shall we begin? There are lines of investigation I would like to pursue today, but I wanted to consult with you ladies first. We were with Lestrade earlier this morning."

"Would you like some tea, Dr. Watson?" asked Mary. "Mrs. Poole just brought up a fresh pot."

"Thank you," said Watson. "And I should go check on my patient."

"Beatrice just went up," said Mary, pouring tea into the cup that Beatrice had not used and handing it to him. "Do drink this first. I know what it's like when you're investigating. If you were with Inspector Lestrade earlier, you probably haven't even breakfasted yet. Mr. Holmes? Tea? Or would you prefer coffee? I'm sure Mrs. Poole could make some." But Holmes was obviously not interested in tea or coffee. He sat down impatiently and said,

"Miss Frankenstein's collapse last night prevented us from telling you about our interviews with the families and friends of the murdered women—or four of them, since Pauline Delacroix had only recently arrived in London. She was a French lady's maid who had been serving in St. James's Place. Her mistress dismissed her without a reference, so she was forced to make her way on the streets. She had no family in this country, and had not been in London long enough to make friends. The woman who ran the boarding-house where she lived could tell us almost nothing about her. But the four others, including the most recent victim, Susanna Moore, had all been recent inmates of the Magdalen Society. Some only for a few days, one—Sally Hayward, the first victim—for several months."

"All four of them? That's too many to be a coincidence," said Mary. "Diana, do you remember hearing any of those names while you were at the Magdalen Society? Anna Pettingill was the other one, I believe, and of course poor Molly Keane."

"I never paid attention to their names," said Diana, putting more sugar into her tea before slurping it down. "They all looked and sounded alike. But I always knew there was something rotten about that place! Well, I'm ready to go back and search for clues."

"You can't," said Mary. "They already know you there. What we need is someone who can get in without arousing suspicion, who can search around. Someone in disguise."

"I'll go," said Catherine. "They don't know me, and I met enough prostitutes when I lived on the streets that I can convince them I'm one. But I'll need Diana—not to go in!" Diana, who had sat up at the possibility of going as well, hunched down in her chair again and frowned. "I'll need her to be my contact outside. You know all the hallways, right? And how to get in and out, over the wall? I assume there's a wall—there always is. And where the director's office is located? I'll need to know where to look. . . ."

"Just a moment," said Watson. He leaned against the wall rather than taking the only remaining chair, at Mrs. Jekyll's desk. "We weren't implying that you ladies should participate in this investigation. I know you're brave, but this is getting far too dangerous. Yesterday, you were attacked. Let the police handle it, or at least leave it to me and Holmes!"

"But you can't get in," said Mary in her most reasonable voice. "Men aren't allowed into the Magdalen Society, and by the time the police force their way into the building, the director could destroy any evidence she might have, anything that might connect her to these poor women, if indeed she is guilty of wrongdoing. I think we proved yesterday that we can take care of ourselves." She remembered Mrs. Raymond's grim face. Could she be connected to these murders, or to the Société des Alchimistes?

"She has a point, Watson," said Holmes, smiling. "And I must admit, I was hoping Miss Jekyll would suggest some useful way of investigating from the inside, where you and I can't go. However, I understand your concern. Therefore, I suggest you accompany Miss Moreau and Miss Hyde as their protector. You can assure yourself in person as to their safety, although I'm afraid you'll have to stay outside the gates."

"That's scarcely reassuring," said Watson. He gulped the rest of his tea. "All right, I'm going up to check on Miss Frankenstein. You mentioned that Miss Rappaccini is up there?"

"Yes," said Mary, amused. Were men always so obvious in their attentions? No, not all men. Mr. Holmes would certainly not be obvious—if, indeed, he paid attention to women at all, as women that is! He seemed to treat women as though they were men in skirts, either useful in his investigations or not.

Watson nodded and put his teacup on the table, then left the morning room, almost too eagerly to be strictly polite.

"And what about me, Mr. Holmes?" said Mary, turning to the detective. "There is another line of inquiry I'd like to pursue." If it was going to be all about investigations, well, let them investigate!

"What is that, Miss Jekyll?"

"I'd like to return to Purfleet. As we left after Renfield's arrest, he recognized Diana. I don't know if you remember, but he told her to tell her father that he had done . . . whatever he was supposed to. Is it possible that he might once have seen Hyde? Or had some dealings with him? And Dr. Balfour said something that didn't strike me until later—he said it was a pity that a respectable man of science should fall into madness. I would like to know what sort of scientist Renfield was, and what drove him mad."

"I can see what you're implying, Miss Jekyll," said Holmes. "Was Renfield in some way involved with the Société des Alchimistes? I don't know if Dr. Balfour can throw light on these matters, but he seems to know something about Renfield's past. I was considering another visit to Purfleet myself. This would be a good day for a trip to the country, I think."

"And I'll come with you," said Mrs. Poole, who had brought in a tray with more buttered toast. "Miss Jekyll of Park Terrace can't go wandering off to Purfleet with a single gentleman, Mr. Holmes. Not even one as celebrated as yourself."

"Mrs. Poole, that's ridiculous," said Mary. "This is the 1890s. Men and women can sit in a railway carriage together, I should think, without accusations of impropriety."

"Not ladies and gentlemen," said Mrs. Poole.

Holmes laughed. "I shall be delighted to have your company, Mrs. Poole," he said. "I'm sure you'll make a charming chaperone."

A chaperone! How absolutely mortifying. For a moment, Mary

was almost angry with Mrs. Poole. Then she reminded herself that she was eating the breakfast Mrs. Poole had cooked, in the house Mrs. Poole had cleaned. She owed so much to the housekeeper. Still, a chaperone . . . It did not help that Mr. Holmes was still smiling at the idea.

"And what shall I do?" asked Beatrice, who was standing by the door. She had come in so quietly that they had not noticed. "Dr. Watson is with Justine. She's finally gone to sleep, thank goodness. He says to tell you that she is in no danger, although she must have absolute rest and quiet until the fever breaks. He mentioned your plans. If you are all planning on being out today, and Mrs. Poole accompanies Mary to Purfleet, I believe I had better stay here. Justine needs a nurse, and my poison is still strong. I should not go out in public again until I am—'normal' is perhaps not the right word. Fortunately, my breath cannot harm Justine. Even weakened as she is, she remains stronger than any ordinary woman. My touch would burn her skin, but I will wear gloves."

"Then we shall be fielding three teams, as it were," said Holmes. "Miss Moreau, Miss Hyde, and Watson shall go to Whitechapel; Miss Jekyll and Mrs. Poole shall accompany me to Purfleet; and you, Miss Rappaccini, shall stay here with Miss Frankenstein."

"Catherine will need to be in disguise," said Mary. "She can't go to the Magdalen Society looking like that. She needs to look like—well, a fallen woman."

They all looked at Catherine. This morning, she was wearing one of Mary's day dresses, a brown tartan with a pleated collar. Her hair was pulled back into a chignon at the nape of her neck. Aside from her yellow eyes and the tracery of scars, she looked like a schoolmistress.

"You're never going to fool old Ma Raymond dressed like that," said Diana. "You need to look fancy, with flounces and furbelows— but cheap. And you need paint."

Flounces and furbelows, as though for a woman of the streets! How in the world could Mary supply those? There was really only one possibility. "Come up to my mother's room," she said. "I may have something."

Catherine and Diana followed her up the stairs, while Holmes and Watson waited below and Mrs. Poole assured them that the girls would be back down in a moment, that matters of dress took time.

In Mrs. Jekyll's wardrobe, Mary found an old tea gown of her mother's, at least ten years out of date. It was the only thing she could think of that was fancy enough for Catherine to wear. "It doesn't quite fit," said Catherine. "A former mistress of mine could have given it to me before I was dismissed and forced to make my living on the streets, like Pauline Delacroix. That's what I'll tell Mrs. Raymond."

"She still needs paint, and her hair done," said Diana.

"Well, I don't know where to buy paint—a theatrical shop of some sort?" said Mary impatiently. What was she, a department store?

"No, you need it put on by someone who knows how. Like Kate Bright-Eyes."

"Kate is the one who knew Molly Keane?" said Catherine. She turned around in front of the mirror, examining herself from all angles. For a moment, Mary felt a pang of guilt—it was, after all, her mother's gown, even though it had not been worn for many years. But surely her mother had wanted her to find out about the Société des Alchimistes, or why had she saved the letters in the portfolio? That information had been left for Mary, she was sure of it.

"Yes, that's Kate," said Mary. "I suppose you could go to The Bells and ask for her?"

"Ha! You see, I do come up with clever ideas!" said Diana.

"All right, that was clever," said Mary. "But is it absolutely necessary for you to dress like that? Catherine needs to be in disguise. You don't."

While Mary had been searching for her mother's tea gown and helping Catherine put it on, Diana had once again changed into boy's clothes. Mary could not help wishing that she looked more, well, respectable.

"Catherine said I might have to climb, and it's easier climbing as a boy." Diana put her hands in her trouser pockets. It was obvious that she was not going to change, nohow.

> DIANA: Respectable my arse! Why would anyone want to wear girls' clothes unless they had to? If you walk around the city as a boy, people don't notice you or ask what you're doing all by yourself, my pretty.

> MARY: Cat, you said you would edit out inappropriate language.

> CATHERINE: I think "my arse" is perfectly appropriate in this context. And I agree with Diana.

Mary was annoyed, sitting in the railway carriage on the way to Purfleet. She had wanted to discuss the case with Mr. Holmes, and instead he was engaged in a discussion with Mrs. Poole on the minutiae of housekeeping! On how various stains set and were to be gotten out, the schedules of tradespeople and their deliveries. He seemed fascinated by these domestic details. "You never know when the most trivial information might help solve a case," he said. "I myself, Mrs. Poole, have written a monograph on the soils around London. Did you know, for example, that there is a distinct difference between the soils of Spitalfields and Shoreditch?"

"Is there really, sir? I would not have thought it!" said Mrs. Poole, and received a disquisition on types of cigarette ash that seemed to fascinate her.

The asylum looked just as Mary remembered, with its brick wall and tall iron gates, over which she could see the tops of the trees. But this time, there was no Joe Abernathy to let them in.

"No, sir," said the attendant who came to answer the bell, when Holmes asked his whereabouts. "He was sacked, along with Dr. Balfour and a whole lot of others, on account of Renfield escaping. Dr. Seward was right angry about it. He was in Vienner, or some such place, and took a train back as soon as he heard about the murders. He arrived yesterday morning and sent everyone who had to do with Renfield packing. He's the one you'll have to see, if you want information. He's with another gentleman right now—I just let him in, a gentleman from London. But I'll ask if you can talk to him. What name should I give?"

"Well, that explains why Dr. Balfour didn't respond to my telegram," Holmes whispered to Mary. They waited in the front hall while the attendant confirmed that Dr. Seward would see Mr. Holmes briefly—although he did not have much time, they were warned. Then they were shown up the stairs to the direc-tor's office. As they came to the door, it opened, and a man with a shock of gray hair stepped out. He seemed agitated and almost ran into Holmes. "Pardon me," he said, then nodded to them curtly.

This office was very different from Dr. Balfour's. It had obvi-ously been used for a long time, but was considerably neater. The shelves were filled with books, and there were documents and letters stacked on the desk. Mary wondered if the letter from Professor Van Helsing had been missed.

"Mr. Holmes, to what do I owe the pleasure of this visit?" said the man behind the desk, sounding as though it was not a pleasure at all. He had a grim, official look about him, and was clearly impatient for them to be gone again.

"Dr. Seward, I presume?" said Holmes.

"Indeed. I can spare you fifteen minutes, but I'm sure you'll understand that we're very busy this morning. You know, I'm sure, that the madman Renfield has escaped from police custody. We don't know if he intends to return here. I've asked Inspector Lestrade to send us policemen, but they have not yet arrived. Oh damn!"

Mary jumped, but this last exclamation was not meant for them. Seward sprang up and grabbed a furled umbrella that had been leaning against the side of his desk. Then he strode to his office door, opened it, and shouted down the hall, "Sam! Sam, Mr. Prendick left his umbrella." Sam must have come back to retrieve it, because Dr. Seward stepped out into the hallway, and Mary heard, "Can you run and give it to him before he catches the train? Yes, thank you, that will be all for now. I'll ring for you when you can let Mr. Holmes out."

Prendick! She would have to tell Catherine as soon as possible. How would Catherine feel, knowing that the man who had left her to die was not only alive, but here in London?

"My apologies," he said, coming back into the office. "Particularly to the ladies . . ." He looked at Mary and Mrs. Poole, clearly wondering who the devil they were and why they had come to see him.

Before Holmes could speak, Mary hastily said, "That's quite all right, Dr. Seward. I'm Miss Jenks, of the Christian Women's Missionary Society, and this is my associate Mrs. Poole. Our society is concerned with saving women who have fallen into sin. Several of the women who were so brutally murdered were on our rolls, as having received assistance from our society, and our patroness, whose name I may not mention, but who is connected with the royal family, insisted that we be allowed to accompany Mr. Holmes. I hope our presence will not interfere with your conversation in any way. We are here simply to observe, and will be as quiet as church mice."

"Miss Jenks and Mrs. Poole were of course most welcome to accompany me," said Holmes. "*Cum mulieribus non est disputandum,* as Cicero says."

"I see," said Seward. His mouth twitched, and he looked at Holmes with sympathy. "Now, tell me what you wish to know about Renfield."

DIANA: Translation, please, for those of us who didn't go to Oxford.

JUSTINE: "There is no arguing with women." And I don't believe Cicero ever said such a thing!

"Anything you can tell me," said Holmes. "His history, his past associations. Did he ever receive visitors? Miss Jenks, do you have paper and a pencil? Perhaps you could make yourself useful and take some notes."

"Of course, Mr. Holmes," said Mary. Did she have those things? A pencil, yes—but paper? Silently, Mrs. Poole opened her capacious handbag, pulled out a pad of paper, and handed it to Mary. For the first time, she felt grateful for Mrs. Poole's presence—then guilty for not having appreciated it before. She flipped past pages of marketing lists. "Is there anything in particular you would like me to note down?"

"Anything of interest that could bear on this investigation. You're an observant young woman, I'm sure." Holmes said this courteously, carelessly, as though simply giving her something to do. Mary looked around the office without seeming to. What did he want her to notice? Or was she mistaken, and did he want her simply to write down what Dr. Seward had to say?

But Seward could, or would, tell them almost nothing. Renfield has once been, "believe it or not, considering his present state," a gentleman, a man of business in the city. His business had begun to fail, and the strain of it had been too much for him. Eventually, he had developed the habits that marked his madness. He had neither wife nor children, and his business partners, fearing for his safety, had him committed to Purfleet Asylum. His fees were paid quarterly by the business. He had never, in all the years he had been in the asylum, received visitors. That was all Seward knew. "Of course, he came here under my predecessor. I myself am relatively new here—I became director only five years ago, whereas some of the patients have been here twenty years. Which is why this incident—well, I've been called before the Board of Trustees. So you can understand why I'm so eager, Mr. Holmes, to have Renfield caught and returned to us. I'm afraid there's nothing more I can tell you. Renfield left no papers or other effects, except some notebooks containing what he called his accounts. Nothing but numbers. I'll have Sam show them to you before you leave."

When he bid them farewell, he added, "I hope you and Inspector Lestrade will do your upmost to catch him, Mr. Holmes. My professional career depends on his return. And the best of luck to you, Miss Jenks, in your good work. What did you say your organization was called again? Perhaps I could send a donation."

What in the world had she called it? Mary hesitated for a moment.

"Thank you, indeed, sir," said Mrs. Poole. "These young women come to us blackened by sin, but by prayer and good works they are washed as white as lambs of God. By which I mean their souls, sir. God may hate the sin, but he loves the sinner, and we hope to see these young women seated at the right hand of the Father when their souls are washed clean. Also, we give them hot soup. Hot soup and prayer, sir, will do it every time. Perhaps we can send you some tracts and a request for a subscription. . . ."

"Yes, yes, quite," said Seward hastily. "Allow me to show you out. I'm sure you must wish to be in London again as quickly as possible, to continue your good works."

Before they left, Sam showed them Renfield's notebooks, but Seward had been right: they contained nothing but rows of numbers—presumably representing the flies he had caught and ingested. Nothing to help them in their investigation.

After they had walked through the front gates of the asylum, which clanged shut behind them, Mary pulled the pad of paper on which she had been writing out of her purse. She had stuffed it in there when they left Dr. Seward's office, but her purse was not as capacious as Mrs. Poole's. She had been worried it might not come out again.

"Is this what you wanted?" she asked.

"Ah, I wondered if you would see it!" said Holmes. "Bravo, Miss Jenks. I memorized the name and location of the hotel in Soho, but it's useful to have your written confirmation. And how clever of you to transcribe the letter as well."

"Whatever are you going on about?" asked Mrs. Poole.

Mary showed her the notebook. On a sheet of paper, she had written,

> *Stationary headed Deerborne Hotel, Soho.*
> *Address too small to make out.*
> *My dear John, I will come as soon as I can, but I know*
> *no more about these murders than you do. Why should I?*
> *Surely you and Van Helsing don't suspect me of being*
> *involved in any way. That is absurd and unjust of you.*

Let me know when you arrive and I will come to Purfleet,
but I swear to you that I know nothing whatsoever.
Edward

"It was upside down, but not too difficult to make out, except for the address," said Mary. "Although all these scientific men seem to have atrocious handwriting! My governess, Miss Murray, would have made them write out a section of Wordsworth's *Tintern Abbey*——that's what she made me do, to correct my hand. This must be the Edward Prendick mentioned in Catherine's story and Professor Van Helsing's letter?"

"Certainly," said Holmes. "I don't know if you saw his face as we passed, Miss Jekyll, but his hair was not gray from age. Whatever he has endured, it has marked him forever."

No, she had not noticed Prendick's face. Mary felt a sense of consternation. She simply must become more observant, like Mr. Holmes.

"I believe our next course of action is to return to London and pay a visit to Mr. Prendick," Holmes added. "Clearly Dr. Seward thought he was involved with the murders in some way, and Miss Moreau indicated that he knew how to make the Beast Men you encountered yesterday. If we had been more precipitous, we might have run into him casually on the train, but that is his train departing now, and we are not on it." Sure enough, Mary could hear the train whistle, and there was a line of white smoke against the sky, across the marshes that separated the asylum from the train station.

"If we can't catch Mr. Prendick anyway, I think there's one more line of investigation here in Purfleet," she said. "What about Joe Abernathy? He's known Renfield longer than Dr. Seward, and he was there when Renfield escaped. He must live somewhere in the village."

"Also, he has just lost his position, and will not be feeling particularly loyal to Dr. Seward," said Holmes. "An excellent suggestion, Miss Jekyll. And I must say, that was masterfully done, Mrs. Poole."

"Ah well, thank you sir," said Mrs. Poole, looking embarrassed. "I was in amateur theatricals when I was a girl. We used to have a sort of club, just among the servants in Park Terrace. Used to call ourselves the Park Terrace Players, and put on Shakespeare as well as popular plays like *The Scottish Lass* and *Maid of the Moors*. I was Titania, once."

Mary tried to imagine the respectable Mrs. Poole as Titania, queen of the fairies, but to this imagination would not stretch.

MRS. POOLE: I was a very good Titania, I'll have you know!

BEATRICE: I have no doubt you were, Mrs. Poole.

How to find Joe was the next question, but Holmes said, "Always ask at the pub, Miss Jekyll. Elementary investigation—the pub always knows. And there I see The Black Dog, so we shall step inside. . . ."

"That she will not," said Mrs. Poole. "You may go where you like, Mr. Holmes, but I will not have her setting foot in a place where men are drinking and ogling, like as not."

"Oh, for goodness' sake," said Mary. Diana was right, it was better to dress as a man. She had never before found being a woman confining, but then she had never attempted to investigate a series of murders before either. She had never attempted much of anything. And now she was finding that as soon as one began moving around in the world, doing things, one ran up against a regular list of You Shan'ts.

"Then I shall return in a moment," said Holmes, and disappeared into the dark maw of The Black Dog. It was closer to a half hour before he returned, and Mary and Mrs. Poole had walked around the central square of Purfleet, looking into all the shop windows—at the hams on display at the butcher's, the buns at the baker's, the ribbons and gloves at a shop for ladies' accoutrements.

"Joe lives with his mother in one of the cottages recently built for workingmen, on a road called Peaceful Row," he told them. "I suppose the builders thought that name might avert strikes among the quarry workers! Miss Jekyll, should you ever find yourself in a pub, despite Mrs. Poole's care, never ask a question directly, for you will never get an answer. I bought a pint and said I had come from the asylum, where I was thinking of confining a relative. But I didn't know if I wanted him in an institution, and might look for a man to care for him privately. I wondered if any employees of the asylum might prefer a private situation and was told that several had lost their positions, including Joe. They were almost pressing his address on me, and I promised that I would go see him as soon as possible."

"How clever of you, sir," said Mrs. Poole.

Well! thought Mary. *I would have been just as clever, if I'd been allowed into the pub. I could have told them that I had a poor mad father, or that my brother was in the asylum and Joe had been caring for him. I could have told them any number of things. . . .* What was the use of propriety when it kept one from getting things done?

They had to pass the asylum gates again, taking care not to be seen—but no one was watching. Peaceful Row was just off the main road, a paved street with modern cottages arranged neatly on either side, each with its own small garden. Joe Abernathy's cottage was at the end of the street, before the pavement turned into a path and wandered across fields filled with clover and buttercups. Several cows looked at them curiously, then went back to tearing up mouthfuls of grass. The cottage was surrounded by a garden in which vegetables grew among the flowers. Several hens scratched in the dirt. To one side of the cottage, a woman was hanging laundry on a line.

"Pardon me," said Holmes. "Mrs. Abernathy?"

"Aye, I'm she," said the woman, wiping her hands on her apron and approaching the fence. "And who might you be, sir?" She looked at him warily, as though he might be selling some sort of patented medicine or mechanical broom.

"I'm Sherlock Holmes, and I've come to talk to Joe," said the detective. He waited, but if he expected her to recognize the name, he was disappointed. She merely nodded and said, "I'll see if he's in." She walked through the side door, then came out again a moment later.

"Aye, he says to go on in. You'll forgive me, sir. What with this lunatic escaping, and then losing his position over it, he's not wanting to see many people just now. Especially not newspaper men, and you have that look about you."

"I'll stay out here, I think," said Mrs. Poole. "You have a way with the linen, ma'am. I've never seen pillowcases so white. What do you bleach them in?"

"Oh, well, I make my own washing powder, but it's the lavender as does it. I lay them out on lavender to dry . . . ," said Mrs. Abernathy, visibly pleased.

"There goes my vanity, Miss Jekyll," said Holmes as they walked through the garden, avoiding the hens, which did not move out of their way. "The look of a newspaper man indeed! But our Mrs. Poole is proving invaluable. She is a mistress of the art of distraction."

The side door led directly into the kitchen, which was spotlessly clean. Joe was sitting at the table, reading a newspaper. When they entered, he looked up.

"Well, if it isn't you, miss! Mother told me Mr. Holmes had some ladies with him, but I didn't expect one of them to be you. What a pleasure to see you again. I'm just reading about old Renfield's escape. You know I lost my position over this affair? Although how they expected me to prevent it, when the man can escape from a police wagon, I don't know. He must be a magician!"

"Well, I don't know about that," said Holmes. "He may have been helped. That's what we've come to talk to you about, to see if Renfield had any associates."

"Associates? I don't know what kind of associates you would be meaning. He was mostly locked up in the asylum. But when he run away, which he did regular, he could have formed associates that helped him escape."

"Dr. Seward said he was a businessman before he became mad," said Mary. "Could he have had business associates, perhaps? Anyone he knew from his life before? Did he ever receive visitors?"

"No, never a visitor. I didn't know he was a businessman. That must be why he kept writing numbers down, as though keeping accounts. Of the flies he was eating, you know, and how much life they were giving him. Although he called them his experiments. He would go on about those experiments of his, how each fly gave him so much life and no more. He wanted to know how much life he could get out of them, and then how much if he fed them to spiders and ate the spiders, and then how much if the spiders were eaten by birds—but we never let it get past spiders, which he could catch himself. 'I'll show them,' he would say to me. 'Someday, Joe, I'll show them my note-books, and then they'll have to take me back. They can't deny me the secret of life.' But when I asked him who would take him back, and who was denying him the secret of life, whatever that might be, he would cringe and whine, saying they would kill him straight away if he told anyone. But that was all part of his madness, miss."

"Yes, although there is often a method in madness," said Mary. "Do you remember anything else he used to say?"

"No, that was about all. Just the flies, and the spiders eating the flies, and then the birds, and he wanted a cat. That's what he wanted most, a cat to eat the birds, and he would eat the cat, I presume. And get life from it."

Before they left, Holmes insisted on giving Joe a half-crown. "Thank you, sir," said Joe. "And if I think of anything else, I'll let you know. I hope they deal with old Renfield kindly when they catch him. I don't believe he murdered those women. He was always a gentle soul, excepting to spiders and flies."

Holmes and Mary walked away from Joe's house in a thoughtful mood. "You're both awfully quiet," said Mrs. Poole, tucking away the recipe for homemade washing powder that Mrs. Abernathy had given her.

"Do you think——?" said Mary, looking at Holmes.

"I think it's a distinct possibility," he said. "You were right, everyone does seem to belong to this blasted society. If Renfield was once a member . . ."

"He might know some of the others," said Mary. "Although if he had once been a member, surely Dr. Seward would have been aware of it? We know he's a member himself."

"Ah, that Dr. Seward was lying through his teeth," said Mrs. Poole. "You can always tell when people are lying. It's when they look at you too straight, as though they were angels here on Earth. And indignant, as though they can't believe you would doubt them."

"Perhaps," said Holmes. "If he knew that Renfield was once a member of the Alchemical Society, he would certainly have reason to lie."

It was a perfect spring day, not raining for once, and as they walked back to the train station, Mary imagined they were simply three people going for a walk in a country town. The sun shone down on the cottages and shops of Purfleet, and in the gardens she could see poppies and the tall blue spikes of larkspur. But then she remembered Molly Keane, dead on the streets of Whitechapel, lying in a pool of her own blood. It could not make her enjoy the day less, but it reminded her that there were still murders to investigate.

CHAPTER XIV

The Twisted Man

Mary wondered if the train ride back to London would be like the one that morning. Would Holmes spend it discussing domestic details with Mrs. Poole? But no, he and Mary went over the details of the case. If Renfield had not killed those women, who had? Evidence seemed to indicate that it was someone connected with the Société des Alchimistes, but whom? Dr. Seward's letter had made clear that he had no knowledge of the murders—indeed, he was alarmed by them. But it was also clear that there were various factions in the society. Could this be the work of a faction that opposed Seward and his friends? Who then were they? It seemed as though they were in contact with Renfield, without Seward's knowledge.

"So on the one hand," said Mary, "we have my father, Dr. Rappaccini, and Dr. Moreau, who all knew each other, and who are all dead. And then we have Dr. Seward and his friend Professor Van Helsing, who knows Mr. Prendick, who knew Dr. Moreau! And then we have Renfield, and the implication that he may at one time have seen Hyde. Three different groups of people. Are they friends? Enemies? In league with one another? And who among them would be murdering women? Beatrice said it was an ancient experiment, the same process that had created Frankenstein's monster a hundred years ago. Why would anyone want to re-create that?"

"Then there is the question of whether this is all connected to the Magdalen Society," said Holmes. "Is it merely a coincidence that four of the murdered women had been inmates of the society? I wonder whether Miss Moreau has any information for us. Perhaps there will be a message when we return."

"What about Mr. Prendick?" asked Mary. "Don't we need to find him—and follow him? Deerborne Hotel in Soho. It shouldn't be hard to find."

"Oh no, you don't," said Mrs. Poole. "Neither of you seems to have noticed that you haven't eaten anything since breakfast. First we go back to the house—it's almost tea time. Anyway, you need to check for messages, don't you? And then you can go following whoever you please."

But when they arrived at 11 Park Terrace, there was no message. As soon as they stepped out of the cab from the station, Mrs. Poole said, "The door's open." And sure enough, the front door was almost imperceptibly open, as though it had been closed by a person who was not very careful.

"Beatrice! Justine!" Mary called as soon as they entered the house. Her words echoed down the hall. There was no response. Then all three of them called, even the respectable Mrs. Poole, who as far as Mary knew had never shouted before in her life.

> MRS. POOLE: Of course I've shouted before. I'm human, aren't I?

> DIANA: Scolded isn't the same as shouted.

There was no response. The house was empty—except, of course, for the Beast Man lying on the floor of Justine's room, but being dead, he scarcely counted. Mary almost tripped over him when she ran upstairs, in a panic, to see why Beatrice, at least, wasn't answering. She screamed just a little, more in surprise than fright, when she saw him on the carpet. The sound brought Mrs. Poole and Holmes upstairs after her. She stood in the entrance to the room, looking at the dead Beast Man. He lay amid a tangle of bed curtains—someone, whether a Beast Man or Justine, had torn them from the bed. And the rest of the room was a shambles. Chairs were overturned, the shaving stand had been knocked over, and its mirror was covered with a spiderweb of cracks. The clock and spill vase had been swept off the mantelpiece. They lay, smashed into pieces, on the hearth.

"Dear Lord," said Mrs. Poole.

"They put up a fight," said Mary. She did not know what else to say.

"They did indeed," said Holmes. "Look at this man's face. Although man is a generous term to use for him. Judging by his hairiness and the shape and size of his teeth, he was once a bear. He seems clumsily made. I wonder . . . well, no time for speculation now."

On his cheeks, the Bear Man had two marks, as though he had been grasped by two red hands.

"That must have been Beatrice," said Mary. "She told us her touch could burn."

Holmes walked around the room, examining the overturned furniture, the tangled curtains. "I want to go outside and check for footprints. No, Miss Jekyll, you may not come with me." Mary opened her mouth to protest. "More of them may be lurking about. So, if you please."

She shut her mouth again, but was not in fact pleased. If there were Beast Men lurking about, two together would be safer than one. And surely she could be of help? But Holmes was already gone. She waited impatiently as Mrs. Poole walked around the room, surveying the damage. "Look at this clock. It came with your mother when she married your father, all the way from Yorkshire. It stood on this mantle for more than twenty years, and I was always grateful, miss, that you couldn't sell it because it ran a bit slow. Well, it won't be keeping time now, that's for certain."

"Surely that's less important than Justine and Beatrice?" said Mary.

"Of course it is," said Mrs. Poole, reproachfully. "But we can't do anything about them at the moment, can we? Do what you can, as my mother used to say, and leave the rest to God. Or Mr. Holmes, as the case may be."

"I would never arrogate to myself the powers of the deity, Mrs. Poole," said Holmes. He reentered the bedroom with his long stride. "There were five of them, including our dead friend. Three wearing boots, two with feet too deformed for human footwear. All their gaits are irregular, as though they were shuffling. I saw their footprints clearly in the mud on the sidewalk, five coming and four going, although they ended at the bottom of the road, where I believe they had a carriage waiting. Going, there is a mark as of someone being hurried along and half dragged, no clear prints, but the foot is smaller than the others. Perhaps one of the ladies was dragged and the other was carried."

"Beatrice must have killed the Bear Man, but she couldn't have handled five," said Mary. "And Justine was too sick to fight back."

"I think Justine must have done some fighting too, nevertheless," said Holmes. "Otherwise there wouldn't be so much damage."

"We need to summon the police," said Mrs. Poole.

"No," said Mary. "The police would never believe us. What would we say? You need to look for a poisonous girl and a woman who is over six feet tall, because they've been kidnapped by a bunch of Beast Men?"

"Miss Jekyll is right," said Holmes. "Lestrade would laugh in our faces. We need to send Watson a message, and find Prendick.

All the clues indicate that Miss Rappaccini and Miss Frankenstein were kidnapped by Beast Men, and Prendick knows how to make Beast Men. You'll need to stay here, Mrs. Poole, in case the others return or try to contact us. And Miss Jekyll . . ."

"I'm not staying here," said Mary. "I'm coming with you. Proper or not, I want to find out what happened to Beatrice and Justine."

"You go right ahead, miss," said Mrs. Poole. "Two heads are better than one, they say. I'll straighten up here."

"If you see Charlie," said Holmes, "send him on to Watson with this message: 'Miss Rappaccini and Miss Frankenstein have been kidnapped, and we've gone to find Prendick in Soho, at the Deerborne Hotel.' He may have simply gotten the stationary there, but hopefully he'll be staying either at the hotel or close by. Come on, Miss Jekyll. We haven't had our tea, but no rest for the wicked, as they say—or for detectives either!"

Together, they set out for Soho. At the last minute, Mrs. Poole had handed Mary a tea cake, saying, "You have to eat something, miss. Otherwise, you'll faint, and what sort of help will you be to Mr. Holmes then?" Mary walked quickly, the uneaten tea cake in the pocket of her mackintosh, worried about the two girls. Where were they? Would they be all right? She had only known them for a few days, but already they felt like family, as though they belonged together.

BEATRICE: As we do.

MARY: Despite our differences.

BEATRICE: Or because of them.

Meanwhile, Catherine had spent that afternoon sewing. Kate Bright-Eyes had done wonders. At The Bells, where they found her, she had worked on Catherine's face and hair. "I have all my things here," she told them. "After what happened to Molly, I can't live alone anymore. I get nightmares! So I'm renting a room at the inn, though it's twice as much as my old lodgings. You're a brave one, Miss Moreau. I wouldn't go into that society, knowing the girls who died had been there, not for a hundred pounds. There, how does that look?" Catherine looked at herself in the cracked mirror that hung in Kate's room. The powder Kate had put on her face and neck covered the scars. In the mirror, she saw rouged lips and cheeks, and a great deal of hair, not all of it her own. Yes, it would do just fine.

Of course, as soon as she arrived at the Magdalen Society, Mrs. Raymond had told her, rather sharply, to wash her face and rearrange her hair. She had wiped off the rouge—it had done its work, which was convincing Mrs. Raymond that she was in need of salvation. But she had not touched the powder, which was the color of her skin anyway. "It's what actresses use," Kate had told her. "You're a bit darker than most of us, ain't you? But I think it will do." With it, she looked . . . entirely human. She liked looking human. And then she had gone to the workroom.

If you asked Catherine what she likes less than sewing, she would say being shut up in a cage, in a ship's hold, for weeks while that ship sails across the Pacific Ocean to a mysterious island. Or, on that island, being transformed from an animal into a woman without the benefit of anesthesia. But that might be it. She would prefer eating rats on the streets of London or being chased by Wolf Men.

MARY: Must you be so melodramatic?

And she is particularly bad at it. Perhaps it has to do with the fact that her hands were once paws, but she is unable to sew even a straight seam, as Sister Margaret reported to Mrs. Raymond.

"She's quite hopeless. I gave her a tea towel to hem, and look at it! Perhaps we can have her do something else—mop the floors, for instance." The new girl's yellow eyes made Sister Margaret nervous.

"We might put her in the cleaning crew, by and by," said Mrs. Raymond. "But for now, I want her under your supervision. There's something about her . . ." She pondered for a moment, then shook her head. "No, I can't place it, not yet. At any rate, I don't want her doing anything arduous. We don't want her to suddenly leave, do we? To return to the base luxury of her life on the streets, like those other girls? Poor Sally Hayward or Anna Pettingill? We want her to understand the value of what we offer here—the comfort and safety of the Magdalen Society. And get her a work dress as soon as possible. I don't want her going around in that ridiculous getup."

> DIANA: How do you know what they said? It's not as though you could hear them.

> CATHERINE: I did, actually. It was the first time I tried reconnoitering, but Mrs. Raymond was in her office. I was right outside the door and heard them. Anyway, it doesn't matter if I got the details exactly right. What matters is whether it makes for a good story.

Whatever Catherine was considering at that moment, it was not the comfort and safety of the Magdalen Society. Her thread had snapped again, which meant re-threading and making sure the new stitches continued imperceptibly from the old, while overlapping enough so that neither end would come loose.

"Why are we sewing, anyway?" she asked. "I don't see why we all have to be sewing. Aren't there other things we could be doing that would save our souls just as well?"

"Hush! Sister Margaret could return at any moment," said the girl sitting next to her. The girl's name was Doris, and she had pimples on her cheeks. She was only fifteen, and rather plump. It was difficult to tell that she had ever wandered the London streets. She looked like any servant girl from Mayfair or Marylebone. "The linens and clothes we sew are bought by charitable women, who buy them to support the society."

Catherine wondered whether her crooked tea towel, the second she had hemmed that day, would help the society. She rather thought not.

"I have a friend who was here, about a month ago," she said. "Her name was Molly Keane. Did you know her?"

"You knew Molly?" said the girl to the other side of Catherine. She was thin and sallow, with dark circles under her eyes. Catherine vaguely remembered that her name was Agnes. "Well, I never. Horrible what happened to her, wasn't it? It's a lesson on the wages of sin, as Mrs. Raymond always tells us."

"No chattering!" said Sister Margaret. They had not heard her come in, but she stood in front of them, pursing her mouth, which made it look as though she sucked limes for the fun of it. "Idle chatter is the Devil's work. Who would like to read to us from Reverend Throckmorton's sermons?"

And that's the problem right there, thought Catherine, ignoring the voice of Agnes, droning on about how Jesus had separated the sheep from the goats, and the lesson Reverend Throckmorton had derived from that text. *There's never any time to talk in this damned place. It's prayers and sermons and work, all day long.*

It had not been difficult to join the Magdalen Society. Mrs. Raymond had taken one look at her and assigned her a bed. Although she had said rather sharply, "I hope you understand that we expect all our girls to truly repent, Miss Montgomery."

"Oh, I will, I promise you," Catherine had replied. "You don't know how grateful I am for this opportunity, ma'am. It's rough on the streets, and after that sailor came at me with the broken bottle, I'd had enough, I can tell you! And my landlady said I wasn't paid up, so she wouldn't let me in the boardinghouse. And my da won't take me back—I'd taint all the other children, he says. All I have is the clothes on my back. I'm grateful you're willing to take me in."

"Well, you just behave yourself here," Mrs. Raymond had said with a frown. Catherine had nodded and signed in the big book, a large leather-bound volume in Mrs. Raymond's office where girls who had come before her had written their names or made their Xs next to the names written for them. She had signed: Catherine Montgomery. The first thing she would have to do was look at that book. She assumed it contained the names of all the girls who had stayed at the Magdalen Society. Catherine would see if the murdered girls were listed. And then? She wasn't sure. But whatever she did would have to wait until that night, when everyone was asleep. In the meantime, she had a seam to sew.

> DIANA: We were so bored waiting in the house across
> the street, me and Charlie. Dr. Watson didn't seem
> to mind. He read all the newspapers, for mentions of
> anything unusual, he said. Once, he pointed out that
> the animals stolen from Lord Avebury's menagerie
> were still missing. The search had been going on for
> a month, but they hadn't been found. "What do we
> care about a bunch of animals?" I asked him. But he
> said any missing animals could have been used to
> make Beast Men.

> CATHERINE: At least you didn't have to sew seams
> and listen to Agnes read sermons! Sister Margaret

had a whole book of them, by a Reverend
Throckmorton, whom she had once met and for
whom I'm convinced she had a secret passion.
They were about sheep and goats, and the saved
and damned, and how one would be saved and
the other damned forever. He seemed to have
something against goats. . . . After several hours
of listening to that, I was ready to rip her throat
out!

JUSTINE: It's not such a bad thing to learn about God.
I could not have lived all those years alone if it
were not for the spiritual lessons my father taught
me before he died. I find it comforting to believe
in a divine Father who observes and knows all.

CATHERINE: Oh, spare me! Religion is a tool some
men use to control others. I saw that myself on
Moreau's island.

DIANA: What Catherine said. If you had grown up in
that damned society . . .

BEATRICE: Please, we've had these arguments before.
Justine will never convince you, and you will
never convince Justine. Cat, go back to your story.
Our readers aren't interested in a theological
discussion.

At last, the bells announced that it was time for dinner. An
entire day of sitting in an unnatural position doing unnatural
work, listening to nonsense . . . Who actually needed tea towels,

anyway? Or the horrible pin-tucked children's smocks the more experienced sewers were making? Not children, who would rather run around naked, like animals or savages. And much healthier it would be for them too!

At tea, Catherine discovered that meals at the Magdalen Society included no meat. Because vegetable matter was healthier, said Reverend Throckmorton—have you ever heard such nonsense? She stared down at what Sister Margaret cheerfully informed her was a vegetable ragout.

"You're not eating," said Agnes, who was sitting next to her. "Are you quite all right?"

"I've decided to fast," said Catherine. "Hunger will remind me to repent of my sins."

"Oh, I understand!" said Agnes. "I felt that way myself, before I found peace and forgiveness for my sins. Those will come to you in time, I promise."

Catherine looked at her thin, earnest face and wondered what she would taste like. Not much meat on those bones, unfortunately. Doris would be more appetizing.

A girl across the table from her, who could not have been more than twelve or thirteen, looked at her curiously, but when Catherine gave her a hard stare, she looked down again at her own plate.

After dinner there was a lecture, and then more prayers, and finally, finally, the inmates of the Magdalen Society were dismissed and sent to bed. "You're not in the dormitory," said Sister Margaret. "Follow Alice. Here's a work dress for you, which you should wear tomorrow, and a nightgown. It's been freshly laundered, so it may be damp. Dresses and undergarments are laundered once a week, sheets once a month. If you have any questions, Alice should be able to answer them."

Alice was the girl who had been sitting across the table from Catherine, the one who had stared at her during dinner. "It's this way," she said. She gave Catherine a curious sidelong glance, but did not say anything further. Catherine followed her up a flight of stairs to the third floor. Here there were a number of smaller rooms. Each had been allocated to two girls, who shared one bed. Besides the bed, the room had only a chest of drawers and a single wooden chair. When Catherine saw the narrow bed she would be sharing with Alice, she wondered how she would be able to sneak out at night. Perhaps Alice was a heavy sleeper?

"I could help you, miss," said Alice. "With those buttons, I mean."

There were a lot of buttons on the dress she was wearing. She had not considered how she was to undo them.

"Thank you," she said. "And you don't need to call me miss. Just Catherine."

"Yes, miss," said Alice. She started on the buttons up the back. "I was in service, you see. Before I came down in the world. When my mistress died, there was no money left to keep servants, so we were all dismissed. It's not so easy to find a job nowadays. I swept a crossing for a while, and then a gentleman offered me money for other kinds of services, but I said no. And a kind lady, seeing as he was importuning me, gave me a card with this address on it. It's not so bad, if you can get used to the food and sermons." She started on the buttons on the cuffs. "This dress now, it reminds me of one my old mistress used to have. Might I ask where you got it, if I'm not being too bold?"

"What?" said Catherine. She had not been paying attention. How was she to sneak out of the bed, and then the room, without Alice waking up?

"The dress, miss. Might I ask where you got it?" Alice folded it neatly, then put it on the chair. Sister Margaret would no doubt come for it in the morning.

"Oh, I have no idea." She briefly considered eating Alice, but she rather liked Alice. And the girl had been so helpful with the buttons.

> ALICE: You did not!

> CATHERINE: Oh, didn't I? I would have eaten Mrs.
> Raymond herself, after that vegetable mess!
> Although I'm pretty sure she would have been
> tough. . . .

"I think one of the other girls gave it to me, when I started on the streets. She didn't need it anymore, and she told me it would be attractive to gentlemen. You know, make me look like a lady. They like us to look like ladies, until they don't." Catherine put her undergarments away in the drawer Alice pulled out for her, then put on her nightgown. She lay down and pulled the thin, rough wool blanket over her. "You're too young to know about such things."

"The gentleman didn't think so," said Alice, getting into bed beside her.

"Ah, gentlemen. Best avoid them," said Catherine. "I haven't known a single one of them that didn't want to ruin a girl, in one way or another. Good night . . ."

The sky was darkening to dusk. Of course, they had not been issued candles. Such an extravagance would not have occurred to Mrs. Raymond or Sister Margaret. Catherine lay with her eyes closed. It would be several hours until she could sneak out of the room, through the long stone corridor, and down the stairs to Mrs. Raymond's office. There would be no light, but that would not bother her. A cat can see in the dark.

She waited, motionless, like a cat that feigns sleep before a mouse hole. Slowly, she heard Alice's breath slow, heard the sounds in the other rooms cease, except for gentle snoring. Slowly, a half-moon climbed the sky. There would be some light after all, but not too much. She didn't want anyone to see her.

By moonlight, she silently rose, careful not to wake Alice, and slipped out of the room. Through the window at the end of the hallway, she could see the moon, floating in the sky like a boat on the ocean. She passed the rooms of sleeping girls, then made her way down a flight of stairs to the second floor. Although she had been to Mrs. Raymond's office earlier that day, the stone hallways and wooden doors of the Magdalen Society looked so much alike that it was difficult to remember where it was located. Thank goodness Diana had described the building so thoroughly, even drawing her a map on a corner of Watson's paper. If Diana's instructions were to be trusted, Mrs. Raymond's office should be right at the end of this hall. . . .

> DIANA: Of course my instructions were to be trusted! I lived in that bloody house for seven years. I should know where her office was—Sister Margaret caned me enough in it. Never Mrs. Raymond: it was always something she left to Sister Margaret. Until one day I turned on her and broke the cane. After that, she never did it again.

> CATHERINE: I'm building suspense. If the reader isn't sure whether to trust you, it builds suspense, don't you see. Anyway, I wasn't sure whether to trust you, then. Sometimes I'm not sure whether to trust you now!

The office was exactly where Diana had described. It was not locked. Catherine pulled the door closed behind her and looked around. The brocade curtains had been drawn for the night; there was just enough light for her to avoid the armchairs, so much more comfortable than anything in the bare workroom, where girls sewed on wooden benches. She walked over thick carpet, soft under her bare feet and welcome after the chill of the stone floors, to Mrs. Raymond's desk. Yes, the book was still there. She pulled open one of the curtains so moonlight would fall on the book. She opened it to the page where she had signed, then began to scan the list of names. Nothing. She turned back to the previous page. There, a name she recognized:

Molly Keane

Several weeks ago, she had entered the Magdalen Society. Why had she left? Catherine flipped back, page by page. And there were the others, scattered randomly among the list of names:

Pauline Delacroix
Susanna Moore
Sally Jane Hayward
Anna Pettingill

More than a month ago, each of them. Even Pauline Delacroix, whom Holmes had not been able to trace, had been an inmate (that was the most appropriate word) of the Magdalen Society. What did it mean? There must be more information, perhaps letters. In the desk? She was about to open the top drawer when she heard footsteps coming down the hallway. Three sets of footsteps: one sharp and decisive, one irregular, one shambling. Who could it be? But there was no time to speculate now. Where could she hide? Quickly, she closed the book, moved it back to its place on the desk, and slipped into the window recess, drawing the curtain closed in front of her. The walls of the building were thick, the windows deeply set. There was plenty of space for her in the recess.

The door opened, and the gas was lit: she could hear the striking of a match and suddenly, the curtains were edged with light. Catherine could not see them, but she could smell them: two human, one a beast.

"I suggest that you moderate your tone with me," said Mrs. Raymond. "I allowed Diana to be taken because I was heartily sick of her. And because you owe me, Mr. Hyde. When should I expect to be paid for the information I'm providing?"

Hyde! This was Hyde? So he was alive after all. . . . Mary had been wrong, then.

"We have always been on good terms, Mrs. Raymond." The voice was hoarse, almost a whisper, as though the speaker were consumptive. He spoke in the cultivated accent of a gentleman, but something about that voice sent a shiver up Catherine's spine.

MARY: Did it really? Or are you exaggerating for effect?

CATHERINE: It did! Really, there was something about his voice. . . . It set my teeth on edge. But there was a kind of desperation in it that made me pity him too.

"Good business terms," he continued. "My associate will pay you as soon as he can, I promise."

"I don't trust this associate of yours any more than I trust you," said Mrs. Raymond. "How am I to know he exists? Twelve girls, I've provided—descriptions, addresses. Twice I contacted the girls myself, luring them into places where you could collect what you desired. I want my hundred pounds. Once I receive it, I'll tell you where to find your daughter."

Twelve girls! And Lestrade only knew about five. The other seven . . . presumably their bodies had not been found. Catherine heard a low growl.

"And your friend here doesn't frighten me. I've seen worse in the alleys of Spitalfields."

"I already know where Diana is, Mrs. Raymond." So the Wolf Men had been his spies! Well, that made sense. And that growl . . .

"But evidently she's not in your possession. Are you having difficulty retrieving her? One small girl? I don't think much of you or your organization, Mr. Hyde, if one small girl gives you difficulty."

"We have not yet retrieved her, no. We have not had time to turn our attention to such a trifle. But once we have time, it will present no difficulty. Our organization is more powerful than you can imagine, Mrs. Raymond."

Was there a way Catherine could see, just a little? She wanted to see Hyde. He sounded confident, but underneath that confidence, she could smell fear. This was Diana's father . . . and Mary's, if her hypothesis was correct. Hyde, the criminal, alive. Could she catch a glimpse?

"My associate is very real, and will reveal himself in his own time. Meanwhile, we need a pair of hands. Delicate hands—he is most specific. Anna Pettingill's hands were rough and chapped. We need the hands of a lady. Another governess, perhaps. Or a lady's maid."

Catherine edged slowly toward the center of the window, where there was a gap in the curtains about the width of an eye. Yes, there—no, she could only see Mrs. Raymond. What was that? A floorboard had squeaked, and for a moment Catherine wondered whether she had stepped awry. But it was across the room, outside the door.

Mrs. Raymond had heard it as well. She wrenched open the door, grabbed what was standing there, and pulled it inside the room.

It was Alice.

"How long have you been standing there, brat? How much of our conversation have you heard?" She held Alice by the collar of her nightgown.

"Just about everything, I reckon." Curiously, Alice did not seem afraid. Foolish of her, thought Catherine. She should be afraid, very much so.

"So the girls have been spying on me! How many of you are there, beside yourself?"

"Just me," said Alice. "And I wasn't spying. That new girl, Catherine, was snoring so loudly I couldn't sleep. So I walked around and came down here to see if I could get a bit of food, dinner not being what they call nourishing. I saw the light, and I came to investigate."

Ah, Catherine had been too quick to dismiss little Alice. She could lie like a champion. But why? She had clearly followed Catherine. Why was she protecting her?

"That will make it easier," said Mrs. Raymond. "There will only be one of you to get rid of. Hold her, Mr. Hyde! And you, whatever you are!"

What was happening? Through the gap in the curtain, Catherine saw Alice crumple to the floor, and then light flash on something in Mrs. Raymond's hand. A knife? No, now she could see it—a hypodermic syringe. Had Alice been drugged? She should have leaped out earlier, when Alice was still talking. When they could both have run. Now, the best course of action was to wait.

"You'll have no use for this morsel—her hands are as red and raw as a scullery maid's," said Mrs. Raymond. "But you might as well take her with you. It's too dangerous to keep her here, where she can talk to the other girls. Dispose of her as you will."

"You, take her," said Hyde. A dark shape leaned down and

gathered Alice in its arms. When it stood again, Catherine could tell that it was a Beast Man, tall and hairy. A Bear Man, judging by the smell. Instinct said attack, but if she showed herself now, she would be caught. Would she be able to fight a bear? She didn't think so. He was an ugly specimen, badly sewn together. Moreau had been cruel enough, but at least he had tried to make his creatures aesthetically pleasing. These creatures were malformed, even for Beast Men.

And then, finally, as the Bear Man turned to go, she caught a glimpse of Hyde. He was small, certainly smaller than she was. He gave an impression of deformity, although perhaps it was simply the way he walked, hunched over, with a queer shuffle. If he had stood upright, he might have been handsome—in his face there was charm, as well as craft and guile. But his sneer would have made most women avoid him.

"Think about what we need, Mrs. Raymond," he said. "Hands, a lady's hands. I'll be back with your payment tomorrow night."

"I should hope so," said Mrs. Raymond. "And no hands until you do! I'm not to be trifled with, Mr. Hyde." She followed him out the door, turning down the gas as she went. And then Catherine heard a key turn in the lock. She was locked into Mrs. Raymond's office.

MARY: Alice, why did you follow Catherine? Were you just curious about where she was going?

ALICE: Oh, I was curious all right, but I didn't care about that, miss. See, she was wearing Mrs. Jekyll's dress. I recognized it right away: there was a darn under the arm that I had made myself when Mrs. Poole didn't have time. Your mother had torn it in one of her fits. And so I thought, *Why is this woman wearing Mrs. Jekyll's dress?* You could have sold it, of course, but I didn't think you would sell your mother's clothes unless you were in desperate straits. Perhaps she had stolen it, but something about her didn't strike me that way. I've known thieves, and she wasn't a thief. And then I saw her hiding in Mrs. Raymond's office, behind the curtain. I could see her eye in the gap, staring at me. I didn't know if she was a bad one, but I knew Mrs. Raymond was, and that little man—Hyde— and the tall hairy one, they weren't right either. So I made a choice.

MARY: It was the right choice, and I'm glad you made it.

ALICE: Thank you, miss.

Catherine turned and examined the windows. They opened outward, and unlocked easily. All she had to do was turn the latch. She waited: there, two men, one of them carrying what looked like a sack of laundry. That must be Hyde and the Bear Man, and the woman following behind was Mrs. Raymond. They walked across the courtyard, and then Mrs. Raymond let them out through the front gate. She locked the gate behind her and returned to the house.

Would she be coming back to her office? The gas was turned down, but not off, so she might be coming back. Quickly, Catherine pushed one of the windows outward and climbed onto the ivy that covered the front of the house. She closed the window as best she could. She would not be able to latch it again, but perhaps Mrs. Raymond wouldn't notice, or would assume that one of the girls had forgotten to relatch it after cleaning. She let herself down the ivy, hoping it would hold—Diana had described climbing up and down it, but Diana was lighter than she was. And it was two floors down to a courtyard paved with stone.

The ivy held. She let herself down onto the cold pavement, wishing she had worn her boots, although they would have made too much noise in the corridors. She slipped across the courtyard, hoping no one was looking out the front windows. There was the gate, but Mrs. Raymond had locked it. How would she get out? The stone wall was too high for her to leap over, and there was no ivy here to climb.

"Pssst." It was Diana, standing on the other side of the gate. "Come on, I've already picked the lock. You should have taken off your nightgown to climb down that wall. You look like a ghost! Anyone could see you from a mile away."

"Well, maybe they'll think I'm a ghost," said Catherine. "Hyde and a Beast Man—they went to the right! They have one of the girls in a sack."

"That was my father?" said Diana. "My father's alive? If I'd known, I would have looked at him more closely. I thought they were both Beast Men. Watson was keeping watch and saw them come out. And then I saw you climb out the window. I told him and Charlie to follow them, and that we would catch up. You can follow them by smell, can't you?"

Yes, she could smell all four of them: Watson's pipe tobacco, Hyde's cologne, the rank scent of the Bear Man. Charlie smelled, surprisingly, of soap.

"Put this on," said Diana. "It's Watson's jacket. He said you might get cold. My father's alive. So Miss Mary was wrong after all—I'm not surprised. Mum always did say that he was clever enough for anything. And he never came for me, all those years. Bloody bastard."

The jacket was too large, but Catherine was grateful for it. At least it covered part of her nightgown. For the rest—well, she would be bare-ankled and barefoot. *Cats don't need shoes,* she reminded herself. "Come on," she said to Diana. "They went that way."

The two girls hurried down the street, into the labyrinth of the London night.

CHAPTER XV

The Streets of Soho

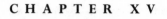

Mary and Holmes waited in a narrow street across from a boardinghouse in Soho. It was a run-down, disreputable place, with shutters that hung awry and a general air of slovenliness. The area itself was not promising: above them hung lines of chemises and undershirts, drying in the tainted London air, and there were piles of refuse in the alleys. In a nearby yard, a dog had been howling off and on for the last half hour. Yet they were not far from the respectable Deerborne Hotel, where they had inquired for Mr. Prendick earlier that evening. They had agreed that there was no time to lose and a direct approach was warranted, so Holmes had shown the proprietor a letter signed by Inspector Lestrade that authorized him to make any inquiries necessary. The proprietor, a cheerful, red-faced man with an elaborate mustache, had said that yes, Mr. Prendick dined there regularly, always arriving as the dinner service began. They had waited in the proprietor's office, on the chance that he might dine at the Deerborne that night.

And he was punctual as clockwork: at seven o'clock on the dot he walked in. Sitting as inconspicuously as possible behind some potted ferns, pretending to read *Punch*, they had watched him eat alone in the hotel dining room. Would he recognize them if he saw them directly? It was doubtful: he had not glanced at them this morning when almost running into them at the asylum. No doubt he had been too upset. Still, it was best not to take chances. After dinner, he paid his bill and made his way to the front entrance, retrieving his hat and umbrella from the hall stand. They had followed him, always staying about a block behind. Finally, he had turned into this street and entered the boardinghouse.

He was still there, in a second-floor room: every once in a while they could see his silhouette cross the window. It is easier than one thinks, Mary realized, to recognize a silhouette.

"Can't we just go confront him?" Mary asked, at last. "We've been waiting for hours, and nothing's happened." Where were Beatrice and Justine? What had happened to them? How were Catherine and Diana doing? Why had Watson not sent word? She could not help worrying about them all.

"Something will happen," said Holmes. "Miss Frankenstein and Miss Rappaccini have been kidnapped. That changes the situation for whoever murdered those women in Whitechapel and created the Beast Men. If Prendick is involved, he will be summoned. If not, he's of no use to us, and we'll need to start from the beginning. But I think he is involved, despite his protest to Dr. Seward. When he passed us in the asylum hallway, the look on his face was not anger, as it might have been if he'd been unjustly accused. It was fear. Wait, there—what is that?"

It was a strange little man, loping up the street. He seemed to be about Diana's size, but his arms were longer than they should be, and he moved hunched forward, as though wanting to put his knuckles on the ground to help his progress.

"Beast Man," said Mary. They were all different, but by this time she could see what was common about them all: the impression of misshapenness, of something inhuman in them. At last, something was happening.

The Beast Man stopped at the door of the boardinghouse, stood upright, and rang a bell. The door was opened by a woman as slovenly as the house, evidently the landlady or a servant of some sort. She stepped back and he disappeared through the doorway, then down the dark hall.

The door closed behind him. They waited: What would happen now? There was Prendick again, silhouetted briefly against the window. Then the gas was lowered. A few minutes later, the two of them emerged through the front door: Prendick and the Beast Man. They turned right and started walking up the street.

"Quickly," said Holmes. "Stay as far behind as you can, but don't lose sight of them."

They followed Prendick and the shuffling Beast Man through the narrow streets of Soho, as inconspicuously as possible. There were gas lamps along the major streets, but many of the smaller streets were dark, lit only by the light from windows. Prendick was traveling by unfrequented ways, streets with few shops on them and fewer passers-by. Mary was glad: that meant fewer people to notice their presence. She could see the moon over the housetops, hanging above the chimneys like a shilling, half bright and half tarnished.

She did not know where they were. She recognized nothing, and she could not ask Holmes while they were in pursuit. Thank goodness she had left her umbrella at home. It would have been a nuisance under the circumstances. If it rained, she would simply get wet. Three times they almost lost Prendick, but each time they saw him again. If it had not rained the day before, they would likely have lost him altogether. Each time, Holmes found footprints that pointed them in the right direction. Prendick's footprints were not particularly distinctive—he wore a brand of ready-made boots bought by many gentlemen, Holmes told her under his breath. But he was walking beside the Beast Man, whose footprints stood out like a beacon in the darkness. After a while, even Mary could distinguish them from the other footprints on the muddy pavement.

On one long, lonely street, they had to wait in an alcove to avoid being seen.

"I think I know where he's going," said Holmes.

"Where?" asked Mary. "And how can you know?"

"By logical deduction: if he's making Beast Men, it must be somewhere his actions will not be noticed. Where the presence of animals will not be remarked upon, where limping men with dark skin and excess hair will be treated not as monstrosities, but as foreign sailors."

"The docks!" said Mary. "I've heard they're the locus of iniquity and vice. Of course, that was according to Mrs. Poole, and she might well say the same of Mayfair. I'm not sure how much her assessment is to be trusted."

"In this case, she's not too far off," said Holmes. "Come, they're almost at the end of the street. If I'm right, they will be turning south."

"Have we been walking east?" asked Mary. "I've lost all sense of where we are."

"Yes, can't you smell the Thames? We've been walking parallel to it almost all this time."

Of course. She blamed herself for not having noticed the rank smell, or for having noticed it but only as a matter of course, as something at the edge of her consciousness but not as a clue. Let that be a lesson to her—one she was not likely to forget.

"They've turned the corner. Come on!"

Mary hurried along the street behind Holmes. Her feet hurt terribly, but that did not matter. They had to find Justine and Beatrice.

They turned where Prendick and the Beast Man had turned before them, toward the river. This street was lined with warehouses. Prendick rapped on the door of the second one on the left. She could hear the sound reverberating. The door opened, and for a moment she could see a rectangle of light. Then it closed behind the man and beast, and the street was dark once more.

Keeping to the shadows, she and Holmes drew closer. Here there were no streetlights, but the street was wider and the moon shone down as it could not in the narrow alleys. They could see the warehouses well enough. The one into which Prendick had been admitted was two stories high and made of brick. It had a great door, most likely to admit carts, and then the smaller door on which Prendick had knocked. Over the great door was the name ALDERNEY SHIPPING, in white paint that was visible even in the darkness. On the second floor were several windows, all dark. On the first floor, there was only one window, in which a light was shining.

"Shall we try to see what's going on?" Without waiting for a response from Holmes, she crept up to the window with the light in it. The shutters were closed, but they were so old that some of the slats had rotted away, and the window itself was broken in several places. She had a clear view of the room, or a portion of it. What she saw caused her to gesture wildly to Holmes. He was right behind her, having followed her almost immediately. He looked in as well at the horrific scene. Mary's blood ran cold in her veins.

> CATHERINE: Now am I being melodramatic?

> MARY: No, it really did make my blood run cold.
> I mean not really, because blood can't run cold
> within the human body. But as a metaphor, it
> accurately describes how I felt at the time.

> CATHERINE: Oh, for goodness' sake!

Even Holmes said "Dear God" under his breath.

MARY: He really did say that. I remember it distinctly.

The room had no doubt once served as an office for Alderney Shipping. An oil lantern hanging from the ceiling lit the center of the room, but left much of it in shadow. The room was lined with shelves that had probably once held smaller packages. Now, those shelves held large bottles that reminded Mary of the Royal College of Surgeons. Swimming in those bottles were parts of bodies. Hands, legs, torsos. Perfectly preserved heads. Eyes closed, they swam in preserving fluid. But surely there were more parts than five girls could have provided? She could see at least three heads, and she did not want to count the number of limbs, of various sorts. Along one wall was a large cage, which had probably once safe-guarded valuable merchandise. Now it held Beast Men. She could see two, or was it three, standing in their hunched, misshapen way close to the bars, but only part of the cage was visible from where she was standing. In the center of the room, under the lamp, was what appeared to be an operating table. Around it stood Prendick and two Beast Men—the hunched, shuffling one that had fetched Prendick, and a tall, hairy one that looked suspiciously like a bear.

On the table lay Justine, still in her white nightgown. Her wrists and ankles were strapped to the table. She was staring up at the ceiling, calmly.

JUSTINE: I was waiting for death and preparing to
meet my Lord.

"There are three of them," Mary whispered to Holmes. "Do you think we could rescue her? The Bear Man looks strong."

"That can't be all of them," he whispered back. "What's in the portion of the room we can't see? Wait and watch. I think we need to know more before we act."

"Well, Prendick? Can you do it?" The voice Mary heard was deep, harsh. It was not a voice she had heard before.

"I don't know," said Prendick. "It's a delicate operation, removing a brain. Moreau could have done it, but I'm not Moreau. I could damage her forever."

"Damn you! You'll do it, and it will work, or I'll strangle you with my bare hands!"

A shape—a man's shape—strode across the room, hands outstretched, as though to show Prendick what exactly he might expect. When Mary saw him, she gasped. He was the largest man she had ever seen, at least seven feet tall, but it was not his height that struck her most. No, it was the breadth of his shoulders, the thickness of his arms and legs, muscled like the strongest of circus strongmen. He was in shirtsleeves, with the sleeves rolled up to his elbows, so the blue veins on his forearms were clearly visible. And then, the pallor of his face, the rough black hair, the black eyes rolling with an expression of fury . . . She had never seen anyone so frightening.

"Killing me won't help you create the woman you want," said Prendick. How could he be so calm? Was it desperation, or exhaustion? Certainly he seemed exhausted. "I can try to replace her brain. It will, at any rate, be easier than creating an entire woman, which was your original insane plan."

"Keep a civil tongue in your head, or I'll tear it out! You can create a woman for me as well dumb as speaking—and I shall enjoy your company more."

Prendick looked down at the ground and said, "All right. I'm ready to start when you wish."

"Do you see what you've driven me to, Justine?" The giant looked down at her. "I give you one final chance. Say that you love me, that you will return to me willingly, and I will spare your life."

"I will never love you," said Justine in a voice that sounded as though she were speaking from a great distance. "I welcome death, and willingly choose it over a life with you, Adam."

The giant roared with displeasure. He turned to the cage where the Beast Men were kept and pounded his great fists on the bars. All the Beast Men cried out, some in fear, some in anger. The shuffling Beast Man leaped up as though startled and gave a high screech, but the Bear Man stood silent and motionless.

"Very well then! Prendick, begin the procedure. Once your brain is replaced with the brain of that girl, that governess, it will be a blank slate, ready for whatever I teach it. I shall be your Frankenstein then, not he—not the cursed father who created us both!"

He took a jar off the shelf. In it was a brain, a human brain floating in preserving fluid. "Do you see this, Justine? This is what will replace you! The brain of"—he looked at the label on the jar, where a name was written—"Susanna Moore. Your body will continue, but you—all that you are—will be gone!"

Justine looked calmly at the brain in the jar and said, "I am ready."

With a growl, the giant handed the jar to Prendick, who put it on a cart next to the table. Still calm, he said, "I'll need time for the ether to work. For an ordinary woman, it would take several minutes, but she isn't an ordinary woman. I don't know the dose that will put her under, or kill her. I'll have to experiment." He looked down at Justine and said, "I'm sorry."

She did not look at him. Instead, she closed her eyes and said, "Notre Père, qui es aux cieux, que ton nom soit sanctifié, que ton règne vienne, que ta volonté soit faite sur la terre comme au ciel . . ."

Prendick took what looked like a sponge off the cart, put it on top of a bottle, and turned the bottle over so the sponge was saturated with the chemical within, then held the sponge over Justine's nose and mouth. If she continued to pray, it was inaudible.

The giant said, "Are you sure the new brain will be blank, that I'll be able to influence it as I wish?"

"No, of course I'm not sure," said Prendick. "That was Frankenstein's theory, but it seems obvious that although you lost your memories, your essential characteristics survived the process. You are the man you were before he brought you back to life—the criminal he found on the gallows, with parts of other corpses where your body had decomposed past recovery. Just as this is still essentially Justine Moritz, the virtuous servant of the Frankensteins. What you will find in the brain of Susanna Moore, I don't know. I can guarantee nothing. Particularly not in this circumstance, when you have asked me to do the impossible with the inadequate. I'm a biologist, not a surgeon."

"You will do as you're told, or I'll send the story of how you betrayed Moreau to your damned society. Do you think they will allow you to live, after learning that you took Moreau's killer as your concubine? The next time you have a guilty conscience, Prendick, do not take opium where others are likely to overhear."

"I've checked on the Italian girl." That voice! Mary shifted position, inadvertently elbowing Holmes out of the way. She could see him: a small, twisted man standing by the door to the storage room. With a gasp, she sat down on the cobblestones, with her back pressed into the brick wall.

"What is it?" asked Holmes.

"That's Hyde. He looks exactly as he did when I was a child. But that's not possible. He died. My father died."

"Hush! Let me hear!" whispered a familiar voice out of the darkness.

Startled, Mary turned toward it. Catherine was crouched beside her.

"How did you—"

"I'm a cat. I've been here, listening, for some time. Now hush!"

". . . will take a while for the poison to work, but it should accumulate quickly within a locked room. The girl should be dead within the hour."

"Wouldn't it be quicker to kill her yourself?" said the giant, impatiently.

"Unlike you, I'm not a killer," said Hyde. "And there will not be a mark on her. Remember that your butchery has Scotland Yard on our trail. Even after I convinced that imbecile to confess, you wanted another brain—fresher, you said! Your actions continually put us in danger of discovery."

"Well, then you have time to assist Prendick," said the giant.

"I'm a chemist, not a surgeon. Although I can appreciate the skill with which Frankenstein created her. A woman Prendick created for you would never have been so finely made, whatever the starting material."

"Thank you for your confidence," said Prendick drily. "Perhaps, as a chemist, you can help me with the ether, which does not, at the moment, seem to be working."

Hyde bowed, a mocking, twisted bow.

"I'm surrounded by incompetents!" roared the giant, once again setting the Beast Men in the cages pacing and calling.

"I think we've seen enough," whispered Mary. She had been transfixed by the spectacle, but now was the time to act. As for Hyde—she could not think about him right now. "We need to rescue Justine and Beatrice before they figure out the ether and start cutting Justine's brain out!"

"Alice too," said Catherine.

"Who's Alice?" asked Mary, but Catherine waved for them to follow her and then ran across the dark road, as lightly as—yes, as a cat. On the other side, she ducked into an alley between two warehouses. There, barely visible in the darkness, stood Diana, Charlie, and Watson.

"Look who I found!" said Catherine.

"Holmes! Good to see you, old man," said Watson. "I was wondering how you were getting on."

"Well, I think, all things considered," said Holmes.

"Oh bloody hell," said Diana. "Just tell us what you saw. And next time, I'm coming too. I hate being left behind!"

In the alley, Mary described what they had seen in the warehouse office—the bottles on the shelves, the operating table, Justine's plight. "And someone is being poisoned, we don't know where. Are they trying to poison Beatrice? How would they do that? But it doesn't matter—we have to rescue them as quickly as possible."

"Who is this Adam?" asked Watson. "He seems to be their leader, and the chief perpetrator of this madness."

"Can you not guess?" said Holmes. "He is the first monstrous creation of Victor Frankenstein."

"But the monster perished," said Watson. "It says so in Mrs. Shelley's account."

"Oh yes, because everything written down is true," said Diana. "Like the rot you write about Sherlock here."

"We don't have time to argue," said Mary. "Who's going to rescue Beatrice? She's locked up somewhere in that warehouse."

"If it's a lock you're talking about, I'm the one to pick it," said Diana.

"I'll go with her, to protect her," said Charlie.

"I don't need protecting."

"Thank you, Charlie. And the rest of us need to rescue Justine before she goes under completely." Mary looked around at the circle of potential rescuers. She could barely see their faces in the darkness. "Four of us against five of them—Hyde, Prendick, the monster Adam, the Bear Man, and that small shuffling one . . ."

"An Orangutan Man, if I'm not mistaken," said Holmes. "They

are—they must be—the animals stolen from Lord Avebury's menagerie, transformed into men, or approximations of men. Lord Avebury sent me a list of the stolen animals. One of the bears and one of the boars is dead. Which leaves—well, if I remember his list correctly, I hope that cage is securely locked. If we had time, we could form a plan—rushing into that room and trusting in the element of surprise is scarcely the wisest course of action."

"I know," said Mary, "but what choice do we have? Our friends are in there. Who knows how long Justine has?"

"Of course we're going in," said Catherine. "Come on, already!"

"Miss Jekyll is right," said Watson. "This is no time to hold back out of consideration for our safety. Although the thought of you ladies going into that warehouse . . ."

"You're not going to dissuade us, Dr. Watson," said Mary. Could this possibly work? It would have to.

"I was going to say, the thought of you going in weaponless . . . But I only have my revolver. Holmes?"

"I have mine," said Holmes. "You'd better keep yours, Watson. I'll give mine to either Miss Jekyll or Miss Moreau. And I shall fight with my fists. I have been trained in baritsu, remember. You misunderstood me, Miss Jekyll. I was certainly not going to suggest leaving Miss Frankenstein in danger."

"I don't need your revolver, Mr. Holmes," said Mary. Out of her purse, she drew her father's revolver. It was small, the sort of weapon a gentleman could carry concealed. She wondered if he had bought it for his excursions as Mr. Hyde. Who was alive . . . which meant her father was alive.

MRS. POOLE: Were you carrying a revolver all that time?

MARY: I put it in my purse before we left for Soho.
I thought if Dr. Watson carried a revolver, I should
as well when accompanying Mr. Holmes. One
never knows when a revolver will come in handy.

MRS. POOLE: Very sensible of you, miss.

MARY: I had to leave my purse in that alley, and forgot
to retrieve it afterward. At least I remembered to
tuck the rest of the money and the house key into
my waistband. I suppose Diana's right—women's
clothes really aren't made for adventures.

DIANA: Told you.

"I don't need a weapon either," said Catherine. "I am a weapon.
Remember that I killed a man with my hands—and teeth!"

"Then follow me," said Holmes. "I shall go in first. These are
criminals, and remember, in this matter I am acting for Lestrade
and Scotland Yard. I am an official representative of the law."

Both the larger and smaller warehouse doors were locked, but
Diana picked the lock of the smaller one with what looked suspiciously like one of Mary's hatpins, which had been stuck through
the underside of her lapel. "I could do this when I was seven!" she
whispered to Holmes, who was standing behind her. Cautiously,
she pushed open the door. It opened onto a dark hallway that ran
the length of the warehouse. At its end was a window, through
which a bit of moonlight shone on a spiral wrought-iron staircase
up to the second floor. Holmes stepped past Diana, revolver in
hand. Mary followed him in, and then the rest of them followed
one by one, as silently as they could until they all stood in the
hallway. Watson, who was in the rear, shut the front door behind

them. On the left side of the hallway, they could see the outline of a door—that must lead to the larger loading area. On the right side were three doors, the first of which had a line of brighter light underneath it. From it they could hear the vague murmur of several voices: that must be the door to the room in which Justine was being held.

Mary whispered, "Diana, try those other doors! If Beatrice is in one of those rooms, and you can free her, you may both be able to help us. If not, try upstairs, and we'll have to go in without you. There's no time to wait."

"All right," said Diana. "Come on, Charlie."

And now we must once again separate our narrative into two parts: one that follows Diana down the hallway, and another that stays with Mary and Catherine.

CATHERINE: I can't write from Diana's point of view.

MARY: Of course you can. You're a writer; you can write anything. Just find your inner Diana.

CATHERINE: I don't have an inner Diana.

DIANA: Ha! You wish. Everyone has an inner Diana.

Diana's thoughts were in chaos. But then, they always were, so this was nothing new. At that moment, her inner monologue sounded something like this: *That was Dad in there the bloody bastard haven't seen him since I was a baby so he is alive after all wonder what Mum would think of that don't know why Mary treats me like a child after all I'm fourteen I can pick locks and climb and bloody well do what the other girls do except poison people and bite them through the throat but I'm as clever as anyone tea was a long time ago I wonder if we'll get anything to eat?*

MARY: All right, you've made your point! Stop
picking on Diana and get on with the story.

It took only a moment for Diana to pick the locks on the second and third doors. Beatrice was not in either of those rooms, which were filled with crates labeled ALDERNEY SHIPPING. She would need to look on the second floor. She waved at Mary and pointed up the staircase to indicate where she was going. The rescue would have to proceed without her. Mary waved back.

Diana mounted the spiral staircase, Charlie climbing after her. "You're awfully good at those locks, ain't you, miss?" he said as they reached the second floor.

She was both annoyed and pleased by his attention. Pleased because it was a fitting tribute to her skill, and annoyed because of course she was good at them. She was Diana Hyde, wasn't she? She had always been able to pick locks and pockets, and climb into and out of windows. She had often thought that if no better opportunity presented itself, she might one day become a burglar.

DIANA: And I still might!

The second floor had doors only on the left—which had, of course, on the floor below, been their right. There was once again a window at the end of the hall, this time overlooking the street. Either it had no shutters or they were open, for it let in just enough moonlight to see by. Once again, there were three doors.

The first room was empty. Just as Diana was about to pick the lock of the second door, she heard a faint moaning from the door at the end of the hall. As silently as she could, she ran to the third door and picked the lock. The room had one window, through which moonlight shone into the room. In the farthest corner sat

Beatrice. Her wrists and ankles were tied together with rope, and there was a piece of cloth tied across her mouth. Across the room from her, beneath the window, lay a girl who was moaning and moving slightly, as though in her sleep.

And there were other sounds, coming through the floor: downstairs, someone was shouting. Whatever was happening down there had begun.

Diana stepped into the room, but immediately stepped out again. A sweet odor wafted out after her, as though the room contained a wonderful garden.

"Don't breathe that!" she told Charlie. "It's Beatrice's poison. Here, do you have a handkerchief about you?"

Charlie produced a large, rough handkerchief from his trouser pocket and handed it to her.

"Open the window," she said, pointing to the one at the end of the hall. He nodded and ran to open it. How nice it was to have someone who, when you told him to do something, just did it— without arguing!

Diana put the handkerchief over her mouth, ran into the room, and struggled with the rusted latch of the window. It took her a few minutes, and finally she had to drop the handkerchief so she could use both hands. The air was so sweet, so fragrant. All she wanted to do was sit down, breathe it in, remain in that garden forever. With a final tug, she opened the latch and pushed the window panes outward. Fresh air! She breathed deeply.

She grabbed the girl on the floor and lifted her to the window as best she could, with her arms around the girl's chest. The girl was not heavy, but she was as limp as a sack of grain.

"Come on, breathe!" said Diana. The girl was not dead, not yet, although she was barely breathing. When she breathed in the fresh air, she began coughing—rough, hacking coughs that shook her body. It was difficult for Diana to hold her up, but she propped the girl's body on the windowsill and held her there, with her head outside the window.

"What can I do, miss?" asked Charlie. There was no need to whisper now: they could hear shouts coming from downstairs, and a loud crash. What was happening? But there was no time to wonder.

"Help Beatrice," said Diana.

Keeping the girl propped on the windowsill, she turned her head—Charlie had taken a knife out of his pocket and was cutting the strip of cloth over Beatrice's mouth, the ropes on her wrists and ankles.

"Oh, I'm so happy to see you!" said Beatrice. "Quick, let me out into the hall so I'm no longer poisoning this room! That poor girl . . ."

"Lean on me, miss," said Charlie, holding out his hand.

"No, my touch will burn." Beatrice helped herself up against the wall, then stumbled past him toward the door.

The girl was leaning out the window, drawing fresh air into her lungs.

"Come on," said Diana. "You're going to be all right. We have to get you downstairs. Can you walk?" The girl nodded.

"Charlie!" Diana said. "Can you get her out of the house?"

"Sure," said Charlie. "Come on, miss. You lean on me and I'll get you out of here. We'll have to go down the stairs to the front door. Do you understand?"

The girl nodded again, weakly.

"I'll go first," said Diana. "We don't know what's happening down there."

From downstairs, they could hear the murmur of voices, but just as they reached the doorway, a shot rang out.

"What's happening? Where are Mary and Catherine?" asked Beatrice.

"Down there," said Diana. "The man who made the beasts—the

Beast Men, I mean—he's going to operate on Justine. Take out her brain and replace it. They're down there with Watson and Holmes. They have guns. They must have shot someone. Come on, Charlie will get you out—I have to go help them."

"I'm going with you," said Beatrice.

Diana nodded. She and Beatrice ran down the hall, their boots clattering on the floor and then clanging on the metal stairs. But they could not worry about the noise now. As Diana reached the bottom of the stairs, she looked up. Charlie was supporting the girl, who stumbled beside him. "All clear!" Diana called up. The hallway was empty. Whatever was happening, it was happening in the office at the end of the hallway. The door to the office was open: a rectangle of light lay across the floor.

"Listen!" said Beatrice. "What is that?" They could hear the most infernal sounds, a cacophony of shouts, screams, and roars, as though a menagerie had been let loose. Then, more shots! They looked at each other with fear in their eyes and ran to the rectangle of light.

DIANA: There was no fear in my eyes!

BEATRICE: Well, there certainly was in mine.

The sight that greeted them through the open door was horrific beyond belief. A menagerie had indeed been let loose: standing by the door of the cage was the madman Renfield. The Beast Men were out—all but one. That one was pacing back and forth, still behind the closed door of the cage.

Quickly, Diana looked around the room: Mary and Holmes were standing in one corner, revolvers raised, guarding Watson. He was lying on the floor, a red stain spreading across his shoulder. A Wolf Man lay dead at his side. Another lay only a few feet away, in front of Mary, still alive but clearly dying. He held a hand up, as though pleading for mercy. But he could no longer stand, no longer even move himself along the floor. Both his wolf and man brains knew that death was coming. He raised his head and howled. In another corner stood Catherine, guarding Justine, who leaned against the wall as though about to faint. How had she gotten out of the restraints and off the operating table? The Bear Man and a Boar Man were both crouched before her, about to attack. Prendick and Hyde were still standing at the table, but the Orangutan Man had hidden under it. Prendick was clutching the table for support. Hyde was holding a scalpel in front of him, like a weapon. At the far end of the room, next to a desk where the manager of Alderney Shipping had once, no doubt, sat to do his accounts, stood the giant, Adam, holding a hand to his chest. On the desk was a lamp, and by its light she could see that his shirt was stained red. But more frightening than the red on his shirt was his face, twisted with fury, pale as a corpse except for the blood running down one temple.

"Do you think you can defeat me? Me, Adam Frankenstein?" he shouted. And as the Wolf Man howled, he threw back his head and roared. The rest of the Beast Men shrieked in response—an unnatural cacophony in the silence of the London night.

CHAPTER XVI

Into the Warehouse

While Diana and Charlie were running up the stairs, Holmes, Mary, and the others were preparing to rescue Justine from her captors. Holmes opened the office door, stepped in, and said, "The game is up, gentlemen. Raise your hands over your heads and step away from Miss Frankenstein. We are armed, and prepared to shoot." Lamplight glinted off the barrel of his revolver.

Prendick and Hyde both looked up, startled. Prendick raised his hands, still holding the ether sponge. Then Hyde raised his. In one hand he held the scalpel, with which he had been about to make the first incision. A shriek rent the air. In a corner of the room, by the cage in which the Beast Men were confined, crouched the madman Renfield. So this was where he had gone! At the sound, the Beast Men in the cage paced back and forth uneasily, all but one who lay in the shadows, by the far wall. How many of them were there? Mary was just behind Holmes, but she could barely see over his shoulder. The Bear Man standing by the operating table growled, as though perplexed by this turn of affairs, and the Orangutan Man jumped up and down with his knuckles still on the floor. Only Adam Frankenstein remained completely motionless. He grinned, a horrific sight on that corpse-like face. Mary shuddered.

"Well, well," he said. "It's a pleasure to meet you, Mr. Holmes. I anticipated that we would meet at some point, although I didn't think it would be so soon. How did you come to find us?" He spoke with an English accent, although with a foreign inflection.

Holmes stepped forward. Mary, Watson, and Catherine stepped into the room behind him, fanning out to both sides. Mary raised her revolver. It was the first time she had aimed it at anything other than a target. Would she be able to use it when the time came? *Of course,* she told herself. *I don't have a choice.* The room had a close, musty smell, no doubt from the Beast Men. She wished she could hold a handkerchief over her nose.

"Catherine!" Prendick looked at her with astonishment. "How is it possible . . ."

"How is it possible that I escaped from the island on which you left me to die?" said Catherine. "Untie Justine."

"And if we don't?" asked Hyde in his rasping voice. "What will you do then, Miss Moreau? That is who you aren't, isn't it? The Puma Woman?"

"Then we will shoot you all, and untie her ourselves," said Watson. "It would probably be easier for you to untie her without the preliminary shooting."

"I suggest you follow Miss Moreau's instructions," said Holmes. "We will not hesitate to shoot criminals."

On the table, Justine moaned. She turned her head to one side, then the other, as though trying to dispel the influence of the ether. The Beast Men gathered at the front of the cage—all but the one who lay by the far wall. They looked on, curiously and with suspicion. Now Mary could see that there were three of them. Another Boar Man, who resembled the one Justine had killed. And two that looked like—dogs? No, wolves. The Wolf Men who had hunted Catherine and Diana.

"Cat, I never meant . . . ," began Prendick.

"Are you mad to come here, Mr. Holmes?" said Adam, disregarding his confederates. "You and Dr. Watson, armed only with those toys? And with two—ladies, if they are, which I rather doubt, since ladies don't go around carrying guns or making threats. We are more than a match for you. It is you who should be surrendering to us. That's logical, Mr. Holmes, and you believe in logic, do you not? For years, I followed your exploits, as recounted by Dr. Watson. In the Alps of my native Switzerland, in the ruined castle I had called home for most of a century, I received them regularly by post. I know your methods. They are impressive, although they are the methods of a calculating machine—you measure and observe, then make your deductions. You are a kind of glorified automaton. I doubt you can understand the methods of a creative mind. The true criminal will always escape you, because he will be able to do what you cannot understand—the unexpected!"

"I would not trust too much to Watson's accounts of me," said Holmes. "He's liable to exaggerate." He fired one shot. It hit the wall on the opposite end of the office. Startled, Mary jumped at the sound. The Orangutan Man screamed and scampered under the operating table. The Beast Men began howling and shaking their bars. Nervously, Prendick untied one of Justine's wrists.

"Fool! What do you think you're doing!" shouted Adam. "The man shoots one bullet into a wall and you're ready to surrender? You're an even greater coward than I suspected, Prendick. Stay where you are, all of you. And Prendick, if you loose her bonds, I will rip your head off with my bare hands. She is mine. She was made for me, and I will not lose her again."

"Mr. Prendick, do as I instructed, or I will have the significant pleasure of shooting you," said Holmes. "Any man who would take God's creations and turn them into these monstrosities is not worthy to live."

> CATHERINE: He did *not* need to say that.
> Monstrosities?

MARY: I don't think he meant you, Cat.

CATHERINE: Nevertheless, it was unnecessary. And
rude.

DIANA: Will you get on with the story already? I want
to hear the part where I come in. That's the best
part . . .

"Adam, can't we just let her go?" said Prendick. "Why do you
need her? Why her specifically? We can go back to the original
plan. Wouldn't it be better to make another woman?"

"There is no other woman! Why do you think I killed those
women myself, rather than sending another out to do it? I had to
make sure they looked like her! Her eyes, her hands . . . There
is no other woman for me. She escaped me once. Now I've found
her; she will not escape me again."

"Oh, but she will!" said Catherine. "She's escaping you now!"

Mary looked at the operating table—it was empty! Hyde was
still standing beside it, although Prendick had retreated a few steps,
as though unsure what to do. Where was Justine? Standing beside
Catherine, leaning on the wall, trying to draw a clear breath. But
nevertheless standing. How had she managed to get off the table?

JUSTINE: When the ether sponge was taken away,
I could breathe again. I pretended to be less
conscious than I actually was. Then, I noticed
that one of my wrists was untied. I reached
over and untied the other. No one was paying
attention to me—everyone was looking at Adam.
Except—I think Hyde gave me a quick glance.
He didn't do or say anything to give me away.

My ankles were already untied, I don't know how,
although I remember seeing him lean down and
say something to the Orangutan Man. Once I was
free, I rolled myself off the table and staggered
over to Catherine. I felt so sick from the ether that
I could barely stand. I was afraid the whole time,
afraid that Adam would see me. But it seems to
me now, thinking back, that Hyde stood between
us. I wonder . . .

MARY: I wonder too. I wonder very much.

Adam screamed with rage and lunged toward Justine. A shot
rang out, then another. It was Holmes—no, Watson, or rather
both of them. They had both shot Adam, and a red stain was
spreading down his shirtfront. He stepped back and put a hand to
his chest, then looked at the red on it, as though surprised. For a
moment, the room was silent, except for the sounds of the Beast
Men in their cage. Then Adam looked up, grinned, and began
moving toward Justine, not as quickly as before, clearly in pain,
but as though nothing could stop his progress.

"You're mine, you will always be mine. You know that, Justine.
You know it in your heart, where you love me, despite yourself—
as I love you. Come to me now, and there will be an end to all
this. Your friends will be safe, no more women will be murdered.
Those murders are on your head, my love. I killed them for you,
for no other reason. But if you come to me, if you love me, everything will be all right again."

Mary raised her revolver, aimed carefully at his forehead, and
shot. The recoil jarred her—she had known it was coming, but it
still took her by surprise and almost knocked her back against the
doorframe.

Adam howled and fell to his knees. Blood ran down his face, from his temple and into one eye. He wiped it with the heel of his hand, presenting an even more horrifying visage than before, with blood smeared over one cheek. He glared at her and said, "Who the devil are you, girl?"

"I'm Mary Jekyll," she said. "Stop, or I'll shoot again."

He threw back his head and laughed. "Jekyll's daughter! Oh, that's rich! Do you hear that, Hyde? Jekyll's daughter, with a toy gun in her hand . . ." The laugh turned into a howl, and the Wolf Men howled with him. The Boar Man shook the bars of the cage.

Mary raised her revolver and aimed at him again.

"No!" It was Renfield, standing by the cage of the Beast Men. "He promised me lives! Many lives, as many as I wanted, if I would be good. And I was good, Master! I said that I killed those girls. I said everything you told me, and I want my lives now."

He turned toward the cage.

"What is he doing?" asked Watson. That corner of the room was dim—too far away from the lantern, and the lamp on the desk did not cast its light so far.

"He has a key!" Catherine shouted. She had been able to see what they rest of them could not, but the result was evident to them all. In a moment, the door of the cage opened with a metallic clang, and the Beast Men were out—all but the one in the corner.

The Wolf Men were coming directly at them. They were men, but they were still wolves—they came with mouths open, teeth sharp and tongues hanging out, slavering. Mary braced herself for a second shot.

But Watson shot first. One of the Wolf Men fell, whimpering, to the floor. The second leaped at Watson and sank his fangs into the doctor's shoulder. Watson screamed—the sound shocked Mary. Holmes stood between her and the second Wolf Man, his revolver still trained on Adam, who was shouting with pain. Mary ducked under Holmes's arm. The room was a chaos of noise and movement, and her arm ached from the first shot she had fired. But she shot again, aiming at what she could, which was the Wolf Man's side. He gave a bark, stumbled, then fell. Watson staggered back against the wall and slid down until he was sitting, his knees drawn up. Mary crawled over to him. The shoulder of his jacket was torn and hung down, but worse than that, the flesh beneath it was torn as well. Blood dripped down the sleeve. She was almost afraid to touch it, but she must do something. What?

"Tell me what to do, Doctor," she said. He looked so pale that she was afraid he was going to faint. She felt a pull on the hem of her skirt and looked down. It was the Wolf Man, not dead but clearly dying. He looked at her with the eyes of a wolf, pleading. He did not understand death, any more than an animal does. He raised his head and howled. For a moment, she pitied him. But Watson would bleed to death if they didn't get him out of there, soon. That was what she must focus on right now.

Mary heard a sound behind her. More Beast Men? Surely there could not be more. She turned—there, standing in the doorway behind them, were Diana and Beatrice. *Thank you,* she thought, not sure whom she was thanking—God, or Diana, or both.

"Do you think you can defeat me? Me, Adam Frankenstein?" Mary turned back to see Adam stagger forward, blood running down his face, once again moving toward Justine. "You can kill these pitiful creations of Prendick's. You can kill them all. But you'll still have to contend with me! And you, Justine. Understand that you were made to be mine! You are mine forever. I would rather kill you with my own hands than see you live without me."

"Come any closer and I'll tear your throat out!" It was Catherine.

She stood in front of Justine, in her nightgown, with Watson's jacket hanging open, and screeched with rage. It was a wild sound, the sound of a puma in the mountains, inhuman and frightening.

> BEATRICE: It was indeed! I'd never heard anything like it.

"Beasts! Bring her to me!" Adam shouted. The Boar Man lunged at Catherine, while the Bear Man turned and lumbered toward Holmes, reaching for him with misshapen hands. Once again, Holmes shot—he hit the Bear Man in the forehead, and with an almost puzzled expression, the Bear Man stumbled forward and fell at the detective's feet.

Catherine leaped at the Boar Man. Griping him with her hands and feet, as though she were still a puma holding onto her prey, she bit down on his ear. He roared with pain, plunging left and right, trying to shake her off. She held on tightly, but he grabbed her by one leg and threw her onto the floor. The Boar Man leaned over her and opened his mouth, aiming for her throat, trying to bite through it. She twisted and turned in his grasp, feeling his hot breath on her skin, smelling the stink of it.

And then she saw two hands reaching above her, grasping the Boar Man's face, the thumbs over his eyes. She looked up and saw Beatrice, beautiful and grim. The Boar Man howled with pain. He stood and tried to shake Beatrice off as he had shaken Catherine, but now he was blind. His flailing arms found her and encircled her, as though in an embrace. He held on as tightly as he could, squeezing her around the chest. Beatrice struggled and gasped for air. "Help me!" she called faintly. Dodging around Catherine, still lying on the ground, Diana tried to find an opening, an opportunity. She waited for the right moment, waited, waited . . . then, she plunged her knife into the Boar Man's back.

BEATRICE: How did you know the knife would not
plunge into my back? We were circling round
and round, that beast and I, as though we were
dancing a waltz.

DIANA: I didn't. In life, you sometimes have to take
risks.

BEATRICE: Thank you . . . I think. At least you didn't
stab me. I suppose that is what matters.

The Boar Man roared and let Beatrice go, but the knife was
too small to do much damage. He swung around, then turned
toward Diana, following her smell. He lumbered in her direction,
swinging his arms wildly. She backed away, but she was no longer
near the door. In her effort to find an opening, Diana had circled
around, and she was now backing into the corner. In a moment,
she would be trapped. Suddenly, light glinted against the Boar
Man's throat. He fell to his knees, and then forward onto the floor.
Behind him stood Hyde, with the scalpel in his hand.

"You must be Diana," he said.

"Hullo, Dad," said Diana. "Nice to meet you, I guess."

"Traitor!" roared Adam. "Who took you in after you left
England? When you were wandering around Europe, friendless,
wanted by the police? Who gave you shelter and safety, a laboratory so you could continue your experiments? It was I! And this is
how you repay me!"

"You're mad, Adam," said Hyde. The Boar man moaned once,
then lay dead at Diana's feet, the blood from his jugular draining
onto the floor. "You told me we were coming to England so you
could challenge the society that had expelled me and would not
admit you as a member. Remember that? You wanted to punish

Van Helsing and his faction. When you recruited Prendick and we started making Beast Men, I believed you. And then we started collecting the women—what for? More experiments, you said. When I told you Justine was alive, it became all about kidnaping her, bringing her to you. This was always about your personal desires. You disgust me!"

"How dare you! You rat, you ape, you piece of refuse that I took in! How dare you insult me!" Adam turned to the cage, now empty, except for one remaining Beast Man—the one in the shadows. "Come out!" he said. "Come out now!" He strode over to the cage and picked up what was hanging on the wall beside it: a long black whip. He swung it, hitting the bars so they clanged and rattled. The last Beast Man started toward the cage door.

Mary, who was still kneeling by Watson, attempting to staunch the flow of blood from his shoulder, cried out. An old poem, taught to her as a child by her nursemaid, who had later become the respectable Mrs. Poole, went through her head: *Tyger, tyger, burning bright.* The Tiger Man had started to undergo the process of transformation, but was still only half man, half tiger. His head was vaguely human, his paws beginning to resemble hands. He walked awkwardly on all fours, with no tail. The scars from a series of surgeries gleamed red and angry.

He growled low in his throat at Adam, but seeing the whip, he turned toward Holmes and crouched, ready to spring. Holmes raised his revolver. Suddenly, the room was silent, except for a low sobbing that Mary realized was coming from Renfield, still crouched in the corner by the cage, with the keys in his hand. Would a bullet stop the Tiger Man before he could crush the detective in his jaws?

Catherine stepped in front of Holmes. Would she spring at the Tiger Man? Surely that would mean her death! She was less than half his size, no match for the power of his animal body. Mary was about to cry "Stop!" when Catherine shrugged off Watson's jacket, then pulled her nightgown over her head and stood naked in front of them all.

"Look at me," she said. The Tiger Man crouched, still ready to spring but not moving, looking at her. Over her brown skin ran the seams of many scars, like the map to an unknown destination. "Smell me. I am like you, Brother. I too was transformed by a Master with a Whip. But do you know what I did, Brother? For all the pain I had endured, I killed him. That was what I did. I turned on him and bit him through the throat. He was not a god, only a man, and he died more easily than I thought possible. Do you understand me, Brother?"

The Tiger Man looked at her with great yellow eyes. Then he dipped his head, still barred with black stripes, almost as though nodding to her. With a roar, he turned and sprang on Adam.

Mary realized she had stopped breathing only when she started again. She had been so afraid the Tiger Man would attack Catherine. . . .

CATHERINE: I wasn't afraid. He was my brother. And if he had attacked me, it would have been a fitting way to die.

DIANA: Oh, come off it. You always say stuff like that, as though you were in one of your own novels.

CATHERINE: Well, at any rate, I would have died so quickly that I wouldn't have felt it! What else was I supposed to do? I acted out of instinct. If I'd thought about it for a moment, we might all be dead now.

The Tiger Man landed with his paws on Adam's chest. Adam staggered back against the desk, but did not fall. The Tiger Man lunged for his face, but Adam hit him in the jaw with a fist—once, twice. With a roar, the Tiger Man fell to one side, landing heavily. He staggered and shook his head, disoriented. Where the paws had been on Adam's chest, his shirt was torn and streaked with red. "Renfield, the keys!" shouted Adam.

"And you'll give me lives? Many lives, Master?"

"Yes, as many as you want! Just throw me the keys, damn you!"

Renfield tossed the keys into the air. They arced, silver in the lamplight, then jangled as Adam caught them. He stepped behind the desk and pushed the chair aside.

"Watch out!" shouted Prendick. "There's a gun in that drawer. We kept it locked because of the Beast Men."

The Tiger Man shook himself once more, then put his front paws on the desk and jumped up so he was standing on top of the desk, between them and Adam. The desk was covered with piles of paper, probably receipts and bills of lading for Alderney Shipping. The piles slid and pieces of paper fluttered as the Tiger Man moved among them. He snarled and swatted Adam across the face. Adam's head snapped back, and long red welts appeared along his cheek. The Tiger Man reared back to strike again.

"Diana! Give me your knife!" said Mary.

"Why?" said Diana, not taking her eyes off the dangerous dance at the end of the room.

"Because I need to cut bandages! And then you need to get Justine out of here."

"What? Why me?"

"Because the rest of us have weapons, and you don't," said Mary. "For goodness' sake, just do as you're told for once! Lead Justine to the rendezvous place."

"What rendezvous place?"

"Across the street! That alley where we all met. Just take her there."

"Oh, all right. I never get to be in on the fun."

"How is Watson doing?" asked Holmes, looking down for a moment.

"Not well," she replied. "We need to get him out of here as soon as possible." She cut strips of cotton from her petticoat and wound them around his shoulder as best she could, but the bites were fierce and deep. If they did not get him out of the warehouse soon, Watson would bleed to death.

Adam snarled back, as though he were an animal as well, and hit the Tiger Man once more across the face. The Tiger Man fell heavily, sending papers fluttering across the desk and to the floor. In the moment that gave him, Adam had unlocked the drawer and taken out a revolver. It shone, cold and metallic, in his hand.

Holmes aimed, but once again the Tiger Man had risen and was between them. He roared, and then there came another roar: Adam had fired the revolver directly into his mouth. The Tiger Man fell back onto the floor in a shower of papers. As he fell, his paws reached for a final purchase. One of them caught the lamp, which toppled and rolled over the desk.

"Oh no, you don't!" shouted Adam to Diana. "You're not taking her anywhere!"

Mary glanced back for a moment. Thank goodness—she could see Justine disappearing through the office door. How would Adam respond?

He was still standing behind the desk, revolver raised. There were papers on the desk, papers on the floor, and now—"They're burning!" shouted Catherine.

Oil spilled from the lamp and spread across the desk. Suddenly, the desktop was in flames. Adam stepped back and raised his hands, as though to ward them off.

"We must get out of here!" said Beatrice. "The chemicals in those jars are flammable."

"Out, now, all of you!" said Holmes. "Mary, can you support Watson?"

"With help," she said. "It will have to be Catherine. He's too weak to breathe Beatrice's poison."

"I'll help," said Hyde. Mary looked at him, startled. Why was he offering to help? No doubt so they would let him escape. . . .

"You're not as strong as I am," said Catherine contemptuously. She put her shoulder under Watson's arm. Mary put her shoulder under the other, and together, they raised him. Holmes still stood with his revolver trained on Adam, who was almost invisible behind the flames on the desk and the smoke rising from them.

The papers on the floor had caught fire as well. Renfield was screaming, a high shriek like a teakettle on the boil. Something bolted out from under the operating table—the Orangutan Man. He ran toward Holmes. More quickly than the detective could respond, the Orangutan Man reverted to his animal nature and, on all fours, slipped between Holmes and the doorframe, then out the door.

"He's not important," said Holmes. "But you need to go! I'll stay and see this through to the end."

They filed out through the space behind Holmes: Beatrice first, then Mary and Catherine supporting Watson between them. Hyde tried to follow them, but "I don't think so," said Holmes. "You're not leaving until I do." As they left the room, Mary glanced back. Holmes raised his revolver and shot at the lantern hanging from the ceiling. The reservoir shattered, and oil spilled over the floor. In a moment, it too was in flames.

Then she saw Adam, in flames, lurching from behind the desk, across the room. How many bullets did Holmes have left? She had not kept count . . .

But she could not stay to help him. There was Watson to get out into the cool night air. She and Catherine followed Beatrice down the hall, stumbling out the door. They crossed the street, with Watson's feet dragging on the stones between them. In the alley, Diana was waiting, with Justine and Charlie. And—

"Alice!" she cried. "What in the world are you doing here?"

Together, she and Catherine set Watson down, as gently as they could, against the brick wall of a warehouse. He was moaning and barely conscious.

"She's from the Magdalen Society," said Catherine. "How do you know her?"

"She used to be my scullery maid, is how," said Mary. "Alice, what were you doing—"

"Look!" said Beatrice. Through the first-floor window, they could see that the warehouse office was filled with flames. And in a moment, they could see flames through the window on the second floor as well. Flames rose to the roof of the warehouse. Where was Holmes? Mary scanned the building anxiously.

"Don't forget, we have a wounded man," Beatrice reminded her.

"Of course." He would be all right. He must be all right. Sherlock Holmes would not be defeated by Adam Frankenstein . . . would he? *No, certainly not,* she told herself. She turned to Charlie. "Can you find some way to get Dr. Watson to a hospital? He needs to be looked at immediately. A cab, or a cart of some sort." Mary checked the bandages on his shoulder. They were already stained through.

"I'll look, miss," said Charlie, "though cabs don't come to this part of the city, and I don't know where I'm going to find a cart, this time of night."

"I'll go with you," said Diana. "It's better than waiting around here!" Before Mary could stop her, she followed Charlie into the darkness.

"Damn that girl! Will she ever learn to do as she's told?" Mary tried to make Watson as comfortable as she could on the cobble-stones. He moaned again and shook his head back and forth—it reminded her of the wounded Tiger Man. Had Holmes come out of the warehouse yet? Resolutely, she brought her mind back to the problem at hand.

"Someone is on fire!" said Justine. "Look—through the window. Is that him? Is that—Adam?" In the warehouse office lurched a form, massive, entirely engulfed in flames. The flames were so high and bright now, blazing through the windows and up from the roof, that they illuminated even the alley.

"It must be," said Catherine. "Who else would be that tall?"

Two shots rang out—who had fired them? And then Holmes was running out of the building, with Hyde at his heels. Mary breathed a sigh of relief on seeing Holmes. But Hyde—for a moment, she wished he could have died in the fire. The thought was wrong, unworthy of her. This was her father . . . no, she was not ready to accept that. Not yet.

When they reached the alley, Hyde looked back at the burning warehouse. "I don't suppose even Frankenstein's creature can escape such a conflagration," he said. "Wait, what are you doing?"

Holmes had clapped a pair of handcuffs on him. "Edward Hyde, you are under arrest for the murder of Sir Danvers Carew. It will give me great pleasure to deliver you to Scotland Yard."

Hyde snarled like a dog, then threw back his head and laughed. "Nicely played, Mr. Holmes. It will be my great pleasure to see you prove your case in court."

"And I will be sorry when you are hanged, Mr. Hyde."

"Wait, where's Prendick?" asked Catherine. "Did he get out? Is he still in there?"

MARY: I was worried you were going to run back in after him!

CATHERINE: Certainly not. I mean, I did think about
it for a moment. Because unlike him, I don't leave
people to die.

"I have no idea," said Holmes. "In the confusion of the fire, he
could have run toward the back of the building and escaped out
the window."

"Prendick always was a coward," said Hyde. "A coward and
a mediocre scientist who lacked imagination. It was foolish of
Moreau to teach him as much as he did."

"That's probably the only thing on which we will ever agree,"
said Catherine.

"Isn't that him?" asked Beatrice.

A dark shape was running across the road toward them. "Don't
leave me! I don't want to die! I don't want to die!" Renfield waved
his hands frantically.

"All right, you won't die," said Holmes. "Just come with us—
quietly, mind—and we'll take you safely home again."

"To my flies?" asked Renfield, rubbing his hands together.

"Yes, to your flies," said Mary. "Big fat juicy ones. You just
need to come with us."

"Since I am inconveniently out of handcuffs," added Holmes.

"Oh, I'll go with you so nicely! I'll be good, you'll see!"
Renfield smiled anxiously. *He can't be trusted,* Mary thought. And
yet they would have to trust him, for now. Certainly he was more
deeply involved in this case—with the Société des Alchimistes,
if not the murders—than they had thought. How had her father,
or rather Hyde, convinced him to confess to murders he had not
committed? And why Renfield in the first place? What was his
connection with the society, and with Hyde? But this was no time
for questions.

With a crash, the roof of the warehouse fell in. They could see burning pieces of it falling into the second floor, where Beatrice had been held captive. The street was no longer dark. Now, light from the fire flickered across the cobblestones, illuminating the London night. Even in the alley, they could feel its heat and hear its roar, as though it were speaking with the voice of the dead Beast Men.

"We need to move," said Holmes. "Both for Watson's sake, and because I need to let the authorities know there's a fire. It could spread through this entire area."

"We found it!" Diana's voice came out of the darkness. She emerged, followed by Charlie, into the light of the conflagration. "There's a steamboat by the docks, and the captain is willing to take us upriver. He swore at us proper for waking him up, and said he wouldn't take us for love or money. But I told him you had lots of money, so I hope you do. He says he won't fire up the boiler until he sees it."

"He can take us to the Royal Hospital! Surely they'll have the facilities to treat even such a wound," said Mary. If only they could get Watson to a hospital quickly. . . .

"Dr. Watson will not live that long, not if he loses more blood," said Beatrice. "We must cauterize the wound."

"How?" asked Catherine. "There's our fire to heat metal, but it's too dangerous to approach. You can feel how hot it's burning, even from here." As she spoke, the second floor broke through and fell into the first. By the time the fire burned out, the building would be a skeleton.

"I can do it." Beatrice rolled back her sleeves. "Mary, remove those bandages. They must be changed anyway—they are soaked through with blood."

"A chemical burn. How clever of you, Miss Rappaccini," said Hyde.

Beatrice looked at him scornfully. "You would have made me

a murderer," she said. Mary had not realized she could sound so contemptuous.

MARY: And I've never heard you sound like that since.

DIANA: Oh no, our Beatrice is always so polite!

MARY: Unlike some.

Mary removed the bandages as quickly as she could, trying not to think about how deep those gashes must be, what all that blood meant. When the shoulder was bare, although crusted with blood, Beatrice touched it—carefully, carefully, with the tips of her fingers. Where she touched, the dried blood bubbled away and the skin burned. But it was clean, as though disinfected by fire. With more strips from her petticoat, Mary bandaged the shoulder again.

"Nicely done. You would make a good nurse, Miss Jekyll," said Holmes. Mary flushed at the compliment, glad it was dark so Holmes could not see. "Now, I must get Watson to the hospital. Charlie, can you find the nearest fire station and alert the Fire Brigade?"

"Of course we can," said Diana. "If you turn left, and left again, there's a road down to the docks. The boat is named *Hesperus*—it's painted on the side."

"No! You stay right here—," said Mary, but it was already too late. Charlie and Diana had melted away into the darkness. "Damn and double damn!"

"Well, Miss Prim and Proper is cursing," said Catherine. "That, I never thought I would hear!"

"You're going to hear it a lot more if she keeps behaving like that," said Mary.

DIANA: And I have! You know, it would do you good
to curse a little more. . . .

MARY: Don't you have something productive to do?
Like, I don't know, drink poison?

"I'll lift Watson, if someone can help me on the other side,"
said Holmes.

"That will not be necessary," said Justine. "I am recovered
from the ether now. I can carry him myself."

What a strange procession they made! Catherine walked in
front, since she was the only one who could see in the dark, wearing Holmes's frock coat over her nakedness. The moon shone
brightly onto the street down to the water, but the warehouses
in this area were old, the streets badly maintained. It was easy
to trip over uneven stones or bits of refuse. Behind Catherine,
Justine carried Watson as easily as she would carry a large pillow.
Behind her walked Holmes, with Hyde at his side in handcuffs,
and Beatrice next to him. He had been warned that if he tried
to escape, either Catherine would bite him or Beatrice would
breathe on him. He did not seem to relish either option. Then
came Mary with Alice, and finally Renfield in the rear, afraid to
be left behind in the darkness.

CHAPTER XVII

A Boat on the Thames

Even in the darkness, Mary could see that Alice had her arms wrapped around herself. She took off her mackintosh and draped it over the girl's shoulders. "There, put your arms into the sleeves and button up the front. It's too cold for a nightgown. How ever did you end up at the Magdalen Society? I thought you were going back to your family in . . . the country somewhere? I don't think you ever told us."

"Will you be angry, miss, if I tell you that I lied to you and Mrs. Poole? There weren't no family in the country, just a charity school. My mum left me at an orphanage when I was only a baby. Guess she couldn't take care of me herself. When I was old enough to learn my letters, I was sent to the School for Impoverished Children in Spitalfields. I've never been outside London."

"But you told me about milking cows and gathering eggs!" It was difficult to believe that Alice—shy, silent Alice—had lied, particularly to Mrs. Poole. Why, Mary herself wouldn't have been brave enough to lie to the housekeeper.

MRS. POOLE: She knows I've forgiven her. Alice is a
    good girl, and won't do it again.

ALICE: Thank you, Mrs. Poole.

"Aye, one of the other girls was from the country," said Alice. "At the school there were two kinds: girls whose parents paid for them, though little enough it was, and girls who had no parents, and who were paid for by subscription. That was me, one of the charity girls. My friend was one of the paid girls—her dad paid for her, because her mother had died and her stepmother didn't like her. We shared a bed, and at night when I couldn't sleep, she used to tell me stories about life on the farm. She was terrible homesick!"

"But why did you lie to us?" They were at the water now. Moonlight shone down on the Thames, and at the dock, among the boats moored there, was the *Hesperus*. Its lanterns were lit, fore and aft, and Mary could see its name written in white paint on the prow. It was a small steam launch, with its chimney already smoking—the captain must have decided to trust them after all.

"Ahoy, there!" called Holmes. "May we board, Captain?"

"Aye, if you'll show me you can afford it," shouted a rough voice. The captain stepped into the lantern light. He was what Mary would have expected a steamboat captain to look like: grizzled, with a knit sweater and flat cap on his head. "A pound for each person, that's what I want. And if I can count correctly, and I can, there are nine of you, and that makes nine pounds even."

"Nine pounds!" said Mary. That was an outrageous sum!

"Aye, that's what I want, little lady. And it looks to me as though you'll pay it, seeing as that gentleman ain't looking too healthy. What did he do, drink too much? And what are you, circus performers? Not that I care, mind you. It takes all sorts to make a world, and there are sorts down here by the docks that would make you think the world was a strange place indeed."

"I'll give you five now, and the rest when we get to the Royal Hospital," said Holmes. "This man is wounded—we must get him to a doctor as soon as possible. I give you my word that you shall be paid."

"Aye, and who might you be, leading a man around in hand-cuffs, followed by loose women in various states of undress? How am I to know you're not a criminal yourself?"

Loose women! Well, looking around her, Mary had to admit they didn't look particularly respectable. At least Alice had a mackintosh to cover her nightgown. But Catherine's bare legs stuck out from under Holmes's frock coat.

"I'm Sherlock Holmes, and I'm taking this man to Scotland Yard."

"Mr. Holmes! Am I supposed to believe that? Then you'll be able to tell me all sorts of things about myself, without me having to tell you." The captain looked skeptical. "Tell me something, Mr. Holmes. Anything about me that you wouldn't know."

Holmes's expressions were usually difficult to read, but even by lantern light, Mary could see that he was thoroughly exasperated. "Your initials are G.M. You smoke a pipe, your preferred tobacco is Old Virginian, indeed you were smoking your pipe as we approached. You were a sailor but were wounded by a bullet to the shoulder, so you gave up the seafaring life to become a riverboat captain. Your wife is a conscientious woman who scolds you for drinking excessively. Is that enough to prove my identity, Captain? My associate, Dr. Watson, is grievously wounded."

The captain looked at him with wonder. "It's like magic, it is! Aye, I'm George Mudge, and you're right about everything, even the old woman, who's far too good for a reprobate like me. How we do like reading those stories of Dr. Watson's on a Sunday evening. It will be an honor to take the both of you— and your companions—upriver. Come aboard, Mr. Holmes! I'll have to tell Mike, who runs the boiler. He won't believe it's really you!"

If Mary had not been so tired, she might have laughed out loud. Next, Captain Mudge would be asking Holmes for his autograph!

What a night it had been: fear and tragedy and absurdity, all mingled. She simply didn't know how to respond anymore.

The steamboat was small, just large enough for about twenty passengers. Under ordinary circumstances, it was probably a pleasure-launch hired for day trips up the river. Justine carried Watson to the back, where he could lie on one of the benches. Holmes followed her, leading Hyde. Beatrice went after him, and Mary was about to follow as well, but . . .

"No, I want to go up front," said Catherine. "It's bad enough being on the water. At least let me breathe fresh air, not that stuff coming out of the chimney."

"I didn't know you disliked water," said Mary.

"Did you ever know a cat that liked it?" Catherine led them to the front of the boat, past the chimney. Mary did not particularly mind the smoke, but to Catherine, with her cat's nose, the stench must be terrible.

> CATHERINE: It was. Most of London smells terrible.
> Except the rubbish heap outside Billingsgate
> Market. That smells of lovely fish heads. . . .

So Mary followed her, relieved that she did not have to sit near Hyde. Eventually, she would have to confront him, but not yet. Alice followed Mary. There, they settled themselves on the seats facing forward, presumably so pleasure-seekers could see where they were going. Renfield stood undecided, not certain which way to go, but finally turned to sit with Holmes and Hyde in the back. Thank goodness the madman would not be sitting with them. Yet another thing Mary would not have to worry about, for a while at least.

When they were seated, Mudge cast off the line, and then they were free of the shore and on the water, steaming up the Thames in the darkness. *I've never been on a boat before,* thought Mary. Yet another item on the growing list of things she had never done. The wooden seat was hard, the air was cold, and there was darkness all around the lantern on the prow, like a large firefly leading them into the night. All around, she heard the lapping of water. The ground under her feet, which had always been so stable, was no longer stable, but swayed side to side, as though she were floating on uncertainty itself.

BEATRICE: That's a lovely image, Catherine.

CATHERINE: Thank you. I rather like it myself.
I may write "cheap popular fiction," as a reviewer recently called it, but I can do symbolism. . . .

Catherine, who was sitting next to Mary, touched her arm and leaned toward her. "Are you all right?"

"I think so. I'm not sure. Probably not. It's the first time I've had a dead father reappear, you know?" She said it low, so Alice would not hear. The last thing she wanted was Alice worrying about her.

"It's going to be all right." Catherine squeezed her arm—the gesture was unexpected, from Catherine. She had been so aloof, so independent, until now. "We're going to be all right. Adam's dead, the Beast Men have been destroyed, and we're going to get Watson to the hospital."

"Yes, I know." Mary wished she could sound more convinced. It was the darkness, the motion of the river, the way it mirrored the uncertainty of her life—of all their lives. "But what about you? Prendick . . ."

Catherine looked out at the darkness. "As soon as you told me he was alive, I knew I would see him again." She was silent for a moment, then added, "He looks different. Older, and his hair's turned gray. I didn't get the chance to talk to him. Perhaps I never will, if he died in that fire. Although if he survived the ocean, he can probably survive anything. But Hyde . . . I mean, your father. You'll have to speak with him, you know. At the very least, you'll have to ask him about the Société des Alchimistes. You need information, if nothing else."

"I'm hungry," said Alice, suddenly. "Begging your pardon, miss. Perhaps I shouldn't have mentioned it, but I had the thought and then it just came out. Must be almost dying back in that warehouse. That would make anyone hungry, I'm sure."

Mary laughed, low so as not to disturb the silence. Not that anyone would have cared, but it was so present, the silence of the boat, the sound of the water, that it seemed almost a sacrilege to speak too loudly. She could not help it—here she was worrying about what would happen tomorrow, and the day after that, when there was plenty to worry about tonight. Thank goodness for Alice. At least her problem had a solution.

"I'm sorry, Alice. I don't have anything, although as soon as we get home, Mrs. Poole—wait, I do have something after all!" The tea cake she had put into the pocket of her mackintosh earlier—could it possibly still be there? "Reach into your pocket—no, the other one. Yes, can you feel something?"

Alice pulled out the tea cake, flattened like a top hat at the opera.

"Well, it will have to do for now, I'm afraid. At least it didn't fall out along the way!"

Alice ate it in small bites, to make it last. They could hear a murmur from the back of the boat. It was Holmes's voice—Mary was sure of it. And then a rougher voice that must be the captain's. What were they talking about?

"I'm sorry I lied to you, miss," said Alice. "See, the head-mistress at the charity school, she weren't a kind woman, or an

educated woman neither, like you and Mrs. Poole. She didn't like
having charity girls—only the Board of Trustees made her take
them so the school could get subscriptions. She always said no
one would want an orphan. So when I was sent to you, to see if I
would do as a scullery maid, I told Mrs. Poole that I had grown up
on a farm. My friend had told me so much about it, because she
was homesick, that I could talk about milking and gathering eggs
and how the hay smelled when it was cut and stacked in the fields.
I ain't never seen a hayfield, really. I'm sorry, miss. I was only ten
at the time, and didn't know better."

"You don't need to apologize. I'm just glad you're safe and
coming home with us! But tell me how you ended up at the
Magdalen Society."

"And why were you following me?" asked Catherine. "That's
how she was caught by Hyde. I was in Mrs. Raymond's office,
looking through her desk, when that old witch and Hyde walked
in. They started talking about the girls—Mrs. Raymond was the
one giving Hyde their names, so Adam could kill them and take
their body parts. And they heard a noise—Alice was outside the
door. Why were you standing outside that door?"

"Well, it were this way. I hadn't nowhere to go, when Miss
Mary dismissed me. I tried sweeping a crossing for a while, but a
big boy took my crossing and the broom I'd bought. The money
Miss Mary had given me for my wages was running out. I slept in
doorways, but the police would tell me to move on, so I would
be walking most of the night. And soon I wouldn't be able to buy
food. So I thought, who can orphans turn to when they can't turn
to anyone else? Why, to God of course, like it says in those books
Mrs. Poole never wants me to read because she says they're so
low, but only a penny. So I went into a church, and the minister
asked about the state of my soul and whether I was afraid I'd fall
into sin if I lived on the streets, and I said yes—although I'd have

thrown myself into the Thames first, which I suppose is another kind of sin. The minister gave me a pamphlet and told me about the Magdalen Society. I was careful to tell Mrs. Raymond that a gentleman had importuned me, thinking she might not let me stay if I just said I was hungry, and she told me to sign that big book. I told that lie to you too, miss," she said to Catherine, "and for that I'm right sorry. I didn't know you were a friend of Miss Mary's, then. So there I was for a week, getting fed regular and a bed to sleep in, although terribly bored, when I saw you."

DIANA: I told you, Our Lady of Dullness . . . and Murder! I guess the murdering part wasn't that dull.

ALICE: I'd rather the dullness, thank you very much, having almost been murdered myself. I'll wear scratchy wool, eat overcooked food, and listen to sermons that make you fall asleep in your chair, if it means not being poisoned.

DIANA: Alice, you have no sense of adventure.

ALICE: Quite right, miss.

"You hadn't yet gotten your Magdalen Society dress when I saw you," Alice continued. "That terrible gray wool we all had to wear! It was when you were coming out of Mrs. Raymond's office. I was mopping the floor on my hands and knees, and got a good look at you as you walked past, though you wouldn't have noticed me then. I thought, *I'd know that dress she's wearing anywhere*—it belonged to Mrs. Jekyll, God rest her soul. It was her lavender tea gown, and many's the time I've helped Mrs. Purvis, the laundress, wash it. And I thought, *I want to find out why she's wearing that dress.* So when we went into the sewing room, I watched you, and then at dinner I sat next to you. I asked Sister Margaret if you could share my bed, since I was lonely at night, having always slept with another servant. That was another lie, I'm afraid. And then when you got up at night, I followed."

"Well, that explains a great deal," said Catherine. She sounded amused. There was just enough light from the lantern to see that she was smiling. "And I have to compliment you on the lying— you seem quite accomplished at it."

"Oh, it's terrible, miss," said Alice. "But once I get started, I can't seem to stop. Going on about gathering eggs in the morning, how warm they felt in my hand, and the cornflowers in the fields, and my two brothers. About how I missed the farm, when I'd never been farther from London than a cab horse!"

"Oh, Alice, if only I'd known!" said Mary. "I couldn't have paid you, but you would at least have had a roof over your head."

"I couldn't tell Mrs. Poole, miss. Not after the terrible lies I'd told."

"Well, we're going to go home and tell her. And then you'll stay at Park Terrace until we can figure out what to do with you."

"Home," said Catherine. "That sounds rather nice—home." She was not sure she believed in the concept.

It does sound nice, thought Mary. And that was what she'd been assuming, without realizing it—the house on Park Terrace would become a home. For Diana and Beatrice, and Catherine and Justine, and now for Alice. They would all live there together, no more going off to join the circus or perform in freak shows. Which might not at all be what the others were assuming would happen.

In the back of the boat, a different conversation was taking place.

"Your initials are on your handkerchief, which is tucked into the sleeve of your jacket. The pipe is in your breast pocket—I can see the stem, and you smell of tobacco smoke. There is ash on the breast of your jacket, which together with the distinctive smell allowed me to identify your preferred tobacco at once as Old Virginian. As you may know, I have written a monograph on the different types of tobacco ash and how to distinguish between them. You have the weathered face of a man who has spent years in a tropical climate and the bearing of a military man, particularly about the neck, so you could have been a soldier. But the knots at the end of your dock lines are distinctly nautical; even if they were made by your subordinate, you would have taught and supervised him. I deduced a man who had served on a sailing ship, most likely in the South Seas, and had come back to London to settle down. It would be easy and logical for such a man to run a steamboat up and down the Thames. You move your left arm stiffly, likely from an old wound, and there is a bullet on your watch chain, no doubt the very bullet dug out of that shoulder. You have the flushed nose and cheeks of a drinker, and your trousers are patched on one knee—a thick patch, carefully sewn around the edges. There is your conscientious and no doubt thrifty wife. Such a wife would object to your nights at the pub, and is not likely to refrain from scolding."

"Ah, well, when you explain it like that, it seems obvious," said Mudge.

"Of course, it always seems obvious once it's been explained." Holmes sounded annoyed, but Beatrice could tell he was scarcely paying attention to Mudge. He was worried about Watson.

"Put your hand on Dr. Watson's forehead," she said to Justine. "How does it feel?"

"Hot. Hotter than it should, I think." Watson's head was on Justine's lap. She held him as tenderly as though he were a young bird in a nest. It is the way she holds everything—when you are as strong as Justine, the world is terribly fragile.

"I was afraid it would be," said Beatrice. "He's running a fever,

Mr. Holmes. If I had my medicines, I could bring down the fever and fight the infection—but I have nothing. I only hope the hospital has what he needs. The state of medical knowledge in London is, let us say, not what one might expect of the largest city in the world."

"I'll get you there as quickly as I can," said Mudge. "I'll tell Mike to stoke up the boiler, then send him back here to meet you. He won't believe it's you, sir. What a night! We came down here because a party of gentlemen, fresh from a club in Mayfair and deep in their cups, wanted to go slumming, see what they called the real London. But they were supposed to be back hours ago. No doubt they're dreaming in some opium den, unless they've been murdered already. I was cursing my foolishness in having agreed to bring them down here, but it's allowed me to meet you. Life's a rum thing, ain't it? If I find a piece of paper somewhere, you'll give me your autograph, won't you, Mr. Holmes?"

Holmes assured him that yes, he would be perfectly happy to autograph anything, if the captain would just get them to Chelsea as quickly as possible.

Mudge went to check on his boiler, and they sat in silence: the detective, the murderer, the Giantess, the Poisonous Girl, and the man who might die that night.

In the bow, Mary, Catherine, and Alice had also fallen into silence. What were our heroines thinking, as the boat moved upriver through the darkness?

> DIANA: Now you really do sound like a penny dreadful! Anyway, how could you possibly know what was happening in the back of the boat, when you were sitting in the front?

> CATHERINE: Because I asked Beatrice, and unlike you, she has an excellent memory.

BEATRICE: Please don't interrupt. I want to know
what we were all thinking. I remember what I
was thinking . . .

Beatrice watched the face of the feverish man. Had she done
enough to sanitize the wound? If there was fever, infection must
be present. Could it be stopped in time? She thought of her father's
garden in Italy. The herbs she had grown there could stop the infection, but where would she find them in England? She remembered
the Italian sun and the hills around Padua, with their vineyards,
their orchards of fig and olive trees. How different from this city,
where it was always cold and wet. Would she ever be warm again?
Once, she had wanted love and joy, but those were gone. She no
longer expected them of life. All she wanted now was freedom. If
she had that, it would be enough.

Catherine remembered another ship, bearing her away
from the island where she had been made. Pretending to be an
Englishwoman although she had never seen one, guessing how she
was supposed to act by what seemed to be expected of her, what
the captain and his sailors were startled by in her behavior. She
had learned quickly: not to climb the rigging, to eat her food with
fork and spoon as well as a knife, to agree that the heat of the
sun made her feel faint and accept a seat in the shade. Anything
unusual in her behavior, she explained as loss of memory from
the trauma of being shipwrecked and having to sustain herself
on a deserted island. And then the long voyage to England as the
ward of Sir Geoffrey Tibbett, wearing white cotton dresses he had
bought for her in Lima, carrying a parasol to shield herself from
the sun. He was half in love with her but unwilling to admit it
to himself. She was not surprised that when he introduced her
to his wife, on the doorstep of his house on Curzon Street, the
woman had welcomed her with a frown and said, "Do come in"

as though meaning the exact opposite. Then scrounging on the streets of London, like one of the stray cats that lived on refuse. Would she have to go back to that life? Or was this a new life waiting for her, a life with these . . . other monsters, for weren't they monsters, after all?

Mary was thinking of the handcuffed man who sat in the back of the boat. This small, crooked man with the sneering face—was he truly the tall, respectable Dr. Jekyll? The father who had perched her up on a laboratory chair and shown her the different colors of the Bunsen burner flame in response to various chemicals? He had not acknowledged their relationship except by a careful nod, which could have meant anything but felt significant somehow—as though he were afraid of going too far, of making a gesture that would be rejected. *As it would be,* she thought. *I could forgive him betraying me, but betraying Mama—never.* Diana might accept him as her father, but Mary never would.

Justine, if she had been anyone other than Justine, would have been thinking of that day's events. Of how she had been kidnapped by the Beast Men and taken to the creature who had loved her so long, with such a cruel, sick love. She would have been thinking of how she had been rescued by Holmes, Watson, and the other women. But she was Justine, so she was thinking about whether or not there was a heavenly resting place where Adam's tortured soul would find peace at last, or oblivion. And she was probably quoting something from Goethe. . . .

> JUSTINE: I was, in fact. I was thinking about Goethe's idea of the soul. It resembles the sun, which seems to go out at night, but is simply diffusing its light elsewhere and will return again when day comes. We cannot see it, but that does not mean it doesn't exist. So, too, with the human soul.

Faith is knowing that the soul is eternal, whether
we see it or not—as God is.

DIANA: Whatever. Can we get back to the story?
This is the interesting part.

Far away, across the city, Diana was being important, and a boy. She was telling the fire marshal that she and Charlie had seen a fire and thought it should be reported before any more buildings were burned.

DIANA: See? You have no problem writing as me,
when you have to.

CATHERINE: When I absolutely have to!

"You rascals probably set it yourself!" said the fire marshal, frowning down at them. "I should have you both arrested. What were you doing down by the docks, anyway?"

"Oh no, sir," said Diana. "See, we was following this gentleman, thinking he might give us a few coppers, like. He looked rich enough, and we thought he might be going to one of them dens of iniquity, as me mum calls them. And he wouldn't mind parting with a few coppers. But he went into that warehouse, and there was another gentleman waiting for him, and they started shouting at each other and going at each other something terrible. 'I'll kill you for that, Prendick!' the other man shouted, and then he hit him, and the one named Prendick hit back, and they was circling round and round each other, grappling like wrestlers, and it was a grand fight! But then they fell on top of the lamp and knocked it over, and soon the whole room was on fire. Like the picture of Hell in the *Child's Own Bible*. That's how it started, sir."

"And how did you see all this, unless you went in after him?"

"Why, we watched it through the window. We didn't want to miss such a grand rumble. And then the Prendick one came running out, and the other fellow, he just lay there, and before you could say Jack Robinson, the building was up in flames, to the second floor! So we come to tell you, and maybe you'll give us some coppers for being such good citizens, eh?"

"Nothing for you! I know what you were about, following a gentleman. Planning to pick his pockets, likely as not. If you'd done so, you'd be going to gaol right now. All right, call out the men, Jensen. There's a fire down by the docks, though precious little we can do about it. Those old warehouses are about falling down anyway. And you two, get yourselves out of here. Someday, I'll see you both swinging from nooses, and I'll say good riddance."

Diana and Charlie watched the men come out of the fire station, the horses pulling the wagon, the men in their uniforms with metal hats gleaming in the light of the street lamps. Then they headed back toward Soho. It would have taken them hours, had they not caught a ride in a wagon heaped with cabbages that was most likely, Diana thought, heading to Covent Garden Market. In this, she was right.

DIANA: As usual.

She did not bother to ask the wagoner's permission, of course. She grabbed the back of the cart, hoisted herself up, and climbed in among the cabbages, crouching down so the wagoner would not notice. Charlie followed her up and into the wagon, catching his foot on the edge and falling against the side, but the wagoner did not hear or turn around. Even if he had, what could he have seen in the dim light? Their clothes quickly became permeated with the smell of cabbage, but they were so tired and dirty that it scarcely bothered them.

They slipped out of the wagon just before it reached Covent Garden. The stalls were not yet open, but vendors were already piling up their produce: turnips and onions that had wintered over, lettuces and peas sown early, strawberries grown in greenhouses, peppers and aubergines brought in ships from warmer climates. As they walked through the market, following the narrow alleys between the stalls, a pale yellow sun rose over the buildings of London. Suddenly, the flower girls began their chant: "Flowers for sale! Loverly flowers, fresh from the country!"

When they had left the narrow alleys behind and were once more on familiar ground, in the streets of Soho, Charlie said, "You know, Diana, you're the best liar I ever heard."

"Ain't I, though?" Diana reached into her pocket and pulled out an apple. "I'm a pretty good thief, too. If I'd told him we were there on a Sunday School outing, he would never have believed us. People are always ready to believe the worst." She took a bite of the apple and then handed it to Charlie. "Here, share and share alike. Not too big a bite, mind, or I'll keep it all for myself!"

The sun was up in the sky by the time they reached Park Terrace. Diana rang the bell. Mrs. Poole answered the door with an "Oh, it's you, is it? Don't you both look a sight! What did you do, sweep chimneys? Come in, then, both of you, and get your-selves some breakfast. And tell me where Miss Mary is, because I haven't seen hide nor hair of her since yesterday. It's mortal wor-ried I've been, and I hope they're all right, those girls!"

CHAPTER XVIII

Back to Park Terrace

"How is he?" asked Mary, rising from one of the wooden benches provided for visitors. This seemed to be a night of sitting on hard benches. But at least they had made it here, all of them, and Captain Mudge had only charged them five pounds after all. "Because it's you, Mr. Holmes," he had said. "Wait until I tell the little woman who I ferried up the Thames tonight. Sherlock Holmes himself, and a bunch of circus performers! She won't right believe me."

"The doctor says he'll recover, but it will be a while before he can use that arm again," said Holmes. "I'm grateful to Miss Rappaccini for speaking with the physician. My medical knowledge is, I fear, too specialized for such a case. And of course to Miss Frankenstein for carrying him to the infirmary." He bowed to Justine, who had followed him and Beatrice up the stairs to the infirmary with Watson in her arms. They had been gone for almost an hour, while the rest of them waited below: Mary sitting on the bench with Alice falling asleep against her shoulder, Hyde handcuffed to one of the rails, Catherine pacing back and forth. Renfield crouched in a corner, muttering about his flies. Once, Hyde had turned to her, as though about to speak, but she had looked down and checked the time on her wristwatch, then wound it as though completely intent on the process. She had no wish to speak with him, not now.

"It was nothing at all, Mr. Holmes," said Justine. Perhaps carrying a man up a flight of stairs was nothing to a woman who could strangle Beast Men with her bare hands.

"Yes, it will take time, but with exercise, he should regain the full use of it," said Beatrice. She took off the surgical mask and gloves she had been wearing while in the infirmary. She had not wanted her breath to foul the air. "Mr. Holmes, when you said this was a hospital, I imagined it would be a medical facility. I did not expect—a charitable home for veterans?"

"Yes, the Royal Hospital has housed the injured veterans of our wars for more than a century," said Holmes. "Here they may live out the rest of their days in peace. I knew if such a wound could be treated anywhere in London, it would be here. And of course Watson himself is a veteran of the Afghan Campaign."

"Mr. Holmes! Hr. Holmes!" A man with a halo of silver hair ran down the hall toward them. "I can't let you go without telling you what a pleasure it is to see you here, and Dr. Watson as well. Although of course we're not pleased he's been injured. Far from it, I assure you. I'm the secretary of the hospital, and if there's anything we can do . . ." He bowed to Holmes, then looked at the women in their various states of undress with surprise.

"You can take care of Watson," said Holmes, "for which service I will be most grateful. Your physician assures me that he will recover fully, in time. Other than that assurance, all I require at the moment is a cab or carriage, so I can take a dangerous criminal to Scotland Yard. Or rather, two carriages for hire, so these young ladies can make their way home as well."

"Is there anything more we can do, Mr. Holmes?" asked Mary. She had wanted to go upstairs too, with Holmes, Beatrice, and Justine. But they could not leave Hyde or Renfield, so she and Catherine had stayed in the hall and waited. It had been frustrating, sitting and waiting, out of the action. She could have done more than serve as Alice's pillow.

"Can you take Miss Frankenstein and Miss Rappaccini back to your residence?" asked Holmes. "They've had a long night. I need to take Hyde and Renfield to Scotland Yard. Miss Moreau, if you could accompany me, I believe they would remain on their best behavior."

Why was Catherine going to Scotland Yard, while Mary was going back to Park Terrace? It wasn't fair. She could have guarded Hyde and Renfield just as well. She didn't have Catherine's teeth, but she still had her revolver . . .

She nudged Alice, and the scullery maid opened her eyes sleepily. "Is it time to make breakfast yet, Mrs. Poole?" she asked, yawning. Then she looked around and said, "Oh!" as though suddenly remembering the events of the night. Mary stood up and rubbed her aching shoulder.

Holmes took her elbow—she was so startled at the gesture that she almost jumped back. He leaned toward her and said, in a low voice, "I don't wish to alarm the others, Miss Jekyll. They believe our enemies have been defeated, but we don't know whether Prendick escaped, or where he has gone. We believe the Beast Men he created are dead, but we can't be sure. Certainly one got away in the confusion. We don't even know whether they had other confederates. I have asked Hyde, but he refuses to speak. It's still dangerous out there. I trust you to keep them safe from harm—Miss Rappaccini, Miss Frankenstein, and . . . that girl, whom I take to be a servant of yours?" He looked at Alice curiously. "As soon as I can, I will return with Miss Moreau and we can reconvene, as it were. I think Miss Frankenstein knows more than she has told us—we need to hear her story."

"All right, Mr. Holmes," said Mary. "I think I have just enough money left for the fare." She was disappointed at being sent home, but he was right. She had to get Beatrice and Justine safely back to Park Terrace. He had taken her elbow, he had spoken to her in confidence. . . . She did not quite know what to think, except that it was new, and she liked it.

When the secretary himself told them the carriages were waiting on Royal Hospital Road, they went out together. Just before Hyde mounted the steps into the first one, he turned to her and said, "Mary . . ." It was the first time he had spoken to her directly.

Mary looked at him: the crooked man with a face that might have been charming had it not borne such signs of past dissipation and malice. He seemed . . . cautious, almost pleading.

She looked away. She did not wish to speak with him, not here, not now. Perhaps later, after he had been charged with the murder of Sir Danvers Carew. Perhaps then she would visit him in prison, before his trial and hanging. Then she would ask him . . . what? Why he had performed those experiments. Where he had been all this time. How he could have treated her mother, and her, and even Diana, so badly.

"At least . . . ," continued the rasping voice. "At least I was able to see Ernestine once more, before she died."

See Ernestine? When had he seen her mother? Mary turned back, but he was already in the carriage, across from Renfield, with Catherine climbing up the steps behind him. "I'll see you at home," said Catherine, then pulled shut the carriage door. Holmes was already in the carriage as well, having entered on the other side. And then, before she could say "Wait!" the driver cried, "Gee up!" and the carriage rattled away across the cobblestones.

She stared after it. The face at the window, the face her mother had raved about before she died. Had it been the face of Hyde?

"Mary, are you all right?" said Beatrice. "You look as though you've seen a *fantasma*—a ghost."

They were all waiting for her—Beatrice, Justine, and Alice, looking at her curiously. She did not know what to say. If her mother had seen Hyde, suddenly at the window, after all those years—what would it have done to her? Killed her, most likely. The window was on the second floor, so how had he—but no, she had seen Diana climb. No doubt Hyde could climb as well. She remembered her mother in those last few weeks: delirious, raving. Then the precipitous decline. Her hair spread out on the pillow . . . Mary could not think about it anymore, not now. She had to get the others back to Park Terrace.

"Come on," said Mary. "Let's go home."

> CATHERINE: There was no need to envy me. I can't think of anything less interesting than taking that sniveling rat to Scotland Yard.

> DIANA: That's Dad you're talking about. And yes, I know how you feel about him, Mary Contrary. It doesn't change the fact that he's our father.

> CATHERINE: I meant Renfield. Going on and on about eternal life, and how he had been promised, and giving Hyde covert glances all the while. And Hyde ignoring him—ignoring all of us. Holmes tried asking him questions about the Alchemical Society. Who was involved? Where was it headquartered? What was its agenda? But he just stared out the window. And when Holmes tried questioning Renfield, he started in on his flies and spiders. Finally, we arrived at Scotland Yard.

He got out, and suddenly bobbies appeared from
I don't know where. One of them ran to tell
Inspector Lestrade. Holmes talked to Lestrade for
a few minutes while Renfield and Hyde were taken
away in handcuffs. Then he got in the carriage
again and we headed back to Park Terrace. He said
he wanted to talk to Justine as soon as possible.
That was it. Pretty disappointing, and not at all an
adventure. Also, you got breakfast before we did.

"What took you so long?" asked Diana. She was sprawled on
the parlor sofa, in yet another of Mary's nightgowns. How many
of them were left? Her hair was wet and combed back, no doubt
the work of Mrs. Poole. When she sat up, it left a damp spot on
the sofa where she had been lying.

"You look remarkably clean," said Mary.

"The ogress forced me to take a bath before breakfast. She would
have forced Charlie too, if he hadn't bolted out of here double-quick.
And I don't blame him, though he didn't get anything to eat."

"Oh, I put something in his pocket," said Mrs. Poole. "I
should have held you under the water until you stopped talking.
Running around London dressed like a newsboy at all hours!
What sort of behavior is that for a young lady? Good Lord, is that
little Alice?"

"Yes, ma'am," said Alice.

"It's a long story," said Mary. "Right now, I think we all need
food—except maybe Beatrice!" For the first time, she realized
that she was famished.

"Just tea for me please . . . ," Beatrice started to say, when
thunk, like a tree falling in a forest, Justine fell over onto the
carpet, exactly where the Pig Man had lain two nights ago.

"Justine!" said Beatrice. She knelt by Justine and examined her without touching. "I think she's fainted again. She's been so strong all night, but I wondered when the strain would begin to affect her. Mrs. Poole, can you bring the *sal volatile*? And if you have any brandy . . ."

Even after Justine had revived, Diana administering the smelling salts with perhaps too liberal a hand and Mary giving her sips of brandy out of a small glass, it took both of them to help her up the stairs to what had once been Dr. Jekyll's bedroom. Which Mary supposed was now Justine's bedroom. Beatrice followed them up.

> JUSTINE: I was so ashamed of myself for having fainted again! After all, I am the Giantess, the Strong Woman. . . .

> BEATRICE: It's not strength. I have explained to you—it's a matter of blood pressure, of how Frankenstein created you. All of us have our weaknesses.

They deposited Justine in bed. "I'll stay with you, *cara mia*," said Beatrice. "Perhaps Mrs. Poole can bring you up something to eat? And you should sleep. . . ."

"I cannot yet," said Justine. "Mr. Holmes said he wanted to talk to me as soon as possible. He wanted me to tell him everything I know about Adam. But you should all have breakfast. You do not need to stay with me, Beatrice."

"Don't be silly. Of course I will stay."

"She doesn't eat anyway," said Diana. "But I'm still hungry."

"You've already had breakfast," said Mary. She turned to Beatrice and Justine. "I'll ask Mrs. Poole to bring up something for you both." Should she stay? This was her house, after all. No, it was their house too. Let Beatrice stay—she did not have to be responsible for everything. Mary felt a sense of relief. There were others to share the responsibility now.

When she and Diana entered the morning room, Alice was already eating a breakfast of eggs and buttered toast, wolfing them down as though she were starving.

ALICE: Which I was.

"Lord, wouldn't Mrs. Poole rag me if I ate like that!" said Diana.

"Alice is a good girl, and you are nothing of the sort," said Mrs. Poole, coming into the morning room with a tray on which there was a pot of tea and another stack of toast. "I want Miss Mary to sit herself down and eat, before she collapses from hunger. Here's more tea, and there's milk and sugar on the table, and butter in the dish, and I almost forgot the orange marmalade. I bought a new jar yesterday, as *someone* seems to have a bottomless stomach. Shall I fry up an egg for you, miss?"

"What about for me?" asked Diana. "I wouldn't mind another egg." She sat on one of the chairs, drawing her legs up under the nightgown so her bare feet were on the chair cushion.

"As though you haven't already had two!" said Mrs. Poole. "If you want more, you can have toast. And try not to sit like a monkey."

Diana stuck a fork into the piece of toast on top of the pile, moved it to her plate, buttered it lavishly, then spread a thick layer of marmalade over it.

"Just toast for me, please," said Mary. She was hungry, but the thought of an egg turned her stomach. She poured herself a cup of tea and wrapped her fingers around it, grateful for the warmth. How long had it been since she last sat at this table? Two days? Could it only have been two days? It was as though time had passed differently. And here she was, back again at the same table, in the

same room, with morning sun streaming through the lace curtains. It seemed completely different.

"Well?" said Diana, after Mrs. Poole had left the room. "Did
you talk to him?"

"To whom?" Mary added two lumps from the Minton sugar
bowl, with its pattern of birds and flowers, that her mother had
purchased as a bride newly arrived in London, and sipped her tea.
Yes, that was exactly what she needed.

"To Dad, of course," said Diana. "Did you talk to him at all?
Ask him anything?"

"No," said Mary. "I'll talk to him when he's properly in
prison." And there she would ask him—what? Whether he had
climbed up the wall, looked in through the window? Whether
he had killed her mother? Intentionally or not, it scarcely mat-
tered. Ernestine Jekyll lay in her grave, in the churchyard of St.
Marylebone.

"Oh, you are so stupid!" said Diana. "Why didn't you talk to
him when you could? I wish I'd been there. I would have asked
him all sorts of questions. Like where he's been for fourteen
years. I bet he wasn't with Adam the whole time. I bet he traveled
around and had adventures. And you didn't even ask him about
them!"

Mary felt an urge to throw her teacup at Diana. "First of all,
he may be your father, but he's certainly not mine. My father died
the day yours took control of his body and life. Second, I have
no wish to know about his *adventures*, whatever they might be. I
want to know where the money went and how he could have abandoned . . ." Her mother. Her. She did not want to tell Diana about
her suspicions, not yet. After all, it wasn't Diana's mother who
had been killed. Mary had been the one to watch her mother die,
to stand by the grave as her mother's coffin was lowered into the
ground. She gripped the teacup tightly. And then she reminded

herself that Diana's mother had died a pauper's death, with no one to care for her or even bury her properly. She put the teacup back down on the table, afraid she might break it. "Third, you do not call me stupid in my own house."

"I calls it as I sees it," said Diana. "And he is as much your father as he is mine, *sister*. Do you think your precious Dr. Jekyll simply disappeared when he turned into Hyde? He's still there. He's always there. He may look different, but Hyde is just another name he calls himself." She gripped the butter knife, as though at any moment she might fly across the table and attack Mary with it.

Alice stared at them both, turning from one to the other, fascinated yet fearful, wondering if there was going to be a fight right here in the morning room.

Just then, the front doorbell rang. "That will be Catherine and Mr. Holmes," said Mary. "I didn't expect them to return so quickly! They must not have spent much time at Scotland Yard." Had they left Hyde there, in police custody? They must have.

A moment later, Holmes strode into the morning room, ahead of Mrs. Poole, who was looking flustered.

> MRS. POOLE: And a good thing too. I don't know what the two of you would have done without him to calm things down.

> DIANA: Good thing for Mary! I would have thrown the knife at her.

> CATHERINE: You mean good thing for you. Why do you think none of us notices anymore when you get angry? You get angry all the time, and then it passes, like a spring storm. But when Mary gets angry . . .

DIANA: When Mary gets angry, she sits there and
stares at you. She doesn't even say anything.

CATHERINE: It's what she does after that. Remember
Count Leopold. We had no idea she was going to
shoot him.

MARY: He deserved it. Also, I don't get angry. I just
dislike it when people are rude to my friends.

[The author feels obligated to point out that this
remark was greeted with a collective snort.]

"Where is Miss Frankenstein?" said Holmes, looking around
the room.

"Upstairs," said Mary. "She fainted again—she's not as strong
as she seems. You must not upset her."

"Forgive me," said Holmes. "My manners are atrocious."

"You could say that again," said Catherine, sliding into the
morning room behind him, around Mrs. Poole. "I won't allow
you to endanger Justine's health, Mr. Holmes. Not even inadvertently. She's strong, but she's also very sensitive, particularly
to emotional strain. Every once in a while, her heart gives out.
Remember that she died and was brought back to life. You can't
treat her like an ordinary woman. Mrs. Poole, are there any
kippers?"

"That's exactly what I want to ask her about," said Holmes.
"With your permission, Miss Moreau, and yours, Miss Jekyll. I can
see how much you all care about each other. May I speak with her,
if I am—less abrupt than I unfortunately can be when pursuing
an inquiry?"

He looked so chagrinned that Mary felt sorry for him. He

had not meant to be rude. He was just—well, he was Sherlock Holmes, and he always would be. She must not expect him to behave in any other way.

"She's in bed," said Mary. "But she's prepared to talk to you. I think it would be all right if you went up to her. I'd rather not make her come down. Catherine, what do you think?"

"Honestly? I'd rather you let her rest, but I doubt she will until she's spoken with you. And I think she needs to talk about what happened, or she won't be able to let go of it. That's how Justine is. But are there any kippers, or maybe sausages?"

Holmes nodded. "Then, if the good Mrs. Poole will countenance such unorthodox behavior, I will go up to her room and speak with her there."

"I'll go up with you," said Mary. "I'm almost done."

"I'm not going to miss this!" said Diana, shoving toast into her mouth.

"Well, we can't all go up," said Mary crossly. "This isn't some sort of circus."

"With Mr. Holmes as Atlas, the Strongman?" said Catherine, pouring herself a cup of tea, as though amused at the thought. "I'm certainly going up, if only to make sure he doesn't give Justine a fit with his line of inquiry! Where is the milk jug?"

Alice handed it to her.

"Are you coming up too?" asked Mary, smiling at Alice. After all that had happened last night, she did not want Alice to feel left out.

"I'm just a scullery maid, miss," she replied, shaking her head rapidly, like a sparrow. "No more adventures for me, thank you. I'll clear up here and then bring something up for Mr. Holmes and Miss Moreau. They need their breakfasts too, I'm thinking."

And then, despite Mary's concern that they would all be too much for Justine, they trooped upstairs: Mary leading the way, with Holmes and Catherine and Diana trailing behind.

Justine was sitting up in bed, looking pale and tired, but composed. Beatrice was sitting in a chair by the bedside, drinking more of that green sludge she seemed to favor. Justine had toast and what looked a bowl of vegetable broth on a tray, but she had not touched it.

When they entered, Beatrice moved back toward the window and opened it a crack at the bottom, to let in air.

"Mr. Holmes," said Justine. "You see I have been waiting. You told me that you wanted me to tell you everything I know about Adam Frankenstein. It's little enough, I'm afraid. Before last night, I had not seen him in almost a hundred years. Even with what I know of him, I would not have thought him capable of such atrocities. Cutting up women! He was always violent, but impulsive, not calculating. I would never have imagined . . ."

Holmes sat on the edge of the bed and took her long, pale hand. "Forgive me, Miss Frankenstein. I do not mean to distress you, but you understand, I'm sure, why we must know everything. Adam, Hyde, and Prendick were all involved with this secretive society, although in different ways, I suspect. Prendick seems to still be a member, Hyde was cast out, Adam was never admitted. And Renfield—what is his connection? Why did Hyde choose him to pin the murders on? You see how complicated this case has become. I doubt Renfield will give us any useful information—he is too sunk in his madness. Hyde may speak, once he has spent some time in Newgate. I have arranged for an interview with him, after he is charged and imprisoned. Meanwhile, any additional information may lead us to the Société des Alchimistes."

Justine nodded. "I will tell you everything I know."

"And Mr. Holmes, I found this on the bookshelf while searching for something to read to Justine." Beatrice picked up a book from the side table and handed it to him. Over his shoulder, Mary saw the title in gilt letters on a green cover:

Frankenstein:
A Biography of the Modern Prometheus

"I believe of us all, only Dr. Watson and I have read it. My father believed it to be an accurate account of the creation and death of Adam. We know now that it is at least partly false—Justine was not destroyed, and Adam did not pursue his creator into the Arctic waste and die there. I do not know why Mrs. Shelley falsified information. Nevertheless, I believe we should all read her book."

"I've read it," said Catherine. "It was on Moreau's island. That's how I knew to look for Justine."

"Well, I shall read it as soon as possible," said Holmes, examining the frontispiece. "A pursuit through the Arctic—it sounds quite the shilling shocker. Miss Frankenstein will tell us to what extent it can be trusted."

CATHERINE: Although it's not at all a shilling shocker. She was a very good writer, you know.

DIANA: Why are you interrupting your own story?

"I've never read it myself," said Justine. "But I will tell you my story, and you can judge. Perhaps if you will all sit down . . ."

Holmes nodded and withdrew to the other chair. Mary and Catherine sat at the foot of the bed. Diana shamelessly plopped in bed next to Justine, sitting cross-legged and with her chin in her hands, as though listening to a bedtime story.

Just as Justine was about to start, Alice brought up a tray with a plate of toast and eggs for Holmes, and a plate of kippers for Catherine. She gathered Mary's and Catherine's empty teacups on the tray, then headed once again toward the door.

Justine sat up against the pillows, took a sip of water from a glass on the side table, and said, "If you will pardon a preamble, I shall begin at the beginning—or my beginning, as it were." Alice stopped and stood, half in and half out the door, leaning on the doorframe, as though even she could not help listening after all.

CHAPTER XIX

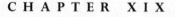

Justine's Story

I do not remember my life before I woke on my father's operating table, except in glimpses: my mother, a widow to whom I was simply another mouth to feed, sitting in her rocking chair by the fire, with my brother and sisters around her. She wore a faded black dress with a white lace fichu around her neck, and looked older than her years. The Frankensteins' grand house on the shore of Lake Geneva, with its walls of gray stone, beneath mountains whose peaks were always covered with snow. In spring, we would gather wildflowers on their slopes and make crowns for ourselves, the upstairs maids and kitchen maids, even the fat old cook. Only the housekeeper was too proud to wear one. The courtroom in which I was condemned to death and the faces of the good men of Geneva, solemn beneath their white wigs, looking at me as though I were an insect, the lowest creature on God's Earth.

I do not remember my first childhood, or how I grew up in the Frankenstein household.

But my father told me my history: how I was sent in service to his family when I was no older than Alice. How I was treated well, as part of the Frankenstein family. How his mother loved me, and how I was considered almost a sister by his cousin Elizabeth, who had lived with the Frankensteins since she was a child. I was trained as a nursemaid for the Frankenstein boys, first for his younger brother Ernest, and then for the youngest, William.

Victor, the eldest, was already in school, and soon to depart for university. He told me that I was a happy girl, always laughing, with golden hair and eyes like the sky above Lausanne in summer. That is what he told me. But I do not remember.

One day, William was found dead, strangled in the woods. The house was searched, and a locket that he had been wearing, with a portrait of his mother in it, was found among my clothes. I was accused of his murder—I, who had taken care of him since birth, who would never have harmed a hair on his head.

It was Adam who had killed him, in a fit of rage when William, meeting him in the woods, called him an ugly ogre. He confessed it all later to my father—confessed to the murder, and to putting the locket in a pocket of my apron. He was responsible—both for William's death and for mine. But the jury did not know of Adam's existence, so I was condemned to death, and then hanged.

CATHERINE: Frankenstein should have told them.

JUSTINE: We've had this argument before. How could
    he have convinced them that he, a university student,
    had created a man out of corpses and brought it to
    life? They would never have believed him.

CATHERINE: He should have found a way. His family
    was one of the most important, one of the richest,
    in the region. The Frankensteins should have
    protected you.

JUSTINE: But they believed me guilty. Only my father
    knew the truth. And remember, I confessed.
    I should not have, but the priest told me I could
    only have absolution if I confessed to the crime.

I thought that without absolution, I would not be able to enter Heaven or stand before God, who knew I was as innocent as the bluebells that grow on the mountain slopes. I know now that God is merciful and would have understood, but I was only seventeen, and frightened.

CATHERINE: I wonder which of them would win, in a contest for worst father? Frankenstein, Rappaccini, Jekyll, or Moreau?

The night after my hanging, Adam came to my father and threatened him. If he did not make a monster out of me, a monster like him, Adam would kill the members of the Frankenstein family, one by one.

MARY: Why you, Justine? Why did he ask for you specifically?

DIANA: Well, she was a convenient dead body. I mean, she'd just been hanged.

MARY: You really are the worst, you know that?

DIANA: What? It's true.

My father told me that Adam has seen me on the day of William's murder. I was worn out from searching for the boy and had fallen asleep in a barn, on a pile of hay. That was when he put the locket into my apron. He must have thought me . . . attractive, I suppose.

So my father agreed that he would do this thing, bring me

back to life—for Adam, to be his mate. But not in Geneva. He had heard of new surgical techniques developed in England, and would travel there, to study at the Royal College of Surgeons. Then he would travel to a remote location, where he would not be disturbed in his work. He preserved the parts of my body and packed them into a trunk—very cleverly, he told me. But of course I remember none of this.

What I remember is the waking, as though coming up through water, up and up until I thought there would be no surface and I might drown. Then I took my first breath, gasping and staring wildly about me. There was a light like the moon, but it was the lantern over the operating table. The first words my father said to me were, "Justine? Are you awake?"

There was pain, a great deal of pain. Catherine and I talked about this, when we were in the Circus of Marvels and Delights. We are both made creatures. That is why I think we understood each other immediately, when she found me. She said, "Do you remember the pain?" And I said, "How can I forget it?" But I healed.

"Can you walk?" my father asked.

I stumbled like a child to a bedroom he had prepared for me. For a week, I lay on a mattress filled with straw, half awake, half in fevered dreams. Then one day I opened my eyes and the sunlight was golden, the sea continually crashing against the rocks below. I could hear birds and insects. The fever was gone. I was alive.

"I was so worried," he said to me later. "I thought I would lose you again." So you see, he cared for me. He loved me . . .

I thought of him as my father because I remembered no other before him. Justine Moritz's father had died when she was a child. It was Frankenstein who gave me life again—the life I have now. I had to learn how to walk, how to eat with a fork and spoon, how to read first words and then sentences. All these he taught me, carefully, patiently. He had brought a woman's dress for me, but it did not fit. In creating me, he had necessarily made me larger, elongated the joints. He was not a trained surgeon, just a university student. He did not have Moreau's skill.

At first, I had to wear his clothes, although the trousers were too short for me. But I found that if I cut the bodice off the dress and sewed a new waistband, I could make a serviceable skirt. I used the same needle and thread he had used to stitch me together. . . . Over it, I wore a shirt of my father's. When it was tied with a sash, I looked respectable enough.

Slowly, slowly, I learned. For months, we lived peacefully in that lonely cottage, with its stone walls and low thatched roof. Once a week, he would take a boat to what he called Mainland, for we were on an island—one of the Orkneys, I found out later. Despite its name, Mainland was one of the other islands, the largest of them. We were on one of the smaller islands. Once a week, he would come back with food—flour, sugar, whatever we could not grow in our stone-walled garden or procure from the few poor cottagers who lived on that island with us. No one bothered us, and I was not seen except by sheep, and once a shepherd boy from a distance.

Our days were simple: a breakfast of porridge, then a walk across the hills or down to the rocky beach, and perhaps a game of ball to increase my coordination. Then study. He taught me so much! I suppose out of sheer boredom as much as a desire to educate me. As Justine Moritz, I had been merely a servant, who could read fairy tales and add numbers as long as she was using the fingers of both hands. As Justine Frankenstein, I read Aristotle and discussed the sorrows of young Werther. My father had brought two trunks, one filled with me, the other filled with books. I soon exhausted them and started reading my favorites a second time.

I knew it could not last. He told me as much. Elizabeth, to whom he was betrothed, was waiting for him, and he would need to get back to his university studies in Ingolstadt. But I was young,

in mind if not in body, and I did not think much about those things.
My world was the windswept stone cottage at the top of the cliffs,
and our meager vegetable garden, and the restless, eternal sea.

> JUSTINE: That's good, restless and eternal. Thank you,
> Catherine. You make me sound so much more
> eloquent than I am.

> CATHERINE: You wrote that, actually. You're a better
> writer than you think.

> JUSTINE: Oh, surely not! After all, English is not
> my native language. If I could have written it in
> French . . .

> CATHERINE: You're just as annoying on this subject
> as Beatrice. Your English is perfectly fine, if a bit
> Miltonic for a modern audience.

And then, one day, he appeared. The monster, Adam.
We were sitting in the sunshine, at the top of the cliff on
which our cottage was situated. I was sketching—my father had
taught me how, to help with my fine motor coordination. He had
brought pencils and a notebook to make anatomical sketches, but
I used them to draw butterflies, or the flowers that grew in the
nooks and crannies. Sketching became my favorite occupation, a
way to record the wonders of the natural world around me. And I
found that I had an exact eye, a skilled hand. Again, I do not know
if that is Justine Moritz, or the Frankenstein in me.

My father was sitting on the grass, reading from *Plutarch's Lives*.
Then suddenly, I heard a roar, as though of a wild animal.

"So here you are, my tormentor! Traitor! How dare you sit in the sunshine, while I live in darkness and despair!" It was Adam. Although I think now that my father should have named him Lucifer. In his pride and fury, he reminded me of the fiend himself.

My father rose and stumbled back. I screamed, thinking he might fall. We were sitting close to the edge of the cliff, with a view of another island across the firth and the waves crashing below. But he found his footing. I remember him standing there, against the blue sky, towering above me although really he was a foot shorter than I am.

"You cannot have her," were the first words out of his mouth.

"Cannot?" said Adam. "She is mine. You created her for me, at my command. And now you dare tell me what I cannot have? Remember, Frankenstein—the lives of your family are in my hands. I have killed William—shall I also kill Ernest, and your beloved Elizabeth?"

"No, no," said my father, putting his hands to his head. "Let me think, give me time to think . . ."

"You've had all the time you deserve," said Adam. "You," he said to me. "Come with me. You were created for me, to be my companion and mate. We shall go off to some desolate corner of the Earth, where we shall live out our miserable existence together."

"I am not a *you*," I said. "I am Justine, and I am a rational creature, capable of determining my own actions. I have no desire to go to some desolate place, nor yet to be miserable. I can guess who you are—my father told me that before me, he created a creature, deformed and malicious. You are that creature, are you not? And now you say I was created at your command. That may be true, but no promise my father made to you before my birth can bind me. I am capable of reasoned thought, and therefore free, so says Monsieur Rousseau. By your threats, you have already proven yourself unworthy of such as I am. I do not choose to accompany you."

Adam stared at me in astonishment. "You have been educating her, reading and discussing with her. As you never did with me! Now I see the full extent of your cruelty, Frankenstein! You created her to mock me, to taunt me with the love I should have had, which you intend to keep from me forever! You rejected me as your son, and she has rejected me as her mate. At your command, no doubt!" He lunged at my father. I stepped between them, attempting to thwart his attack, but he was stronger than I was. He thrust me aside as though I were made of straw. And then I saw his hands around my father's throat. I screamed again, and beat his back and arms with my fists, but to no purpose. I saw my father's face go red, and then his body go slack, and there was nothing I could do to save him. I think there is no man on Earth stronger than I am, but Adam was not a man, not as ordinary men. He had the strength of Lucifer himself. In a moment, my father lay dead, strangled by the foul creature he had created. Adam lifted him up, then threw him, as though he had been a stone, into the churning waters below. And that was the last I saw of my father, Victor Frankenstein.

Adam turned to me. "Take me to your house," he said. I led him to our cottage, farther down the cliff, where a hillock gave some protection from the wind.

And so began a period of my life that—I do not wish to dwell upon. For months, we lived as man and wife. I did what he bade me—the housework, preparing our food. Soon, we ran out, and although we had money, neither of us could take the boat to Mainland. He told me with what fear and cruelty he had been treated, how even children had pelted him with rocks. He was certain we would meet with a similar reception. Instead, he foraged among the hills, bringing back herbs and roots, sometimes an entire sheep stolen from a herd.

He spent his days looking at an atlas that was among my

father's books, determining where we should go. To the wilds of South America? To parts of Africa where the natives had never yet seen a white man? The Arctic? He wanted a place where we could live undisturbed and raise our children—for he wished us to have children. He did not know it was impossible, that in the process of assembling me, my father had removed the organ popularly believed to cause hysteria. From an excess of caution, I suppose. I am like any other woman, but—I cannot bear a child. I feared Adam too much to tell him the truth, and seemed to accept his plans. What else could I do? He was stronger than I, and ever watchful.

He tried, I think as well as he could, to make me love him. In the evenings, we sat by the fire and he would talk to me— of philosophy, history, literature. Indeed, if he had not been my father's murderer and my captor, I might have been charmed. He was as intelligent as my father, perhaps more so, and I could speak with him on many topics. I learned much, during those conversations. But always, as the fire burned down, he would say, "It is late, Justine. Come to bed." And I would remember that I was not a free woman.

I knew that if I left while he was foraging for our food, he would follow me. He had the senses of an animal, and I was the only one of his kind—his mate. If necessary, he would follow me to the ends of the Earth.

"We are man and wife," he would say to me.

"Not in the sight of God," I would say. "Not until we are united by a minister." And then he would rage against religion, like a freethinker and radical.

Lying beside him at night, in the bed where my father had once lain, I thought of throwing myself off the cliff. After all, I was already dead. Surely God would not punish me? But then I thought, *What if I am still Justine Mortiz, with an immortal soul? A soul that belongs to God and not myself, which will one day reunite with its true*

Creator? No, I could not kill myself. Not while I believed myself to still be God's creature.

And then I thought that perhaps I should kill Adam. He had already killed William and my father. He would never appear before a jury, as Justine Mortiz had. Perhaps I had a duty to be his judge and executioner. But even if I could find a way to overcome his greater strength, I lacked the courage. I could not kill the spider that wove its web in a corner of the ceiling. I had never killed anything in my life, and could not do so now, in my death-life.

One night, he was sitting in my father's chair, waiting for me to finish making our dinner. My father had brought several bottles of whiskey from Mainland. He used to drink a glass after dinner, to aid digestion, he said. I thought it was foul stuff myself, but then I have never liked the taste of spirits, not even as Justine Moritz. Adam had found the bottles and taken to drinking, first after dinner, and then during the daytime. That night, he had already drunk several glassfuls of the amber liquid. And he was excited: he had finally decided that we would go to Africa. With our superior strength, we could traverse jungles and deserts that made the interior of the continent dangerous for white men. We would see what no European had ever seen. Surely the rude savages would worship us as gods. All day, he had been talking about it, asking if I wished to go to Africa with him, there to start a new race, more than human. I would be his Eve in that distant paradise. Eventually our children would return to Europe and rule over civilized men, who had grown weak and overconfident through their use of technology. I said yes, of course I was excited at such a prospect. I agreed with him so he would not get angry, to keep him in good humor.

I was cooking potatoes in lard over the fire, stirring them in a skillet with a wooden spoon. The skillet was set on a metal grill directly over the flames. I was trying not to burn the potatoes, and although I said that yes, we would go to Africa, to start a new race there, I suppose my distracted assents did not satisfy him. Suddenly, he was next to me.

"You are going to love me, are you not?" he asked. He smelled of whiskey. "Justine, look at me. Tell me that you will love me, in time."

I looked up at him, startled. This was a question he had never asked before. I did not love him—I loathed the sight of him, and at that moment he saw the truth in my face. He roared with rage and caught me by the throat. "I shall make you love me! You shall either love me or die."

I gasped for air. What madness was this? We were the only two of our kind in the whole world, and he would kill me? I, whom he had called his Eve, whom he considered a mate and the mother of his future children?

But he was enraged, and the whiskey was clouding his mind. Slowly, I could feel his hands closing around my windpipe. I still had the handle of the skillet in my hand. I swung it toward him, flinging the hot lard and potatoes into his face. He screamed and let go of my throat, stumbling back and clawing at his eyes. I did not give him time to recover—if I had, he surely would have killed me. I swung the skillet, hitting him on the side of the head. Over and over I swung it, hitting him about the head as he staggered back, then fell on one knee, roaring and still trying to see, in pain. Blow after blow, for he was so strong that it took many to fell him. Finally he lay on the ground, still.

I did not know if I had killed him or merely rendered him unconscious, but as soon as he was no longer moving, I dropped the skillet and ran, out of the cottage and down to the shore where my father's boat was pulled up beyond the tidemark. I lifted it and carried it to the water, then pushed it out as far as I could. I got into the boat and began to row. I had never done such a thing before, and it took a moment to adjust to the oars and the buoyancy of the water beneath me. But I had seen my father do it, and I stroked as he had. Slowly, but steadily, I rowed away from that island, south toward the Scottish shore. I worried about missing it, not knowing how the ocean currents might carry me, but I consigned myself to God and prayed that He would guide my boat. If He wished me dead upon the seas, that was His prerogative. At least I would not die by Adam's hand.

Night fell, but my father had taught me about the stars, so I continued to row, heading always south. When the sun rose, I saw that I had reached a rocky shore, and I breathed a prayer of thanks that I had not crashed upon it. I did not know where I was, but I pulled my boat up on the rocks and climbed to the highest point, a hill of scrubby grass. There, I looked about me. As far as I could see, there was nothing: the sea on one side and barren hills on the other. What could I do but walk, following the shore, knowing that sooner or later I might reach a fishing village? To the west, the shore veered south, so I went both westward and southward at once, with the wind howling over the hills on my left, and the sea crashing on my right.

After three days of walking, I came upon a village, a small one tucked into a cove. It was clear that the village made its trade from the sea, for there were fishing boats in the harbor. I know now that it was a tiny place, scarcely a hamlet, but at the time it was the largest I had ever seen.

I was starving. I had been walking for three days, all day and most of the night, sleeping as little as possible, curling into what crevices I could find. I could go for a long time without food; nevertheless, I felt the pangs of hunger like any other creature. I had eaten some berries that grew on the low shrubs—no berries were poisonous to my constitution. I had eaten mussels washed up on the shore, and some snails, raw because if Adam was following me, a fire might alert him to my presence.

I knew how the people of that village would treat me, for Adam had told me how men and women treated our kind. Even the children had thrown rocks at him, called him monster, driven him from their midst in fear. But the town had a bakery, and I could smell bread, fresh because it was still morning. It stirred a distant memory of Justine Moritz taking a basket of bread, fresh from the oven in the great kitchen of the house in Geneva, to her mother's house. I imagined what that bread would taste like and thought, *What if they kill me?* Perhaps I deserved death after all, not for my actions, which I thought had been justified, but because of what I am. That is what hunger and tiredness will do to the mind. At last, even the instinct of self-preservation begins to go.

I walked into that village, my clothes stiff with mud and saltwater, my hair tangled like a bird's nest. The fishermen saw me first, back from their morning's catch, gutting their fish or mending their nets. They stared at me, as at an apparition that had walked into their midst. Then a boy who had been kicking a ball in the village square saw me, and called to his playfellows. They shouted at one another, but not with fear, neither with hatred. No, it was . . . excitement. Even a sort of delight. I looked at them curiously.

Several of the fishermen left their boats and walked toward me. *Ah,* I thought. *Now the stoning will start.* But I could not make myself turn and walk away. These were the first men I had seen, apart from my father. I wanted to stay with them and continue to smell the tantalizing scent of fresh bread from the bakery.

One of them, roughly dressed, his face red from the sun and wind, stood before me and said, "What are ye, then? Some sort of freak?"

But I did not understand him, for my father had taught me only French, which was his native language and the language of Justine Moritz.

"*Pardon, monsieur, je ne comprends pas ce que vous dites,*" I said. "*Je suis fatiguée et affamée, et je prie que vous puissiez me donner un peu de pain.*" A little bread, that was what I wanted more than anything on Earth.

"She's a furriner," said another one of them.

"She's a giantess!" said the boy with the ball. "Like the one at the fair, but even taller. I wonder how strong she is?" He pulled up his sleeves, clenched his fists, and made muscles, as though he were a strongman himself. "Are you strong, giantess?" he asked.

Giantess . . . *la géante.* They were not afraid of me. I was, to them, a figure out of a fairy tale. I pulled up my sleeve and showed the boy my muscles. They were not particularly impressive, for my arms were as slender then as they are now. He looked disappointed. I smiled and lifted a wheelbarrow that had been left by the side of the square over my head. It's not large muscles that make you strong, I wanted to tell him.

He laughed, delighted, and the other boys applauded, and then the fishermen. They asked me to lift more things: a log that had been cut for a mast, a rather large pig. Hearing their shouts and laughter, the shopkeepers came out of their shops: the butcher and grocer, the baker with his apron still on. Soon I had a circle of villagers around me, all wanting to see me perform feats of strength. One of them threw a coin at my feet, and soon there were other coins, not many but a few. They clinked on the cobblestones. I gathered them up and put them into the pocket of my skirt. I was starting to tire, for I had walked long and slept little. I bowed to the villagers, signaling that I was done for the day. They clapped and began to disperse, but the baker's wife ran into the bakery and brought out a loaf for me, with a smile and a shake of her head to indicate that I would not have to pay for it. I blessed her in French, but I believe she understood me.

As I left that square, most of the loaf under my arm, the rest in my mouth, I looked at myself in the bakery window. I had never seen my own reflection. My father's cottage had no mirror, and I had not passed a lake or pond or even puddle, no water still enough that I could see myself in it. I stared at myself. I looked . . . ordinary. Taller than women are, but there was nothing hideous about me. I could pass among human beings.

It came as a relief. You have seen Adam—his hideous countenance. Any part of it would be handsome enough, but all together—my father had made him from corpses that had lain dead some days, taking what body parts were not yet corrupted. He had not been preserved carefully, as I was. And my father had been younger, less experienced. I was no longer the pretty girl who had called herself Justine Moritz, but I was not a monster.

I continued walking south along the coast. I slept in meadows and pastures, finding what shelter I could—beneath a tree, or in a barn or shepherd's hut. Sometimes I stopped in the villages. In one, I saw a man painting a boat with pitch to make it waterproof, and I begged him, in gestures, for his brush. On a broken piece of wood I painted, in black letters, GEANTESSE STRANG WOMEN. These were the words I had heard the villagers speak. When I showed my sign in the towns, which were getting larger, I would be given coins, with which I could buy bread and cheese and onions. By this time I had a canvas bag, and a pair of men's shoes, and an old hat to gather the coins in. But I kept on moving, always afraid that Adam would find me, afraid he would hear of the "geantesse" who performed in the towns. Perhaps I had killed him—but no, although I tried to tell myself that he must be dead, something in me did not believe it. My only safety lay in the fact that men ran from him or attacked him, instinctively.

Although I did not know it, I had made my way down to Cornwall, in the south of England. There, one night, I was showing my strength in a town square when a man staggered out of a tavern and challenged me. He was drunk and wanted to wrestle, to show that he was stronger than me. What was I, after all? A woman, and no woman was stronger than a man. I understood this, in part—I was learning English from my encounters with Englishmen, although all of them seemed to speak in different accents—and what I later realized was Welsh, I could not understand at all. I thought for a time that I had wandered into another country. . . .

This man was challenging me, it was clear, and I waved my hand to signal that no, I would not wrestle with him. *"Non, non,"* I said, clearly I thought. But his companions came out of the tavern and surrounded me. Then, he lunged. . . .

I had meant to step aside, to let him stumble past. But as he came, all I could see was Adam, coming toward me, hands outstretched. He was not Adam, not a monster, only a man—so I reached toward him, grasped him by the throat, and snapped his neck. He crumpled as his companions looked on, dumbfounded, not certain what had happened. There was an opening in the circle they made. I turned and ran through it, leaving my sign and hat behind on the pavement. I ran and ran, knowing what would happen now, what human justice was. Had I not been hanged once? I had no wish to be tried again for murder, although I deserved it, for I had killed a man. This time, I was guilty.

> CATHERINE: Although you know perfectly well it was
> in self-defense.

> JUSTINE: But this is *my* story, as I know and feel it.
> In my heart, I knew myself to be a murderer.

That night, I longed to die.

I was afraid to surrender myself to the justice of man, but wished that the justice of God would strike me down. I ran through the night, following roads headed I knew not where, away from the town where I had committed such a heinous crime. Overhead, clouds alternately concealed and revealed the sliver of a moon, which threw the shadows of trees across my path like bars.

DIANA: Oh please! Cut the symbolism already.

Like prison bars! At last the roads dwindled down to mere paths, and then I was stumbling across fields, with the stubble of mown hay scratching my bare legs above my shoes. It grew darker—clouds covered the moon, so I could no longer rely on it to give me a sense of direction. The fields gave way to rockier ground on which I was in danger of twisting my ankles. I scarcely noticed when the rain began, at first a few drops I brushed off my hair, and then as though the heavens had opened up, a deluge. I stood in a field and looked up at the sky, water streaming down my shoulders and over my arms, soaking my clothes. Then and there, I prayed God would strike me down with a bolt of His lightning. Surely that was in His power, and surely I deserved to die.

But He did not strike me down.

There was nothing to do but trudge on through the darkness, not knowing where I was going. And so I trudged.

I did not see the wall—I simply walked into it. Then along it, feeling my way, my hands on the cold, slick stones. At last I felt something—the wood of a door. There was a handle, which turned under my hand. And then I was inside, my shoes squelching on the floor. I took them off and walked carefully, feeling my way. Where was I? A barn of some sort?

There was something soft under my feet—and then something hard against my knee, something I had walked into with a thump. I cried out in pain, and the cry echoed, as though I were in a large

space. A barn then, I was certain. I felt around me—there was a
sort of pallet, covered with cloth. I could do no more. Without
light, I would only wander aimlessly. Whoever discovered me
here in the morning might take me to prison—I was so tired and
wet that I no longer cared. I clutched at the pallet and fell upon it,
sobbing with exhaustion. And then I believe I lost consciousness,
overwrought with the fears and horrors of that night.

The next morning, I woke and looked around me with astonishment. Sunlight streamed through the windows. I was in a large
room, as magnificent as any in the Frankensteins' house. The floor
was covered with a carpet in dim, rich colors. On the walls were
paintings of men and women in the garb of previous centuries,
and shelves upon shelves of books—hundreds of books. Sunlight
glinted off the gold titles on their spines. The pallet on which I had
fallen the night before was a sofa, upholstered in velvet, and what I
had bruised my knee on was a low table with designs inlaid in ivory
and exotic woods. It was the library of a wealthy family—Justine
Moritz knew that. But everywhere, there was a sense of neglect.
The carpet was moth-eaten. The books and furniture were covered with dust. The curtains that hung at the windows had faded,
and there were cobwebs in the corners of the room. The barn I
thought I had stumbled into was a grand house—magnificent, but
utterly deserted.

I wandered through that house in astonishment, my bare feet
cold on the floors. Everywhere it was the same—dust and decay.
I did not know, until much later, that the house was the seat of an
aristocratic family. When the old earl died, his son had inherited
the property, but had so indebted himself that he could no longer
afford to live there or keep it up. Neither could he sell, for the
property was entailed. The house, its contents, and the surrounding estate could not be sold, but passed automatically to the next
heir. The son had gone off to farm in Africa, and his son after him

stayed there, never returning to England. So the house was left to the moths and spiders.

And to me.

I had nowhere to go, no one in the world to whom I belonged, for I did not consider myself bound to Adam. That morning, I found a broom and swept away the cobwebs from the moldings and chandeliers. I took the rugs outside and beat them until you could see their colors again, like jewels. I wiped the tables and chairs with a soft cloth, and promised them I would find beeswax, so they would shine as they had before. I washed the windows with white vinegar from the butler's pantry. Finally, I dusted the books, as Justine Moritz would have done. Remember that I had been a maid. What I had known best in the world, before my father taught me philosophy and literature, was cleaning. I knew how to launder fine linen, polish silver, keep a great house. My brain might have forgotten, but my hands remembered. I found myself a room, one of the maid's rooms, for I did not wish to be presumptuous. When I was done cleaning, I washed my clothes and myself in a tub I filled from a well behind the house. It was a relief to be truly clean for the first time in weeks.

But I was hungry, and there was no food. Whatever had been left in the house had been eaten long ago, probably by mice, for I found their droppings. So I went outside. Through the second-floor windows, I had seen a walled garden beyond the hedges that surrounded the house. I discovered it was a kitchen garden, large although neglected. It had once provided produce for the entire household, and I could still see vegetables among the weeds. Beyond it was an orchard, also walled to protect the fruit trees from the sea winds. I could not tell what kinds of fruit grew there, for I did not know how to distinguish apples and pears and quinces, but Justine Moritz remembered they would someday be good to eat. Slowly, I began to discover that there would be enough food for me: now there were asparagus and lettuce, later there would be cabbage and cauliflower and courgettes. If I tended the garden now, there would be a full harvest in autumn, and for winter I could store the cabbages that were already developing.

The house stood on a high cliff above the shore, but there was a path down to the rocks. There, I found mussels and snails, which I already knew I could eat. Later, I would find a way to fish—I had seen men do it with nets, and there must be a net somewhere in that house. I stood on the rocky shore, eating the green sprouts of asparagus and broccoli that I had brought with me to assuage my hunger. Yes, I could live here. I had food and water, a bed for the night. I had that library of neglected books. What more did I need?

I was completely alone, except for the mice and the owls that nested in the attic, whom I did not disturb. It was my own Eden, and I was its Eve. I thought it was paradise.

I will not tell you the story of those years, for there is no story to tell. Season after season, I planted my garden, fished from the sea with what had once been a tennis net, and read the books in the library. It had been the library of an educated man, so I read the philosophers and great poets. I taught myself English and Latin, and also a little Greek. In what had been a lady's chamber, I found pencils and paints, and amused myself by sketching and painting until my supplies ran out. Sometimes I found a honeycomb and stole part of it from the bees. Their stings could not wound me. I always felt like a thief, but what sweetness! Once, a stray cat came, and her progeny lived with me for the rest of my time there, keeping down the population of mice.

I rarely left the environs of the house. Although I did not realize it, the estate surrounding that house was extensive, and no one had reason to trespass on it but poachers after hare. Sometimes I saw and disabled their traps. I thought, surely someone will come? A caretaker, if no one else? I kept a bag packed, ready to flee should

I need to. But no one ever came. I lived simply and happily enough, although I missed my father and my kind, the companionship of another with whom I could converse. I had everything I needed but a friend.

I did not realize that a legend had grown about the Cornish Giantess, who roamed that stretch of shore. I suppose I had been seen searching for food among the rocks. That is how Catherine found me.

One day, it was in late summer I think, for the gourds were hanging heavy on their vines, I looked up and there, sitting on the garden wall, was a woman. She was bare-headed and barefoot, in a simple linen dress, with a straw hat on the wall next to her. She had strange yellow eyes, and she sat looking at me as though she had been there a long time.

It had been so long since I had seen another of my kind that I stepped back and shrieked. It sounded like the call of a bird—one of the falcons that sometimes circled overhead. How long was it since I had last spoken?

"Do not be afraid," she said in English. She pulled down the collar of her dress, which was unbuttoned at the top. "Look. I, too, am made. I, too, am a monster. *Monstrum sum.*"

> CATHERINE: I wasn't even sure if she would understand me. What if she spoke only French or German? But I thought she would understand the scars. As to who she was, that was a guess on my part. I was traveling with the Circus of Marvels and Delights through Cornwall. One day, a man said to Lorenzo, "You should get the Cornish Giantess, you should. Make a fortune!" He told the story of a giantess who had lived by the seashore for a hundred years. Lorenzo thought it was only a story—after all, it was a hundred

years old. But I began to wonder. Moreau had
talked about Frankenstein's experiment. Victor
Frankenstein had gone to England, specifically
to England, to create a female monster. But he
had never completed his task. Afraid that his male
and female monsters would reproduce, he had
disassembled her and thrown her body parts into
the sea. That's what I knew from Mrs. Shelley's
account.

MARY: Which is a pack of lies.

CATHERINE: Yes, I began to suspect it was inaccurate
when I heard of the Cornish Giantess. But *why*
did she lie, Mary?

MARY: To protect Frankenstein. To protect the Société
des Alchimistes.

CATHERINE: I don't think so. What I think is . . .

JUSTINE: Please, can we finish my story?

I had no food to offer this Cat Woman, who had guessed my
identity and sought me out. At that time I ate only vegetables and
what I could scavenge from the sea, which I did not even cook
for fear of attracting attention to myself. But she said she was not
interested in eating. She was interested in listening.

"And so you've lived here ever since," she said to me after I had
told her my story, such as it was.

"Yes," I said. My throat ached from talking so much.

"Alone, all this time."

"Yes, but it does not seem so long. I have books, I have my garden . . ."

"Justine, you've been living in this house for almost *a hundred years*."

It startled me, that so much time had passed. I had no clock, no calendar. I had not kept track of the passage of time. I did not age, and evidently I could not die. I knew many winters had come and gone, but . . .

"I did not know," I said, feeling for the first time a sense of desolation. Everything Justine Moritz had known was gone.

"You can't stay here forever," she said. "For one thing, the world is changing. The nineteenth century is coming to an end. Although you don't feel it here yet, the towns are growing larger and there are more people in them. Soon, they will be everywhere, even here. And this house has been sold. I heard people at the sideshow talking about it. The current heir is a woman, raised in Africa and rich from a coffee plantation. She sued to break the entail and won. People don't like entails much, anymore. The land will be developed—it will become a grand hotel, surrounded by seaside cottages. There is a mania now for going to the seaside, I can't imagine why. For another, you can't live alone your entire existence. That's not right. It's not . . . no one should have to live alone for so long. And I happen to need a friend. And the circus does not have a giantess."

That is how I left my place of refuge and solitude. I joined the Circus of Marvels and Delights. And the rest . . . you know.

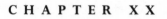

CHAPTER XX

The Athena Club

When Justine finished her story, the room was silent, except of course for the sound of Diana chewing the last piece of Justine's toast. *Damn that girl,* Mary thought—really, her language was deteriorating with Diana around. She would have to make sure that Justine got a proper breakfast.

Finally, Holmes said, "And no one came to the house, not for a hundred years? That seems . . . unusual. I've heard stories of such entails and the difficulties they cause, particularly when a case goes to chancery. But surely there would have been a caretaker of some sort."

"Truly, there wasn't," said Justine. "Well, there was a boy, once. It was when I had been there—half a century, perhaps? He came to find the giantess. The people on that coast were poor farmers—they had no interest in whether the legend was true. It was enough for them that their fathers and grandfathers had spoken of a giantess—they repeated the stories they had been told. They were simply trying to survive. But that boy—he was different. He wanted to know for himself. I say boy, but he was already half a man, seventeen or eighteen perhaps. He was already more mature than men twice his age."

Holmes looked puzzled. "Was he connected with the estate in any way?"

"Not as far as I know. He said he was from up the coast, and had come to a local village during his school vacation. He was the sort of boy who collects seashells, who digs up bones and shards of pottery. He was inquisitive, and particularly interested in the geology of that area. I showed him the library and told him that he could read whatever he liked. He would visit once or twice a week. He helped me to practice English, and we even talked a little in Latin. We became . . . friends. Then one day he told me that he could not come anymore. His landlady had become suspicious about his long walks, and he did not want to put me in danger. So he stopped coming. He promised that he would never tell anyone about me."

"Did he ever ask you about yourself, who you were and how you were made?" asked Holmes. He sounded—skeptical. Suspicious.

"I do not remember him asking, but I told him . . ." Justine leaned forward as though suddenly struck by the thought. "I told him about the Société des Alchimistes."

"Could he have been a member of the society?" asked Holmes.

"I do not know. But he was so young—surely not?"

"Frankenstein was young when he created Adam," said Catherine. "But you know who he was—you told me his name, remember? William something."

"Yes, William Pengelly. I called him Will, and sometimes, when I was particularly pleased with him, Guillaume. My one friend in all that time, other than the cats of course . . ."

"Miss Frankenstein!" said Holmes, clearly astonished. "William Pengelly, the geologist? Pengelly, who excavated Kents Cavern and proved the Earth could not possibly be six thousand years old, as Bishop Ussher had suggested?"

"You know him, then?" said Justine. "Oh, perhaps I could speak with him again! How I would like that." She smiled a pale, wan smile, as though remembering their friendship with pleasure.

"Speak with him! No, he died several years ago, an old man. I did not know him myself, but he was well-known to anyone with an interest in science and the inductive method of reasoning. He

was a respected member of the Royal Society. He could not possibly have had anything to do with the Société des Alchimistes.
And yet, there must have been a reason for him to be there. It
could not have been a coincidence. Just as one part of this case
begins to make sense, it becomes more inscrutable."

"Then you don't believe he was simply my friend?" said Justine,
looking as sad as Mary had ever seen her.

"Of course he was your friend," said Catherine. "I have to
admit, this is starting to sound—well, clearly he wasn't just a
village boy. But that doesn't mean he wasn't your friend, Justine."

"My brother Mycroft has contacts in the Royal Society. Perhaps
they can tell us more about this Pengelly," said Holmes. "It seems
clear that we have solved one mystery: we know who committed
the Whitechapel Murders, and why. Now we must solve the
mystery of the Société des Alchimistes. What is it? Who are its
members? Is it still carrying on its illicit activities, particularly in
England? But I promised Lestrade that I would return as soon as
I could—I left him with very little information, just enough to
charge Hyde with the murder of Molly Keane." He stood, looking
both worried and impatient. "Miss Jekyll, if you'll excuse me, I
will go trouble Mrs. Hudson for a meal of some sort and another
coat, since Miss Moreau is still wearing mine, then take a cab
back to Scotland Yard. I have a lot to tell Lestrade, and I'm not
sure how much of it he will credit! He's not the sort to believe
in hundred-year-old giants or Beast Men. He will likely dismiss
it all as a fairy tale and look for the most ordinary explanation—
that Adam was a madman, and the more improbable parts of the
story are simply figments of my imagination. From long association, I know how he thinks, you see. Then I must send a message
to Lord Avebury, who will not be getting his menagerie back,
although who knows, the orangutan may head home, if he indeed
escaped the fire."

"Of course, Mr. Holmes," said Mary. "And we will see you . . ." *When?*

"Tomorrow, perhaps. I will of course bring you news of Watson. But you—I believe you should all get some rest. It has been a difficult night for you all."

Mary nodded. Yes, it had been difficult. But exciting too, she could not deny that. Did she want to experience any more such nights, stalking a suspect through London with Mr. Holmes, solving mysteries? Well, not tonight, that was for certain!

Holmes bowed and said, "Until tomorrow, then." With a couple of long strides, he was out the door. As he passed her, Alice started, as though remembering where she was, and then followed him out, still holding the breakfast tray.

Mary heard the voice of Mrs. Poole below, then the front door closing. And then silence.

Suddenly, she realized they were all looking at her—Justine leaning back against her pillow, Diana sitting cross-legged on the bed, Catherine with her legs curled under her like a cat. Beatrice in her chair by the window. They were all waiting for Mary to speak.

"Well?" said Diana. "Now what?"

Now what, indeed. She knew what she wanted to say, but would they agree? The only way to find out was to ask. "What I'd like is for you all to stay here. I've lost all the family I had . . ." Hyde did not count, of course. "I think we've all lost our families, haven't we? Diana has no one. Beatrice may still have relations in Italy"—Beatrice shook her head—"but anyone Justine knew is long dead. And Cat—well, she had no human family, at least. I want us to be a family for each other. Anyway, we still have a mystery to solve. As Mr. Holmes said, we know who committed the Whitechapel Murders, but we know almost nothing about the Alchemical Society. What sorts of experiments were our fathers conducting? What were they trying to prove? We know it had to do with biological transmutation, but there were papers . . . they met to give papers, remember? Are there papers about Beatrice, or Catherine, or even Justine? Is there a journal? Societies usually have journals, don't they? Beatrice, didn't you mention a journal of some sort? There's still so much we don't know. It seems clear that the society was not directly responsible for the Whitechapel Murders. My father had been cast out of the society, and Prendick, who is still a member, was hiding his activities from them. Adam was an experiment, wasn't he? Rather than a scientist. And he mentioned that they, whoever they are, wouldn't let him join. But the society did sanction the creation of . . . well, of monsters. Girl monsters. Is it continuing those activities? If so, it must be stopped. I have no idea what we're going to live on, because we'll run out of money soon. Still, I think we should all stay here and find a way."

There, she had said it. Now she waited to see how they would all respond.

Justine nodded. "Yes, we should certainly try to stop the Société, although it will not be easy. You are right—we must solve this mystery together. We are—like sisters, are we not? I lost my own sisters when I was sent into service, and then when I died and was reborn. I would like to have sisters again."

"Speak for yourself," said Diana, with an expression of disgust. "I have one sister, and she's bad enough. Anyway, what about Poison Breath? I saw what happened in that warehouse! Are we all going to die in our sleep?"

"That was scarcely her fault!" said Mary.

"No, Diana is right," said Beatrice. "I will always be dangerous. If I stay here, I must spend most of my time in the laboratory, so my poison does not affect you all. I agree that we must try to stop the Société des Alchimistes. But are you certain that you wish me to stay?"

"No," said Diana, and "Yes," and "Yes, of course," said Mary and Justine simultaneously.

"Catherine?" said Mary, realizing she had not yet spoken.

"I don't know," said Catherine. "We'll fight, inevitably. I don't just mean Diana sticking knives into people, which doesn't count. What I mean is that we're opinionated. We'll want our own way. Except maybe Justine, who has to be gentle because she's so strong. It won't be a peaceful life, with all of us here."

"I know," said Mary. "But families do fight, don't they? Anyway, I think we're stronger together than apart."

"Maybe." Catherine frowned. "Anyway, I'm a puma. I'm solitary and secretive, according to the *Encyclopaedia Britannica* in your father's study. Yes, we need to stop the society, if it's still creating— well, more of us. But I'm not sure I want to be anyone's sister."

"But you've been like a sister to me," said Justine gently.

Catherine merely shook her head and said, "I'll have to think about it."

"Perhaps we should all do that," said Mary. "Let's get some rest. We all need it. And then we can talk again later? I'm sure if I ask nicely, Mrs. Poole will make us a proper tea. With sandwiches and cakes. And sausages, of course," she said, looking at Catherine. "And delicious green goo," she added, for Beatrice's sake.

Diana stuck a finger in her mouth and pretended to vomit. Presumably commenting on Beatrice's choice of nourishment?

"You know," said Mary dispassionately, "you may not have to wait for Beatrice's poison. I'm seriously considering smothering you with a pillow while you sleep, just to keep you quiet for a while."

Suddenly, Justine started to laugh. She put a hand over her mouth as though embarrassed, trying to hold it in. But then Beatrice started as well—elegant, musical laughter, as one might expect from Beatrice. Catherine threw her head back and laughed heartily, without restraint. Mary looked startled, but then even she started, and could not stop until her sides hurt. She had not laughed since . . . well, when had she ever laughed? It was painful, yet it brought a sense of release, as though a key had turned in her chest and opened a lock she did not know was there.

"I'd like to see you try!" said Diana indignantly. "Anyway, I'm going to my room. I had a long night rescuing Poison Breath over there, in case anyone's forgotten." She yawned conspicuously, crammed the last of Justine's toast into her mouth, and walked out of the room, nose in the air, with a smear of marmalade across one cheek, like a damp, barefoot duchess.

"*Her* room!" said Mary. "When did it become *her* room?"

"Just now, I think," said Beatrice, wiping tears from her eyes. "You said you wanted us all to stay, didn't you? Including Diana. But I think we had better go to our rooms as well. Justine is getting no rest with us here."

Before they left, Mary persuaded Justine to finish the vegetable broth. Then she took the tray back down to the kitchen and checked with Mrs. Poole to make sure the housekeeper still had enough money for necessities.

Yes, Mrs. Poole told her, for the moment. She was being economical, but the rates were coming due, and Diana would eat them out of house and home for sure. Mary thought again about her bank balance: forty-one pounds, twelve shillings. How would it feed seven—herself, Diana, Beatrice, Catherine, and Justine, plus Alice and Mrs. Poole? Well, six, since Beatrice barely ate—she assumed green goo was cheap. But she was too tired to think about it right now.

She walked back upstairs to her room. On the way, she checked on Justine, who was fast sleep and snoring gently under a blanket that did not quite cover the more than six feet of her. Catherine's door was closed, but Mary supposed she was asleep as well. Diana was still awake, lying in Mary's childhood bed with her knees up and a book propped on them. "Go away," she said, sticking her tongue out. Mary went in and kissed Diana on the forehead, as her mother had kissed her when she was a child. Why had she done that? She did not know—instinct, she supposed. To her surprise, Diana did not actually hit her, but she did rub her head as though wiping away the offending kiss. "Gross," was all she said.

DIANA: And it was. And it still is.

MARY: But you didn't hit me. You never hit me when I do it.

DIANA: Is that supposed to mean something? Because it doesn't.

CATHERINE: Not hitting people is how you show affection.

She lay down on her bed. Just for a minute . . . then she would get up and change into a nightgown. In just a minute . . . By the time that minute had passed, she was asleep.

Diana had not wanted to sleep. Mary had told her to sleep, so she wouldn't. When she got to her room, she sat on the floor, looking at the bookshelf. These must be the books Mary had grown up with. *A Child's History of England*—boooring. *Poetical Fancies*—who named these books? *Alice in Wonderland*—that looked better. She took it off the shelf and into bed with her. Ah, this was more like it! Soon, she was down the rabbit hole and in a land as chaotic as her own mind, with caucus-races and Cheshire Cats that disappeared, leaving their grins, and Mad Hatters holding tea parties. She particularly admired the Queen of Hearts.

DIANA: See? You can write perfectly well from my
perspective when you want to. Told you so.

Catherine had gone to her room and shut the door, wanting to
be alone. She was secretive and solitary, right? The room, which
had been Mrs. Jekyll's, had an air of delicate femininity: blue silk
curtains matched the blue silk coverlet on the bed, and the furniture stood on slender mahogany legs as though about to start
dancing. Catherine had the urge to scratch it all up. It reminded
her too much of Lady Tibbett's house. She took off Holmes's frock
coat, which she had been wearing since last night—it seemed a
thousand years ago. Surely there must be something for her to
wear? From the wardrobe, she chose a pair of drawers and an
embroidered chemise. That would do.

She opened the window. Below her was the courtyard that
separated the main house from the laboratory, where Beatrice was
probably sleeping. She looked up: there was a drainpipe running
all the way to the third floor, close enough that she could reach it.
How strong was it? Would it bear her weight?

She climbed out the window and up the drainpipe. It was
sturdy enough to support her weight, but ran up only to what
must be a third-floor bathroom, or more likely a sink and water
closet. If she could just reach from where the drainpipe ended to
one of the window frames, and from there to the gutter . . . In a
moment, she was up on the roof, among the chimney pots. It was
a clear day—clear for London, anyhow—and she could see across
the tops of the houses. London seemed to go on forever.

She turned and crossed the roof. She felt a savage delight in
being up so high, the delight she must have felt on a cliff in the
Andes, before Moreau transformed her into a woman. In one
direction was a succession of alleys and mews. In the other was
Regent's Park, with its green treetops swaying in the wind. How

strange life was! She had been born in the mountains of Argentina, then born again on Moreau's island. Now here she was, at the center of the largest city in the world.

Somewhere in that city was Edward Prendick. One day, she would meet him again, and then, she would tear out his throat.

DIANA: And you all think I'm violent!

CATHERINE: I'm supposed to be violent. I'm a puma, remember?

DIANA: As though you let us forget it.

But for now . . . should she stay here? She could go anywhere, she could survive under any conditions, but Justine needed a home. This one would do, at least for now. After all, she had enjoyed the camaraderie of the circus. She supposed that was the human part of her, the part Moreau had created. She would have to tell Lorenzo what had happened to his performers. He had always treated her well, and he deserved to know—not the whole story, but at least that she and Justine had found another home. And then, they would begin a new life. It would, in some ways, be not much different from the circus. Both the circus and the house on Park Terrace had their monsters. . . .

CATHERINE: Yes, Mary, I know how you feel about that word. But I'm not going to stop using it. So you can stop cluttering up my story with your objections.

The adventures of the previous night had not tired Catherine as much as the others—she was nocturnal, after all. But she, too, needed rest. She clambered down the drainpipe and climbed through the window, then curled up under the blue silk covers and fell asleep, twitching as she dreamed of hunting deer on the slopes of the Andes.

> JUSTINE: I like Catherine's writing. It's dramatic—
>   perhaps overly dramatic at times. But I can see
>   what she saw, feel what she felt, as an animal
>   transformed by Dr. Moreau. That is good
>   storytelling, I think.

> CATHERINE: Thank you! And if any of you want to
>   write this book, you're more than welcome to try.

Beatrice was not asleep. She looked around the room that had once been a laboratory, and before that an operating theater. Yes, she thought it would do. The glass dome let in plenty of light. She could put plants on the desks where students had once sat observing dissections and demonstrations. The laboratory could become an indoor greenhouse. Some of the plants would be poisonous— would Mary allow that? She did not know.

She climbed up the stairs to the office. What had happened here, so long ago? How had Dr. Jekyll falsified his own death, to escape as Hyde?

The room itself was spotlessly clean. The only pieces of furniture were a desk and chair, two glass-fronted cabinets, empty now, and the sofa on which she had slept the first night she had arrived. In one corner stood a cheval glass. What must it have seen so many years ago? Jekyll's transformations into Hyde, she guessed. She looked into its depths, but saw only herself—a woman of uncanny beauty.

> BEATRICE: Catherine, you know I don't think of
>   myself that way.

CATHERINE: Well, everyone else does. Really, your
modesty is one of the most annoying things
about you. That and your absolute mania about
Votes for Women and Dress Reform. And no,
you can't comment here about the importance
of the suffrage movement or the dangers of tight
lacing.

DIANA: Is this one of those scenes where the monster
looks in a mirror?

It had been one of the most terrible nights of her life. She had
almost killed another human being—a child, this time. She must
never do that again. Here she could stay secluded, away from
others. And perhaps her medicines could heal—making up in
some measure for the deaths she had caused.

Beatrice lay down on the sofa and pulled a blanket over herself. She was so tired . . . not from lack of sleep, but from a
sense of hopelessness that had been with her since the death of
Giovanni. Here, she thought, she might find . . . not happiness,
but peace.

Beatrice closed her eyes and dreamed whatever flowers dream.

BEATRICE: That's very poetic, but they don't dream
anything. Flowers have no cerebral cortex.

CATHERINE: Oh, for goodness' sake. Can't you be the
romantic heroine? Mary is too sensible, Diana is
too impulsive, and Justine is too tall.

BEATRICE: But I'm not a romantic heroine. I'm a
scientist.

When Mary woke again, it was almost dark. She looked at her wristwatch, but could not make out the hands. She must have slept all day! And in her clothes, too.

She heard voices downstairs, and for a confused moment she thought it must be Enid and Nurse Adams. Then she remembered the events of the past week. Had it all really happened? It must have—she could not have made such a thing up. Not Poisonous Girls and Beast Men and Adam Frankenstein.

Who else was awake?

When she went downstairs, rubbing her eyes, she found they all were. The gas had been lit in the parlor, and there was a fire in the grate. Catherine, Justine, and Diana were sitting around the tea table, on which there were cakes and sandwiches, as she had predicted. Beatrice was still sitting away from the group, by the window.

"We didn't want to wake you," said Catherine. "We've been making plans."

"What sorts of plans?" Were they going to stay? Or had they been talking about going back to the circus? Even Beatrice could make a good living in the circus sideshow. Mary hoped, more than she had hoped anything in the past week, that they would be staying. After all they had been through, she wanted them together, in this house.

Just then, Alice walked into the parlor, holding a glass filled with . . . well, it was green. "Mrs. Poole sent me up with this, miss," she said to Beatrice, handing her the concoction. "She says she'll be up herself in a moment."

"That's very kind of you, Alice," said Beatrice. "Particularly since I almost poisoned you. I cannot apologize enough—"

"Oh, that weren't your fault. You couldn't help it, being all tied up."

Beatrice sipped from the glass and smiled. "Mrs. Poole is a genius, I think. This is perfect. Will you tell her from me, Alice? And—if I am to remain here, if this is to become my home, you

must call me by my name. I have no intention of standing on cer-
emony with anyone."

"Yes, miss . . . Beatrice," said Alice. "If you'll excuse me . . ."
And then she was gone again, like a mouse that disappears into the
woodwork before you've had the chance to blink.

"I hope she's not afraid of me," said Beatrice, sipping her green
sludge. What in the world had Mrs. Poole put into it? It looked
like weed soup. "After all, I almost killed her."

"No, she's just shy," said Mary. "She always has been, since she
first came here. I would never have expected quiet little Alice to
be as brave as she was last night. So . . . what were you talking
about before I came in? Will you stay?"

"Of course we're going to stay," said Catherine, as though it
were obvious. She picked up a sandwich, looked at it, and said,
"Watercress. That's pig food." She handed it to Justine. "Where's
the ham?"

Just then, Mrs. Poole came in with the teapot.

> MARY: Mrs. Poole, do you realize that you're always
> coming in with tea?

> MRS. POOLE: It's a good thing I am, or you girls would
> never eat, with all the gallivanting you do.

Alice followed carrying the tea tray, with cups and saucers
and all the usual implements. She arranged the cups and saucers
on the table, and Mrs. Poole poured out a cup of tea for each of
them.

"Mrs. Poole, would you please sit down for a moment?" said
Mary. "You too, Alice, and take my tea, won't you? I'll get myself
another cup in a moment. I need to ask you both a question."

Mrs. Poole sat down in an empty armchair. Alice took Mary's

teacup with visible reluctance, as though it were one of Beatrice's poisons.

"Oh, for goodness' sake, do sit, Alice, or you'll spill your tea," said Mrs. Poole. "I can see that we're going to be thoroughly modern in this house. What Mrs. Jekyll would think of it, I don't know. She had such strict notions of order and propriety. Well, at least you're all here safe and sound for one night."

Alice sat down on the carpet by Mrs. Poole's chair and drank her tea in small sips.

"That's what I want to ask you about," said Mary. "What if all of us were to live here together? I've asked Diana, Beatrice, Catherine, and Justine to stay. And I'd like to ask Alice as well. But Mrs. Poole, this is as much your home as mine. You've lived in it longer than I have. What do you say?"

Mrs. Poole looked at them all appraisingly and shook her head. "You girls will be a lot of trouble, no doubt. Especially that one." She nodded at Diana, who had just taken two sandwiches at once. "But I think you belong here, together. All I ask is that you let me know what you're doing, so I don't worry that you've been kidnapped or murdered!"

"And we'll help with the housework, Mrs. Poole," said Beatrice. "And do have some cake. I'm sure it's delicious."

"How would you know?" said Diana. "You don't even eat."

"Well, I'll believe that about the housework when I see it. But I don't mind if I have a slice. Getting that oven to make cake was a triumph of mind over metal. It just goes to show that even at my time of life, you can learn new tricks!" Mrs. Poole cut herself a generous slice of cake.

"And Alice?" said Mary. "Will you stay? Not just until you find a new situation, but for as long as you wish."

Alice nodded. "Aye, miss. So long as I don't have to go on adventures. Or, you know, die."

Mary smiled. "Our first adventure, I think, will be finding a way to support ourselves. We're going to run out of money quickly if we don't find work of some sort."

Beatrice drank the last of her sludge. "Thank you, Mrs. Poole. That was very refreshing. As I was saying before Mary came down, we should find work that suits our various talents and capacities. If you allow me, I will grow medicinal herbs. The laboratory, with its skylight, is a perfect environment for them. I noticed what a limited pharmacopeia the Royal Hospital has. Even the Royal College of Surgeons lacks some of the medicines my father was able to develop from his plants. I believe if we all gave it some thought, we could find ways to earn our keep, to pay for this house and our living expenses."

> MARY: And so we have. Beatrice's medicines sell consistently, and your books bring in royalties, Catherine. Justine's paintings are increasingly popular. The one of the girl with the lilacs is going to pay the water rates.

> DIANA: *Lilac Time.* What an absolutely rotten name.

> JUSTINE: But people like it. They like to see things that are happy. And I am good at flowers. . . .

> CATHERINE: Leave Justine alone. She can paint whatever she wants, and she brings in more money than you, anyhow.

> DIANA: Once I'm a famous actress, I'll bring in more than the lot of you. You'll see!

MARY: Well, for now you're just in the variety show, so don't get too high and mighty. And I'm not sure you should be in that! It's barely respectable, and you really should be in school.

DIANA: Respectable my arse! And as for school . . .

CATHERINE: Here I interrupt my narrative, and Diana's subsequent diatribe, to inform my readers that my first two novels, *The Mysteries of Astarte* and *The Adventures of Rick Chambers*, are available for sale in bookstores and train stations for only a shilling. The third novel in the series, *Rick Chambers and Astarte*, will be appearing for the Christmas season, followed by *Rick Chambers on Venus*, unless the publisher calls it *Rick Chambers and the Caverns of Doom*, or something else entirely. I'm currently working on the fifth novel, and it would go much more quickly if this monster of a narrative didn't take up so much of my time!

MARY: I don't think your readers want an advertisement in the middle of the story.

CATHERINE: My readers appreciate hearing about my forthcoming publications, thank you very much.

That was the first meeting of the Athena Club. Oh, we didn't call it that, not then. Not until several months later, when Justine suggested the name. Readers who remember their classical mythology will immediately realize its significance: Athena, born from the head of her father, Zeus. We do not claim the wisdom of Athena, but we identify with her dubious parentage.

But that night was when the club started, really. With all of us sitting in the parlor having tea, telling Mrs. Poole what had happened the night before, to her shocked horror. Discussing what we were going to do, how we were going to investigate the Alchemical Society. The next day, we would continue to talk about practicalities: how we were going to support ourselves and live together without Beatrice poisoning us all, or Mrs. Poole strangling Diana. But that was the moment when we knew, when it became real.

Now, when you approach the front door of 11 Park Terrace, you will see a brass plaque directly over the bell pull: THE ATHENA CLUB. That is what we are, a very exclusive club. For monsters.

MARY: Except we're not monsters.

DIANA: Says you.

The next day was Sunday, so we all went to church except Catherine, who said religion was a fraud and a sham—we were all idiots for believing that God the Father lived up in the sky, and would bless us if we were good, punish us if were bad. Like Moreau in his compound.

"Why do I have to go if Catherine doesn't?" said Diana.

"Because you're still a child, and you need to be raised properly," said Mrs. Poole, who was helping us with our gloves and hats. Mary had somehow found enough gloves and hats for everyone.

"But I'm fourteen, and she's only ten," said Diana. "I mean, from the time she became a human being."

"You have to count in cat years," said Catherine. "As a puma, I was already on my own and ready to mate."

MARY: What about your human years? Do they count
as human years? Will you age at a normal rate now?
I mean for a woman?

CATHERINE: I don't know. Pumas only live about
fifteen years in the wild. It would be rather awful
to die at fifteen, don't you think? But I simply
don't know. I don't think even Moreau knew—or
cared about that effect of the humanizing process.
He ignored his Beast Men after they were created.
It was the act of creation itself that interested
him. So I guess we shall simply have to see. No
man knows how long he has to live anyway, right?
Justine couldn't have guessed she would live for
almost a century. It's just . . . the way things are,
and one has to deal with it as best one can.

Mary, Diana, and Alice went to St. Marylebone Church.
Beatrice and Justine, who were Catholic, went to St. James's
Church, across from Spanish Place. Mrs. Poole said she would go
to an afternoon service. Catherine sat up in her room, opened a
notebook, and started writing: "No man who has seen Astarte has
lived to tell the tale but one: I, Rick Chambers, Englishman." *Yes*,
she thought. *That sounds just right.*

By the time Mary returned with Diana and Alice, and Beatrice
and Justine returned together, Mrs. Poole had prepared Sunday
lunch. So we all sat around the large table in the dining room,
since the morning room table was too small. It would become
our room for club meetings and plotting strategy. But that day,
we were eating creamed ham (Catherine and Diana), cauliflower
soup (Justine and Mary), and something wilted (Beatrice). And
we were making plans. How could we live together? What would

we live on? We all thought of ways to make money: Beatrice would sell her medicines, Justine wanted to try painting, Catherine would write. Diana wanted to become an actress, but no, said Mary. Being an actress wasn't respectable, and anyway she had to go to school. As did Alice. "I just want to be a housemaid, miss," said Alice. "I almost died, remember? I would rather not almost die again, if you don't mind." Mary had insisted she eat with us rather than in the kitchen. (She was picking at the ham.)

"Well, we can't afford school fees anyway, and I suspect that sending Diana to school would be a disaster," said Mary. "So we can educate you both at home. Beatrice can teach you science, and Catherine can teach you literature, and Justine can teach you French and Latin. And I used to be rather good at history. But what can I do to bring in some money? I have no artistic talents. I could be a shop girl or typist, but I've already tried all the agencies . . ."

"How about becoming my assistant?"

We all looked up, startled to hear a masculine voice. There, in the doorway of the dining room, stood Sherlock Holmes.

"I'm sorry, miss," said Mrs. Poole. "He didn't wait for me to announce him. Just strode in here . . ."

"Forgive me, Mrs. Poole," said Holmes. "I'm afraid I have rather urgent news. You see, Hyde has escaped."

"From Newgate?" said Mary. She looked astonished, as well she might.

"From the depths of Newgate itself. And I assure you that he was well guarded. This morning, the warden found the lock picked and the prisoner gone. Has he tried to contact any of you?"

We all shook our heads.

"I don't suppose Renfield has escaped as well?" asked Mary. "That would be a bit too much."

"No," said Holmes. "I telegraphed this morning, to make certain. He's safely locked up, according to Joe Abernathy, who's been rehired at the asylum. I suspect Dr. Seward heard of my visit to Joe and wants to keep an eye on him. The good doctor looked at the both of us suspiciously when I returned his madman yesterday afternoon, after I assured Lestrade that he was not complicit in the murders. As of this morning, Renfield was in his room at the asylum, in a straightjacket. Only Hyde was gone. Lestrade is alerting the ports, and if he's seen, he will be arrested. However, he managed to escape the first time, and I suspect we have seen the last of Mr. Hyde for a while. I'm sorry." He looked at Mary with concern. "I know this must be a blow to you. You wanted to question him, and there's no possibility of claiming any reward in his absence."

"And what of Mr. Prendick?" asked Justine. Catherine looked away. If there was any information on Prendick, she did not want to know, although she knew Justine was asking for her.

"Lestrade is also having his boardinghouse watched, although if Prendick has any brains at all, and I suspect he does, he won't return there. What he did is not technically a crime—there is no statute on the law books forbidding the creation of Beast Men. But I wager he does not want the Alchemical Society to get wind of his activities. He was clearly hiding them from Dr. Seward. When Seward summoned him, suspecting that he was somehow implicated in the murders, Prendick denied any knowledge of them. I wager he does not want the society to know he was involved with the likes of Edward Hyde and Adam Frankenstein."

"Prendick is gone. I'm sure of it," said Catherine. "He's a coward. He's always been a coward."

"Well then," said Holmes. "Where does that leave us? With Adam Frankenstein dead and the Beast Men destroyed, but Hyde and Prendick still on the loose. Although that orangutan may have gotten away as well—I'll tell Lestrade to keep an eye out for him. It may be difficult to press charges against Mrs. Raymond now, since there's no direct evidence of her involvement. I was counting on Hyde to testify against her. However, I've told Lestrade to keep an eye on her, and of course he will continue the search for Hyde. He can't take credit for having solved the Whitechapel Murders without a murderer, preferably behind bars."

"But Mr. Holmes," said Mary, "while these two men have escaped, there is also the Société des Alchimistes itself. It is secret and unscrupulous in its methods. We may have solved the Whitechapel Murders, but the mystery of this society remains. Who are its members? What does it do? Is it continuing the experiments that created Beatrice and Catherine? Surely this mystery is not yet solved."

> MARY: I like how neatly you have us talking, when
> really of course it was a babble of "Do you think
> they'll catch him?" and "I bet he's headed back to
> Switzerland." and "Can I have more ham? I'm still
> hungry."

"I agree," said Holmes. "I have not forgotten about the society itself. It has been operating in England for . . . well, we don't know how long. And here in London—or at least it was, while Jekyll was conducting his experiments. London is my city. If there is a secret organization in it, I want to know what it's doing." His face as he said this was grim.

"And what did you mean just now, when you said I should become your assistant?" Mary was almost afraid to ask. Surely he did not mean that she would be another Watson? Solving mysteries with him, traveling around England as a detective? Well, detective's assistant. But still. After all, she had helped solve the Whitechapel Murders. . . .

"I mean that I need someone to organize my papers. You've seen yourself that at present, they are in disarray. I know where

everything is, of course. But I need someone with a clear and logical mind, such as you have, to devise an organizational system that
will make all my files easily accessible. It's clerical work, but you
asked for work, and I have some for you. Are you interested, Miss
Jekyll? I can offer two pounds a week."

Mary put her soup spoon by her plate. She aligned it precisely, then folded her napkin beside it. We already knew her well
enough—at least, Catherine already knew her well enough—to
see that she was disappointed and not showing it.

JUSTINE: I knew it also.

BEATRICE: And I.

DIANA: I thought she always did that. Just because
she's Mary. Doesn't Mary always do that?

"Yes, thank you. I should be very glad of two pounds a week.
When would you like me to start?"

"Today, if possible," said Holmes. "I need to get back to
Lestrade at Scotland Yard, and I would like you to accompany me.
As a temporary Watson, to take notes. In Watson's absence, I lack
a reliable secretary. Of course he doesn't thinks of himself that
way, but his notes are often useful to me, before they become
the melodramatic stuff of his stories. If you're done with your
meal . . . will you come?"

"Of course," said Mary. Scotland Yard! Well, she might be
stuck in 221B Baker Street tomorrow, but today at least she was
going somewhere interesting.

"And how is Dr. Watson?" asked Beatrice.

"Much better this morning," said Holmes. "I saw him first
thing, before meeting with Lestrade. You may visit him if you like,

but I suggest no more than two of you at a time. I hope you won't be offended if I say that all of you together can be . . . overwhelming. Particularly for a man in his delicate state."

"I'd like to go see him," said Beatrice.

"I'll go with you," said Catherine. "For protection."

"Thank you, Cat, and of course you're welcome to come with me. But I think I can protect myself." Beatrice looked as though her pride had been wounded.

"Not to protect you. To protect the British public from you. Particularly until you become less poisonous. I can already see the headlines: *Italian Beauty Poisons Londoners!* The newsboys would be crying it all over the city. . . ."

"And what about me?" asked Diana. "I want to go somewhere or do something! Why don't I get to do anything?"

"Diana, will you stay with me?" said Justine. "I am not yet entirely recovered, and if any danger were to threaten, if Hyde were to return for instance, I'm not sure I could defend myself, or Mrs. Poole and Alice. We would need someone as clever and resourceful as yourself on our side."

"Oh, well, if you need me. I suppose I can stay." Diana shrugged, but looked as pleased as a cat that had gotten into cream.

Mary was not sure she approved of Justine's maneuver. Surely that sort of praise was bad for Diana? But at least it would keep her from following one of them without permission.

"Well then," said Holmes. "Let's be off on our various errands. Miss Jekyll, if you're ready?"

"Yes," said Mary. "Yes, I'm ready." She rose from the table and pushed back her chair. "Let's go." It would be an adventure. And perhaps not the last.

MARY: Of course not the last. Think of all the things that have happened since then!

CATHERINE: Yes, but I have to end with at least a little
    suspense.

MARY: What about what happened after that? You
    know, immediately after. You were all there.

"Just a moment, Mr. Holmes," said Mary. "I've forgotten my
umbrella."

They were already outside the door of 11 Park Terrace—I
mean, the Athena Club. It was a late spring day in London,
which meant it was about to rain. Mary had indeed forgotten her
umbrella—she did not add, deliberately. Because she had to know.

Holmes nodded, and she ran back inside. Catherine and
Beatrice had their coats on. Well, her coats. Their coats now.
Justine and Diana were standing in the hall, seeing them off.
Quickly, because she did not want Holmes to come back in and
hear her, she said, "Diana, where is that pin you used to pick the
locks in the warehouse? The hatpin you probably stole off my
dressing table."

Diana looked at her with astonishment. "What hatpin?"

"You know perfectly well what I mean. Tell me the truth."

"I have no idea what you're talking about." Diana shook her
head, eyes wide, all innocence. Which meant of course that she
was lying. We were beginning to know her now, to know each
other. We could tell things about each other that others would not
be able to. That's how it is with families.

"You gave it to him, didn't you?" Mary spoke accusingly.

"Well, he's our dad! Whether you want to admit it or not."
Diana crossed her arms and looked petulant.

"So you did! I knew it. As soon as I heard he had escaped from
Newgate, I wondered what he could have picked a lock with, small
enough to hide from the guards. You must have slipped it to him

before you ran off with Charlie, when he was already in handcuffs. It's your fault a criminal has escaped from prison. It's your fault a man who is dangerous to the public, and potentially to all of us, is still out there. Don't you realize—it was *his* watch fob in Molly Keane's hand. Adam wasn't a member of the society. He might have killed her, but our—*your*—father was just as responsible for her death. He was probably the one who cut out her brain—with a scalpel! Do you even understand what you've done?" Mary took her umbrella from the stand, as though she might run Diana through with it. *And he may have caused my mother's death*, she did not add. That was not something she wanted to discuss, not yet. Instead she added, although it felt irrelevant now, "It's your fault we lost even the possibility of a reward for finding the murderer of Sir Danvers Carew."

"*He's our dad*," said Diana. She looked utterly immovable. Which is how we have learned Diana often looks.

Mary glared at her for a moment, then made the sound a lady makes when she is thoroughly angry. (It's a sort of low growl.) Clutching her umbrella like a sword, she walked out the door into the rainy London afternoon.

> MARY: Do you know what Mr. Holmes said to me in the cab? "Miss Jekyll, I know you and your friends haven't told me everything. I won't enquire into your secrets, beyond what is necessary for me to solve the mystery of the Société des Alchimistes. They are safe even from me."

> BEATRICE: That shows he is a gentleman.

> CATHERINE: It shows he had already guessed what we weren't telling him. After all, he's Sherlock Holmes.

And he wanted Mary to understand that he could
be trusted. Haven't you noticed how he is around
Mary? Do you seriously think he needed an assistant
to organize his files? He wanted to keep her close,
that's what he wanted. For more reasons than one,
I'm guessing.

MARY: Why would he want that? Anyway, his files
were a complete mess. With the organizational
system I devised . . .

CATHERINE: Oh please.

CHAPTER XXI

The Letter from Austria

It was August, three months after the night we had decided to live together at 11 Park Terrace. We were sitting in the parlor with the windows open to let in any breezes that might be flitting around the stagnant streets of London. The weekly meeting of the Athena Club was about to start.

The parlor did not look the way it had three months ago. Justine had painted it yellow, and there was a band of flowers around the top of the wall, close to the ceiling. That had been Beatrice's idea. She insisted we must do away with the darkness and drab of previous centuries—we must have beauty and light. Also, she liked flowers. So we had yellow and green and blue walls, and the furniture had been re-covered in Indian fabrics, and there were Japanese porcelains on the mantelpiece. She had bought them cheaply at a church rummage sale. She and Mary argued about the expense, but since Beatrice brought in more money than the rest of us, it was only fair that she should spend some on fabric and porcelain if she wanted to. We had to admit that we rather liked her taste, so we let Beatrice decorate and try to talk us into supporting the Labor Movement, Aestheticism, and Rational Dress. Mary retorted that we were conspicuous enough without dressing differently from everyone else, but she had bought a bicycle. Mrs. Poole was scandalized. Those three months had brought certain changes to our household. Justine talked more, although it was usually about the meaning of life. We tended to stop listening when she said "Rousseau" or "Kant." Surprisingly, Diana was the one who listened to her most often. Sometimes she even tried to read Justine's books, although we had seen her curled up on the sofa with her head uncomfortably pillowed on the *Critique of Judgment*. We had taken down the walls between the servants' rooms on the third floor, and Justine used that space as a studio. The entire third floor smelled of turpentine. She particularly liked to paint flowers, and children, and pastoral scenes. Catherine was working on her first novel, and two short pieces of hers had been published in *Lippincott's Monthly Magazine*. During the day, we often heard the *click-clack* of her typewriter. Beatrice's plants had taken over the laboratory, spreading over the tables and up the walls. Except for Justine, we only went in there briefly, because the air itself had become poisonous. It would make you start to feel faint, and eventually you would lie down and die. But nothing could harm Justine, so she visited Beatrice whenever she liked.

Every weekday morning, Mary walked across the park to assist Sherlock Holmes. She had, to her great pleasure, participated in solving several mysteries. In "The Case of the Missing Finger," by Dr. John Watson, published in *The Strand*, she had even been described as "a young woman of prepossessing appearance." We were worried that Watson, whose wound was almost completely healed, had developed a secret passion for Beatrice. Whether it was requited or unrequited, we did not know.

> BEATRICE: Don't be silly. He has always been simply a good, kind friend.

Diana continued to be a trial to us all. We were considering poisoning her with one of Beatrice's concoctions. No, not really, although Catherine swore that if Diana used her typewriter and messed up the ribbon one more time, she would bite that girl through the throat, just wait and see.

> DIANA: I would have liked to see you try! You were so annoying, always moaning about how difficult it was to write a novel. And look at you now, Miss Author.

> CATHERINE: The first one was hard! Almost as hard as this one . . .

Alice continued to insist that she was only a housemaid and not at all interested in adventures, thank you very much, but she was getting particularly good at Latin, almost as good as Beatrice. And Mrs. Poole was still Mrs. Poole. She would probably never change.

> MARY: She never has. She's still the same Mrs. Poole she's always been. Only more so.

Since his escape from Newgate, we had not heard of or from Hyde. We assumed he had made it to the continent, where he could stay hidden for years if necessary. Prendick had disappeared as well. To Lestrade's consternation, the Whitechapel Murders were still considered unsolved, and learned men wrote treatises advancing possible solutions, all of them wrong. We continued to investigate the Société des Alchimistes, although we had not yet found out as much as we would have liked. Our investigations were ongoing.

It was Saturday, the day of our official club meeting. We were all sitting on the sofa or in the armchairs, except Diana, who sat cross-legged on the floor. Even Beatrice was sitting in an armchair rather than by the window, since she was less poisonous now.

DIANA: She's still poisonous enough!

Mary was presiding. She usually presided over our meetings, although we had no official club president. But she was the best at organizing and keeping us all from talking over one another. As usual, our first order of business was finances. What had we made that week?

Mary: Two pounds.

Justine: Ten pounds from a commissioned portrait. This was not a usual sort of payment and could not be counted on again. But two of her paintings had been accepted into a gallery in Soho.

Beatrice: Five pounds seven shillings.

Catherine: Nothing. She had already received an advance for the novel she was writing, and had no magazine sales to report.

Diana: Nothing, yet. She was trying to persuade Mary that she should become an actress. If Mary would just let her appear at the Alhambra . . . Yes, the girls showed their legs, but so what? We allocated ten minutes for Diana's arguments, and one minute for Mary to say "No."

That made a grand total of seventeen pounds, seven shillings for the week. Not bad, much better than we had been doing at first. It was difficult feeding seven mouths and maintaining a large house. But we were managing.

Second order of business: What had we learned about the Alchemical Society? Catherine, who sometimes wrote in the British Library Reading Room, had found mentions of the society in eighteenth-century manuscripts. The society had been less secretive then, and many prominent Englishmen were members, but so far she had found no information on what experiments, if any, they had been conducting. She would continue her research. Mary reported that Dr. Seward was still in Purfleet. Joe, who was watching Seward for us, had told us he was planning on going to Vienna again, but at the last minute the trip had been canceled. Why had Seward canceled his trip? We did not know. It was frustrating knowing so little. Ten minutes for complaints about how little we had discovered so far. Beatrice said it was natural for our investigations to go slowly.

Third order of business: Mrs. Poole had found two stray kittens in the backyard. What should we call them? The names Alpha and Omega were proposed and unanimously approved. We had kittens! Mrs. Poole insisted she was letting them stay only because they would eventually catch mice.

Fourth order of business: Mary said, "I received this letter yesterday. You remember I said there was one person in the world to whom I could recount the events that brought us together? That person was my former governess, Miss Murray. I wrote her a letter several months ago, not knowing she had moved. My letter seems to have been forwarded from address to address, but it finally reached her, and she has written back. I think I'd better read you her response."

We waited, wondering what the letter was about, knowing Mary would not have told us about it if it were not important. She started reading.

> My dear Mary,
>   I'm sorry it's taken me this long to respond to your letter. As you can see from my address, I am no longer teaching school in England. To explain why I am in Vienna would take much longer than I have at present. For I, too, have been living an adventurous life, sometimes too adventurous for my taste. It has,

strangely enough, intersected with yours in a sense.
You will perhaps understand more when you read the
enclosed. If I were in a position to help the writer,
who is the daughter of a dear friend, I would. But I
need to leave Vienna almost immediately. I told her
that if she wrote to you, I would forward her appeal—
it is the most that is currently in my power. I hope—I
very much hope—you can help her. And forgive me
for my brevity. I will write more when I can. My
love to you, now and always (and I think you need no
longer call me Miss Murray).

Mina

"And?" said Catherine. "What is the enclosure?"

Mary stared at a second sheet of paper folded in the first, as
though trying to decide what to do with it. But really, she had
already decided, or she would not have brought it to our meeting.
She began.

Dear Miss Jekyll,

Our mutual friend Miss Murray has told me
who you are, and of the Athena Club. You do not
know me, but I take the great, the very great, liberty of asking you to help me in my dire need. I
am the daughter of Professor Abraham Van Helsing,
a doctor and researcher associated with several
important universities, in England and on the continent. My father is also a prominent member of a
certain Société des Alchimistes. Miss Murray has
assured me that you know of this society, and that
you and your fellow club members are aware of
its activities. I am, against my will and sometimes

without my knowledge, the subject of certain experiments carried out by my father. As I result, I am . . . changing. And I am afraid. The one person who could protect me, my mother, is locked away in an asylum for the insane. I am not yet of age, and have no resources of my own or friends to whom I could turn. I do not know what to do. Please, if you can, help me, I beg of you.

> Lucinda Van Helsing
> Vienna, Austria

For a moment, we were all silent. Then, "Where's Austria?" asked Diana.

"We wanted to know if they were still making monsters," said Catherine. "I think we have our answer. The Société des Alchimistes, or at least some of its members, are still experimenting on girls. Lucinda Van Helsing doesn't tell us how. . . ."

"She may not know herself," said Justine. "This Professor Van Helsing must be stopped. We cannot allow such experiments to continue. I speak only a little German, but could learn quickly, I think."

"Austria is near Switzerland," said Beatrice. "I stayed in Vienna briefly, trying to find a cure for my condition. The nights will be getting cold there, although the days are warmer and sunnier than in London. We shall have to pack sweaters and wool coats."

"I'll have to ask Mr. Holmes for some time off," said Mary. "I think he can survive without an assistant for a while. But this isn't the sort of thing we can rush into. It must be planned carefully. Has anyone seen the atlas?"

"I was using it to plan Rick Chambers's escape route," said Catherine. "I'll bring it into the dining room. Meet me there in five minutes."

"You're not going to leave me behind," said Diana. "You're always leaving me behind."

And then we sat around the large mahogany table: Mary, Diana, Beatrice, Catherine, and Justine. Mapping travel routes, calculating expenses. Planning the future adventures of the Athena Club.

> **AUTHOR'S NOTE:** Mary refuses to listen to me, but I am after all the one writing this story (with frequent interruptions), so I'm going to add a note about Mrs. Shelley—also named Mary—and the book she is most famous for writing: *Frankenstein, a Biography of the Modern Prometheus*. We authors have to stick together, even when one of us is long dead.
>
> (Those of you who are interested only in adventures may wish to ignore this part and go directly to reading one of my other books. I won't mind.)
>
> Mary says the book is a pack of lies, and accuses Mrs. Shelley of writing it to protect the Société des Alchimistes, as it was constituted in her time. After all, she never mentions the society. She implies that Frankenstein was working entirely unguided and alone, which was not the case. Most readers nowadays assume the book is a work of fiction anyway, as Watson did, but it's not. Neither is it entirely lies. The early story of Victor Frankenstein is almost entirely accurate, as we know from Justine. Mrs. Shelley fails to mention that as a student at the University of Ingolstadt, Frankenstein was inducted into the Société des Alchimistes by his chemistry professor. We have seen both their names, Victor Frankenstein and Adolphe Waldman, in the records of the society,

in Budapest. (To find out how we were able to access those records, read the second in this series of Adventures of the Athena Club.)

MARY: That's quite clever of you, actually. Making them want to read the second book.

Frankenstein created Adam, as Mrs. Shelley describes. Then, he created Justine. And this is where the biography becomes, as Mary calls it, a pack of lies. It concludes with an implausible and melodramatic chase across the Arctic, with Frankenstein pursuing the monster he created, for "revenge." Seriously, even I write more believable fiction than that! Those of you who have read the book will have noticed how different those chapters are from the earlier ones, which recount entire conversations verbatim, and describe Frankenstein's experiments in detail.

To understand her motivations, you have to understand the complicated woman who was Mary Wollstonecraft Shelley, only nineteen years old when she started writing the *Biography*. She was the daughter of Mary Wollstonecraft, author of *A Vindication of the Rights of Woman*, and one of the few female members of the Société des Alchimistes at that time. She died when Mary was only a child, although we know that Mary identified with her mother and often read her writings. Mary's father, the political radical William Godwin, was also a member. Mary herself never became a member of the society—we do not know why. Her husband, the poet Percy Shelley, was a member, as were Lord Byron and his friend Dr.

John Polidori. Evidently, it was quite fashionable to be a member of the society in the early part of the century. It was not as secretive as it later became, and just scandalous enough to tempt men like Shelley and Byron.

So, think of who was gathered at the Villa Diodati that summer in 1816 when Mrs. Shelley began work on the *Biography*. Percy Shelley, Lord Byron, John Polidori, and Claire Clairmont, Mary's stepsister, who was pregnant with Byron's child. About halfway through the summer, they were joined by Polidori's friend Ernest Frankenstein, Victor's younger brother and the sole remaining member of the Frankenstein family. It was an unusually wet summer for Switzerland: rain kept the inhabitants of the villa indoors. To pass the time, they told stories, and that was when Mrs. Shelley learned the details of Victor's life, from Ernest himself. In the records of the society, there is a letter from Ernest to the president of that time. I record here a portion of it:

"Although you will scarcely credit it, Monsieur le Chevalier, the Creature came to me himself to tell me of my brother's death in Scotland. He gloated over his vile crime, which I did not hesitate to call patricide, and vowed that he would revenge himself upon all the Frankensteins, forever. And upon that she-creature my brother had so unadvisedly made for him. I told him that she was likely dead already, if not of drowning then of exposure and starvation, and indeed I have heard nothing more of her. If I do, I will destroy her myself. Such an abomination should never have been allowed to walk the Earth. It is bad enough that my brother created Adam, but that he would create an Eve both stronger and more clever than man? That should never have been permitted, and if Waldman had known, he would have brought the full wrath of the society down on my unfortunate and misguided brother's head."

Ernest knew how his brother had died. He knew about Justine. In that company, among members of the society sworn to secrecy, and Mary Shelley, daughter of trusted members, I believe he revealed the truth. So why did Mrs. Shelley write her book, and knowing the truth, why did she lie?

It must have been, in part, to deflect attention from the society. If Adam appeared in Europe, he would be seen as the creation of a lone university student who had already paid the price for creating a monster. He would not be connected with the Société des Alchimistes.

MARY: I told you so.

But Mrs. Shelley also did something else: in her *Biography*, Justine is never created. Frankenstein decides a female monster would be too dangerous, and throws her body parts into the sea.

Why did Mary Shelley never join the Société des Alchimistes? Because she was the daughter of Mary Wollstonecraft and the stepsister of Claire Clairmont, whom Lord Byron was treating as a mistress he had already tired of. He would later abandon her daughter Allegra, who died in a convent in Italy. She knew the truth: that Frankenstein had created a female monster, and that the female monster had escaped. And she hid that truth. Knowing of Justine, she did the best she could, for another woman. She erased her from the story.

MARY: That's highly speculative, you know.

CATHERINE: But I'm convinced it's true. Look at the sympathy with which she wrote of Justine Moritz.

That summer, Mary Shelley was only nineteen. She had run away from home with Percy, who was already an acclaimed poet. She was in the home of the famous and scandalous Lord Byron, among men who were learned and powerful. And in their midst, she did something revolutionary. She allowed Justine to write her own story.

JUSTINE: I like to think it's true, and that in her own way, Mary Shelley was also a sister to me. . . .

As I've written this book, I've sometimes wondered what she would have thought of us and our adventures, and of course the book itself. I think she would have excused its defects (yes, Mary, I know there are some, don't act so astonished) and praised it as an accurate portrayal of a group of women trying to get along in the world as best they can, like women anywhere—even if they are monsters. Sometimes I imagine her sitting in my room, in the chair by the window, as I write—marveling at the typewriter and how much faster it is than a quill pen! Whenever I'm not sure what to say, when the words don't come and I sit there staring at my notebook, she says something encouraging, one author to another. I swear, sometimes I can see the shadow she casts. . . . And then I nod at the chair, as though she were really present, and get back to writing.

ACKNOWLEDGMENTS

This novel began as a question I asked myself while writing my doctoral dissertation: Why did so many of the mad scientists in nineteenth-century narratives create, or start creating but then destroy, female monsters? I didn't get a chance to answer that question within the dissertation itself, so I tried to answer it here, in a different way.

This novel would not exist without the help of a great many people. I would like to thank John Paul Riquelme and Julia Prewitt Brown, the first and second readers of my dissertation, for letting me write about monsters, and for their tireless patience with a graduate student who was already, at that point, transmuting into a writer. Before this was a novel, it was a short story called "The Mad Scientist's Daughter." I'm grateful to Karen Meisner, who purchased and edited it for *Strange Horizons*, and to John Joseph Adams, who reprinted it in *The Mad Scientist's Guide to World Domination*.

Once I started writing the novel version, Alexandra Duncan and Nathan Ballingrud workshopped an early draft of the first three chapters. Ellen Kushner, Delia Sherman, Catherynne M. Valente, and C. S. E. Cooney read and commented on a later draft of those chapters; they showed me who my characters were and how I could write the rest of the novel. Haddayr Copley-Woods generously read the entire novel once it was drafted. This novel would not exist in its current form without their smart, honest, and insightful feedback, and I am so grateful for their help. During the writing process, I traveled twice to England to do the necessary research. Thank you to Farah Mendlesohn and Edward James for letting me stay in their beautiful house in London, and for suggesting so many of the resources I ended up using. And thank you as well to Terri Windling for showing me her lovely corner of Devon, so I could get a sense for the countryside Justine travels through. Finally, many thanks to Joy Marchand for a lesson on translating into Latin.

My agent, Barry Goldblatt, was involved with this project from the beginning: we started talking about it long before I wrote the first draft. I'd like to thank him for his faith in me and this novel, and for waiting so patiently until it was done. And a heartfelt thank-you to my editor, Navah Wolfe, who saw all the places my manuscript could be stronger, as well as the entire team at Saga Press who created the book you hold in your hands, including Bridget Madsen, Tatyana Rosalia, and Krista Vossen. I'm also grateful to Kate Forrester, who created a cover illustration more perfect than I could have imagined.

Finally, my thanks to Kendrick Goss, who waved away my doubts, and most of all to Ophelia Goss, who read the final draft before it was submitted and told me that she liked my girl monsters. This book is written for her. It is so much better for the help of all the people who have read and commented on it in one form or another. Its mistakes and deficiencies are, of course, my own.